Forty-eight enthralling stories fr⟨
science fiction, fantasy, and horror wɪ

A monk accidentally summons a disgruntled lesser demon....
— "Please Hold" by Georgia Cook

In the world of fashion, a stylist takes matters into their own tentacles....
— "The Fashion Police Are Watching" by Jane Brown

Extraterrestrial beings discover the Voyager craft and send a message......
— "Out Here" by Scott Beggs

The last true maskmaker in Venice offers a mask that will change minds......
— "The Mascareri" by Izzy Varju

When a woman can't afford the proper burial spell, she's left with an unsettling alternative....
— "Grave Concerns" by Aeryn Rudel

A man journeys through an endless fog in search of the mysterious Falls of Imoletta...
— "The Falls of Imoletta" by Thomas Canfield

A family evacuates their home planet, leaving everything behind...
— "Twinkle Twinkle" by Matthew Keeley

... and many other short tales of wonder, shock, and awe.

THE BEST OF METASTELLAR YEAR TWO

"*MetaStellar* supports diverse narratives from around the world, which is always encouraging!"

— Todd Sullivan

"*MetaStellar* magazine has been a pleasure to work with. I am proud to see my work alongside so many talented writers in the Year Two Anthology."

— Jason Lairamore

"*MetaStellar* is at once a valuable source of great fiction, reviews, and related content, and a wonderful community to be involved in as a writer."

— Andrew Dunn

"*MetaStellar* is ... well ... stellar! The magazine is visually slick, informative, diverse, and relevant. There is always something interesting to read. Articles are well-researched and conscientiously written. I've worked with their various editors and found them on point and efficient."

— Nina Munteanu

THE BEST OF

METASTELLAR

YEAR TWO

Edited by Melody Friedenthal,
Marie Ginga, and Geordie Morse

METASTELLAR PRESS
MetaStellar.com

Table of Contents

Note From the Fiction Editor

By Geordie Morse

Here we are, *The Best of MetaStellar: Year Two*. In some ways I think a sequel deserves higher praise than the initial production (outside of Hollywood franchises). One means you made it to your goal, but two and beyond means you managed to stay there. And to be fair, we've done far more than stay consistent; *MetaStellar* experienced incredible growth in terms of readership and exposure in the past year, in a trajectory that we might dare to label "exponential".

I'd like to think the quality of our original fiction has followed this trend of improvement. As of this writing, we've just finished our fifth open submission period for original flash fiction, although you'll have to wait until Year Three publishes to see the latest stories we've picked.

With each new cycle I see more authors whose names I recognize from previous years, and I get to send their stories to be judged by other authors whose stories have already been published on our site; community-building, some might call it.

The board has also been honored with increasing distinction by readers and writers as not just another fiction market, but a particular fiction market that stands out from the others. The countless hours of volunteer effort from our board are well worth it to be mentioned by name as a speculative fiction magazine that publishes great stories with a professional, punctual staff.

Perhaps the biggest change we've dealt with this year is the looming presence of AI writing in the fiction marketplace, an elephant in the room for many years until the explosive advancement of AI, spearheaded by the public release of ChatGPT 4, shattered the pachydermal silence.

Several other major markets closed their submissions against a tidal wave of procedurally-generated content, for both logistical and ethical reasons. How can a magazine's staff process potentially thousands of story submissions generated within minutes, and is it fair to give space to stories that are written by a language model, rather than a person?

As for *MetaStellar*, we've been lucky so far to not have our submission box similarly inundated with AI writing. This may be due to our model of a limited biannual submission cycle, rather than a year-round open window and a big slush pile. The latter question was more pertinent for us to answer, and we decided that we would diverge from the majority of markets on this point. Since the start of 2023, we accept stories that have been created with the aid of AI tools.

For more about this decision, flip to the back of this book, where our editor-in-chief, Maria Korolov, summarizes the discussions we had as a board. She is herself a journalist who has been covering the development of AI for many years. If the rise of AI in creative spaces is of concern to you, as it is to all of us on the editorial board, I hope you'll give it a read and a think.

As *MetaStellar*'s lead fiction editor, I'd like to do my part in encouraging anyone who likes to write stories to consider submitting their work for publication- not just to us — though we'd appreciate it! — but to any magazine, journal, publishing house or anthology that seems like a good match for their style.

Many people, my past self included, have kept stories hidden away in drawers or computer folders because we couldn't imagine anyone aside from ourselves enjoying our work. But to surprise yourself, the first step is to try, and trying is worth everything. So let the stories in this anthology be an inspiration to those who need it; these same authors whose work is now printed here in book form started from the same place, and now we have more stories out in the world.

MetaStellar fiction editor Geordie Morse works primarily as a personal language coach, developing curricula and working with clients remotely. His first book, Renna's Crossing, is out now. His various other projects are cataloged on his site Arnamantle.com.

Note from the Reprints Editor

By Marie Ginga

Time goes by quickly when you're loving what you do. And I do. Choosing the best reprint submissions for this second anthology was no easier than the first one. What we ended up with is a hefty volume of can't-stop-reading stories.

It was another great year for our readers to feast on a glorious smorgasbord of speculative fiction. Although we have some regular contributors, it's nice to see a continued presence of authors new to *MetaStellar*. It is part of our mission to be a venue to help up-and-coming authors to get some visibility and we do a great job, if I do say so myself.

We link authors' stories as many ways as we can, often connecting to Amazon and other sales platforms, as well as social media and web pages. We create an author page for each of our contributors. We also share the wealth by giving other publications a boost when we link our printing to theirs.

Any author can request to be a guest on our podcast, Long Lost Friends with Elizabeth Eve King and Andrea Goyan, accomplished authors and artists in their own right. And we are always looking for volunteers at our magazine, which is run by an all-volunteer force.

We continue to receive a constant stream of quality short stories in all speculative genres. The submissions represent not only a cross-section of genres, but also a wonderful representation of the diversity of our authors. Young (our youngest is 14) and old; all shades of white and brown; local to us here in Massachusetts and internationally—as far away as Korea and New Zealand; LGBT and neurodiverse. I'm happy to bring readers great stories and I'm happy to give authors a great opportunity to be seen.

Nearly 500 fiction and non-fiction authors have invested their creative energy in our magazine. That, coupled with a great cast of editors and a video team, has established *MetaStellar* in the top five spec fic magazines online.

I'm proud to be a part of it.

Marie Ginga is the reprints editor for MetaStellar Magazine. She's also an accomplished writer under her pen name, Marie LeClaire, with five novels and a collaborative anthology to her credit. You can find her on many reading platforms and at Amazon.com/Marie-LeCLaire and at her website, MLeClaire.com.

Please Hold

By Georgia Cook

Brother Gregor bent close to his work, his hands trembling as he lifted the taper. Candlelight flickered in the gloom; incense sticks pierced the fetid air. A drab gray light trickled through the tiny windows, illuminating the chalk circle drawn across the floorboards.

Two more candles to go...

It was bitterly cold in the turret room. Positioned high above the cloister, the monks had been using it as a storage space. A stiff breeze howled through the rafters, the air smelt of dust and ancient pigeons, the floorboards creaked at every footstep.

Not, by all accounts, the ideal place for a summoning.

The flame flared, seemed almost to snuff out, then caught, flashing a spectacular green. Brother Gregor allowed himself a sigh of relief, then moved to the fourth candle, chanting softly under his breath.

The forbidden parchment crackled at his feet, spotted with sweat and ancient wax. The eldritch symbols transcribed across it caught the candlelight in such a way that they seemed to twist and change in the air.

With a trembling hand, Brother Gregor lit the final candle.

The chalk circle began to glow. Tongues of eldritch flame crackled across the ceiling. Brother Gregor jumped back with a cry as smoke poured across the floor, extinguishing the candles and wrapping the room in an eye-watering mist.

In the midst of the swirling smoke arose a figure, thin and hunched. It was much smaller than Brother Gregor had expected— although, he supposed, demons were capable of taking any number of forms—he recalled an entity in The Book Of Bolem (a lesser demon of malice by the name of Helector) whose favored form was a demonic flea, and was renowned for sucking men's brains out through their spines. But the smallness of this particular demon seemed less deliberate than unavoidable. It was lanky and thin, with a shock of bright red hair and a narrow, unhappy face. Its lips were small, its cheeks were spotted with what Brother Gregor could only describe as Demonic Pustules.

"Gods!" the demon groaned, waving the smoke out of its eyes. It had a thin, reedy voice. "More bloody incense! Why does he always send me to the bloody incense summonings?" It fixed Brother Gregor with a petulant glare. "What are you looking at?" it snapped.

"T-the Great...Demonic Lord Warenlgameth?" asked Brother Gregor, in the voice of one who has poured over every forbidden text and ancient tomb, memorized the name of every lesser demon in existence, and is now overcome with a pressing uncertainty. "He of the...Drowning Valleys, Lord of Endless Nights, King of—"

"Yeah, nah, sorry," the demon scratched a pimple. "He's off right now. 'Getting Coffee' apparently, as if anyone takes two hours to make a blessed coffee. And as if he'll remember to get me one, which he won't." The figure sighed and seemed to reemerge from its cocoon of misery just long enough to shoot Brother Gregor a second glare. "You got a message?"

Brother Gregor squinted. The demon was wearing a loose striped shirt and baggy breeches, its straggly blond hair swept back with a not inconsiderable amount of grease. A small white square attached to its chest bore the legend: Hi! My Name Is Jeremy! followed beneath, in much smaller print, by Have A Damned Good Day!

"You are not... the Great Demonic Lord Warenlgameth?"

The boy snorted, "Sure. Whatever man. Like he'd make me manager. I work for him."

"You work for him?"

"Yeah, and lemme tell you; for a Lord of Endless wossname, he's not even that impressive."

"Are you...a lesser demon?" Brother Gregor looked the boy up and down, "A...lesser, lesser demon?"

"Certainly bloody treats me like a demon," the boy (and now Brother Gregor felt certain this was a boy; not even the demonic lords themselves were that good at acting) adopted a low, rumbling voice, "'Jeremy, man the summoning circles. Jeremy, no portals to the Bahamas on your lunch break. Jeremy, what have I told you about calls on company time?'" He pulled a face, then stuffed his hand nonchalantly into the pockets of his trousers. "Teaches me to sell my soul for a bloody Ford Focus."

"This...is what happens...when you make a deal with the Great Demonic Lord Warenlgameth?"

"Yeah, and between you'n me: the overtime is whack." The boy leaned back, smirking slyly. "Why? You thinking of signing on? Cos' I get some sweet employee benefits once I claim my first soul; we're talking first dibs at the coffee machine, employee parking—"

Something rumbled, far back in the smoke.

"—What?" The boy glanced over his shoulder, listening to a voice Brother Gregor couldn't hear. His face went red. "No, I'm not messing with the stupid— ...I'm taking a summoning. Like You Asked." Another pause. Jeremy went even redder. He turned back to Brother Gregor.

"You better be selling your soul right now man, or I'm toast."

Brother Gregor stood in the darkness a moment, weighing his options; there were many things he was willing to sell for the price of eternal knowledge; many dark paths he was willing to walk. But the words 'Employee Parking' sent a shiver down his spine no dread curse had yet managed.

As the boy turned again, distracted, Brother Gregor lunged forward and extinguished the remaining candle. The boy vanished with a cut off "—oi!" and the room plunged into darkness.

Brother Gregor stood in the gloom for a long moment, breathing hard. Then he turned and very deliberately began to snuff the incense sticks. He'd bury them tomorrow, somewhere far away from here, and tell the Abbot the summoning had failed.

It was all well and good selling your soul, but some hells just weren't worth the risk.

Georgia Cook is an illustrator and writer from London. She is the winner of the LISP 2020 Flash Fiction Prize and has been shortlisted for the Bridport Prize and Reflex Fiction Award, among others. She has also written for numerous podcasts, webcomics and anthologies. She can be found on Twitter at @georgiacooked and on her website at GeorgiaCookWriter.com.

Tik Tok Man

By Andy Rafferty

Gerry leaned back in his chair, stretching, rolling his head and shoulders. His neck cracked. He wiped sweat off his forehead with his t-shirt, reached over and clicked the desk fan to the highest setting. The black cat lazing on the bookshelves gazed down at him with her habitual contempt.

He considered breaking for lunch—he was having pot noodle sandwiches and had been looking forward to them since about five minutes after he logged in to the works intranet. He'd been astonished how easily he'd dropped back into the habits of his student years, once the lockdown kicked in and the whole office started working from home.

PING

He tabbed out of the spreadsheet to Messenger. Notification. Alex.

>> This is so cool! Run it through yor headphones for best effect. A TikTok video.

Gerry rolled his eyes, but he was very warm, and very bored, and very sick of spreadsheets. TikTok videos were one of the few things that made lockdown slightly more tolerable.

He clicked the link, and the video started playing. It began with an androgynous figure in a badly lit room.

YOU WILL ONLY HEAR THE WORD YOU ARE READING!

The words were superimposed in the top half of the screen.

Gerry had seen a few of these already. He was a little disappointed, but these things were only ever a few seconds long and he had nothing better to do.

The figure raised its hands, pointing to the top of the screen. The header vanished. Two words appeared, floating above the figure's fingers.

On the left, in a dark yellow bar: CLOUD WAVES. On the right, in a light orange bar: LAKE SHORE.

There was a burst of synthesized sound. Gerry heard CLOUD WAVES. The figure inclined its head as if it had performed an act of consummate magic and then the video started again.

YOU WILL ONLY HEAR THE WORD YOU ARE READING!

The same burst of sound.

LAKE SHORE.

The diversion was already wearing thin. Gerry typed a quick LOL into Messenger and went to tab back to the spreadsheet. Another *PING* interrupted him.

Alex again.

>> Try it with yor eyes closed. It's weird.

Gerry almost shut the messenger window down and got back to his spreadsheets, but on an impulse decided to give it a go. He expected he'd hear one or other of the words, but idly wondered if it might be something more interesting.

He clicked the video again.

YOU WILL ONLY HEAR THE WORD YOU ARE READING!

He shut his eyes.

The burst of sound—

—tore through his brain like a chainsaw, grinding and tearing, ripping into his awareness, sundering his sense of self. His jaw locked with a click, his head snapping back and to the side involuntarily, muscles cording his neck with unnatural force.

A palsy slammed through his body. His right hand, still gripping the mouse, jerked to one side, his left opening and closing convulsively.

The darkness behind his eyes was overwhelmed with clouds, and eyes, and crackling chiaroscuran dots, a fractal pattern exploding again and again. The five second burst of sound cycled over and over, breaking against his thoughts like waves against a levy, overwhelming him, washing him away.

He jerked again and was completely still, eyes closed. A droplet of blood oozed from his left nostril and hung there for a moment. With deliberate slowness, he reached up and wiped it away, smearing it on the back of his hand.

Then he opened his eyes and looked at the screen. There had been nobody to see what happened to Gerry except the cat, and she was profoundly indifferent.

He clicked to copy the URL of the TikTok video, closed the messenger window, and began methodically going through his contacts list, his fingers a blur on the keyboard, copying the video and typing the same message over and over.

>> This is so cool! Run it through yor headphones for best effect.

Then he just sat there, motionless, sweat beading on his forehead, waiting for the replies.

Andy Rafferty lives in the north-west of England with his partner and cat. In his day job he works for Profound Decisions, a live-roleplaying company creating scenarios that give people opportunities to argue with each other. In his spare time, he writes about things that scare him and panders to his cat. Support him on Patreon at @AndyRafferty and you can also find him on Twitter at @wulfboyraff.

Con of the Dead

By Stephen Patrick

"Honey, I already told you, I'm headed downstairs now. Yes, I checked the rooms. Yes, even under the bed and the drawers. Sweetheart, enough already. I'm in the elevator. I'll meet you in the lobby."

The yellow elevator lights pinged down from nine to eight and Paul felt gravity latch on to him. Two Louis Vouitton bags stuffed with vacation clothes and makeup tugged on his right arm while a single, faded brown leather travel case adorned his left.

Paul's cell phone chirped. He looked down to see a new text message from his wife reminding him to have cash ready to tip the bellhop. Ping. Another floor down as the red LED flashed from six to five. His phone rang.

"Yes, Honey," he answered. "Your book is on top." The elevator pinged and Paul stepped out. "You can get it out once we're in the airport."

His phone buzzed with three new texts from his wife, each sent while he was talking to her. Damn that Bluetooth headset he bought her for Christmas!

Behind him, a high-pitched whistle was followed by a terrible thump.

"OK, OK, I'll be right there." Paul snapped his phone shut.

Another thump, then another. They boomed in cadence as they came closer.

He turned toward the sound, but his vision was blocked by a flash of gray steel. He ducked instinctively as the sharp edge of a Klingon Bat'leth sliced through the air. He spun around, barely dodging another spinning ceremonial blade. The thumping surrounded him as a dozen Klingon-garbed accountants and computer techs marched in lockstep around him.

"Bah, foolish human," growled one man through thick glasses.

"You're ruining our parade" screamed a portly man through his salt and pepper beard.

The clanking of steel on leather drowned out his screams as Paul ducked and darted to avoid the spiked knees and armored shoulders of the advancing horde. He braced his feet beneath him and leaped at the first gap that emerged between the part-time Klingons. As he slipped past them, he caught the edge of a Mek'leth on his thigh and screamed out in pain. He was hurt, but he was free. His hand darted to his thigh to check on his injury, but his momentum still carried him forward. He stuck his other hand out to stop himself, but his hand hit the gap between two doors.

The doors gave way, sending him tumbling into another room. Unlike the throbbing steps of the Klingons, this room was quiet, deathly silent. He pulled himself up to a knee, but realized that although the room was silent, the room was full of people. Each pair of eyes from the packed room was locked on him. Three men and two women sat behind a table at the front of the room. In front of them, books about Star Trek and Stargate SG1 sat upright like billboards. The names on the books matched the paper name cards in front of each person. Not a single word was said from the audience or the celebrities at the dais.

Paul smiled a sheepish smile and stood. "I'm so sorry, folks." His hand brushed his thigh. He was bruised but not bleeding. "I... um.... I fell. I'll be going now."

He stepped back toward the door, pausing to listen for the boots outside the room, but they were gone. Behind him, one of the men on the panel snatched a book from in front of him and frantically flipped through the pages.

His finger trailed down one glossy page before stopping midway. "Ladies and gentlemen," he called out to the audience before gesturing toward Paul. "Let me present our final panelist, Dr. Thomas Braynes, author of the lost 23rd episode from Star Trek: The Next Generation, season two."

A roar swelled in the crowd. "Oooooooo!" Everyone's eyes were locked on him. Then a single word spread throughout the room.

"Braynes." It started as a whisper but grew into a moaning chant that filled the mouths of everyone in the room.

"Braynes." They chanted from their seats. Hands darted up from the audience members, each vying for his attention.

"Braynes," they repeated. When he did not respond, the ones on the row closest to him stood up and reached out toward him.

"Oh my God," Paul screamed.

More hands reached for him, as the audience began leaving their seats and filing down toward him. Some held pens and autograph books, others filled with dog-eared amateur screenplays. Paul threw open the door and grabbed his cell phone, frantically hitting redial. Before the phone connected, a red plastic sword blade slashed across his right wrist, numbing it and sending his phone skittering across the carpet floor.

To his right, two men dressed in brown tunics and tights slapped blinking plastic swords together in a swirling battle. One wore red and black paint that was smeared from the sweat pouring down his forehead.

"What the heck?" Paul asked.

Without breaking from the fight, the man spoke to him. "I'm sorry, dear Padawan, but the Force is strong with this one."

The other man lunged forward, slashing with his blinking red sword. The blade whistled through the air, and the first man dropped to a knee, clutching at his gut. He handed his sword to Paul.

"I die, Padawan. Now you must defeat the Sith Lord."

"Maybe later," Paul answered.

The man let the sword fall slowly, waiting for Paul to grasp it. Paul spied his cellphone down the hall near a table covered with movie posters, swag items and a charity book donation box. As the plastic sword fell to the ground, Paul ran toward his phone.

After two steps, four hands pulled him backward, clutching at his shoulders. Two notepads were thrust in front of him while two men in matching Spock t-shirts stabbed their pens at him.

"Braynes," they shouted in unison.

He violently shrugged his shoulder and slipped off his jacket, leaving it behind in their clutching fingers. In two steps, his phone was in his hand again. He flipped it open, but the chants of "Braynes" had grown so loud, he could not hear the phone. A pair of double doors led into the dealer's gallery and his only available avenue of escape. He stepped hard to his left as a feint, before twisting to his right and ducking through the double doors.

As the doors clicked shut behind him, he looked down at his phone. "No service" blinked back at him. He slapped the phone shut and contemplated throwing it against the nearest wall, but that wall was draped with a wall of t-shirts depicting Ewoks urinating on various automobile brands and some odd jokes about Spock's phaser. The wall behind him was lined with worn paperback books, sitting behind a table stacked high with all sorts of leather and stone trinkets, goggles and cogs for machines that no longer existed. The air was thick with the scent of mothballs on Wookie costumes and stale Frito pie. He leaned against the table to catch his breath, feeling the glossy covers of brand-new paperback books beneath his fingers.

A soft voice came from behind him, "So, are you a fan of post-apocalyptic vampire comedies?"

Paul looked down. His right hand had curled around a paperback book depicting a masculine woman in cutoff jeans and a John Deere hat punching a blood-soaked zombie in the face. "Um?" he blushed as he withdrew his hand like it had touched a hot stove. "I guess so?"

"That's just the first book," said the woman. "I've got five others in the series."

"Wow," he stammered. "That's very impressive, I guess."

Her claw-like hands reached toward him, filled with five more books. "Would you like me to autograph them for you?"

He held his index finger in front of him. "Yes, let me go find a pen."

Paul was already moving when she pulled a pen from her shirt pocket. He stepped quickly, navigating a sea of book sellers and buyers toward the doors at the opposite end of the room. Behind him, muffled cries of "Braynes" grew louder as the steel doors opened and a throng of fans flooded into the room.

One man was tracking Paul's flight through the room. "There he is."

"Who?" asked the woman, still holding a pen.

"Thomas Brayne."

"TNG-Episode 23," said the crowd in unison, as they turned toward Paul.

Paul raced toward the door. He slammed against it, but the door didn't open. He jerked at the handle and the door flew open, knocking him backwards and onto one knee. The parade of chanting Klingons stomped through the open door, bearing down on him. The floor shuddered beneath him at the steel and leather onslaught. Paul crawled forward, dodging spiked boots and clanging weapons until the parade had passed. He reached the door just before it latched shut. His heavy door pinched his fingers, but he had enough leverage to pull it open.

The footsteps behind him stopped, leaving a silence that was broken by a guttural command in Klingon. A dozen boots scraped across the floor in a military about-face. Behind them, a pasty white face appeared over the shoulder of a shorter Klingon warrior.

"That's him," said the pasty-faced man, pointing at Paul. "That's Thomas Brayne."

The orderly procession dissolved into chaos as Batleths clanged to the floor. Instead of weapons, the Klingons stepped forward with pens and notebooks.

Paul grabbed a pad from the closest man. He flipped past scrawled signatures from Brent Spiner and Hugh Jackman to find a blank page. He scribbled wildly onto the paper and held it above him, drawing everyone's attention to the fluttering paper. Paul stepped back slowly, cautiously moving backward as the crowd stepped forward. The crowd pressed forward, and Paul stepped out of the room. The hallway behind him was lined with planters and couches, but the only doorway was at the far end. He turned and ran for it. As soon as his back was turned, the crowd thundered after him. He stopped and turned back, holding the paper up in front of him. The crowd skidded to a halt, recoiling from the paper, all mesmerized by the precious in his hands. A few reached out for it, but most simply stared at it. Paul walked backwards, under the protection of the paper. The ping of the elevator rang out behind him. When the door opened, he reached inside and pressed as many buttons as he could reach. When the elevator pinged again, he tossed the paper inside and stepped away. A dozen fans dove into the elevator, scrambling for the page. Paul watched their faces as they read Paul's hastily scribbled, and incorrect, signature. Their glee turned to a scowl as the doors closed on them. "Braynes?"

Paul ran down the hall toward a spiral staircase. He bounded it three steps at a time. The last leap led to the slick marble floor of the hotel lobby and his sneakers squeaked as he skidded to a stop.

A woman in black slacks and a ruffled maroon sweater stepped out of the bar. "Paul? What took you so long?"

"Honey, we've got to go. Have you already checked out?"

"Yes, why?"

"Just go. Now!"

Paul grabbed her by the arm and turned toward the door. After one step, he slammed into a luggage trolley. His momentum upset the delicate balance of suitcases and garment bags, sending a wave of luggage crashing down around him. One by one, he was bludgeoned by Samsonite cases and leather attaches covered in travel stickers from Vulcan and Alpha Centauri.

Behind him, the elevator pinged open and a dozen men stepped out screaming for "Braynes." Above him, footsteps clamored down the spiral staircase. He looked up at a plastic sack hanging precariously from the top rack of the luggage cart. He tried to move, but his arms were caught in the tangled straps of two Imperial Stormtrooper garment bags. A box was visible in the bottom of the sack, a sharp edge poking through a torn seam. The tear grew larger, stretching around a DVD boxed set collection. The thin plastic gave way, sending an orange box tumbling toward Paul. On the back of the box, Paul saw the listing for Star Trek season 2. It stopped at episode 22.

Paul grabbed his wife's arms and raced toward the rotating doors that led to their tram to the airport. As he passed the check-in booth, he heard a man talking to the clerk.

"Yes, ma'am. I'm sorry I'm checking in so late. My name is Thomas Braynes."

Stephen Patrick's stories have appeared in Dark Recesses Press, The Writer's Post Journal, Aphelion, and Bewildering Stories among others. His most recent work appears in the anthologies Road Kill: Texas Horror by Texas Writers, vol 1 and vol 2. He currently lives near Dallas, Texas.

The Old Red Schoolhouse in the Forest

By Katherine Bergeron

We live in an old red schoolhouse in the forest. The forest is thick and woolly, and at night you can hear the wolves sing.

It is safe here.

Before the red schoolhouse, the adults lived in a city. They told us the city had trains and tall buildings and bad people who lurked in the shadows, ready to kill you for money or for fun.

It is safe here.

We knew about the city because the adults gave us picture books of sad cartoon people living in gray buildings, taking dirty buses to factories and offices, and eating bad food. When one sad cartoon person got stabbed in the street, the other cartoon people moved around them, like river water around a rock.

It is safe here.

Yesterday we found a trunk in the basement of the red schoolhouse. It had shiny, floppy books with pictures of beautiful people with paint on their faces and dressed in colorful clothing. They posed in front of buildings like the ones in our picture books, but the people did not look afraid and there were no lurkers or stabbers.

Underneath the books were clothes we had never seen before—they felt soft like petals and smelled like lavender, so unlike our scratchy uniforms. A small wooden box at the bottom of the trunk was full of tubes and jars filled with paint, just like in the books. We put on the too-big clothes and drew the paint on each other's faces and danced around until we realized the adults would be home again soon. We changed back into our old clothes and ran to the creek to wash off the paint—we were ashamed but did not know why.

At dinner, we asked if we could visit the city. The adults wiped their mouths with their napkins and told us it was too dangerous. We would get sick, or shot, or kidnapped. When we asked what kidnapping was, they told us a kidnapper was a bad person who stole you away and never brought you back. When we asked where the bad person would take someone, the adults told us that was enough questions for one night and it was time for bed.

In bed, we whispered to each other guessing where a kidnapper would take us. A castle. A prison. A mountain. An island. A city. The moon. Then one of us said, a red schoolhouse. We stopped talking and tried to sleep.

This morning we quietly rubbed deer fat all over the adults' bags while they slept. We waved goodbye to the adults when they left for their daily walk. Then we sat in a circle inside the red schoolhouse, waiting. At dusk, we heard the wolves howl their feasting cry. When the usual time for the adults' return came and went, we smiled at each other. We stood up, had supper, and went to bed. Tomorrow we will walk to the city—we agreed it can't be too far.

We will be safe there.

Katherine Bergeron's writings have been published by The Haven, Queen Mob's Teahouse, The Satirist, The Bigger Picture, All Worlds Wayfarer, The New North, and Circlet Press. She studied film at Emerson College, and later publishing and communications at Harvard University. Coverage of her work has been featured in print and television, including The Boston Globe, The Boston Phoenix, The Dig, and WCVB-TV's Chronicle. She lives in Boston. You can visit her website at DameCore.com, on Instagram at @damecoreinc and on Twitter at @DameCoreInc.

The Not-So-Duff Duff-Duff

By Tanja Cilia

The plan was perfect. At least, so it seemed, on paper. I was chosen to bring to fruition a Sting Operation for the Government of Zirconia, with the aid of the Secret Service.

I was to go, find a huge house, buy it, and insinuate myself into the community. I would work undercover and help nab all the bad apples that passed my way... that is, members of the Five Families that went by the oldest documented surnames in Zirconia—Allard, Catteja, Faljon, Glech, and Lenponi.

How I would do so was up to me—but money was not going to be a problem, because I had the backing of the Zirconian Government. I would play it by ear.

Ironically (although I was not supposed to know this), members of these secret syndicates are proud of the fact that their Clan names date back to Angevin times.

Just for the record, The Angevins were one of the four distinct British Royal Houses, the other three being Lancaster, Plantagenet, and York. Henry II was the first Angevin King, and John the last one.

My knowledge of history is a little murky, but I seem to recall that in 1158, Pope Adrian IV (the only English Pope), is said to have issued the papal bull Laudabiliter, which ostensibly authorized Henry to invade Ireland. Henry did so, albeit 14 years later.

But I digress. Being fat and short, I qualified for the newly minted "duff" (designated ugly fat friend) position of the members of the Ladies' Circle. Of course, I had to work hard to earn their confidence, because the Zirconians are rather (read: very!) insular and parochial and provincial and close minded and...

But I learned the language... and made them laugh at my attempts to pronounce the most difficult word in their language—trqidq, which means "flour." And it was this which actually set my plan in action.

My cover story was that I was a rich widow, which is why I did not have to work. But of course, there is only so much window shopping you can do, and so many long walks you can take. I had to find something else with which to occupy my time—that was my story, anyway. I dropped details about how the large windfall helped me quench my Wanderlust, and I had read so much about Zirconia that I had decided to make it my forever home.

I launched a Cookie Exchange Scheme. Of course, my house was big enough that I could install ovens in the basement, which the members of the Ladies' Circle could use if they so desired. The stingier ones appreciated the fact that they would save money if they used my electric ovens instead of their household LPG-powered ones. The lazy ones liked it that their cooking session would not have to be followed by a cleaning one, because my maids would see to it; and the chatty ones valued the excuse of a community gathering to give them an excuse to be out and about.

I was not supposed to know that some of them were wives, mistresses, sisters and daughters of the local Mafia. They took great pains to hide Family rivalries from me, because they acted as if they were one big happy family. But sometimes, a side-eye glance at another woman not of their fraternity, betrayed them.

At the time, in Zirconia there was a great to-do about the Data Protection Act. Moreover, the General Elections were coming up, and the Zirconians are rather hot-headed about politics. I always said I was apolitical, so I would not be drawn into any of their polemics about which politician was a candidate for sainthood, and which was the devil incarnate.

I took advantage of this, and I sweetly suggested that because they were all meeting at my house once a week, I had to have their details on file—if they wanted to give them to me, ("informed consent!") that is, just in case someone saw them enter and reported me for holding clandestine meetings of "more than four people" as is the law.

I have already said I look like a duff, but actually I look like a duff-duff... you know, duff as in pudding. That, in their minds translated to "harmless."

One afternoon, while bustling about, off-the-cuff, I told them to write just their names and physical and e-mail addresses, and telephone numbers in one of those old-fashioned school exercise books.

I made the silly joke that there would not be any computer cookies, but just our usual ones... and not all of them got it. I went upstairs to look for the exercise book, albeit I knew perfectly well where it was, to leave them to discuss my request amongst themselves. I did not want to raise suspicions, if they spoke about this with "outsiders."

In any case, I also had the excuse that I ordered baking-related stuff for them from abroad, and thus I could be able to inform them when it was delivered to my hub.

So, I was privy to at least some of their personal data. My bosses were delighted—and I got a raise. Not that I wanted or needed it, but anyway... The details provided them with several leads.

This went on for quite a while, so that they would be lulled into a feeling of security. After a few months, someone came up with the idea that we should begin a mail-order service, because this would be fun and give them an opportunity to sell the cookies far and wide—literally.

I pretended I was an IT klutz and let a couple of them set up an eBay shop. That did not work out, so they set up a Facebook page, and it was a brilliant move.

When I thought it was feasible to do so, I told them I was going to see my aunt, who was terminally ill. This was true. I added that I would use the trip to have an extended holiday—but they could have the run of the basement, to continue production.

However, I did not want them snooping around the house, so I had air freshener cameras installed in the bedrooms, and nanny cams in my kitchen and other rooms.

When I was in Britain, I copied Zilla van den Bornused, the young lady who tricked her entire family into thinking she had had a five-week exotic vacation. Only mine was three months long!

The Secret Service helped, of course, so I didn't have to do the Photoshop tricks myself.

I even had the digital photos printed into a physical album, to show them when I returned to Zirconia. There was I, talking to a Jain with a mountain as a backdrop; wearing a luau on a Hawaiian beach; eating Korean food from a street vendor; scuba-diving and surrounded by clown fish (there is a moral there, somewhere!); having my face painted by a clown in Ho Chi Minh Square in Saigon, and more.

All the time, of course, I was ensconced in Headquarters, and when I went out for shots that had to be taken in the open air before they were manipulated, I always wore a disguise. In the meantime, we also worked out The Sting operation that was the raison d'être for my having been sent to Zirconia.

I would tell them I didn't get a tan because I always slathered on sunblock, since I preferred to remain pale and interesting. I was sure this would raise a couple of laughs—and yes, it did, indeed.

The Officers kept tags on my cameras; and, sad to say, there were a couple of attempts by "my friends" to go to my living quarters... I'm sure it was not because they suspected anything about my double life, but just because they were nosy.

I sent them photos on Facebook Messenger, but I asked them to keep them private. I asked them how sales were going, and they were so proud of themselves, that "our" going concern was operating in the black, and they could make donations to worthy causes.

I gently suggested that we have an actual event where we would invite dignitaries to attend a Cookie Exchange. This, of course, was only a cookie exchange in name, because actually it would be a grand affair. There would be entertainment—a live band, a concert, and a sale. All proceeds from ticket sales would go to charity.

The trap was set. It now remained for the targets to swallow the bait.

This being Zirconia, they all knew someone who knew someone who could put up a sound stage, manage the lights, paint the backdrop, sew the costumes, print the programs, etc etc.

It sort of hurt me to see women who trusted me work so hard to get their men trapped; but all is fair in love and war.

The ruse worked out far better than I ever hoped. I asked the women to send out separate invitations to all branches of their extended family, to make it easier for me to get the Boss of Bosses to attend.

It was a long shot, but it worked. There he was, resplendent in a starched white shirt with gold tips at the collar, and reeking of aftershave, trying to behave as if he was just an ordinary proud husband.

The proceedings went without a hitch. Like clockwork, when random people left the venue, some of them were followed by a Secret Service car and arrested far away enough from the venue so that no one could pin the blame on me.

The headlines of the papers, the next morning, were the cherry on the icing on the cake.

Tanja Cilia is Maltese, Mediterranean, and European—in that order. She writes in between editing and proof-reading. Read more from her at PaperJacketBlog.wordpress.com.

For Love, I Tear

By Zach Shephard

When I tore the first layer from Zolan's body, I found a different person beneath.

On the outside, he was a charcoal-skinned, sharp-jointed creature, with eyes like captured fireflies. Ever the charmer, he insisted I was the most beautiful woman in all the land: my smile, he said, shone brighter than the tumbling prisms of Baraxia's Crystal Falls.

That was outer-Zolan. The man inside was something else.

He never wanted me to look beneath, but I persisted. On our tenth night together, in a silk-draped forest-bed, he acquiesced.

I ripped, shredded, pulled. Zolan screamed. I exposed the hidden layer.

He was a shriveled, pink creature, one eye swollen shut, with a hunched back and three limp tails. I passed him a mirror, and he nodded at his reflection. We talked until daybreak.

Nothing was the same.

I'd loved Zolan, but I did not love the creature inside. I left him to scoop up the pieces of his shredded outer layer. We never crossed paths again.

I wandered the world, seeking the next Zolan. Around me, rumors of war grew: great armies crossed the plains, abolishing alien ideas, sending monsters to the graveyards of legend. Time was running out: I needed to find love, before I was forgotten.

✸ ✸ ✸

Zolan was not the first, nor would he be the last. For centuries I'd cared little for companionship; I thought it beneath me. Then someone found me. Felia? Fellena? Her name escapes me. But at the time, I'd thought her the one—my true love. I was wrong. Her inner layer was a hideous thing: black, bubbling tar, oppressive and hot as the desert sun. Still, she'd given me a glimpse of what life could be like with love. So began my obsession.

After Zolan was Marok, a soldier in the war. His shoulders were broad, his arms tattooed with glittering sapphire curves. Despite his profession, he nurtured a love of poetry and dance. I asked to peel away a layer. He refused. I stayed with him, and in two months' time, his exterior sloughed on its own, like a snake's skin.

Beneath was a complicated creature—a mess of sharp angles and thorns, like a human rosebush seen through a cracked lens. He still claimed to be a soldier, a poet, a dancer—but his movements were jerky and insecure, and there was darkness in his chest.

I stayed with him another year—whether out of love or pity, I'm not sure. In that time, he shed another layer, revealing a skeletal figure with loose limbs and a fractured neck. There was no love there, for either of us. I left.

I pursued companionship aggressively, determined to make up for wasted time. In all corners of the world I searched: the lakeside village of Luce, where Danton's reptilian inner-layer broke my heart; Aria City, with its golden towers and rose-pink cobblestones, and politician who didn't warn me of the bloody bear-traps at her core; the countryside prowled by Rogash the Wanderer, who would rather kill me than show his true self. I left his bones under the peach tree where we'd first kissed.

All the while I heard tales of battle, their outcomes disconcerting. In my travels I encountered a woodland shrine devoted to me: the blood-adorned stones had been toppled, the bone-charms stomped. Before long, the last few who revered my kind would be smothered by the tide of war, and I would be swept up with them. I wasn't ready to go—I needed more time to find that which my heart sought.

In the bakery, I met Kai.

He brought me the honey-cake I'd ordered, along with a raspberry tart for himself. He joined me at the table outside, where we chatted and laughed under sun-gilt clouds. Kai let me try his tart—the best item from his kitchen, he said. My joy must have been evident after that first taste, because he insisted the rest was mine.

Kai was as sweet as the treasures he baked. Everything he did was for me. I'd been worshiped before, by strangers who never quite knew what I was, but no one had ever loved me like Kai.

Naturally, I was skeptical. After all the others, how could I not be? Kai's outer layer loved me, yes—but what about the rest?

I wanted to wait—to let Kai reveal himself naturally. But the end of war was rapidly approaching, and I didn't want to leave that world before knowing true love. Every day, I cursed myself for all those wasted centuries—for not starting sooner.

I asked Kai to let me dig—to expedite the process. He agreed.

I tore away his outside, revealing a dark-eyed, stubble-cheeked man beneath. His hair was thick, and just long enough to run my fingers through.

He was the same Kai I'd just shredded. The same Kai who held me at night when thoughts of war brought tears to my eyes. The same Kai who loved me.

I'd never met a mortal who didn't change from one layer to the next. It was unsettling.

With permission, I shredded another layer. We shared the same laughs and smiles we always had. War tore through the countryside. Kai continued holding me, even when he grew sick.

I didn't understand. I removed another layer.

Kai remained unchanged, though his health deteriorated. Marching legions approached the city, abolishing memories of my kind. Kai, weakened, still held me, telling me everything would be all right.

When would I finally see his true self?

I shredded another layer, and another. Each time, I found the same Kai—weaker, smaller than before, but always smiling. He loved me completely.

With tears in my eyes, I removed one last layer.

Lying on the bed, in the room above the bakery, was the same man who'd brought me a honey-cake and shared his raspberry tart. He died holding my hand.

For years I sought love, thinking I knew who I was. But with Kai dead by my hand, I've finally seen my innermost layer. My worshipers were right all along. I stand on Kai's balcony, watching the advancing armies, sun low at their backs. I could flee and prolong the inevitable, but why? At my heart, I'm the darkness of this world. I understand that now. And soon, so will the rest.

The sun sets. I shred my final layer. Night's army approaches, and I drift from the balcony to meet them.

Zach Shephard's fiction is generally either bleak or humorous, without much of a middle-ground. His stories have appeared in places like Fantasy & Science Fiction, Flash Fiction Online and the Unidentified Funny Objects anthology series; for a complete list of published works, check out ZachShephard.com.

Reflections on a Loaf of Rye

By Shelly Jones

I sing to the children across a field of lacy white flowers, harvesting caraway in my apron: "Pockets full of caraway, ovens full of rye. Knead and eat your cares away, until it's time to die."

They look at me disdainfully, sluggishly yank a handful of weeds, hold them out to me. "That's not caraway," I say, inspecting the half-dead stalks. The girl shrugs, drops them to the ground while the boy watches, a finger picking at his ear. "Don't you want to help me make bread when we get home?" I ask, hoping the promise of a crisp loaf will tantalize their taste buds, tame their tempers.

"We don't like bread," comes a defiant voice. "We like sweets!" They flee over the hill, leaving me to finish the harvesting alone. They do like their sweets, I think, remembering how many times I have pulled them from the bakery window in town, their hot breath fogging up the glass, obscuring the treasures within: confections, doughs, delights their mother knew how to bake. I follow their laughter through the fields until we reach home.

✳✳✳

"Mother always baked us sweets," the girl bemoans, looking at the dark oats on the table.

"You'll have to teach me how," I say, pulling out a wooden bowl.

"That's not how it works," the boy pipes up. "You're supposed to teach us!" He swipes an errant finger through the flour, shoves it in his mouth, and coughs a dry puff.

"No one ever taught me how to make sweets. All I can bake is bread. Wouldn't you like a nice rye loaf?" They roll their eyes and rush out of the hut, leaving a trail of dusty footprints across my clean floor. I knead the dough, the heel of my hand stretching and pressing into the sticky paste until it smoothes into a silky ball. Satisfied, I let it rise, knowing the wait is worth the promise of the dough.

✹✹✹

She comes to me in a dream, a crown of spun sugar, a milky gauze covering her face. She casts her hands over the children, asleep on the floor in the straw. It is then I see the glint of metal on her finger, a ring more precious than the tin that pinches me. She smells of yeast and dead leaves, of chocolate and blood.

"Mine," a voice whispers in my head, claggy and deep. "Let them come to me."

✹✹✹

The children balk at my bread. They stare at the thin slices on their plates, a sliver of butter smeared across. They poke at it, as if testing the proof, examining my work. "It smells funny," says the girl, nose crinkling.

"That's the caraway," I reply, chewing my own slice carefully, hoping they will mime me. "Remember when we picked those flowers in the field near the crossroads? I used them to spice the bread."

"We're eating flowers?" the boy asks, disgust coating his tongue.

"Mama used to make us flowers from marzipan. Do you know what that is?" the girl asks.

I swallow and shake my head. The rye loaf squats on the table between us, sad and misshapen. Their father says nothing.

"It's delicious. It's made of almonds."

"And sugar," her brother offers.

"And she'd carve the most lovely shapes for us—flowers and vines and cherries that we'd wear tucked behind our ears like jewelry." She smooths her hair, primps and preens.

"You can do that with real cherries too. We'll pick some next summer. Maybe you can help me make jam."

The girl slumps back in her chair, legs swinging beneath the table. "It's not the same."

It is only then I realize how much she reminds me of my sister. I imagine her foot trampling on the loaf as if it were a steppingstone in a river—the bread crumpling, crumbling beneath the weight of her. I cannot bear it. I remove the rye from the table, wrap it carefully in a tea cloth. Outside, they cannot see my tears as I unpin the laundry, fold it until it is too dark to see what I am doing. When I come back, the children are asleep, and I am grateful for the silence.

"I could take a position in town," I whisper to him. "I can mend or clean. Perhaps the bakery needs a good bread maker."

"The town is too far to go to each day and return each night," he rationalizes. It is a long way—too far to walk, and he needs the horse to carry wood from the forest. "We could sell the children. The boy would make a good sweep or stableboy; the girl could learn to cook."

"Sell the children?" I ask, a knot swelling in my stomach. I glance at their sleeping forms, tawny hair askew. "They are your children, but to sell them..." I think back to the dream, the metal ring that matches his. "She wants them," I manage.

"Who?" he asks with a yawn.

"Your wife. She came to me in a dream. She wants the children to come live with her."

"My wife is dead."

"She came to me, spoke to me. She is in the forest. We'll send the children to her. If she is not there, if it's all a lie, they'll return to us— and we'll start anew."

He is silent for so long, I fear he has fallen asleep before hearing my plan. I am about to give up, to roll over, when I hear him sigh. "I'll take them to the forest in the morning."

The knot unravels. I sleep dreamlessly, wake rested.

In the morning, I pin mint to their coats for warmth, tuck a sprig of rosemary in their pockets for protection. Wrapping a fresh loaf in a cloth, I hand it to the girl, who accepts it begrudgingly. For a long time, I watch them from the doorway, the boy trailing behind her as they wind their way towards the woods.

Shelly Jones is a professor of English at a small college in upstate New York, where she teaches classes in mythology, folklore, and writing. Her speculative work has previously appeared in Podcastle, New Myths, The Future Fire, and elsewhere. Find them on Twitter at @shellyjansen and on her website, ShellyJonesPhD.wordpress.com.

Conscription Day

By S.R Malone

An officer with a square-set jaw greeted us at our front door.

"Daddy, who is this man?" Myra asked.

"Oh, this kind gentleman is from the army," I crouched by her side, "He's here to take you to space camp."

Liar.

She stared at me with wide, innocuous eyes; the eyes of a firstborn whose lawful duty was to serve for five years off-world in the military. More importantly, the eyes of a daughter who does not wholly believe the truth, nor understand it, but cannot help but trust the word of her loving parents.

"Have a fun holiday, pumpkin," I said, choking on tears.

Myra squeezed me as tight as she could while her mother passed her backpack to the serviceman. He smiled, dutifully. She sniffled, clutching Myra. They wept together, until the officer gently led our child down the pathway to the curb.

Over the tops of the neighborhood gleamed the upper struts of the launch pad, towering over rows of spotless prefabricated houses. Unified Earth flags stood sentinel on countless lawns, blowing mockingly in the breeze.

I watched Myra join other innocent faces in the convoy, all prepared for their holiday.

Fury bubbled under my flesh as her pale face pulled away from our street, the row of black SUVs fading to dots in the distance, like a chain of ants as they rounded the corner and climbed the hill to the launch pad.

This day was one I had been dreading for seven years. Ever since I held the waxy black and white stills of Nora's womb back then, a concoction of pride and anxiety swelling in my stomach.

My foreman rang the house earlier, giving the all-clear for my absence today; such is the way of the world now when your eldest is called up.

And that evening I stared heavenwards as the craft's retros fired up and it ascended into the misty dark blue. I settled on the edge of the porch, watching it soar free of suburbia.

Every night I sit and impatiently await its return, as others do.

I did not anticipate the acidic sorrow that would fill my veins, casting red eyes over Myra's room, a dark museum to her memory; a baseball bat slunk in the corner, her dolls arranged as she had left them, having a tea party. Her plastic crossbow with foam darts; her little brother Ryan has one too, but he is too young to understand why they are never played with anymore.

The Mathesons from No.10 pass me tonight, waving and smiling their sympathetic greetings. I'm perched here every night, and the neighborhood knows it. The neighborhood likes to discuss it.

"Conscription Day," sighed Emmett Matheson, the last time they'd invited us for dinner, "It isn't easy. But it's our duty to the planet, and that's something worth the sacrifice." He'd led me into the study, and we'd shared a Scotch. I'd positioned myself near the window so I could watch the skies. "We can't fight it, and nor would I want to— no, sir." My gaze had wandered to the photo of him and his lad, a picture a decade old.

Tonight, I blow a kiss to the dying embers of the day as the milky yellow glow from the living room presses out against the gloom of the porch.

Myra would be ten years old today.

I just hope, pray even, that she had a brilliant day.

In the dusk, the spotless homes lining the street like fireflies.

This was what we sacrificed for.

This, our utopia.

S.R Malone is a writer living just outside Edinburgh, Scotland. He has been published in Synthetic Reality Magazine, 365 Tomorrows and Entropy-Squared. When he is not writing or reading, he likes to spend time with his family and their dog, going for walks in the Scottish wilderness. Get in touch on Instagram at @s.r_malone.

The Finite Magic of Little Monsters

By Audri Salinas

Magic is not just a Gift, despite the commonly used misnomer. To view it as such can lead to irresponsible delusions and wasteful practices. Rather, Magic as understood by the Guild is a limited resource that needs to be carefully controlled and allocated for peak societal impact. We take this duty seriously and strive to invite only the most visionary Witches and Warlocks into our ranks. In this way, we protect and cultivate the Coven of the Arts. ~ Edict of Redistribution, section 1, article 2.1.

Guildhall had been Hanna's dream ever since she was old enough to understand what dreams meant.

From the moment she registered the significance of that spiky black insignia, her life had been spent chasing it. She'd dragged her exasperated parents and disinterested brother into endless craft stores and galleries, steering family vacations toward exhibitions of Magic or Coven signings. She'd spent long hours at the local mystic shop, eyes scraping over swirling orbs, singing statues, and tittering paintings of rosebud ladies, their smudged, impressionistic parasols spinning behind them. She'd read every book she could find on the Guild and watched countless interviews of new witches and warlocks, inhaling the minor details of their lives as if she could repeat their success by osmosis. Her childhood bedroom had a poster of Guildhall dominating one wall (which her mother called "nightmare fodder" and had promptly ripped down when Hanna moved into the city). She'd worked herself to the bone developing her unique Gift, perfecting her Little Monsters, applying every year for the chance to take the Exam. Her father wouldn't talk about it and Cody didn't understand. But, despite her mother's nervous doubt and gentle suggestions to maybe do something else, Hanna had blown on the coals of her dream with relentless ferocity.

Finally, finally, here she was.

Guildhall.

The mansion was huge and imposing, as mysterious as the power it represented. Innumerable windows glinted at her like so many eyes, eerie even in the bright midday sun. Ivy stretched long fingers up the encircling stone wall and curled around the top of heavy wrought-iron gates. The cobblestone path was hemmed in roses. On either side, bushes cut into sharp animal shapes prowled with silent grace, tethered by their roots but still roaring and swiping and howling at the clouds.

Magic.

It's even more impressive in person, Hanna thought, tilting her head back to trace the spiral turrets that rose into the sky like smoke.

Despite a lifetime of envisioning herself in this exact place, Hanna still felt like an intruder. She was a mundane smear of gray on an otherwise beautiful painting, a pebble among gleaming gems. She shifted her weight, suddenly all too aware of how dull and unremarkable her jeans, Chucks, and ratty cotton pullover might seem.

It doesn't matter, Hanna told herself sternly, trundling her enormous rollaboard through the gates, down the path, and toward the great gilded doors. The Coven doesn't care how you look. They sent the invitation. They wanted you to come.

Hauling her oversized suitcase up the age-warped stone stairs, Hanna paused. Took a deep breath. Lifted the knocker.

The door swung open, ripping the brass ring out of her fingers.

Hanna swallowed her surprised gasp, stuffing it back into her chest as she faced the tall figure in the now-open door. It was an elderly woman, forebodingly elegant, wiry gray hair pulled in a high, tight bun. She wore a deep crimson turtleneck that hugged her bony frame like a bloodstain.

"Hanna Ramison, I presume?" said the woman in a voice that reminded Hanna of old church bells.

"Y-yes." Hanna coughed, reining in her frayed nerves as she pulled the acceptance letter out of her back pocket. "Yes ma'am, I'm here for this month's Exam." She held out the crimped paper, worn soft by her endless, incredulous rereads.

When it had materialized on her tiny kitchen table, Hanna hadn't believed it. At first, she thought it was a hallucination. Or worse, a joke. But when she'd seen the invitation scrawling itself across the thick, cream-colored parchment as if by an invisible hand, she'd known. The bristling black cursive manifesting her dreams before her was the truest, strongest Magic Hanna had ever felt. It had to be real.

Now the acceptance letter looked small and mortal next to the majesty of Guildhall.

Like her.

The woman arched one brow, inscrutable eyes sweeping down. Hanna could almost read the thoughts on her forehead, written in the same barbed script. A video game T-shirt? Jeans? Sneakers? What kind of witch do you think you are?

But Hanna didn't flinch away. Instead, she hitched her expression into the warm southern belle smile her mother had taught her, clutching the suitcase handle that was her tether to the world.

In that suitcase were her tools, her clay, her paints.

Everything she needed to make her Little Monsters.

Give me a chance, Hanna tried to say with her smile. I'll show you what I've got. Let me prove you wrong.

After a long, breathless moment, the old woman stepped aside to let Hanna in, turning away in half dismissal as the door crashed shut behind them.

"I am Headmistress Oswall." She clicked into the entrance, Hanna jogging to keep up. "I will be overseeing your efforts for the next month and conveying my..." she flicked a glance back, "thoughts to the rest of the Coven. Our final evaluation will take place on the last day of the lunar cycle, in the gardens."

Hanna swallowed, eyes still adjusting to the sudden darkness. She already knew that. She knew everything there was to know about the Exam.

Including what happened to those who failed.

"You are not committed to anything until you step onto one of the Reservoir crystals," the woman continued as Hanna blinked, taking in the akimbo arms of the master staircase, the cavernous entrance hall, the rows and rows of portraits around her, half of them familiar, all of them famous. "Until then, you have the option to leave at any time. Do you understand?"

"Yes, ma'am," Hanna said, hating the drawl that came out when she was nervous. She wondered if Headmistress Oswall could hear it.

"You've been assigned a room on the third floor. Do not leave the Guildhall grounds. Do not attempt to go through the GuildGate or access the Reservoir. Do not speak to any Coven member or associate. You will fraternize only with the other aspirants until you have either passed your exam or returned to the common population."

Headmistress Oswall swung around, a key dangling from one finger and glinting like a knife.

"Any questions?" she snapped.

Hanna swallowed again and it felt nauseatingly like a rodent was trying to burrow into her chest.

Be brave, she thought. For Cody.

She accepted the key, clutching it tight enough to leave teeth marks on the flesh of her thumb.

"No ma'am."

"Then good luck," Headmistress Oswall said without emotion. "I'll be watching."

✳ ✳ ✳

Should aspirants prove themselves worthy conduits of Magic, they will not only be allowed to keep their Gift but will also be granted full support and exposure. They will never want for supplies or mystical assistance. Their work will be featured in our galleries and distributed by our infrastructure, and they will be guaranteed a position of honor among the Magical elite.

Those who fail to prove themselves at Guildhall will offer their Magic to the Reservoir, to be redeployed as the Guild sees fit. ~ Edict of Redistribution, section 2, article 5.6.

✳ ✳ ✳

Hanna was surprised to find someone already in her room, a wild-haired girl with perfectly round glasses and baggy harem pants who introduced herself as Deja Bisset.

"I'm from Quebec," said the girl in a thick accent, rising from the nest of her paint-splattered sheets.

"Roanoke," Hanna said, hefting her suitcase onto the bare, plastic-coated mattress. "Virginia," she clarified when the girl's eyebrows puckered.

"That's a big suitcase for just a month, no?" Hanna could feel Deja's breath on her neck as the other girl leaned in close. "I brought only one change of clothes. You seem to have many."

"It's my supplies."

Hanna edged away just enough to not seem rude. Deja didn't seem to notice. She only frowned, strangely cat-like as she cocked her head. "But they are providing everything we need, are they not?"

A flush rose up Hanna's neck. Her mother had said the same thing.

45

Honey, if they don't have the right supplies that might mean they aren't interested in this, er, kind of work.

Hanna shoved the voice to the back of her mind, to the bleak grayness that existed at the edge of her ambition.

"Just wanted to be safe," she said to Deja instead, stretching her back and peering around her new room. "Woah... are these yours?"

Hanna leaned in to examine a beautiful painting of the sea, one of several hanging on the wall over her new roommate's bed. They were majestic, the paint actively crashing and blending with so much force that Hanna found herself wondering how they didn't fall off the wall. Deja's work was silent, of course. Like the hedges outside. And yet still gorgeously kinetic, alive, pulsing with Magic.

"Yes," Deja answered in an unsure voice. "My Gift manifests as ocean landscapes." The other girl scratched her blue-splattered arm, eyes bug-like and magnified by her thick spectacles. "I hope that headmistress woman likes them."

"She'd be an idiot not to," Hanna said, unable to tear her eyes away from the azure progression of the sea, the snowcap crest of foam punching into tender sand. The closest painting seemed to gain force as she watched, waves pumping faster, wilder, in rhythm with her heartbeat, somehow channeling Hanna's tension into each violent surge.

Her fists clenched.

Doubt — that old, malevolent friend — slinked into her mind, tried to sink its fishhook claws into her certainty. *Can my Gift really compete with this? Will they choose her instead of me? Maybe I should leave, keep what I have, return to my studio and the small life of a local magician?*

But she forced herself to take a deep, calming breath, lifting that well-worn memory of her brother's gleeful laugh as a shield.

If her work could delight a lonely boy with autism, surely the Guild would recognize how much good her Little Monsters could do.

Hanna swung to face Deja, hitching a smile on her face.

"So," she said, offering her best lets-be-friends smile, "where do we eat in this place?"

✳ ✳ ✳

While it is a common, pedestrian idea that there is "enough space for all kinds of Magic," the reverse is actually true. Not only is Magic limited, but there is only so much space for it in the market. Imagine if every enchanted bauble or sketch was given the Guild's stamp? It would be chaos. There would be no way for the Giftless to be guaranteed quality Magic. And worse, if the Coven couldn't depend on support from the Reservoir, then standards would drop even lower. Therefore, it is for the consumer's benefit that we curate what falls under the Guild's stamp, so it can always be trusted. ~ Edict of Redistribution, section 3, article 9.11.

✳ ✳ ✳

Over the next few days, Hanna met the other aspirants. Besides Deja and herself, there was Tommy Holt with his black-and-white Emotographs that could make any of them cry or laugh or tremble with fear. Giorgio Yang, with his mosaics that would shudder with lightning or waver like a summer haze, depending on the mood of the observer. Mildred Parks, whose films saturated the room, the ghostly shapes of actors walking off the screen to wave and strut and dance in the real world with the conviction of more than mere projections. And Jemma Juarez, whose colorful skirts and frothy tops were as expressive as hackles, rising and ruffling with her erratic tempers.

It was enough to make Hanna sleepless.

Not that any of them slept much. They had a month—a mere month—to bet against their futures. So, Hanna was far from the only one spending every waking hour in the studios. Mildred ate lunch in front of her computer as she edited; Jemma could be found bent over a sewing machine until well after dusk; Deja's hands were always layered with paint. Even aloof Giorgio had a goggle-burn from spending so much time hovering over the furnace to bend and warp his glass.

But all that went away every time one of Hanna's Little Monsters came to life.

With meticulous care, she carved and painted each one, setting them on the table to dry. When they were ready, she would breathe her Gift into them gently, maternally, seeding each one with its precious core of Magic. It felt like holding a hot cup of tea in her hands, or maybe a beating heart. Her palms would glow, and her face would flush, and suddenly the tiny figurine would come to life.

When she set them down, the Little Monster would salute her or dance or sing a ludicrous yodel. Each one was as different as a new alien species. Some had antennae or fur, others eccentric but harmless spines. There were bright feathers and dull horns and tombstone teeth and baggy coveralls. But no matter how strange they looked, all of them were cheerful and wild, radiating a larger-than-life silliness that warmed Hanna's heart.

Even in the cutthroat miasma of the studios, her Monsters managed to make her laugh.

Unless Headmistress Oswall was around, of course.

"That woman feels like the personification of a raincloud," Tommy complained one night when they were sprawled around the garden, all of them trying not to look at the heavy stone arch that represented everything the aspirants wanted. They'd spent two weeks living under its shadow and the strain was beginning to show.

"I wonder if she ever smiles," Jemma said, offering one of her own as she passed the flask to Deja.

"I think she does not," Deja answered after a heavy gulp of the harsh gin Giorgio had smuggled into Guildhall and shared without explanation. "But perhaps she would with the right... incentive."

At that point, they all knew what kinds of lurid incentives Deja meant.

"Too bad you don't do portraits," Tommy said with a wink.

"Alas, the Gift comes in its own way." Deja toppled back on the grass with a dramatic flourish.

Hanna giggled, watching one of her Little Monsters do cartwheels on the flower bed beside her. Mildred and Giorgio watched emotionlessly, as dour and serious as ever.

"What do you think it feels like?" Tommy asked after a silent moment as Giorgio took back his flask and finished it. "To stand on those?"

As if pulled by a gravity stronger than Earth's, six faces turned to stare at the crystal circles embedded in the center of the garden, bright against the smooth lawn of grass. There were ten in all—the largest class Guildhall could accommodate. Perfectly round, smooth, and glowing with an inner energy that reminded Hanna of those deep-sea plankton that created their own bioluminescence, the stones pulsed with a deeper, more ancient power than any of them could possibly channel.

The Reservoir.

"I've read that they hold you there," Hanna said, her voice cracking on the last word. She cleared her throat. "Frozen. Until you pass, of course."

"And then you go through the gate," Tommy said brightly.

Jemma scoffed. "If you're lucky."

That was enough to make them fall silent again. It was easy, under a blanket of stars and shared exhaustion, to believe they were friends. But a sinister groundwater ran beneath them, the looming scepter of rivalry.

Because the coven had never, in the entire history of Guildhall, passed an entire class.

"We can do it," Hanna said, grinning as her Little Monster began to toss handfuls of mulch in the air and watch delightedly as it rained down like autumn leaves. "You guys are all such amazing artists, I'm sure we can make it."

Mildred rolled her eyes. Giorgio remained silent. But Jemma, bless her, laughed.

"That's the spirit, Hanna."

Hanna helped a drunk Deja stumble to their room that night, tucking her roommate into bed and almost believing they could care about each other, that they could do more than just survive the Exam.

It would be the last time any of them would take a break.

The Guild recognizes the freedom of small-time magicians to practice outside the jurisdiction of the Coven. That cannot be helped. But the witches and warlocks we select are the true pillars of Magic, the mystical voices of our world. It is through their leadership that we glimpse the great power and majesty of the beyond. It is under their guidance that we see into the soul of existence. There is no greater calling than that. ~ Edict of Redistribution, section 13, article 1.

When the man walked in, Hanna wondered if her eyes had stopped working. It wouldn't be the first time that her feverish exhaustion had blurred the lines of reality in the studio. But no, the figure striding across the wide workshop was real, tangible, his cape flapping behind him.

Warlock Benedict Yosef.

Hanna blinked, looking up from the Little Monster she'd just finished. The figurine was tilting at her thumb with a floppy, harmless lance, but she ignored it. Warlock Yosef was the man responsible for the trimmed bushes in front of Guildhall, the leafy panthers and leggy green giraffes. His work was coveted by every wealthy family from here to Japan. An original Yosef could elevate any common estate to one of taste and elegance. When she was thirteen, Hanna had spent a whole summer begging and cajoling her parents to take her to the Richmond Botanical Gardens to see a full exhibition of Yosef's work. When they'd finally relented, the pure bliss of the experience had sustained her for half the school year.

Now Hanna gaped as one of her childhood heroes marched through the flurry of Jemma's fabric trimmings, the steady rumble of the sewing machine covering up the click of his boot heels.

Hanna rose, drifting over to Jemma. Tapped her on the shoulder.

The sewing machine fell silent.

"What do you—?"

Jemma's irritable question died as her eyes found the newcomer.

Warlock Yosef didn't seem to notice them, striding up to Headmistress Oswall as if the aspirants weren't even there.

"I need to access the Reservoir," he said without preamble. "I've been commissioned for a project in D.C. that requires a bit more... oomph."

Headmistress Oswall's lemon-pinched mouth didn't slacken, but she bowed her head. "Of course, if you'll follow me to the garden..."

The Headmistress's voice faded as she turned to leave. But Warlock Yosef hesitated. Glanced back.

And caught their gaze.

It was a split-second acknowledgement of their existence, a dismissive heartbeat of a look. But did Hanna imagine the pity in his eyes? The jaded acceptance that some of them would have to sacrifice on the altar of his success?

Before Hanna could puzzle out his frown, Yosef turned away, disappearing down the corridor after Headmistress Oswall.

"Asshole," Jemma said, bending back over the sewing machine.

"I mean, he's not allowed to speak to us." Hanna massaged her sore fingers, cramped from the long hours of carving and painting.

"No." Jemma's voice was rough with sleep deprivation and determined rage. "We're not allowed to speak to him. There's a difference."

The ruffle that ran down the spine of Jemma's blouse began to sharpen into a ridgeline of spikes. Hanna recognized the dismissal.

"I'm gonna go tell Deja," she said.

Jemma didn't respond, so Hanna made her way into the great hall and up the staircase, thinking about Warlock Yosef.

Would she be like that, as a registered witch? Would she offer only vague, skeptical pity to the aspirants she met in the future? Maybe she would. Maybe after years of watching faceless youths try and hope and fail, she would harden to protect herself from the onslaught of pain, of rejection, stride past as if it didn't touch her.

No, Hanna vowed as she stepped into the third-floor corridor. I won't be like that. I'll support every aspirant's dreams, no matter how unlikely. I'll inspire the Coven to be better. Do better.

A small, unwelcome voice echoed up from the chasm of her doubt.

If you get the chance.

She shook away the thought, throwing open their bedroom door. "Deja, you aren't gonna believe—"

But Hanna fell silent as the wild-haired girl swung around, her eyes even rounder and more manic than usual.

Deja was sobbing.

"W-what is it?" Hanna stammered, stepping inside and closing the door softly behind her. "What's wrong?"

"I can't... do this," Deja wailed, falling into Hanna's arms. "I'm going... to fail."

Hanna stroked Deja's hard spine and held her close, closer than she was strictly comfortable with.

"Of course you won't, you're doing great," Hanna whispered. "You've worked so hard. Look at your new paintings, they're better than ever."

"It's not... enough," Deja gasped, collapsing to the floor. "I know it's not... enough."

Squatting next to her roommate and the closest thing she had to a friend in Guildhall, Hanna stroked and whispered and did her best. But nothing she said could console Deja. The frenzied, desperate, exhausted push had worn the already-eccentric girl so thin that she was bending, a tree in the wind, an old bridge about to snap. Hanna felt it too. All the aspirants did. There were only a handful of days left until their Exam, a deadline of hours to prove their worth. Every one of them was giving their all to convince Headmistress Oswall they were worthy.

Statistically, only a few of them would.

"You're okay," Hanna said, fighting the urge to retreat into her own space, her own mind. "You're going to be fine."

Warlock Yosef's face swam back to her as Deja continued to weep and shudder, his faint pity as sharp as ever.

Maybe this was why he didn't speak to them. Because the memory of his own Exam was still raw enough to bleed.

Guild-certified Magic goes beyond mere entertainment. It's deeper and richer, at once reactive and resonant. Its value cannot be classified by the difficulty of spells or its effects on the Giftless. Rather, it must channel that indescribable other, breathe fully formed mystery into the world. Because of that, witches and warlocks themselves must be more than mere practitioners. The aspirants we choose to join the Guild must embody Magic in every element of their being and present themselves to the world as accurate representations of the Coven. Our time-honed craft of recognizing such outstanding individuals is what sets the Guild apart. ~ Edict of Redistribution, section 15, article 3.

Hanna had never been so frightened in her life.

As she followed her fellow aspirants into the garden, she wondered if her shaking legs were strong enough to keep her standing. All around her was evidence of the Reservoir's power, throbbing with the tidal pull of moonlight. The night air itself seemed to glitter like fresh frost, moving around them with a strange, prodding intelligence that made the hair on Hanna's arms stand on end.

"Jesus, fuck..." Jemma whispered, fists clenched.

Hanna's mouth was too dry to respond. She imagined the others remained silent for the same reason. Even Giorgio looked like he was about to vomit all over the softly lit grass.

Headmistress Oswall stepped onto the dais where the GuildGate waited, the air inside it glistening like an oil slick. Lined up on either side were draped, hooded figures, their faces lost in shadow, their hands tucked into heavy sleeves.

The Tribunal.

Hanna tried to imagine herself striding past them, disappearing through the arch and claiming her Gift once and for all. But the image in her mind warbled, rippling in the earthquake of her terror.

She swallowed.

"Aspirants," Headmistress Oswall said in a carrying voice. "We have reached our verdict and now so must you. Should you choose to leave, there will be no punishment. You will be allowed to keep your Gift and do with it what you will."

The Headmistress paused, her raptor eyes darting from face to blanched face. No one moved. Hanna met the old woman's gaze with her own determination. She was here for Cody, and for all the little girls and boys like him. She planned to finish what she'd started.

"Very well," Headmistress Oswall continued. "If you wish to stand trial for the chance to join our ranks, then take your place in sacred covenant to accept the decision we have made."

Quivering like a plucked guitar string, Hanna offered Deja a small smile.

We've got this, she tried to say with her eyes, but Deja only clutched herself, stepping onto her own lustrous stone. Hanna followed, choosing a blue-tinted circle at the edge of the group. She planted her feet and clenched her fists, raising her chin to face what was coming.

The Reservoir's glow deepened, darkened, pulsed. The air itself seemed to rumble as if lightning had just struck nearby.

And then Hanna felt every muscle in her body freeze.

Her fear mutated into panic, into feral regret.

I shouldn't have done this. This was a mistake. Oh God, what have I done?

Struggling to control a violent cascade of warring instincts, she focused her unblinking eyes on Headmistress Oswall as the old woman pulled out a long sheaf of snowy parchment, tracked with names.

Hanna was too far away to read them.

My name is on it, she told herself, trying to believe it. I'm on that list.

"First of all," Headmistress Oswall said to the frozen statues of the aspirants. "I want to thank you all for coming to Guildhall. We depend on young magicians like yourselves to keep the Coven supplied with fresh Magic, whatever form it takes. So well done, all of you, for supporting the important work we do."

The old woman's face remained pinched, emotionless, only half sincere. But Hanna didn't care.

Just read the list, she thought desperately. Please, just tell us. Get it over with.

"You should also know that your class had an unusually high success rate. Previously, fewer than one in four aspirants were welcomed through the GuildGate, but this month a full half of you were deemed worthy of the passage."

Three people. That's three people. Hanna wished she could look around, but her head was locked in place, wide eyes drying as Headmistress Oswall consulted her list.

"The new initiates are," she began, squinting at the parchment. "Jemma Juarez."

Hanna watched as a weak-kneed Jemma stumbled up the stairs. The hooded figures on either side of the gate clapped politely as she all but tumbled through the purplish surface of the GuildGate and into the grounds beyond.

Two more names, there are still two more names.

"Giorgio Yang."

Hanna's breath would have caught if it could have. A sob of desperation ricocheted around her belly like a loose projectile with nowhere to go. She watched Giorgio stride up the stairs as if he was born to it, showing none of the nervousness that had stained his features just moments ago.

One more. That's going to be me. Hanna Ramison. Read the name. Hanna Ramison.

"And our last initiate to the Coven," Headmistress Oswall said as Giorgio disappeared through the gate, "is Deja Bisset."

It was perhaps lucky that she couldn't move, because Hanna had no idea how she would have reacted. A scream of agony ripped at her throat, clawed at the cage of her ribs, but she was locked, trapped, helpless as Deja stepped off her circle.

Deja glanced at Hanna. In the other girl's enormous, magnified eyes was a mirror-image storm, Hanna's pain reflected back as tentative excitement, guilt, horror.

Pity.

"I'm sorry," Deja whispered.

"Quickly now, we don't have all night," Headmistress Oswall said, rolling the parchment back up.

Deja turned away, toward the dais and the GuildGate and her future.

Hanna's legs were going numb, her hands tingling with all the pent-up rage she wasn't able to express. Headmistress Oswall stepped forward, blocking their view of Deja disappearing through the Gate. The Tribunal's polite, almost bored applause died away as the Headmistress addressed the three remaining aspirants.

"I'm afraid to say that your Magic has not manifested in quite the way we're looking for. However, your Gifts will still be useful in augmenting the Coven's work. Take heart in the knowledge that your Magic will make the world better, if not directly by you."

Hanna realized with suffocating dread that it wasn't rage making her legs go numb. It was a chill creeping up from the stone, inching up her legs and spine, leeching away something she hadn't even known was there.

"You three will gather your things and leave Guildhall as soon as possible. Should you still wish to pursue careers associated with the

Guild, there are plenty of supporting positions you may choose from. We welcome your assistance and hope you will do what you can to help the Giftless appreciate Magic the way you once did. Thank you again and goodnight."

Headmistress Oswall was turning away, and Hanna wanted to scream and thrash and claw the woman's ice-cold eyes out of their sockets. She wanted to sprint for the Gate, break into the grounds beyond, force them to accept her or even just give back her Gift. But as the glowing Reservoir stone released her, Hanna found her strength gone, as if it was Magic and not muscle that had kept her aloft all these years. She collapsed to her knees, accompanied by twin thumps on either side.

"Come... back..." Hanna whispered as she struggled to lift her head.

But the dais was already empty, the Headmistress and the draped figures of the Tribunal disappearing through the GuildGate and leaving behind the three who could not follow.

While not everyone can be a practitioner of Magic, we must value and support those who have spent their lives cultivating an appreciation for it. Those who fail the Guildhall Exam will be welcomed as Official Distributors and granted the solemn duty of marketing and distributing the Coven's work. We hope they will find fulfillment supplementing the mystic work of the Guild. ~ Edict of Redistribution, section 9, article 7.1.

It had been two years since Hanna lost her Gift, but she still sometimes felt the undertow-pull of Magic or the vague, distorted craving to pick up her tools. Her boss at the gallery said it was like a phantom limb, that it would never really go away. And he should know, having failed out of Guildhall more than a decade ago.

Hanna tried not to think about it.

Selling and stacking and organizing all the Guild-stamped examples of real Magic, Hanna found herself wondering what happened to the others. What did Tommy do, without his gut-wrenching Emotographs? What about Mildred, who would never make the grinning actors walk off the screen and drift around the cinema again? Did they still dream of their work, like she did? Or had they moved on with their lives to do... something else?

She probably should too, but Magic drew her like a moth to flame. It might kill her eventually, but at least it would be warm.

Hanna sighed, straightening a colorful, abstract painting that tugged at the corner of her mind, inviting her to see the world in technicolor splatters. She glanced at the name. No one she knew.

"Hey!"

Hanna spun around to find the large, burly shape of her boss hauling in a crate stamped with that spiky black insignia.

"Help me with this, would you?" Sander said, a bead of sweat dripping into his beard.

She grabbed a crowbar off the counter.

"Do you think they use these huge wood boxes just to torment us?" Hanna said with a halfhearted grin, jamming the crowbar's teeth under the lid and hauling back.

Sander snorted. "Honey, they don't give that many shits."

Together, they managed to pop off the lid and shove it aside. Wood shavings burst out with the rush of air, scattering like petals across the shop floor.

"Damnit," Hanna muttered. "I just mopped."

"What have we here?" Sander said to himself, grabbing the descriptor card. "Oh, it's a new line of figurines. Apparently, they're supposed to be funny."

Hanna froze in the act of gathering corkscrew curls.

"They're calling them Little Monst—hey!"

Hanna didn't hear him. She was a woman possessed, diving into the crate, ripping through the packaging like a child digging into a snowbank. But there was no joy here. Just the choking, claustrophobic feeling of sinking into quicksand.

"No, no, no." Her fingers found something. Clutched it too tight, too hard.

It wriggled in her hand.

Staggering backwards, Hanna gaped stupidly at the thing in her palm. It was short, colorful, feathered. Not one she'd made, but she could have. Years ago, she could have.

The Little Monster grinned at her with benign fangs, cocking its head like a puppy ready to play. Turning the figurine upside down, Hanna blinked away tears to read the sharp script on its foot beneath the black Guild stamp.

A hand-carved original by Deja Bisset.

Audri Salinas is an Hispanic writer of science fiction and fantasy. She's worked for seven years as an assistant at the NYC Pitch Conference and editor at Del Sol Press and her novels are currently represented by the Talcott Notch Literary Agency. When not writing, she can usually be found entertaining her pandemic puppy. More about her can be found at AudriSalinas.com.

The Fashion Police Are Watching

By Jane Brown

"I'm definitely a summer," Lucy says, flicking through the rack of blue dresses.

I groan internally. Another "What season am I?" convert. I twist my lips into a smile. "But of course you are! Look at that beautiful ash hair and rosy cheeks. We have many items in blues, purples and pinks that will look très chic on you."

Lucy beams with the usual twenty-something selfie-obsessed exuberance. She gazes around the plush carpet and gold furnishings of my empty shop. "All these amazing clothes but zero customers? You need a social media presence. I didn't know the Jolie Femme Boutique existed until I got the email. Talk about a hidden gem, tucked down this alleyway." She laughs. "You know, I can't even remember entering the competition. But wow—a one hour styling session plus a free robot. What a prize!"

A few minutes later, after Lucy's ignored all my style suggestions, we head to the change rooms with the items she's chosen.

She pauses when she sees the plastic sheeting covering the walls and floor.

"Redecorating," I say.

She shrugs and enters with her complimentary champagne, drawing the heavy crimson curtains shut behind her.

"Call out if you need help with sizes," I say, before locking the door to the changing rooms and walking back out front.

✳ ✳ ✳

Darkness. I sense Lucy wake. She flails her arms and legs against the straps that bind her to a wooden chair in the middle of the boutique. Her fingers strain to reach her jeans pocket.

I could watch this scene for hours. Instead, I flick the lights on.

"Looking for this?" I hold up her phone, then smash it on the floor. She screams like I've broken one of her physical appendages, not a virtual one. "I've been watching you for a long time, Lucy," I say.

"What?" she says groggily, pulling at her straps. "I only met you today, weirdo."

I chuckle and reach under my chin, ripping off the skin façade.

"G-G-Gary from Accounts?"

I chuckle again. This time when I reach under my chin, my true form is exposed.

Lucy gasps, even vomits a little. I rub two of my tentacles together with glee.

"W-w-what are you?" she says.

"You know the saying: when a baby first laughs, a fairy is born?"

Lucy nods slowly.

"When a teenager first says, 'OMG what is she wearing?' one of us is born. We exist to save the world, eliminating one fashion disaster after another."

"Fashion disaster? What are you talking about? I have great style."

"Oh, Lucy." I shake my head. "Yesterday you wore tartan pants to the office. You are the definition of fashion disaster. Luckily, we believe in second chances. For the next hour, your job is to sit there nicely, absorbing my Fashion Essentials 101. Then your test begins— three chances to choose an acceptable outfit. Three fails and..."

"Fails?"

I wheel out the sleek red FB-6713X. "Latest model. Programmed to scan outfits and calculate a fashion score out of 100. Anything less than 75 equals failure. Bonus: pass the test and you get to take the robot home with you."

Lucy makes a weird noise, a cross between a sob and a squeak. She mumbles, "This isn't happening."

I hit play on my PowerPoint presentation. "Let's begin."

✳ ✳ ✳

"I'm ready to choose my first outfit," Lucy says after I undo her restraints. Instead, she bolts to the front of the shop and desperately tries to open the door. She yells and screams.

"Soundproof," I say.

After a few seconds, she sobs and sinks to the floor.

"Did I mention there's a time limit for the test? Better get cracking."

Lucy drags herself to the closest rack and removes a purple dress and orange shoes.

I sigh. "I fear you are not taking this seriously."

I click a button and the wall between the front and back sections of the boutique retracts. Two of the plastic covered changerooms contain ladies, each gagged and strapped to a wooden chair.

Lucy yelps, putting her hand over her mouth. "Mom?"

The lady's eyes bulge. Her arms strain against the ropes. Lucy runs towards her, but I wrap my tentacles around her waist, yanking her backwards. "Ready to start taking this seriously?"

Lucy sobs, then looks at the other woman. "Who's that?"

I mock surprise. "You don't recognize your old childhood friend Tammy? The one who helped shape your fashion sense? The one who told you it was okay to wear double denim?"

✳ ✳ ✳

The robot whirs and blinks before finally displaying the number 13.

Lucy looks down at her innocent green T-shirt and white shorts incredulously.

"Strike one. Weren't you listening at all? White shorts are a big no-no. Time to say good-bye to your friend." I press a button and a blade erupts from the wall and decapitates Tammy. Blood spurts from her torso as her head rolls back and forth on the floor.

Lucy screams. Her eyes grow wild. She grabs a pair of stilettos and stabs all four of my eyes before my tentacles can stop her. I stumble around blind, then something heavy falls on top of me. Blackness.

✳ ✳ ✳

Thirty minutes later, my eyes have regenerated. I push the shelves off my body. Lucy's gone. The mom's missing too, her hacked-off bindings dangling over the side of her chair. The still closed can't-be-opened-by-humans front door has scratch marks all over it. Damn. I only just repaired that after last time. "Lucy, come out, please. There is no escape. You have two chances remaining to pass the test."

I turn the FB-6713X's thermal imaging sensor on and immediately spot them, huddled together under a pile of winter coats. Idiots. Winter is so last season.

✳ ✳ ✳

It's been a month since Lucy's replacement started at the office. She began well—tailored suits, pumps, the whole deal. But yesterday, she wore polyester pants—ugh. I've got the email ready to go. It all depends on her outfit today.

Jane Brown is a web programmer and short fiction writer who lives by the beach in Australia. Her stories have been published in The Centropic Oracle, Etherea Magazine and Every Day Fiction. She can be found on Twitter at @janebrownau or on her website at JaneBrownWritesAU.wordpress.com.

The Tended Field of Eido Yamata

By Jon Michael Kelley

Somewhere in the distance, the faint tinkling of a bell...

In the serenity where he now found himself, Yamata still retained the vista of his previous life.

Sitting meditatively, he could recall every moment of that existence with uncommon clarity. However, he did not recognize from those memories the child standing before him, a girl of obvious Japanese descent, about eight years old, wearing a simple knee-length white dress that seemed remarkably clean and bright, given that her bare legs and feet were black with dirt. A rice hat made of bamboo sat confidently atop her head and hooked in the bend of an arm was an ikebana basket of similar weave. But there were no flowers.

Except for not having a mouth, she appeared normal in every other way.

But then, Yamata had to look no farther than his own desiccated body to know that, here, "normal" was not to be the dominant theme. Obviously, the afterlife was amenable to showcasing his wasted form, one achieved in the previous one through self-mummification. But that such a gaunt and withered state had escorted him so authentically into the next realm was rousing some concern, as he could only slightly turn his head, and to a greater degree his right arm.

Am I to remain forever a rigid corpse? he wondered.

As it had for the better part of his life, a yellow robe draped his body, though with much less resolve given his strangled girth.

Interestingly, he was able to speak, and had done so upon his relocation; a kindly greeting to the girl. She'd responded only with an unenthusiastic wave of her hand, her brown eyes staring on, mildly curious.

Beyond the girl was a vastness that Yamata was still trying to grasp. And, like the girl, there was nothing he could recall from his previous life to make its comparison; a life spent mostly in the Tōhoku region of Japan's Honshu Island, in search of purification. To all points on the horizon, barren furrows radiated outward from where he sat, a lotus posture that was the very hub for those tilled spokes. He was reminded of a naval flag, one belonging to a country that only had his compulsory allegiance: The land of the Rising Sun, its red ensign's beams flaring outward in strong allegory. And similar intentions were at work here, he suspected, as neither from the east nor west did this sun rise, but instead beat down relentlessly from a perpetual noon.

Although his time here was (in the vaguest sense) relatively new, the tropes for enlightenment were ageless.

The atmosphere was leaden with quietude, as if becalmed eons ago by some great inhalation and had since petrified while waiting for the ensuing release. Once here, Yamata had intuited an acceleration of awareness. Not the passing of time (although there were sequential aspects to the construct), but rather a kind of hastened shedding; a sloughing of absolutes, and things now obsolete, receding away like dreams do upon waking. And very much like dreams, those references slipped no further than the periphery of his erstwhile life; lingering there, close by and ready should they be called upon to offer up sobering testimonials. Witnesses to a world that was more devoted to the conservation of falsehoods than to their dismantling. That Hell was eternal was just one of those; that death was the end of learning and bettering oneself, another. No fires burned hotter than those of the physical world, the fires of greed, lust, anger, hatred, sickness... Heaven, he believed, was anywhere such conflagrations had been doused.

Not so unlike his previous journey, the one he would begin from here would be chaperoned by contemplation. He would be careful of being too prideful, and to always remember that it was never about what life had denied him, but rather what he had denied life.

Yamata considered again his permanent seat, his cadaverousness, the hushed girl, the vast field stretching in all directions...

A field unproductive yet, aside from the growing anticipation.

And that fixed ceiling of sunshine. On a profound level, Yamata accepted the unfailing brightness as obligatory to the venue, for the most crucial lessons were often the most evasive, and to achieve their understanding required keeping any and all shadows squarely underfoot.

That, or the enduring sunshine was simply here to nourish what was clearly an imminent crop of inestimable scope, and aspirations.

In what was without doubt a land of extended metaphor, he considered a myriad interpretation, from the obvious to the abstruse.

Upon those very thoughts, the little girl stepped closer and tipped her basket to allow him to see its contents. Only a few remained of what appeared to be some kind of seed. With much effort he tilted his head and, beyond her, looked again upon the rows, this time focusing on proximity rather than distance. He saw her footprints, deep and purposeful, marching along the soft trenches. Even closer, he saw the tiny indentations where her finger had pushed seeds into the soil. And he could now see that her impressions weren't just localized but disappeared into the staggering distance; toward a horizon not teetering upon the curvature of a round world but poised securely upon the blaring infiniteness of a flat one.

A determined girl! Yamata stared at her again and thought she might even be unusually pretty. But the unnatural smoothness below her nose was influencing that illusion. When having first seen the mouthless girl, Yamata thought of her as stage dressing to his soliloquy, a caricature of quiet innocence. A projection, perhaps, of his immaturity in this new place. He now suspected her reason for being here was as much practical as it was chaste metaphor. She was to be, among other things, the assistant to his immobility.

A less liberated person might have called it servitude, but Yamata saw the potential for a collaboration, though he was yet unclear as to what his reciprocal role might be. And that she could read his thoughts wasn't entirely accurate, as he believed her to be, to some degree, the very extension of them, of his mind. His duality.

Regardless, there was no question that those omitted lips accentuated the expression in her eyes. She was smiling in her agrarian achievement.

He smiled back, then impulsively wondered: Does her white dress suggest virtue? Purity? Or is it to represent the absence of beguiling color? After all, beyond the gold tint of his robe there was only a monotonous blend of bucolic hues.

Abruptly, the girl gave a sighing motion with her shoulders, slowly shook her head, then began walking a tight circle, eyes down and focused on her dirty feet.

Watching the demonstration, Yamata was struck with the notion that she was communicating her annoyance with him.

Have I become tedious with my musings? he wondered. That it is not truth I am chasing but my own tail instead?

If she agreed with these thoughts, she gave no sign.

Finally, he said to her, "Giving into the assumption that you have no name, even if you could speak it, I shall call you Uekiya."

Upon hearing the word, the girl looked up and nodded to the unfailing field, accepting her new title: Gardner. Then she lowered her eyes once more and resumed etching a tight circle into the loamy soil.

Again, considering the girl's inability at speech, Yamata recalled a quote from Lao Tzu, the founder of Taoism, and wondered if she was the exemplar for such wisdom: "He who knows, does not speak. He who speaks, does not know."

Then, to confirm that she either was or was not, in fact, substantial, Yamata reached out his workable hand for her. Stiffly, she stopped going around and round and regarded the gesture with narrow eyes, then slowly shook her head, as if to say that was not appropriate.

Why? he wondered. Am I being reminded that something's authenticity doesn't necessarily lie in its solidness? Or was there still lingering within him a tactile need? One not quite disassociated yet from his former self?

Then there was sudden growth in the field. Already the girl was bent over and studying the nearest sprout, a thing that vaguely resembled an asparagus spear, no larger than his littlest finger and appearing just as corpselike. A reaffirming sign that this was going to be a harvest most different from any other.

Still bent over, hands on her knees, Uekiya turned her attention to him. Where triumph could not insinuate itself in a smile, so it sparkled doubly in her eyes.

From behind him came once again the tinkling of a bell. A declarative echo, perhaps, of his resolve to achieve Sokushinbutsu, the practice to reach ultimate austerity and enlightenment through a most ambitious art of physical punishment: self-mummification. For a Shingon Buddhist, it was an enduring commitment. For many years the devoted monk would practice nyūjō, adhering to elaborate regimes of meditations, physical activities that stripped the body of fat, and an exclusive diet of salt, pine bark, nuts, seeds, roots, and urushi tea. This tea was especially significant. It was derived from the sap of the urushi tree and was highly toxic and was normally used for the lacquering of pottery. When ingested, vomiting and dehydration followed. Most importantly, it ultimately made the body too poisonous to be eaten by carrion insects and their ilk. If the body absorbed high enough levels, some believed it could even discourage like-minded bacteria.

Finally, when sensing his end drawing near, the monk would have himself locked inside a pinewood box, one barely large enough to accommodate his body, wherein a permanent lotus position was assumed. Some monks would insist on having coal, salt, or even lime heaped around them to stave off the slightest moisture.

Once confined, the practitioner's only connection to the outside world was an air tube, and a bell—one he would dutifully ring every day to let those listening know that he was still alive. When the ringing stopped, the air tube was removed and the makeshift tomb tightly sealed.

After a customary three years had passed, the body was exhumed. Of the many who attempted to achieve such a hallowed state, only a very few triumphed. Most bodies were found to be in normal states of decay. However, those who accomplished their own mummifications were regarded as true Buddhas. Highly revered, they were placed into the temples for viewing.

For their tremendous spirit and devotion, admiration was still paid to those who failed in their endeavors. But for Yamata especially, that was modest esteem—and certainly not the sort he ever hoped to gain through compromise.

Uekiya had dropped her basket and, arms dangling at her sides, was now staring intently at something behind him. And by the tilt of her gaze that something was alleging to be looming from a great height. Her awe was absolute. Had she the proper hinges, Yamata thought, she would have been left slack jawed. He then became both exhilarated and frightened. What could exist among these rural and most modest trappings to provoke such veneration? If he were prone to such expectations, he might have believed she was beholding a god.

That she was witnessing a massive thunderhead instead was the likelier explanation. After all, from a parched point of view, threatening rain clouds could easily provoke the same respect as any passing deity.

Moisture. Yes, it would be the remaining ingredient needed to placate the construct's agricultural objective. Being unable to turn his head fully to either side, Yamata's visual range was limited, thus leaving the matter most tantalizing. Yet another clue that the lessons here would not be easily learned.

After what may have been a mere moment or the passing of centuries, the girl reached down and retrieved her basket, her wonderment either spent or the spectacle had finally retreated.

Another burst of growth in the rows, now appearing as a more recognizable plant. Although still spindly and emaciated, the stalks were more pronounced and now home to little brown offshoots that were unmistakably leaves, semi-translucent in their infancy. A quality that he found to be strangely reminiscent, but of what he couldn't yet say.

Whatever relevance this germination had to the setting remained unclear. Yamata continued to employ his wisdom, always mindful that this was by its very nature a land of illusion.

Yamata again reached out for the girl, his compulsion growing fierce. This time, Uekiya wheeled and violently slapped his hand away, nearly breaking off the first two fingers. With utter disbelief, Yamata stared at those digits, both dangling now on withered tendons and pointing obliquely, if not forebodingly, to the ground.

The pain was sudden and intense—and disconcerting. He had not anticipated there to be such measurable discomfort beyond physical life. But he did not react instinctively and withdraw his arm. Instead, he left it out there for her to see. A testament to her brashness, to her insolence.

With something akin to compassion, Uekiya's eyes softened. Then she made her way to the closest plant and began plucking its leaves, placing each one carefully into her basket. As Yamata watched, his curiosity grew into trepidation as he realized that those lucent leaves were the same color and texture as his dried, wrinkled skin. After having gathered only a few, Uekiya stepped up to his extended arm and began carefully applying the leaves to his broken fingers, bringing them back together at their fractures then wrapping and gently rubbing the new tissue into place, manipulating and messaging it until it was indistinguishable from his own layering. When she was through, she turned his hand this way and that, regarding her accomplishments with satisfaction.

Yamata flexed his fingers and found them restored to their original, albeit intransigent, state. But any appreciation of Uekiya's handiwork was quickly dissolving, melting into an anxiety unlike any he had ever known, confirming that the most profound realizations were often the most unsettling.

Within the rows there was yet again another acceleration of growth, this time even more telling as a small whitish bulb had become evident at the top of every stalk, each of those now taller by another eight inches, and with heartier girth.

Are they the rudiments of a flower? Yamata wondered of the spheres. A fruit? Or are they the beginnings of something I dare not try to imagine?

His determined outlook, he realized, was growing dim. A dread had begun building in the thick atmosphere, but there was no beating heart to accompany it to crescendo. Just his quivering essence.

And still the plants grew, now four feet high, their bulbs even whiter and plumper, where within those a restlessness festered. As he stared, they disconcertedly reminded him of caterpillar nests, the larvae inside those silk pouches squirming to break free.

Yamata turned his eyes to Uekiya, as if her own might provide an answer, or at least a concerned recognition of his plight.

He balled his right hand as best he could, and vehemently condemned her speechlessness. "Are you to remain forever silent, or must I say just the right thing, ask just the right question to elicit a response?" But her attention had once again been drawn to something behind him. Something gargantuan was still his impression.

It was then when Yamata noticed that something had gone missing from the construct. He searched his restricted view; frantically so. It was vitally important to remember, he was sure. Everything presented here had dire meaning and was only expected to change or disappear altogether once its purpose had been understood. Or so he expected.

Then there was movement. Of the nearest plant, its bulb had begun weeping milky rivulets; viscous streams trailing down the stalk with the ambition of warmed honey. Then Yamata realized that the discharge was not composed of any liquid but was made up of hundreds of pale white worms. And maggots. Upon reaching the ground, the creatures struggled in the loose soil, their frantic undulations less confident but still maintaining a fixed progression toward his still and sitting form.

Bent over once again, hands on knees, Uekiya was watching the bugs' advancement with rapt wonderment.

The first worms to reach Yamata reared up and attached themselves to the lowest parts of his feet, then began burrowing through the brown, shriveled skin. Sparkles of intense pain began dancing behind his eyes, and a shrill, strident noise stung his ears; the pinched squeal, he quickly realized, of his own dry voice.

The pain of them entering his body was memorable, but the kind they ignited once inside was astonishingly bright and bellicose. A feast not on mere shriveled bone and muscle, he feared, but upon a profound and everlasting food source: his soul. And it too screamed. Sounds not birthed from a decrepit throat but instead the collected resonances of isolation and grim oblivions, now to be intoned upon an unending existence.

The internal writhing of the worms was equally insufferable, and he cried out for a boyhood god; one he had no occasion to revisit, until now.

Finally, mercifully, the pain slowly receded after the remaining worms had inserted themselves. It was a momentous reprieve. But another look at the burgeoning rows beyond confirmed that such amnesties would be fleeting.

Leisurely filling her basket, Uekiya had set about plucking leaves from the offending plant. Yamata stared out across his field, one that was now growing a perpetual supply of sutures; grafts to outwardly mend the external damage caused by an equally eternal progression of the most vile and ravenous creatures.

But what about the internal damage? he desperately wondered. How will she mend that?

Uekiya was now kneeling before him, messaging the leaves onto the chewed holes in his feet, restoring the dead tissue.

When finished, she went back to staring at the anomaly behind him.

Yamata prayed that the girl was, in fact, witnessing a storm. Prayed for a deluge to drown the crawling masses. For lightning to scorch them thoroughly, then let typhoon winds scatter their seared remains across the farthest reaches of this perpetuity.

Prayed for any blight that would dissuade his punishment.

Once, his great profundity did not abide the generic concepts of an eternal and torturous perdition. Now, he was being forced to reconsider. Ironically, what remained intact of his fracturing philosophy was the reverberation of his most insightful expression; that it wasn't about what life had denied him, but what he had denied life.

And life, it was being made very clear, was not going to be denied him.

Despite his most sincere, consecrated motivations, he had accelerated his own death and thereby corrupted those intentions. To tear away the shiny tinsel of devotion revealed the harsher truth of a prideful suicide. But his biggest sin of all was saturating his body with urushi tea. Having done so, he had denied the carrion eaters their due; had disallowed the natural progression of things and had done so vainly and with utter disregard for consequence.

The bulb of the second closest plant had opened, releasing its own white undulant stream. Yamata looked beyond the advancing worms and out upon the incalculable vastness, and within that silent horror was revealed the thing that had gone missing. The bell. It was no longer being rung. And on some instinctive level, that awakened in him a fear more primal than the worms themselves.

Uekiya's growing devotion to the unseen behind him was inviting its own species of fear. Her wide brown eyes had assumed a tragically revering expression, and Yamata was now on the brink of admitting that no less than a god could warrant such reverence.

But what sort of god captivates a child while hiding behind an atrocity of infinite proportions?

Yamata one last time contemplated Uekiya's absent mouth, and out of all the convoluted, Byzantine reasons he could think of for it not being there, he finally decided on a most austere one. Once in hell, there is simply nothing left to say.

Jon Micheal Kelley's credits include stories in the multiple award-winning anthology Qualia Nous by Written Backwards Press, Firbolg Publishing's ambitious literary series Enter at Your Own Risk: Dark Muses, Spoken Silences, Sensorama by Eibonvale Press, and Triangulation: Lost Voices by Parsec Ink.

Masques

By Mike Adamson

Murder has almost vanished from the spectrum of human existence. Not from any elevated moral sense or spiritual refinement, but merely because it is no longer true that dead men tell no tales.

The afternoon is bright and warm, and the terraces of the glittering vertical architecture of New Johannesburg are thronged with passers-by, robots going about their tasks. I stroll in the sun, enjoying the breeze from the sea, and the peace seems inviolate. I barely remember my original name, I must consult my files, but at the moment the detail is not important. There is someone I must meet, but my heart is ambivalent. Will I thank this person, or twist his head off with the hydraulic power hidden beneath svelte, ebon arms?

Toward the end of the 23rd century, the human race has spread across the stars, our vessels have touched over a hundred new worlds, and Old Earth is shaking free of the devastation of its past. Population is a fraction of its old levels, while technology has redressed many a shortcoming. And among the utopic inventions of a race new-born to the universe are the many strategies by which death has ceased to be a certainty.

Death came for me in an accident, the failure of a sub-runner, one of the bullet trains which streak across the world by magnetic induction in vacuum tunnels. The passengers were saved by the many failsafes, but I was unlucky to be in the way of a collapsing stanchion as the mass of the passing Cairo-New Jo'burg express shook plascrete and reinforced alloys to pieces. I was told afterward there had been no time in which to suffer. A quick, clean exit.

It was only later I discovered there had also been doubt. My body was damaged, but not beyond local systems to suspend and repair. Eyebrows were raised in some circles, reviews promised, but I heard nothing more; until a concerned doctor passed me the confidential finding that the supervising medical technician had not pursued the possible options but selected immediate cyber-incarnation.

Cyber-incarnation is the standard fallback by law, in which the personality is downloaded from the chemical matrix of the brain and stored, pending reanimation in any of the available prostheses— cyborg, android, hardlight hologram, whatever the individual prefers. Only the rich can afford their own new body, of course, the rest of us make do with a time-share arrangement, and while it's sometimes inconvenient, there are consolations.

Yesterday I was a surfer riding high, glassy walls coming down on the ocean beaches; the day before, I delighted in music, accessing hardwired routines in the hologram I phased with—I never played piano before but certainly want to again. Today I am in a body I would have envied before my untimely passing, long and dark, and dressed to impress in flowing blues. She draws eyes and I revel in the fact no one knows who I am. Only the dead recognize each other, sensing the simulacra we have become, and trade knowing smiles as we pass, for we are now an elite.

I see the one I'm after, taking a seat at an outdoor café at the foot of the cliff of glass fronting a hotel, its landing pads high above throwing cool shade; this is his lunch hour between shifts. I walk with confidence, the strike of my heels almost lost in the sounds of strolling people, until I slide into a seat opposite and hold his eyes silently. He is not unhandsome, fair hair thick above a strong-boned skull with firm jaw; indeed, his rejuvenation is superb, retarding his 120 years to a comfortable 30, and I sense he appreciates this glove of flesh and alloys I wear. "Doctor Rensburg," I begin, a statement.

A robowaiter hovers nearby. Rensburg softly orders tea—for two.

"You have me at a disadvantage," he murmurs. "Isn't that how they used to put it?"

I offer a fine hand before I smile and at last recheck—Onika, yes, that was my name. "Onika Kabila."

He frowns, clearly not recalling. "Have we met?" He grins now. "I'm sure I would remember one so charming."

I flash him the smile his words earn, then sit back to stare off at the sea as the drone returns with fine china and a glass pot. When we cradle cups of fragrant blend, I have made up my mind. After all my soul-searching, I will not kill him.

Instead, I raise my cup in salute. "Thank you," I whisper, my smile suddenly very genuine. "You could have dropped me back into my living body, but you prematurely reassigned me. I know you earn a gratuity from the cybernetics manufacturers for every patient you send into hard backup, keeping the android industry in full swing, and for a long time I meant to kill you for it." His eyes widened and my electronic senses see pulses race, pupils dilate, a dozen other tells. "But they would only pour you back onto another harddrive, and I'm not so hate-filled I would destroy your brain entirely to prevent it." My stare holds his eyes like glass knives as he pivots upon the uncertainty of the instant. "But you know what? I like where I am now. It's not so different, and better in some ways." I sip again, then rise, lean across the table and speak softly by his ear. "So, I'll wish you good luck and long life, but hope you'll leave the choice to your patients in future."

I rise and walk on in the sun, losing myself among the crowd on the terraces, and know Rensburg is trembling with shock, a very human thing of which I am no longer capable. But that's a small price to pay.

Because I have learned that life really does begin at the end.

Mike Adamson holds a doctoral degree from Flinders University of South Australia. After early aspirations in art and writing, Adamson returned to study and secured qualifications in marine biology and archaeology. He has been a university educator since 2006, is a passionate photographer, master-level hobbyist and journalist for international magazines. For more about him, check out his website, Mike-Adamson.blogspot.com.

The Mad Scientist's Brother

By Jason Lairamore

Once, upon a craggy mountainside, where each and every day was distinctly gray and gloomy, there lived and thrived the most prodigious of scientists. He was (he had overheard the villagers say) most assuredly mad. But they, being the simple and rustic commoner stock, whose knowledge ranged only to the next hillock or two, possessed opinions to which he paid little heed.

What did they know of the great discoveries made during his jaunts of exploration both hither and yon? He would wager they knew even less than those white flecked, furry beasts they cared for.

Take, for example, his current feat of scientific achievement. It was, just now, on the verge of fruition. If only Igor, that imbecilic cow, would hurry with those last few ingredients. He'd never borne witness to such slowness of foot.

Why, the pot was already a-bubble over the coals. The lava stones from the fabled mount Drovinia were just now about to wreath themselves in ephemeral blue. The blackish-green sulfur aeries were already afloat. They looked like ghost orbs upon a fitful breeze. And they were ready to pop. All they needed was the proper incantation.

But still, he waited! Drat that clubfooted, hip-dysplasiated assistant. He should have gone out himself. That was what he should have done.

The bright little rectangle of thick parchment he'd received last week once again caught his eye from where it rested atop his roll-top desk. That letter had traveled all the way from America to his very dooryard. That was what the shaky-faced postman said, anyway. America. Might as well have said the stars. From this deep in Romania, America was but a fairyland dreamplace, a funny-sounding word.

He pushed himself up from the table, careful not to disturb his haphazard array of corked vials and staggered his way to the open roll-top desk where the said missive lay.

There were vials upon the floor as well, so many vials, so many colors. He had as yet not had the opportunity to label them properly. Such a mundane task was so tedious, and the tedious was best left to the tedious. Blast that moronic Igor. If the slug was one tenth the slower, he would slip from time's grasp altogether to become but one more rock on the roadside.

Bah, he was getting tired of so much elixir making. Weeks had passed and he'd had nary a wink of sleep. He'd eaten naught but the bite of bread Igor had seen fit to feed him, and he'd taken to licking the dewy, rock walls of the castle for his water. Such behavior could not be maintained, not one moment longer.

This would be his last elixir, he decided. After this one, his greatest concoction by far, he'd set Igor to the task of labeling each and every vial strewn about this monstrous hall of a laboratory.

He reached the desk with only a few clinks and clanks of vial glassware and picked up the bright parchment. The paper felt odd in his hands, foreign. He almost believed it did come from America. It was such a fantastic thought.

The paper was thickly corrugated, layered so densely as to be unseen by the naked eye. And the pigments were brighter than anything he'd seen in life. Not to mention the gloss! It was downright magical. The little rectangle even had a coat of some chemical to prevent water damage, a chemical unlike any he'd ever seen before.

The words written upon it were of little consequence to him, for he doubted their validity. It was one thing to fiddle with the fantastical notions of America. Fantastical thoughts made the world go round. It was quite another thing, however, to believe the nonsense written upon the surface of the strange. Why, any fool could write. It took but the most basic of instruction. And, in his experience, what a fool had to say wasn't anything he wished to pay any mind.

Still, he tended to read the words every time the bright little parchment found its way into his hands. Such strange words they were, very strange, and less likely true than America itself.

Dear Dr. Bodgen Vasile,

Our mother has passed. Her dying wish, as writ in her will, was for me to meet you. It appears we are brothers, Dr. Vasile. I look forward to meeting you very soon.

Sincerely,

Benjamin Martin

In his wilder moments, he let loose the idea that maybe he did have some lost brother out there. Why, a lost brother would know, surely, that he required some tangible proof, something beyond words. And what better proof could there be than the wonder of the strangely made letter itself?

He read the words again then heard Igor's approach. It was downright ridiculous for a person's incoming to be heralded by his very breath taking.

Next came the squealing of a pig. At least Igor hadn't forgotten that ingredient. Hopefully Igor hadn't forgotten any of the things he'd been sent out to collect, for now that his mind was made up to be done with elixir making, he found that his patience for the art was worn thin.

"Igor, hurry along. I dare say, tell me you didn't forget anything."

"Yess, yess, master. I gots the feathers, I gots the rocks, I gots the tanner liniment and this demon's own piglet. Master commands. Igor gets."

That was good. Feathers plucked from a virgin goose on Saint MaryJoseph Day were a must. As were the mercurial meteoritic rocks that landed in Farmer Dorin's field last fall. Why, those pockmarked chunks had eviscerated one of the farmer's milk cows. That had been a bloody business, it had. He couldn't do without the urine of the tanner, either. There was no better binding agent than urine, not a thing. As for the pig, why, albinos were lucky, everybody knew that. Besides, he could go for a good chop once this business was done.

"Well, don't just stand there gawping about. You see the aeries. Time is of the essence."

With Igor's slow, labored help, which was little help indeed, he quickly rendered the ingredients into acceptable forms and added them to the bubbling cauldron. A quick guttural word or two followed by just the right number of stirs, and his masterpiece was completed. He corked off the vial and set it among the others in record time.

"I did it, Igor. It is done. I've an apothecary worthy of the greatest hall of any king."

"Yess master. And master—"

"Now, Igor," he spoke over Igor's slow lisping drawl. "Get the labels so that you might write the identity of each of my magical spirits. Hurry now, we haven't the night." He was thinking of what remained of the piglet.

"Yess master. Igor obeys. Master's brother from America will have to wait, he will. Yes, I see the light of that. Yes, I do." And he limped away toward the desk and the labels.

Bodgen tore his eyes, as well as his mind, off of the mostly whole piglet carcass.

"What nonsense are you spewing now, Igor? I've no tolerance for tasteless jokes."

Igor turned from his slow meandering and nodded his head up and down. His one good eye, which was larger than the other, was wide with wonder.

"'Tis true, master. I seen him draw forth in his grumbling iron box myself. Put him in the stable, I did. Bid him wait till I fetch you to attend his detail."

"Yes, yes, attend his detail," Bodgen murmured. He fought hard to keep his calm. His brother from America was here! Such could not be true.

"Well, fetch him to me, then. Let's get this done."

"To the lab, master?"

"I can think of no more august a locale. Regality reeks from the very walls."

"Yess master. Igor obeys."

He didn't see the miserable hunchback leave. Such was the state of his nerves. Surely this anxiety was caused by his lack of sleep, or the lack of a decent meal, or, most likely, it was caused by one of the various fumes wafting about. He'd made so many different types of elixirs. So many.

For the one time in the history of Igor's existence, the crippled-up creature seemed to hurry with his task. No sooner had Bodgen smoothed out his stained and wrinkled lab coat than Igor was once again wheezing his way back into the lab, this time with Bodgen's supposed American brother in tow.

Bodgen clasped his hands behind his back, lest they show their shakiness, as the man entered the lab.

At once, Bodgen was certain of two things. One, this man was his brother. He looked more like their father than Bodgen himself. And two, he was not from Romania. The clothes he wore bore insignias Bodgen had never before seen.

"Master," Igor bowed. "I present Benjamin Martin."

"Ben will do," Ben said, nodding deferentially toward Bodgen. "Dr. Vasile, I presume."

"Please, call me Bodgen."

"Bodgen, yes. And your father was Razvan?"

Bodgen nodded. "You look just like him."

Ben frowned. "And your mother? Was she named Lidia?"

"Father always said Mother died in childbirth."

Ben shook his head. "My mother, Lidia, always told me my father was a crazed mad scientist from Romania. I'd thought she was joking."

Bodgen smiled but said nothing. He wouldn't dignify such a remark with further elucidation. Genius was a lonely occupation. That others thought it mad was a foregone conclusion.

Their short stint of silence was broken by a flickering of orange from outside the window.

"More visitors, master," Igor said, stating the obvious.

"Yes," Bodgen said. "It would appear so. Attend the door, Igor. I'm not to be disturbed."

Igor bobbed his head and limped out, locking the door behind him.

"Igor?" Ben asked. A sardonic tint entered his tone.

"It's a common enough name," Bodgen said. He was having a hard time getting a read on this man who looked so much like his father. His mannerisms were odd. He presented a both bold and sloppy frontage, forceful, yet uncaring, like an intense nonchalance. He wondered if the bearing was a specific American trait.

Ben looked about the laboratory. His eyes lingered over the treasure trove of elixirs lying about.

He pointed to a few of the vials. "You deal in medicines?"

"Some of the time," Bodgen replied.

"I only ask because I am pharmacist, by license."

Bodgen nodded. "We've many that deal with farms about here. Luck be with them that licensure is not involved. I dare say we'd all starve to death."

Ben turned his head to the side and looked at Bodgen. "A pharmacist deals with medicine. I create compounds for physicians. I mix salves used in iontophoresis and phonophoresis. It's my specialty, actually. Hydocodone, lidocaine, basic aspirin, cortisone. There are many. It's used in ultrasound and electrical current technologies."

Bodgen's spirit soared with every syllable heard from his newfound brother. Before him stood a kindred spirit, a man with a brain. He'd not heard a sensible voice like that since his father's passing.

"Electricity," Bodgen said, latching on to the last thing Ben mentioned. "I've many trials, have written many books. Why, Igor can tell you firsthand of my catching lightning, of the storage container I invented, of the various modes of delivery and their effect. He was a most useful specimen of experimentation."

"Igor, Igor. Come here. Don't dally," he called.

He turned to the door to find it smoking.

"I say, Igor. What are you about?"

There was still no answer. He walked to the window and chanced a look. The entire town was outside his residence. They carried torches and pitchforks. They were burning the entire grounds.

"Igor?" he said, quieter, looking once more at the smoking door.

Ben, too, looked out the window. After a quick scan, he turned his attention back to Bodgen. "Well, this is great." He paced. "I fly all the way to Romania, drive out in the middle of the mountains for half a day in a rental car, all so I can get killed by an angry mob just like Dr. Frankenstein. Thanks, Mom." He looked to the ceiling. "What a great idea it was, rekindling brotherhood."

"What did you do?" he directed toward Bodgen. "Did you make a monster or something that got away and terrorized the town?"

"I've made several," Bodgen said offhandedly as he began putting elixirs in a canvas bag.

"What are you doing now?" Ben asked.

"They've killed Igor and he's a worthless sack of bones. I don't plan to give them a chance at me."

"You know a way out of here?"

Bodgen wouldn't be able to take all the vials. There were just too many. It hurt him to leave them.

"Of course, I have an escape," he snapped.

"Then wave your magic wand, and let's be about it."

Bodgen looked at his magnificent lab one final time.

"They say luck is like glass, when it shines it breaks, but this time the old saying looks to be wrong."

"Luck?" Ben asked. "You see luck somewhere around here?"

Bodgen tore his eyes from all his wonderful things. "You," he said. "Your coming here, on this day of all days. That is fortune beyond fortune. Perhaps it was the albino pig." He'd sure have liked to have eaten one of its chops.

Ben shook his head. "Luck for you maybe. Not so much for me."

Bodgen had his bag as heavy as he could make it and still carry it.

"Well, let's be about it then." He moved one of the pictures on the wall, a picture of Razvan, his father, and a trap door opened in the floor. "I can get us to your conveyance. From there, you can get us to safety."

"And once we're safe," Ben said. "What will you do?"

"Why, go to America with you, of course." Even saying the words had a dreamlike quality. America. He couldn't pass up the chance. It was just too good to be true.

Ben shook his head but didn't say anything. They started down the stairs.

After a series of dark passageways that Bodgen knew by heart they came to the stables where sat Ben's conveyance. Bodgen blinked at it and turned his head one way then another. It was unlike anything he'd ever seen. He reached a hand out, tentatively, to touch its shiny black hide. His hand shook.

A metallic slamming made him jerk his hand back. Ben had gotten inside the metal beast somehow. He saw him through the thing's windows.

"Bodgen, think you can hurry?" Ben asked from inside. His voice was muffled.

Bogden just stared. How had Ben gotten inside?

"Bodgen, I'd hate to state the obvious and all, but this barn IS on fire."

The outside world crashed in around him. The walls were alight with oranges and yellows.

Ben leaned over and did something that caused the far metal panel of the vehicle to open.

"Get in," he said.

Bogden did as bid. It was becoming hard to breathe, and a little too warm for his taste. Once inside, he pulled on the metal panel, and it shut with ease. He was inside.

Then a roar issued from the machine, and he nearly lost his skin.

"Keep it together. We're getting out of here," Ben said.

The conveyance jerked ahead, through the flaming stable wall, and onto the wagon road that led through town. Bodgen's stomach churned from the jerking about. Never before had he felt anything remotely like this.

"This road isn't quite made for a car," Ben said as they sped along. Bodgen looked out the window to the burning castle that'd been in his family's name for generations. The townsfolk all turned to stare open mouthed as they made their escape. Their eyes were wide in cow-eyed wonder.

"I'm sorry about your friend," Ben said once they'd cleared the town and the first hillock.

The car had settled down to a steady jostling. Its vibrations were soothing. Bodgen, who had had so little sleep of late, found the effect very relaxing.

"Friend?" he asked. He was a scientist. What need him of a friend?

"Igor," Ben said. "I'm sorry."

Bodgen shook his head and settled himself better in his seat. "Igor was an experiment. He's not gone. I will get him back in due course."

Ben said something under his breath, but Bodgen didn't hear. His elixirs clinking from his bag in the back seat were reassuring. He had enough there to start anew.

"Luck or no," he murmured, "I owe you my life."

He drifted off.

And was woken in what felt like an abbreviated moment. The light of day was full upon them. But that bright orb was not what had woken him. The roaring of some great beast thrummed overhead. He rubbed his sticky eyes and witnessed a winged creature zooming away, gaining height as it flew.

"Good, you're awake. We're leaving. I managed to get you a temporary visa due to a death in the family. It'll give you a few days in America. After that, we'll have to figure something out."

Ben might as well have been talking gobbly-goo. Had he not seen, nor even heard, that monster roar through the skies? He pointed at where the thing was still gaining elevation.

Ben glanced at it. "Yes, we are going to fly."

Bodgen shook his head. He was lightheaded and felt sweaty all of a sudden.

"I don't believe it," he said.

"You don't have to," Ben said. "But we have to hurry. The plane leaves now."

"I may be sick." The thought of riding a monster through the air all the way to America was just too much to absorb, even for him.

Ben dug around in his coat and pulled out a strange-looking bottle. From it, he withdrew two white tablets.

"Anxiolytics, for your sickness," Ben said.

Bodgen liked the sound of the name and immediately popped them in his mouth. Ben gave him some water to assist in the swallowing.

"Now hurry up, or the plane will leave without us."

The medicines took immediate effect, or so it seemed. He really probably should have eaten something before dropping drugs into his system.

At first, it was as if a great coat of form-fitting iron had suddenly slipped from his shoulders. He basked in the freedom of it and enjoyed the ease his spirit had so quickly attained. Then Ben was at his hand and pulling him from the car. He let him lead him forth to a great, flimsy building located just up the way. He could feel his feet hitting the ground, the impact imparted with each step, but found, with every additional footfall, a lack of registered importance.

He took to weaving as they crossed into the big building. His upper body kept losing its mooring to the lower. His center of gravity became like a slippery pig at a county fair.

Ben noticed his meandering and took firmer hold of him as they waded into a literal sea of humanity. Bodgen was at a bemused loss of thought as he viewed the spectacle. Before him lay a grand socio-experiment where people were squished together in a construct and then set loose to see what happened.

"We should leave the anthills to the ants," he said.

"Focus on your walking or they won't let us on the plane," Ben said. "Those meds shouldn't have reacted so strongly. How long's it been since you ate. I don't know how blaw, blaw, de blaw."

Bodgen turned his head to Ben and frowned. Ben was still talking, but Bodgen could no longer understand. He didn't care to understand. It didn't matter if he understood.

After a few more steps they reached a counter where a beautiful woman said a few blaw blaws. Ben said a couple blaw blaws back and handed her some paper. The woman smiled at him. He tried to speak, to tell her that her eyes looked like jade jewels, but he could not. He couldn't summon the will to speak. It just didn't matter enough whether he spoke or not.

They walked down a narrow corridor next, and through an oval looking aperture to an arced room where there were any number of seats. Ben led him to one and he fell into it. A seat had never felt as fine as the one he now sat upon. He'd found Plato's ideal chair and it was wonderful. He closed his eyes to better enjoy the sensation.

When next his eyes opened, the arced room was mostly darkened. His mouth was dry. Ben sat next to him reading some sort of text. He coughed to try to get some moisture going in his mouth. Ben put his book away and handed him a clear flask of water.

"There is a meal set aside for you when you are ready," Ben said as Bodgen drank.

"I'm ready," Bodgen said. His jaw ached at the mere mention of food.

Ben called over a waitress and before he knew it, he had a steaming plate of goodies before him.

"Sorry about the meds. I gave you too much," Ben said.

Bodgen waved his concern away as he ate. The meds had been good. Very potent. A good indicator of Ben's skill. Bodgen was proud.

"Tell me of your book," he said. "What matter of study is it?"

Ben picked up the book and showed Bodgen the cover. On it was a man covered in shiny metal fighting a giant, winged lizard. A big-bosomed beauty in a revealing gown waved down from atop a stone tower.

"They have fantasy novels in Romania?" Ben asked.

Bodgen shook his head. He didn't know what Ben was talking about.

"Well, I've not read many myself either," Ben continued. He showed him the cover again. "This one was recommended by a friend of mine."

That wasn't the real reason. Ben was holding back. He could feel the tension radiating off him. That could mean only one thing.

"There's a woman involved in this somewhere," Bodgen said.

Ben tried to feign ignorance for a moment, but it was a weak show. He knew he'd been called out.

"Yes, there is," Ben said. "Her name is Nancy. She's my neighbor. She recommended the book."

Bodgen pushed his empty plate away. "And?" Here was something Ben wanted. It very well could be the means by which he repaid him for saving his life.

Ben looked away. Bodgen picked food from his teeth as he waited.

"In America," Ben said after a pause, "women like to be swept off their feet. They all want Prince Charming to come slay the dragon and save them from the tower." He showed Bodgen the cover one more time. "Just like this."

Bodgen nodded. "And I assume this Nancy is not in need of saving."

"She's not about to be lynched by a mob, if that's what you mean."

"I see," he said.

Just then, he felt a deep trembling in his seat which nearly made him jump.

"Finally," Ben said. "Home at last."

Bodgen had been so wrapped up in his food and Ben's story that he'd completely forgotten where he was.

"We're in the belly of the flying beast at this moment?" he asked, his eyes ever widening.

Ben smiled at him and nodded. "Welcome to America."

The landing was frightful, but not overly so. The others onboard showed none of the nerves he felt, which made it all the more bearable. Once the vibrations had stopped and his ears had popped a few times, they were let out of the beast and were once more awash in the human anthill experiment. Bodgen stayed close to Ben as they collected their bags and found Ben's car.

The drive to Ben's home was made in the dark, but still the sounds and colors of America were a wonder more amazing than his imagination could conceive. There was too much to ever process in so short a time.

Ben seemed tired the moment they entered his house. Bodgen looked around at all the odd contraptions here and there and decided Ben truly was a tinkerer just as much as he was. One could not simply accrue all the things Bodgen saw lying around without being a purveyor of the scientific arts.

"Let me show you to your room," Ben said. "Then I'm going to bed. I didn't sleep a wink the entire flight."

They went up a flight of stairs and Ben showed him to a room with a bed in it.

"I'll be right down the hall if you need me. Make yourself at home. I'll see you in the morning."

With a yawn, Ben walked away. This left Bodgen to his own devices, which was very good for Bodgen, for he had a plan. He was going to repay his brother for saving his life. And he knew just how to do it.

The sun was just coming up as he crept into Ben's room. He'd found, during his exploration of the house, a most useful crossbow. He had that particular item in his hands, loaded up and ready, as he eased his way to Ben's side. As a means to wake Ben, and also to deliver a most spectacular concoction, he'd arranged one of the syringes he'd found among Ben's things.

Without much ado, he jammed the needle into Ben's arm and depressed the plunger.

Ben jerked himself to sitting.

"Wha!" He exclaimed. He saw Bodgen as he rubbed at his arm. "What did you do? Why do you have my crossbow?"

Bodgen backed out of the room. "Come outside and see, Brother. That potion will begin working in just a moment. And you're going to need it. I've a surprise for you."

Before Ben could say another word, he slipped out of the room and made his way to the back door of the house.

The light outside was soft and growing with the rising sun. A cool breeze was on the wind. There wasn't a cloud in the blue sky.

Bodgen stood in the backyard facing the door as Ben came out. Beside Bodgen sat a most docile German shepherd dog.

"What are you doing with Nancy's dog?" Ben asked as he came out fully into the back yard.

Bodgen didn't answer. He glanced to the roof then back to Ben.

"What was in that shot you gave me?" Ben asked. There was real worry in his voice.

"It will make you strong, fast, and nearly impenetrable, for a short time. You're going to need all the help you can get very soon."

He glanced to the roof again. It was time.

"Ben, look!" He pointed to the roof and took a step away.

Ben's mouth hung open; such was his shock. Bogden smiled.

"Is that Nancy? Why is she tied to my chimney?" Ben stuttered.

"Your lady in her tower, awaiting your rescue," Bodgen announced.

Nancy wore a revealing bit of night clothes. Her mouth was tapped shut. Bodgen had not wanted her to ruin his surprise. Not that it should matter now. The potion he'd given her should have her nice and relaxed. She wasn't going to cause any trouble.

Ben turned and stared at Bodgen. "Are you crazy?"

Bodgen nodded. "Wait, there is more." He retreated yet farther away and pointed to the dog. It panted happily away.

"In a moment the dog will become a Balaur, a great winged lizard, just like in your book."

Ben pointed up to Nancy. "We have to get her down."

"Oh, I know," Bodgen said. "You'll have to save her. She'll love that."

"I'm serious, Bodgen. This isn't Romania."

"Look," Bodgen said and pointed at the dog.

The moment stretched and nothing happened. Bodgen frowned. That elixir should have been working by now.

Ben shook his head and looked up at the roof. "Don't worry, Nancy, I'm coming. I'm so sorry."

He took off at a jog that quickly turned into a sprint that would have made a horse jealous.

"Careful!" Bodgen yelled, just before Ben crashed completely through the brick wall of the house. He'd forgotten to warn Ben about how powerful that shot was he'd given him. It ramped up his system many fold.

He took a step toward the new hole in the wall, and a deep guttural grumble issued from the roof. He looked up to see that Nancy had turned a bright red. Her skin smoked. Her eyes stared down at him, trying to pin him to where he stood.

"Rahat!" he cursed. He brought the crossbow to bear, aimed it at Nancy, and fired.

His bolt didn't even come close. He'd never been much of a shot.

He took off at a run to the house. He had more antidote dipped bolts inside. He'd not really planned on using the crossbow. It was meant to be a secondary measure only.

Nancy screamed, sounding like a mix between a person and a hissing snake. He chanced a look just before entering the house. She'd grown wings, big bat-like wings.

He grabbed the bolts and went to check on his brother.

Ben was sitting in the middle of the living room, which was littered with brick rubble. Thick dust had yet to settle. He looked up as Bodgen came before him. There was a sizable knot forming on the right side of his forehead.

A shriek tore the air, followed by a whooshing sound.

The ceiling started to smoke.

"She's breathed fire on the roof!" Bodgen exclaimed. "Quick, we must get outside."

"Breathed fire?" Ben asked as Bodgen dragged him outside through the hole in the wall.

Once outside, Bodgen looked up. The Balaur was high overhead, a great black shape, circling the house.

"The house is on fire!" Ben said, as if he'd just now noticed. "What happened to Nancy? Nancy!"

Bodgen thrust the crossbow toward Ben, who ignored it. "Ben, I hope you are a better shot than me. You must shoot her. The bolts contain the antidote. They are the only thing that can save her."

"What?" Ben asked. Bodgen pointed up. Ben looked up.

"Is that a dragon circling the house?" Ben asked. He rubbed at his eyes and touched the bump on his head.

"I mixed up my elixirs," Bodgen said. "They weren't yet labeled."

Ben held up a hand. "Is that a DRAGON flying above my BURNING house?"

Bodgen nodded and let a little pride enter his voice. "My greatest elixir ever made. I created it just as you arrived and saved my life. It was as if I'd made it for just this moment."

A strange combination of fear, awe, and shock did battle on Ben's face.

"So, I have to shoot it with a crossbow?" Ben asked after a pause.

"Yes," Bodgen said.

Ben shook his head but took the crossbow. He jogged off, hopefully to find a better vantage point from which to shoot.

"Master?" Bodgen heard and spun around. The dog was sitting there staring at him. "Master, what has happened?"

Bodgen would know that tone anywhere, in any creature, regardless of the strange, animal accent.

"You died, Igor, and before labeling the elixirs," Bodgen said to the dog. "Now I've gone and used the wrong ones. You are to blame, as usual."

"Ever so sorry, Master."

A screech of pain sounded from above.

"Got it!" Ben yelled.

"Better watch out, Master," Igor said. "There's a winged Balaur crashing in the yard."

"Of course there is," Bodgen said. "Didn't I just tell you I used the wrong elixir because of your ill-timed mishap?"

The Balaur hit the ground hard enough to bounce. Once down, it commenced to snort and slobber in great sparkly showers of tears and snot as it trounced around the yard swaying this way and that.

In a matter of moments, it'd converted fully back to Nancy, who fell to the grass, asleep, none the worse for wear. Even the crossbow bolt hadn't left a mark. The bolt had entered converted flesh and had fallen free once she'd changed back to her original form.

Igor came to sit beside Bodgen as Ben walked up. Ben eyed Nancy, naked in the grass, then looked to the house, which continued to burn merrily away.

"You burnt my house down," he said. The sounds of sirens could be heard from a distance.

"Yes," Bodgen said. "As I said, the elixirs were not yet labeled."

"'Twas my fault, it was," Igor said.

Ben touched the bump on his head again as he looked first to the dog and then back to Bodgen.

"So, it's Nancy's dog's fault that a dragon burnt my house down?" He asked.

"Don't worry, Ben," Bodgen said. "Nancy will wake up and not remember a thing. It will be like a dream to her."

Ben didn't say anything. He just looked from Nancy to the fire and then to Bodgen. His face was pale. He looked like he was going to be sick.

Bodgen sighed, pulled a needle from his pocket, and jabbed Ben in the neck with it. He fell immediately to the grass to lie next to the naked Nancy.

The sirens drew ever nearer.

"Well, that was a complete waste of effort," Bodgen said. "It didn't go anything like I had planned."

"What'd you give him, Master?" Igor asked, nodding to Ben.

"A shot of forgetme, of course. You saw him. He was in complete shock. Now I'll have to find some other way to repay him for saving my life."

"Yes, of course, Master, of course."

Bodgen frowned down at the inert bodies, chin in hand. The sirens were nearly upon them.

"Master, we must go."

"Yes, I suppose," he murmured.

Igor ran off quick as anything.

"Wait for me, you worthless cur."

"I'm sorry Master," Igor said, dropping back.

That moronic creature was too fast by half.

They left the scene walking side by side. America, the land of dreams, lay before them, ready and waiting for them to explore.

He glanced back once as a great, red vehicle arrived. He'd return one day, he vowed, to repay his brother for saving his life.

One day.

Jason Lairamore is a writer of science fiction, fantasy, and horror who lives in Oklahoma with his wife and their three children. He is a published finalist of the 2012 SQ Mag annual contest, winner of the 2013 Planetary Stories flash fiction contest, a third-place winner of the 2015 SQ Mag annual contest, and a Writers of the Future contest Semi-Finalist. His work is both featured and forthcoming in over 90 publications.

Before

By Andrew Dunn

Before we were forgotten, we were myths. People read of us and learned about us in school. The day we set sail on a column of fire was still a holiday—one celebrated with sales and bar crawls by all but the truest adherents. The true believers still shot miniature rockets skyward by day and looked for us among the stars through telescopes at night.

Before we were myths, we were flesh and blood legends. Top actors portrayed us in dozens of movies people downloaded. Our memorabilia was sold everywhere, down to stylized body suits that copied the silver-blue coveralls we wore into space. People still remembered that once we cleared Earth's gravity, we'd undress and climb naked into our pods so that cryogenic sleep could regale us with centuries of dreams. The idea of two people naked and alone, hurtling through space, stirred some to wonder whether we'd found intimacy one last time before we were sealed in our pods.

Before we were legends, we were curiosities. The world saw us as two exquisite specimens when we were unveiled. Our initial interviews were awkward at first, until public relations dressed us in contemporary fashions. Coaches were brought in to help us speak with the modern cadence and slang of a dozen languages, which we used on television shows, earning ourselves millions of fans. On some shows we were challenged to solve equations that normally took genius minds months—we solved them in minutes.

Before we were curiosities, we were one man and one woman, selected young for our bodies and minds. Even as children our training was rigorous. We had to be able to survive our voyage. Once we reached our destination, we had to be able to start our lives again fresh from our pods in even the most challenging of worlds.

Before we were selected, we were a theoretical project to send human beings toward a peculiar radio signal emanating from beyond our solar system. It was a monumental endeavor, one scientists hoped would lead to technological advancements that would someday make interstellar travel faster, and eventually, as common as short hops to the moon or Martian colonies.

Before our spacecraft entered orbit around the blue-violet sphere well-within the Goldilocks Zone, systems woke us from 372 years of sleep. We were weak at first, but barely aged. Our coveralls had deteriorated slightly but were wearable. We made rounds to see how our craft had weathered the years, then floated through a narrow tunnel into the ship's bridge. Sensors there were rampant with data about the planet growing larger through thick rectangular windows.

There were satellites in orbit. Sporadic radio transmissions in unusual dialects of languages we understood crackled through speakers. Sensors said there were a handful—a dozen or so—populated towns on the planet's surface. Flying machines were moving slowly among the towns.

Before we were discovered, we were the forgotten mythical figures from four centuries past, drifting into the planet's orbit.

Our ship began a sequence of pre-programmed radio messages that had once been cutting-edge technology. Periods of silence between broadcasts gave us time to listen for a response and wonder if it would come.

Before, we had spent our youth strengthening bodies and minds to survive even toxic extraterrestrial environments. Now, we were leaning into an embrace, and wondering if we were ready to meet what humans had become lifetimes after we left.

Andrew Dunn writes science-fiction and fantasy from the state of Maryland, often drawing ideas from jogs through forest trails at sunrise. His work has previously appeared in AntipodeanSF, 365 Tomorrows, Daily Science Fiction, Penumbric Speculative Fiction, and in MetaStellar. His work has also been short-listed in several writing contests. Dunn welcomes reader feedback at dominobeanbag@gmail.com.

The Thirteen Quixotic Temples of Light and Darkness

By William C. Burns Jr

1: Egress on Route 9

It's the dead of summer and Shalott wonders where you get an expression like that: "Dead of summer?"

Top down (yes, she has one of those T-birds)—her hair is going to be a mess, but she doesn't care because it feels so good.

She careens down route 9, just before you get to Chestnut Hill Road.

Four days left on her "vacation of discovery." And, you know, it was such a good idea that no one wanted to come with her. Forget the "Office Rats," she is on a quest for local color.

Suddenly, a handwritten sign, "Shalott—I have your beads." What the…? She locks up the brakes and almost hits the ditch.

Backs up to re-read the sign: "Shalott—I have your beads," shoe polish on cardboard. What a stupid sign. Was she looking for a sign?

She starts to turn around right there, to head back for the comforts of home—but she doesn't.

She looks for people, looks for any sign of people, only to find a strip of tarmac cutting through a forest primeval, a blacktop road as old as the mountains through which she was so peacefully gliding—before this sign.

She looks at the offending sign one more time. This has to be one of Bengie's jokes, but how could he have known? How many women have the same name as her and what would be the distribution on this rural mailing route? Couldn't have been Bengie, she remembers that she had no plans to travel this road till this morning. Chosen quite on impulse. No way he could have been behind this.

A car comes up behind and blows its horn as it swerves to miss her.

It's still there, "Shalott—I have your beads".

She decides to get to the bottom of this and puts the 'Bird in drive. The wheels squeal.

Shalott comes around a curve, and there, big as life, "Beads—Beads—Beads"! Same shaky lettering as the first sign.

A ramshackle old fruit stand covered in a Universe of bangles, bobbles and beads. Oh, it's delightful, complete with wizened old crone and multi-colored tourists in various stages of buying trinkets.

She starts to drive past, gets on the other side, and pulls over on the shoulder.

She pulls a scarf over her hair, walks in her practical shoes to the "Hillbilly Bazaar." Honestly, she expects the sounds of banjos at war.

She is not an expert, but there is literally every kind of bead known to humankind, every conceivable color and shape (and some that aren't) strewn about the weathered pine boards of the stand.

Then she sees it, the tattered sign above the crone, "Beads from The Thirteen Quixotic Temples of Light and Darkness." It reminds her of the lettering she saw on the wizard's wagon in the Wizard of Oz.

Oh, it's fabulous. Shalott snaps a few photos while waiting for the other tourists to complete their transactions, so that she might talk with the old woman in private.

The wilderness grows quiet as the last minivan departs. The now motionless beadmonger meets her eyes. Shalott realizes this is no old woman, this is barely human and it's staring right into her eyes. She breaks eye contact.

A crackling creaky voice from myth says, "Shalott, I was so afraid I'd miss you."

"OK, how do you know my name?"

"You are Shalott, are you not?"

"How do you know this?"

"If you are Shalott, I have your beads."

"Stop it! I mean it. Stop it."

The old woman(?) draws back as though frightened, "Shalott? Have I upset you? He would be mad if I upset you."

Shalott is feeling a little exposed. She's wishing another minivan would pull in and relieve this awkward moment.

The crone, befuddled and baffled in a harmless way, is not unlike her grand Aunt Alice. Like Aunt Alice looking for her keys when her car had been sold years ago.

Shalott tries to comfort the crone, "Look you startled me because you know my name and I do not know you. How do you know my name?"

"He brings the beads—he teels me your name—and he is a very good man. I can teel these things. He is so much concerned for you. He gives me these." The crone pulls out the most extraordinary string of beads Shalott has ever seen.

The textures and colors : some clearly ancient, some small wonders of nanotechnology, others, tiny little pocket universes, tiny little stories, all of them one-of-a-kind exceptions in a world gone mad with mass production.

The crone offers, her hands tremble. Shalott's face softens a fraction. She asks, "Grand Aunt, what is your name?"

"Archna, you call me Archna."

"Aunt Archna. "

"Archna—please call me Archna," the crone interrupts.

"Archna, one of my friends is playing a joke on the both of us."

The crone calms and offers the beads a third time.

Shalott opens her hand. The crone places the string across the young woman's palm and the world disappears...

2: Through the Anteroom of the Twelve Doors

Shalott is standing in front of a broken mirror. Shalott is six years old.

Her grandaunt's stupid mirror is broken, and Shalott is holding the doll. The bad doll that broke the mirror. And now her aunt is going to be mad because this bad doll got mad and hit the mirror.

Sweet Aunt Alice comes into the attic and finds her there with the bad doll.

"Oh Shalott sweetie, what happened?"

"Are you mad at me Aunt Alice?"

"How could I be mad at you child...?"

Shalott interrupts, "This doll, she broke the mirror."

"Child, don't blame the doll. It's not her fault. She is really a very good little doll."

"No she isn't. She breaks things."

"Shalott—Let her break things then. Better she should break everything in the world then you be angry at her. She really is a very good doll."

Shalott looks at the mirror and realizes that she can walk through it, pass through the cracks. And she does.

3: The Temple of Broken Glass

A young woman named Shalott comes to awareness in the lobby of an old movie theater. She quickly realizes that she saw something like this once in an old black and white photograph in her aunt's hat box.

An old movie theater: broken plate glass windows in every direction, rubble and dust on every surface. It looked like the Germans had bombed London, or something.

The crunch of broken glass behind her, she turns to see a man approaching. A man neither tall nor short, not fat or thin, a man that you have to force yourself to actually see because it is the natural tendency of your eyes to slide off him onto anything else in the room.

"Shalott... "

"OK, this is getting out of hand. How does everybody know my name?"

In her hand, a string of beads, excellent beads. She is holding the one that looks something like a shattered marble.

He stops and holds up his hands. It's like he's surrendering or something. His expression: enigmatic.

"Shalott, my name is Finton and I am here to explain a few things."

"OK, Finton, where the freak am I?"

Finton flusters as he pulls a small black notebook out of his pocket. "Right to the point I see. I guess this is only to be expected. You are at the beginning of an adventure, a tour of the Thirteen Quixotic Temples of Light and Darkness. This structure is your point of embarkation. These are the twelve doors."

"I'm not going anywhere."

That got his attention. He consults several pages in the small black notebook and looks even more confused, "You are Shalott? Shalott de Bailey?"

She doesn't answer.

"If you are Shalott, then all of this is for you. If not, there has been a terrible mistake."

"How do you know me?"

"I don't know you personally, "

She interrupts, "How do you know my name?"

"It's written right here, "

"Where am I?!"

"Technically, you are at a road side, at a 'hillbilly bazaar,'"—air quotes—"I believe you called it, on route 9, just before you get to Chestnut Hill Road, with four days left on your 'vacation of discovery'"—again with the air quotes.

"You're not real, so how is it that I see you?"

"I am your guide on said 'vacation of discovery'."

"How is that possible?"

He attempts to show her what looks like technical schema in the little book. "You are between heartbeats. It happens all the time." He sighs, looking somewhat worn, "Look, you can go back if you like. Nothing is keeping you here."

She scuffs her foot, moving a shard of glass through the dust. He is waiting patiently.

Without making eye contact, she asks, "What's the deal?"

"Not sure I know what you mean, Shalott."

"What's going to happen to me?"

"Technically, nothing at all. You may choose to go to the thirteen temples, of which this is the first, and witness the many things there, or you can return the way you came."

He is waiting. She is still there and he takes that as encouragement. He says, "You may exit at any time, just drop the string of beads."

She looks at her hand. The broken glass marble bead has cut her palm, though not badly, one drop of blood. He offers a handkerchief, but she wipes it on her pants leg.

She asks, "How does this work?"

"You chose one of these doors. You take the next bead in your hand and you walk through the door."

"Something bad is going to happen to me when I walk through."

"Drop the string," he interrupts.

"What?"

"Drop the string of beads and go home. It is clear you don't want to participate in this journey."

"I'll drop it when I'm ready."

The man turns without further comment, and walks through the wall.

She fingers the ceramic head bead that is next on the string.

4: Rapa Nui—The Temple of the Grooved Spheres

She steps from the shadow of the jungle, and there is nothing for miles, but grass. The wind cuts wakes through the unkempt grass growing like hair all over the place.

She looks to a perfect cyan sky and if she looks long enough, she might see that it really is a painting of a sky on some kind of perfectly smooth vault. Her eyes drift to the horizon.

She walks East, according to the painted sun that actually is as bright as the real Sun, for no particular reason. Over the rise, she sees Rapa Nui cupped in a picture perfect little valley. It reminds her of a drawing she saw in one of her world culture books, Aztec pyramids somewhere.

Except that these pyramids have carved stone heads at the corners. Huge heads from—no, she can't remember.

Each head has a mysterious metal sphere at its apex: grooved spheres of a solid bluish metal with flecks of white.

She looks at her hand and sees the string of beads.

She looks to the temple.

Dancers in rhinoceros costumes cavort down the stairs on the pyramids and, while there is no music she can hear, they spin and whirl around their temple, round and round, all around. They seem to be trying to do some kind of aggressive martial arts movements but only manage to trip all over themselves. Suddenly they stop. All watch as one climbs to the apex of the temple. He seems to be having a lot of trouble with his horn. He pulls the fake horn off and screams "This can't be happening. This is the end of the World."

The others go mad and throw themselves on the ground.

"This carnage stops right now, you hear me? Right now."

The others call out, "This is the fall of the Western Empire. What can we do?"

"I will build a great wall to keep Them out! Why do we build the wall? Because they don't want us to."

With sticks they draw caricatures of the mad god, Chaos in the sand. Monstrous diagrams with whirling eyes and drool running down its quivering chins. They are clearly using his image as a template.

He shouts, "What the soothsayers are seeing and what you're hearing is not happening. We don't have victories the way we used to."

They shout, "The thunder will eat our ears and rot our brains," (as through Fear, the brother god of Chaos, wouldn't do the same).

He shouts, "Don your headgear so that your eyes won't deceive you!"

Shalott watches as they put their heads in burlap sacks and run into one another.

She notices the Moon rises, much as it should, the Stars wheel and preen as they should. The Sun returns and the Cosmic Wheel turns, just as they always have, despite countless centuries of predictions to the contraire.

She tires of the show and walks to the horizon, which is strangely near.

She finds the crack in the World, and fingers the next bead. The bead that looks like a fragment gizmo from a computer. She takes the computer bead into her hand and steps through the crack.

5: Schen Tal—The Golden Temple of the Ancient Model Aircraft

Shalott is in a hallway made entirely of those small twinkling lights that they twine in the branches of fig trees in nice restaurants. There is no apparent pattern, but subtle light animations seem to flicker in and out of reality. She has seen something like this once when she was a girl. It was raining and as she watched the standing water on a parking lot, she could almost see patterns arise and disappear.

She lets her eyes unfocus and she can see the glittering demons flicker, glide and scream within the Temple. Each has its own special shape, its own sound. Such tiny little creatures of light contrasting with shadow, they cavort and ripple. They call to one another and play the most baffling games.

The golden tooth with wings is Reason. Reason, the most beautiful of all the demons gathered there hover before her.

She smiles, holds out her hand.

Reason flutters just beyond her reach. In a twinkling it twitters and turns, joining the swarming masses.

She leaves by the Southern door.

6: Baian-Kara—The Temple of the Dropa Stones

Shalott steps into the middle of a street, a Suburban street. It smells like fresh-cut lawn and the end of a long day. A young girl notices her immediately, and after a moment, comes over to talk.

"My name is Kachina, and I bet you're here to see the Phantom Planet."

"Hello, Kachina, my name is Shalott and I don't know about this Phantom...", and then she sees it, just hanging there, bigger than the moon.

Kachina takes her hand, and leads her to huge stones that have been gouged out. They fit like recliners. Kachina says, "These are the Dropa Stones. Have a seat.'

"Kachina, tell me about the Phantom Planet."

The girl says, "The Phantom Planet suddenly appeared in the sky three months ago, and no one knows how it got there. I mean, it looks bigger than the moon, but the man on TV said it wasn't bigger, just closer"

Shalott leans back and lets the little girl tell the tale.

Kachina says, "People were running around all over the place shouting 'It's the End of the Known World,' and things like, 'Repent, repent, repent!' Like that, but even though it looked like it was moving closer the scientists told us it had become a satellite which means it's just standing there, not really moving."

The girl's voice becomes conspiratorial, "Now I was looking for Space Monsters with big teeth and weapons of mass incineration. Mom expected Angels of Wrath. Come to break things to cleanse the Earth. Who knows what Dad expects."

"Everybody thinks they know, but no one expected it to just stand there, and that is exactly what it's doing—I sit here on these winter nights and it's warm here in the Dropa Stones. No one can explain it, but it's safe here, safe and warm.

The colors, I love the colors, all swirling and flowing."

Shalott and Kachina sit and talk about all kinds of things for most of the night.

7: Shalott Returns to the Temple of Broken Glass

Shalott pushes through an ancient door and finds herself in the lobby of the old movie theater.

He's there, standing quietly with his little notebook in hand, "Shalott...?"

"Finton?"

Awkward silence.

"How's it going, Shalott?"

"OK," she pulls her hair back, a nervous habit from her childhood, "Finton, what is this really?"

"This is your adventure."

"Who set it up?"

"You did"

"When?"

He riffles back and forth in his ever-present black notebook, finds whatever it is he was looking for, examines several pages, "Says here you set this in motion on your thirteenth birthday"

"I did this?"

"Yes."

"Why?"

Finton looks very confused, scratches his head, turns away and walks out through the wall.

"Thanks bunches, Finton," she shouts to the place where he exited.

She examines the beads. This one that looks like a swan.

8: Leda-Tyndareus—The Temple of the Broken Swan

Shalott is struggling for air; she is underwater. Her thinking brain is somehow detached as her hindbrain galvanizes her into the thrashing of a drowning child. She breaks the surface. She coughs till it feels like her lungs will fall out her mouth. Her feet can barely touch bottom. The waves try to capsize her.

She wipes at her eyes. She slogs toward the beach.

She falls face down in the hot sand, and for the longest time she tells herself to get up. She would wipe at her eyes some more, but her hands are caked with sand. She crawls toward the tree line.

She collapses in the dancing palm frond shadows, and dreams of a world where everything is clean and white, and enameled, a Land of Fine Appliances.

Later (days later?), she swims into awareness. She is on her back, watching a sky untroubled by clouds, through a kaleidoscope of palm fronds.

At length she sits up and there it is, the most frighteningly picturesque shipwreck ever. A swan ship out of Fantasy, not so much wrecked, as Fallen. A shattered ebon-blue swan wrecked on the sand. The unnatural, gaping hole in the bow, biting the sand. A banshee screaming silence, a cygnae's eternal lament for her idyllic exotic home. A home now lost forever. The swan ship orphaned on this alien shore. Defeated. Deep melancholy, transience and decay...

Shalott walks across the burning sand and wishes she had shoes. She finds the name on the bow, "Andromache," wife of the broken warrior.

She tries to find a way onto the deck, but can't. She tries to enter through the mouth, but it's too small. She tries to pry a hole big enough and only succeeds in nearly breaking her arm.

Shalott sits in the shadow of the ship and tries to talk to it. The ship will not answer. Shalott talks about our diminished age; compares our art with the greater ages that are behind us, ages from which we are exiles, tiny ships of flesh tossed by the hidden currents of Time and Fate, currents coursing the endless oceans of existence.

Shalott watches as the sun quenches itself in crimson robes as she tells the ship of turquoise waters, waters of infinite depth illuminated from below, a strange eerie and disturbing glow that terrifies her. This abyss, unlike any in the natural world, where Time eats all actions, dreams and desires. Swallows even the words she speaks. Sequesters her litany of how all stories end in Silence and all voyages end in the Abyss.

The tide comes in and touches Shallot's feet, with just a slight coolness, like a shadow brushing over her.

She looks at the string of beads; she has been holding the swan bead.

Shalott stands and brushes the sand from her clothing. She takes the next bead, a triangular bead of citrine crystal, in hand and walks down the shore.

The ship doesn't say goodbye.

9: Bishapur-Veta—The Temple of Water, Fire and Stone

Shalott finds herself in the middle of an ancient roadway, holding the triangular crystal bead. She walks in a southerly direction on a beautiful spring day.

She sees a sign in the distance. She reads "Bishapur" followed by archaic runes. It might be a mile marker, or something.

She walks about two hours in a south-westerly direction. She passes a beautiful and shallow lake, a waterfall, a stand of oak trees.

At length she comes upon the ruins of... something. Some kind of ancient site becomes visible. Orange blossom fragrance drifts through her, a gift from a nearby orchard. The sky is cyan, the weather clement.

Shalott can feel muscles that have never relaxed, relax.

A river flows from the east to places further westward. City walls and an ancient gate speak of a grander time, a time now passed.

She enters. The floor is carved green stone tiles shot through with veins of obsidian. Occasional marble pillars still hold segments of roof; others are cracked, split and crumbling.

Shalott tries to picture the people responsible for building this temple.

Everywhere there were serviceable pools set in geometric patterns, aching in the dryness of the desert night. This temple seems to have been built for giants rather than mere mortals. An Altar—stairs leading upward and then it hits her. This vast Emptiness, no one— not a single soul.

The wind tugs at her sleeve, but there isn't a sound. She can hear her own footfalls; it is not as though she has gone deaf. Somehow this silence is deeper than that.

A runic inscription on an eastern wall, she can't read it. Was it placed there to encourage or dissuade, to tell of the future or lament the past?

She tops the stairs and finds a huge arena.

She enters the arena through the closest gate, emerging in the middle row of the viewing gallery.

This place is vast, tier upon tier of empty seats with aisles radiating from the center like the spokes of a cosmic wheel.

She decides it is an outdoor theater. The center of the theater is a tawny sand floored oval with a low stage at the end nearest her.

She hears the wind now as it walks the aisles between the seats, and stirs dust devils across the field. The seats have been carved of a jade colored stone.

Shalott sits in one of the seats and leans back. She wonders how she knows this is to be her ordeal, wonders who will test her.

Every nerve in her body is alive. There is no sound save the wind; it is as though everything in the universe is listening.

She gets out of the seat to go down to the field. She has a strange feeling that a part of her stayed in the seat to watch. She does not turn to look, "Well, I am to be the audience as well as the show, am I to be the Tester too?" she asks in a loud voice as she sets foot on the oval. The word "Too" echoes through the arena.

She laughs.

She had imagined so many monsters in this testing, but there are no monsters to be found. So many ordeals she had rehearsed and re-rehearsed and yet here she stands, at the final moment, alone.

She looks back to where she had sat and if she holds her head just right she can see herself up there. She waves to herself and the reclining figure waves back.

From the field she shouts, "Take notes, there may be a quiz!"

"Got it, no problem," comes the reply.

Shalott walks to the stage and sits facing the far end of the field.

There is a distorted blur in the light at the end of the arena; a single figure emerges from the distortion, walking in Shalott's direction.

"Right on time, I see," the figure calls, as her features become clearer.

"I always try to be," she answers, trying to be so casual, so cool.

The approaching woman's face is not clear, but there is something very familiar in the way the other carries herself.

"It appears that the testing will be delayed," Shalott offers the stranger.

"Far from it, this testing is concluding," the stranger says just as Shalott recognizes her face.

The Shalott in the stands beholds Shalott walking up to herself on the stage. She is overjoyed.

She shouts, stamps her feet and applauds.

The two women on the field embrace, while the third one in the stands shouts and cheers like its New Years.

10: Et'-Poth-Ra—Temple of the Rain

Shalott steps out of the woods.

She knows this house, this is the house of the first man she ever loved.

She remembers a time before. Remembers that just before the Tsunami comes, there comes a terrifying stillness. A time when the Sea is drawn back like the blankets on your parent's bed, revealing many strange—things. Things wriggling in the sand and when you see an old lover, it feels just like that.

Before the Tsunami, there comes an out-rush of the air. Before the tidal wave, the wind leaves the land like exhaled breath, whistling through tattered palm fronds, and the sound of breath leaving your body.

Disheveled and unkempt, he stumbles from the house.

His eyes—wild, caged.

He hands her scribbles on a napkin and a fist full of currency. Says, "Build it—build it soon."

She considers. She reflects, and at length, mercy flowers in her heart.

In the sunlight she pieces together ten thousand shapes, ten thousand surfaces. She assembles shiny pots and pans, small bits of copper, tin plates, shards of glass, even sheets of semi-translucent plastic, with a little mortar and wood to hold it all tight.

Her work is true and she finds a kind of pride blossoming in her heart as she steps back. It is a thing of non-Euclidian beauty.

And then comes the rain.

Rattle tink, rattle rattle, tink tink. Ten thousand tiny voices gurgling in the mist. Chirping and hiss-wishing, clattering and plopping, and somehow the noise washes away the wind blowing from the abyss in her. Shalott is satisfied.

He's standing there beside her and she doesn't love him anymore, nor does she hate him. Somehow that is a good thing, somehow that is enough. The sound of the rain is like bacon on a spring morning.

She takes the string of beads from around her wrist, grasps the one that looks like a tiny glass eye, gives the man a friendly kiss and walks back into the woods.

11: Cahya-Zhi—The Temple of the Analakeeha Anomaly

Shalott is in some kind of tunnel, passageway, or something. The passage changes as she moves toward the center, it seems dimmer now. She turns on the electric torches and shadows dance the walls.

She tries to ignore the scurrying shadows down the cross passages and something to the right is calling her name in a deep booming voice.

Rivulets of ooze trickle down the leathery walls. There are patches that rhythmically bulge and contract like the abdomen of a breathing leviathan.

She comes to a choice between a left branch and a right. She goes left. She finds the top of a stair twisting down into the gloom. There is a wall to the right and nothing, as far as the torches can pierce, to the left.

It's like she has been on this stair her whole life, spiraling into the abyss.

At the bottom there's a dimly-lit room. She rests on the stairs for a moment.

The room is filled with thousands of statuettes; some human, others alien creatures. And there in the very center, a bigger-than-life statue of herself with some kind of octopus creature wrapped around her legs.

She laughs a dry and dusty laugh, devoid of any real humor. Not a pretty sound. There is a motion and to the left a heinous two-faced figurine turns to regard her. Every hair on the back of her neck stands erect as she screams.

Something is in the room with her. A shattering crash comes from across the chamber. Her eyes cannot register this moving mass of...

She runs on instinct. A million hallways and an eternity later, she bursts into an egg shaped chamber. The walls rough, glistening, white stone coiling up into a ceiling that is a vast bluish lens. The chamber hums with sizzling energies from the focused beam coming through the lens.

Screaming!

It's in the passageway outside the chamber. She moves further into the chamber to get away from the door.

She sees it clearly for the first time. The hideous heads come through the door and it snags, the shoulders and bulk of the beast are too big for it to fit through the entrance. It's writhing and squirming, enlarging the opening. Several of the legs have worked through the door and the heads are whipping around. The writhing reminds her of when, as a child, she watched a snake die.

One of the spines on the heads slices through the beam and is vaporized.

Bedlam!

Her head cannot contain the sound.

She backs away, further into the chamber, toward the beam running ceiling to floor.

It will come.

She will wait, standing with her back inches from the sizzle of the focused beam.

The light in the room is shifting, becoming more intense. Somewhere up there, dawn must be breaking.

The beast is in the chamber now. First one, then the other head regards her or perhaps the beam behind her.

"Come on baby," she coos.

It rears up.

She step backs

It hesitates.

She feels the beam on her back, "Come on."

It leaps and they fall back into a world of exploding light, where nothing hurts anymore.

She is back in the lobby and Finton is there.

12: The Third Visit to the Temple of Broken Glass

"Finton."

"Shalott?"

"Hey, look, Finton, I'm sorry. No. Really, I am sorry."

She uses her foot to doodle-draw a snake in the debris of the floor, "Finton, there are so many things happening to me, happening inside me. Things I thought buried, things I thought lost."

Finton offers her a perfectly folded, monogrammed handkerchief, because for some reason she is crying. His eyes are the color of kindness.

"Finton, what's this all about? Am I dead?"

The man tries to suppress a laugh, "Shalott, you are certainly not dead. You are perhaps more alive than you have ever been."

"But, what is this all about?"

"As with Life, it's about whatever you chose for it to be about."

"OK, that's just crap, but I get it. One thing, Finton, why are you in this rundown old movie house?"

He chortles again, "Technically, I am not from around here. This place is of your making. I must say I don't really care for the decor, but it serves."

She grasps a tiny silver mirror bead.

13: Salve' deFilmo—The Temple of Flesh

Shalott steps out of a mirror.

She hates this place, mirrors, mirrors everywhere, and not a drop to...

This mirror makes her look fat.

This one makes her lips look—pouty.

This is one of those that bend you every which way.

In this mirror she is comparing herself to others.

In this one she is always alone.

This one says things like, "Diet, stay out of the sun, men don't make passes at girls who wear..."

Shalott turns away only to confront another saying, "Start an exercise program, play sports and eat healthy food." This one says, "Straighten up. Smile and look straight ahead. You'll look and feel more confident,"

She tries it. It doesn't work.

There. Did you see that? Just as she turned, she caught a glimpse. Something—someone—is in one of the mirrors, but when she looks right at it all she can see is herself.

She turns to walk down the hall, and runs right into a mirror, thump.

She thinks about it, extends her hand, and walks back in the direction she came.

Damn. There it was again. The gypsy woman?

"OK, come out, I know you're in here." Her voice echoes strangely.

Nothing.

This twisty mirror looks like rippling water, and she can't make out her own reflection. She says, "You can come out now. Look, all I have to do is drop the bead in my hand and I'm out of here. So?"

She turns to face another mirror with no apparent distortion. She can see her whole body. The outline on the left gets fuzzy and her grandaunt Alice's reflection detaches from Shallot's reflection.

She sees lines in the kind old face. She sees things she never saw before. She discovers that she loves this woman with all of her heart.

"Alice?"

"Don't be so hard on her."

"Hard on whom?"

"You know she is a good little girl. I can just tell about these things."

"Alice, hey—look at me. Yes. Hi. Hey Alice, tell me what's the problem."

"I don't care about that stupid old mirror. I never liked it. And poor little Shalott, she was so upset when it got broken. I just wanted to tell her that I loved her and I didn't care about the—mirror. Dear, are you crying?" It's as though Alice has suddenly recognized Shalott.

"Yes, mam."

"Oh Shalott, don't cry. There's really no point. You know what dear, cry all you want. A good cry is what we all need from time to time."

"Thank you mam."

"How are you?"

"But Aunt Alice, I am a bad person."

"Hush, now none of that."

"But I've hurt people and I am so alone, and…"

"Honey, you aren't alone. Try getting old, now that makes you alone."

"But Aunt Alice—it was my fault."

"Your fault? Your Dad was an asshole, and your mom was too concerned about herself."

"Alice. I've never heard you talk like that."

"High time you did then."

"But I broke your mirror."

"No problem. My mother-in-law gave me that awful thing. I always hated it. Why do you think it was in the attic?"

"But I blamed the doll."

"Shalott, hon, did you think I was so stupid?"

"No, of course not— I am sorry."

"Hey, I was glad you didn't cut yourself."

"Aunt Alice, thank you."

"Honey, what's the problem?"

"I am so alone. Weren't you alone?"

"Shalott, I had you. Even when you weren't there, I could feel you. Oh child, you were my salvation."

"Aunt Alice. I never knew."

"Kinda makes you wish you'd paid more attention, huh?"

"Yes."

"Honey, you're never alone."

"How's that?"

"I'm inside you little one. How can you ever be alone?"

14: Enoch-Tor—The Temple of the Cloud Dragons

Shalott is falling in Darkness.

How long has she been lying here? She opens her eyes and quickly snaps them shut.

There is no ground. She is in free fall with no up, no down, no anything.

Shalott throws up and finds that vomit in free fall is a real nuisance.

She curls into a fetal position for an infinite time. She is in her head. She can hear the sound of a breeze. Her heart beats in her ears.

She fiddles with the strand of beads around her wrist.

She opens her eyes and finds a vast something filling a fourth of the sky. She will call it a planet. Tries to remember a movie where this guy named a planet. It is a very fuzzy and hazy thing, maybe even rounded.

Shalott decides the planet, as yet unnamed, is down.

There are things, clusters of jellyfish balloon things, undulating and meandering the ocean of air all around her. Myriad clouds, debris, everything but a kite, tumbling and floating in the air around her.

She swishes her hands and feet to get a better vantage point. She decides to relax and about that time a massive clump of green streamers passes between her and the planet. There are things crawling on the air-weed, there are things swinging around it.

The sky is crystal clear.

And then she sees it, one of the Magnificent Cloud dragons of Enoch Tor. It resembles nothing so much as a windsock she had painted for her dad when she was thirteen.

The head is a cluster of eyes and feelers. The long sensuous body snakes out for miles behind it. The body striped with that iridescent green you sometimes see on the heads of mallard ducks. The intervening stripes are a pulsating maroon. It has three major fins at 120 degree angles, near the head.

It moves, it slides, and it twists all around her, but makes no move directly toward her.

She is weightless in a sky suddenly alive and the iridescent dragon comes gently to stare into her face.

There are no words.

Beauty beyond…

No words.

And it's gone.

15: E'Teli-Kapus—The Temple of the Four Muses

Shalott is in a bar, more correctly a tavern, a pub. Across the table sits a handsome man she has never met, a man she has known all her life. Shalott is feeling strangely mellow.

She says, "Tell me a story."

"A story? You want a story?"

"Yes, it might help to pass the time."

He scoops a handful of peanuts. "Oh, OK." The peanuts and a portion of the beer disappear.

"Once there were four men in the desert, four turbulent and troubled men. One was named Reason, another named Magic, the third named Poetry, and the last one named Art."

"All men, no women?"

"All right three men and a woman, named Art. That's short for Artilina."

Shalott makes a face.

"They were regents in their own right and owned many things of great beauty and worth, yet they were unhappy. They had come to the desert to forget the future and deny the past.

The man called Reason had concluded that he was disconnected from everything else in the universe. Magic had become dark and filled with Dark visions of pain, blood and decay. Poetry had become a diseased lover, perverted beyond recognition. Art had become disfigured in a war and could no longer bring her to think of anything except her own despair."

Shalott says, "You're making it up as you go along, aren't you?"

The man continues unperturbed, "Well they traveled for seven days without incident. On the eighth day, they met a young man full in his prime."

"What was he wearing?"

"A loin cloth."

"You wish."

"Hush a minute, this is my story.

Well, Magic spoke first saying in a loud voice, "I am death and life, and how do you greet me?" And the man replied "I embrace you."

Wrathful with the man's response, Magic grew wings and talons and attacked the man. The man ducked and slapped at the thing that attacked him. In the struggle the man lost his right eye, but finally he managed a grip on Magic's throat. He pulled Magic up to his face and looked deep with his remaining eye into the eyes of Magic, only to find that there was nothing really there."

"Next, Poetry came up to him and said, 'I am your lover and your disease, how do you greet me?'

The man replied "I dance with you."

Poetry began the dance. It rippled and flowed in the sun and the man kept step. Often it seemed that Poetry would outreach the man, but then the man would pull from some inner oceanic soul and keep the step. The two blurred into one form. It was hard to tell one from the other. In time, Poetry gave out and fell dead on the sand. The dance had badly hurt the man such that he could barely stand."

Art came to the man and looked up at him with fearful eyes, "How will you greet me?" The man did not answer.

Art caught fire and a deep passion came over the man. He forgot his pain and tried to embrace the flame. In a frenzy he screamed, only to find he was alone with nothing but ashes in the wind."

Reason was the only one left. The man feared Reason, but Reason approached. The man, half hobbling, ran and Reason ran after him.

Despite the man's injuries, they ran thus for a full day and a full night. Finally, unable to run any farther, the man stopped and turned to face Reason.

"What have you to fear," asked Reason, "For I have brought you the things that you will need."

Reason gave the man a new mechanical eye to replace the one destroyed by Magic. Reason gave the man a new knee joint that worked almost as well as the old one, although the man still walked with a noticeable limp. Then Reason gave the man a heart-augment designed to keep his blood rich and flowing. This did not keep the man from feeling that his heart was breaking, but kept the guilt from killing him.

The man took all these things and set off to wander the world, in fact, he wanders the world even now."

Shalott sits staring at the man in silence.

16: Amun-Srete—The Temple of the Antikythera Mechanism

Shalott looks around. She is in her room—actually she is in the room she used to live in before she left home.

She watches a younger version of her hesitating at the door of her room.

Today is the first day of the rest of it, the rest of her life, and she hesitates there in the door.

She says to no one in particular, "What will we do today? Will the other kids be mean? What if the bus driver forgets me? How long before anyone notices, and what could happen to me then?"

She looks about the room at all her things and considers just staying in this room for the rest of her life. Considers going into a nunnery. Considers...

She walks through the door to breakfast, which is not such a new thing after all.

Time swirls and a slightly older, young Shalott hesitates at the living room door. She is touching the couch like it's her best friend, "Will I have to take a nap, because I don't think I could just sleep. Do these pants look OK?"

She sees the photos on the wall and suddenly wants to just look at them forever.

Another point on her timeline, she hesitates getting into her mom's car, "I think I have bronchitis. Jennifer Tomlin doesn't like me, and she will be there you know. And all those boys, I hate boys. They stink and they're stupid. Why do girls get stupid when they talk to boys?"

She hesitates at the bathroom door and considers what the cool kids will be doing when she goes to middle school.

"Why do I have to go? They don't teach me anything. Just a bunch of middle aged jerks. Yes, mam."

Time swirls and she hesitates at the gym door. Her prom dress is less than she wanted and Jimmy Farthing. I mean Jimmy Farthing, really?

Still he is nice to her and he doesn't look nearly as bad as he usually does.

She hesitates at her dorm room door. What if she hates her roommate? What if she flunks out? What if she has all these student loans that force her to work in a job she doesn't like and stay in one place when she really wants to roam?

Time coalesces and there he stands (I mean isn't there always one of these guys in all the stories she likes?). And he is holding something in his hand. He's smiling one of those enigmatic smiles.

She's not sure if she trusts him, not sure he's actually there and then he speaks. His voice is the color of kindness. He speaks of many things in her past and it is as if he has always known her.

She still doesn't trust him, but she wants to see what he has in his hand, so she asks him to show her what is there. His eyes are warm and weathered and he steps close enough to not be threatening.

In his hand is the Antikythera Mechanism, a bronze device the size of a tea saucer and dancing across the facets are all the things that have ever been, all the things that will ever be. And it's all so much, and it's all so small that she can't make out any of it and she certainly can't see her role in all this.

She says, "I'm not asking which to choose. I'm not even asking for a shove in the right direction. What I want is some clarity. I want to know what I'm choosing between. I want to know what I'm taking with me and what I'm leaving behind in the dust."

"Young one, you are choosing between the opposites of human existence, and you've been choosing all your life. Choosing whether to go or stay, whether to run or play, where to go and what to do. It has always been you choosing."

He offers and she withdraws her hands. She says, "But some of those choices sucked and things have been broken and face it, I've always been stubborn."

"Strong willed perhaps, but that's why you never chose drugs or took the easy ways that lead to true despair. And yes, you have made mistakes, but you have learned from each of them."

She indicates he might hold the thing up for her. "Why can't I simplify all the stuff on that stupid disk? Why are there no equations? Hell, I'd even settle for some probability studies, just something."

"Some things can be simplified into equations and some things can't. When you're looking at the Total Life Equation, it must be expressed with Chaos elements if it is to be Real."

She is distressed.

"I don't like that. It makes me afraid."

"No one expects you to like it, but that is the definition of courage, is it not? 'She was afraid, but she went on anyway,' and for the most part succeeded."

"What are my choices?"

"The same as all your life: to go into the next room or stay where you are, to let Love course your veins, or remain pure and chaste. To take a chance on hurting yourself on the thorns that grow along the path to the future, or to play it safe in your room. You know most of these choices are not always in yin/yang pairs, and the odds are you will live through most of your mistakes."

He pauses. She can't tell if it was just for effect. He says, "You will choose whether to remain a child or become a woman, whether you face each day as a challenge or a curse. No one can make this choice for you, but you are not alone. You will never be alone."

The stranger places the disk in her hand, and she tries to give it back. She says, "I can't take this; It's much too valuable."

"I hesitate to say this gentle one, but you must take this. Consider it an offering."

"Where did you get it?"

His eyes grow winsome and a smile glows at the corners of his mouth. He takes off his hat and bows to her, "Time is not linear, dear one. You gave it to me when you saved me."

17: Tahl Sheeah—The Temple of the Eternal Moment

Shalott returns to the lobby, but Finton cannot be found. She lays the disk shaped object on the abandoned concession stand.

She examines the last bead; a smooth shiny sphere, blacker than a black hole.

She looks away for a moment, afraid of what this bead might bring. She considers leaving before trekking to the last temple.

She heaves a sigh. Picks up the Antikythera Mechanism and notices that there is a perfect hole in it, exactly the right size for the last bead. She places the bead in the hole and it disappears.

When she looks back up, she can see intense light coming from all around the last door. It seems to permeate everything.

She grips the disk, leans against the door.

Shalott is no longer falling or walking or breathing, and somehow that is OK.

She is under the Sea and though she has never seen Atlantis, she finds herself beside a perfect Atlanten pyramid in the central square.

Dim and murky, who knows how long she's floated there. Something glowing in the distance, there is another, several now. Pinpoints of light moving toward her. She saw these lights in the eyes of a man in a dream when she was a little girl. She called them fairy lights.

There is a sound, a myriad of sounds actually, not unlike an orchestra tuning up. But it's bedlam, total discord.

The first of the fairy lights swims by her. It's a tiny flickering fish. She watches it taking a position on the pyramid and its song locks in. In fact, as each fish assumes its position, a part of a Universal chord engages.

There is a resonance building between the structures that surround her and the square. Iridescent resonant chords folding back on themselves. Harmonic frequencies undulating and subtle, in the eddies and cross currents of temporal flux. Standing waves gelling into matrices, coalescing in concordance with the indisputable laws of an infinitely hydrodynamic Universe. Energies coalescing into stratified sheets of clarified existence. Whisps interlocking into non-linear relationships, spiraling, collapsing, self-recursive fractal spirals curling and unfolding, twisting into deceptively simple vortexes of the ever opening flower of Reality.

Across the ten dimensional crystalline matrixes of the hyper conductive underpinning of the Universe electric dragons of dynamic oscillation cavort, attesting the rightness of the Universal pattern templates.

And building within the chord, a single, tight, searing note rakes the darkness. Pressure building—building—building, unable to release.

Shalott screams, "What's it for?"

A ripping.

A rending.

A shattering. It is the sound of perfect symmetries breaking. It is that thunderous instant when a kernel of Wanting bursts into everything we know!

Alive for the first time, she stands, a stardust thing still quivering in the echo.

18: The Temple of Hope (Formerly Temple of Broken Glass)

She comes to awareness in the lobby of a brand new movie theater, huge plate glass windows in every direction. And she realizes that there are people in the theaters. Some watching comedies, some dramas, a few action-adventures.

"Hey Finton..." No answer.

She looks in her hand and finds the now familiar string of beads sold to her by the crone. She gingerly shoves them into her pocket.

She looks all around for Finton, can't find him, and buys a box of popcorn and a Doctor Pepper from a guy named Jeremy.

"Outrageous price," he says. He still takes the money.

She waits, but he doesn't come.

She gives it one last look around and walks out the door. She doesn't see the man reflected in the mirror behind the concession bar. A man neither tall nor short, not fat or thin, and a man that you have to force yourself to look at because it is the natural tendency of your eyes to slide off this man onto anything else in the room.

He's waving goodbye to her.

19: Return to the Ante Room of the Twelve Pathways

Shalott sees the little girl playing with her doll. The girl is kinda happy there in front of the mirror. Shalott notices that her grandaunt's mirror is unbroken.

From below there comes the sweet voice of Aunt Alice.

Shalott slips out of the attic.

20: Entrance on Route 9

The crone offers, her hands tremble—Shallot's face softens a fraction. She asks, "Grand Aunt, what is your name?"

"Archna, you call me Archna..."

"Aunt Archna..."

"Archna... please call me Archna," the crone interrupts.

"Archna, one of my friends is playing a joke on the both of us."

The crone calms and offers the beads a third time. Shalott opens her hand. The crone places the string across the young woman's palm. Shalott laughs with her whole body as the circle of time completes itself.

The crone is pleased.

Shalott digs in her pocket and pulls out far too much cash.

The crone refuses at first, but Shalott insists.

Shalott climbs into her T-bird, takes one long last look around. Everything is totally electric and for the first time in years, the young woman breathes. How long has she been holding her breath?

She starts the car, shifts gears and is never seen in those parts again.

William C. Burns, Jr. has won the Greenville County Library Award for haiku, and has been published in To Be Men, After the Orange: Ruin and Recovery and Confessions: A Nightmare in Five Acts. He also published in Star*Line, The New Press Literary Quarterly, South Ash Press, and Slug Fest. He is a regular contributor to MetaStellar magazine. He's a full-time writer whose previous lives include being a bioengineer, a teacher of electrical power, microprocessor control systems and a set designer for local theaters.

Out Here

By Scott Beggs

[Message 082010-031924]
[SulNraeu Sproec oaomleir...]
[Language decode complete...]
[Message text]

One greeting.

A century ago, a question blossomed in our awareness that has tormented each subsequent generation's brightest scientific minds. Since other intelligent life must be out there in a universe so vast, why haven't they found us yet? Billions of stars in our system, planets much older than ours to support intelligence, all those eons to develop the necessary tools, and, sadly, a silence so pure and final. We call this [DECODE FAIL: MISSING COMPONENT] Paradox.

Some believed we felt alone because [DECODE FAIL "Fircieon"] intelligent life existed too far apart, over too great a timespan. Some believed a great cosmic conspiracy purposefully hid everyone else from us. The nihilistic among us believed destruction always came shortly after the search.

The simplest answer was that we were alone. It was an answer many of us could not accept.

The [POSSIBLE MATCH "religion"] believed this loneliness was a signal of purpose for a singular creation.

Some of us continued the work in spite of the silence. Intrepid optimists sacrificed large amounts of capital building machines to listen for transmissions. They handed down their admiration and knowledge to a new generation of listeners who handed it down to us. Those of us tasked with this auspicious [DECODE FAIL "oKnhloet"] had accepted a life of maddening patience of not knowing but believing.

All we have known is failure.

Throughout the decades, we have listened, hearing nothing. We have looked, seeing nothing. We have reached, feeling nothing.

Yet not everyone gave up hope.

Then, by improbable chance, we stumbled across your Voyager craft floating through the darkness. We found the gold discus it contained. Its elemental etchings were radiantly clear.

We calculated the craft's trajectory and found your planet along the path. The map you left confirmed your position. It was a moment of unparalleled elation for us, but we are saddened to say we have no name for your home, only a scientific designation of [DECODE FAIL "tT-1129"].

We had to destroy part of the discus to learn to use it. We tested its material. We built a new machine that could draw out its information but heard nothing.

We waited in disappointment, only to hear a faint, low noise near its conclusion. We retested, adjusted the sounds to our higher frequency, replayed it, and heard a thrilling burst of life.

The tones, rising and sweeping. Some falling into harmony and some fighting against one another. Some placid and some angry. Markers of such [DECODE FAIL "jMel"] and vibrancy. Each emotion carried through, miraculously recognizable from such an immense distance. The complicated music of your star.

Most thrilling was what we recognized with greatest intimacy: the undulating chorus of a thought scan. An electronic map of consciousness representing the organ propelling all other inquiries.

Your craft revealed your existence. The sounds, your life. The scan, our connection.

One prominent [POSSIBLE MATCH "religion"] leader called you our sibling. There is truth in that poetry. We live together, separated only by time and by space.

After deciphering the discus, we agreed to form and send this message. We now lack the means to send travelers to you, but we estimate the capability in fifty years, and that, by then, we will be able to move even faster than this message can travel. By all measures, we may arrive shortly after this message does.

We are renewed. We send this message with overwhelming [DECODE FAIL "laehiHm"], hope, and joy, and wish you to receive it with the same. Following this message are sounds from our planet converted to a range of 2000-5000Hz so you can hear us clearly and know us.

Seeing you after staring so long into dark infinity, hearing you after listening so long in silence, we are sure that you have been waiting, too. Let this message from your neighbors be a comfort that you are not alone in the universe. We are out here.

Scott Beggs keeps an eye on the stars. His short stories have appeared in PseudoPod, Dark Moon Digest, MYTHIC Magazine, and All Worlds Wayfarer. He moves around a lot with his family, and he wants to be Buster Keaton's best friend. Follow him on Twitter at @scottmbeggs and visit his website at ScottBeggs.com for more.

The Way of Water

By Nina Munteanu

She imagines its coolness gliding down her throat. Wet with a lingering aftertaste of fish and mud. She imagines its deep voice resonating through her in primal notes; echoes from when the dinosaurs quenched their throats in the Triassic swamps.

Water is a shapeshifter.

It changes yet stays the same, shifting its face with the climate. It wanders the earth like a gypsy, stealing from where it is needed and giving whimsically where it isn't wanted.

Dizzy and shivering in the blistering heat, Hilda shuffles forward with the snaking line of people in the dusty square in front of University College where her mother used to teach. The sun beats down, crawling on her skin like an insect. She's been standing for an hour in the queue for the public water tap. Her belly aches in deep waves, curling her body forward.

There is only one person ahead of her now, an old woman holding an old plastic container. The woman deftly slides her wCard into the pay slot. It swallows her card and the light above it turns green. The card spits out of the slot. The meter indicates what remains of the woman's quota. The woman bends stiffly over the tap and turns the handle. Water trickles reluctantly into her cracked plastic container. It looks like they have another shortage coming, Hilda thinks, watching the old woman turn the tap off and pull out her card then shuffle away.

The man behind Hilda pushes her forward. She stumbles toward the tap and glances at the wCard in her blue-gray hand. Her skin resembles a dry riverbed. Heart throbbing in her throat, Hilda fumbles with the card and finally gets it into the reader. The reader takes it. The light screams red. Her knees almost give out. She dreaded this day.

She stares at the wTap. The dryness in the back of her throat rises to meet her tongue, now thick and swollen. She gags on the thirst of three days. Just like her mother's secret cistern, her card has run dry; no credits, no water. The faucet swims in front of her. The sun, high in the pale sky, glints on the faucet's burnished steel and splinters into a million spotlights...

Hilda read in her mother's forbidden book that water was the only natural substance on Earth that could exist in all three physical states. She'd never seen enough water to test the truth of that claim. She remembered snow as a child. How the flakes fluttered down and landed on her coat like jewels. No two snowflakes were alike, she'd heard once. But not from her mother; her mother refused to talk about water. Whenever Hilda asked her a question about it, she scowled and responded with bitter and sarcastic words. Her mother once worked as a limnologist for CanadaCorp in their watershed department; but they forced her to retire early. Hilda tried to imagine a substance that could exist as a solid, liquid and gas, all in the same place and at the same time. One moment flowing with an urgent wetness that transformed all it touched. Another moment firm and upright. And yet another, yielding into vapor at the breath of warmth. Water was fluid and soft, yet it wore away hard rock and carved flowing landscapes with its patience.

Water was magic. Most things on the planet shrank and became more dense as they got colder. Water, her textbook said, did the opposite; which was why ice floated and why lakes didn't completely freeze from top to bottom.

Water was paradox. Aggressive yet yielding. Life-giving yet dangerous. Floods. Droughts. mudslides. Tsunamis. Water cut recursive patterns of creative destruction through the landscape, an ouroboros remembering.

She'd heard a myth—from Hanna, of course—that Canada once held the third richest reserve of freshwater in the world. Canada used to have clean sparkling lakes deep enough for people to drown in. That was before the unseasonal storms and floods. Before the rivers dried up and scarred the landscape in a network of snaking corpses. Before Lake Ontario became a giant tailings pond. Before CanadaCorp shut off Niagara Falls then came into everyone's home and cemented their taps shut for not paying the water tax.

When that happened, her mother secretly set up rainwater catchers on her property. Collecting rainwater was illegal because the rain belonged to CanadaCorp. When Raytheon and the WMA diverted the rain to the USA, her cistern dried up and they had to resort to getting their water from the rationed public water taps that cost the equivalent of $20 a glass in water credits. It didn't matter if you were rich—no one got more than two liters a day.

Hilda and her mother hadn't seen a good rain in over a decade. Lake Ontario turned into a mud puddle, like Erie before it. The Saint Lawrence River, channelized long ago, now flowed south to the USA; like everything else.

One day the water patrol of the RCMP stormed the house. They seized her mother's books—except Wetzel's Limnology, hidden under Hilda's mattress—and they dragged her mother away. The RCMP weren't actually gruff with her and she didn't struggle. She quietly watched them ransack the place then turned a weary gaze to Hilda. "We were too nice...too nice..." she'd said in a strangled voice. She didn't clutch Hilda to her bosom or tell her that she loved her. Just the words, "We invited them in and let them take it all. We gave it all away..." It took a long time for Hilda to realize that she'd meant Canada and its water.

CanadaCorp wasn't even a Canadian company. According to Hanna, it was part of Vivanti, a multinational conglomerate of

European and Chinese companies. When it came to water—which was everything—the Chinese owned the USA. When China finally called them on their trillion dollar debt, the bankrupted country defaulted. That was when the world changed. China offered the US a deal: give us your water, all of it, and we'll forfeit the capital owed. And they could stay a country. That turned out to include Canadian water, since Canada had already let Michigan tap into the Great Lakes. That's how CanadaCorp, which had nothing to do with Canada, came to own the Great Lakes and eventually all of Canada's surface and groundwater. And how Canada sank from a resource-rich nation into a poor indentured state. Hilda didn't cry when her mother left. Hilda thought her mother was coming back. She didn't.

A tiny water drop hangs, trembling, from the wTap faucet mouth, as if considering which way to go: give in to gravity and drop onto the dusty ground or defy it and cling to the inside of the tap. Hilda lunges forward and touches the faucet mouth with her card to capture the drop. Then she laps up the single drop with her tongue. She thinks of Hanna and her throat tightens.

The man behind her grunts. He barrels forward and violently shoves her aside. Hilda stumbles away from the long queue in a daze. The brute gruffly pulls out her useless card and tosses it to her. She misses it and the card flutters like a dead leaf to the ground at her feet. The man shoves his own card into the pay slot. Hilda watches the water gurgle into his plastic container. He is sloppy and some of the water splashes out of his container, raining on the ground. Hilda stares as the water bounces off the parched pavement before finally pooling. The ache in her throat burns like sandpaper and she wavers on her feet.

The lineup tightens, as if the people fear she might cut back in.

She stares at the water pooling on the ground, glistening into a million stars in the sunlight.

Hanna claimed that there was a fourth state of water: a liquid crystal that possessed magical properties of healing. You could find it in places like collagen and cell membranes where biological signals and information traveled instantly. Like quantum entanglement. The crystalline water increased its energy in a vortex and light. Hanna seemed to know all about the research done at the University of Washington. According to her, this negatively-charged crystallized water held energy like a battery and pushed away pollutants. She told of an experiment in Austria where water in a beaker, when jolted with electromagnetic energy, leapt up the beaker wall, groping to meet its likeness in the adjoining beaker. The beaker waters formed a "water bridge", like two shocked children clutching hands.

Hilda's mother had dismissed Hanna's claims as fairytale. But when Hilda challenged her mother, she couldn't explain why water stored so much energy or absorbed and released more heat than most substances. Or a host of other things water could do that resembled magic.

Something Hilda never dared share with her mother was Hanna's startling claim about water's intelligent purpose. She cited bizarre studies conducted by Russian scientists and some quasi-scientific studies in Germany and Austria suggesting that water had a consciousness. "What if everything that water does has an innate purpose, related to what we are doing to it?" Hanna had once challenged. "They've proven that water remembers everything done to it and everywhere it's been. What if it's self-organized, like a giant amoebic computer. We've done terrible things to water, Hilda," she said, sorrow vivid in her liquid eyes. "What if water doesn't like being owned or ransomed? What if it doesn't like being channelized into a harsh pipe system or into a smart cloud to go where it normally doesn't want to go? What if those hurricanes and tornadoes and floods are water's way of saying 'I've had enough'?"

None of that matters now, Hilda thinks rather abstractly and feels herself falling. They are all going to die soon anyway. Neither water's magical properties nor Hanna's fantasies about its consciousness are going to help her or Hanna, who disappeared again since last month...

"I can't do this anymore with you," Hilda ranted. She paced her decrepit one-room apartment and watched Hanna askance. Hanna sat on Hilda's worn couch like a brooding selkie. Like a sociopath contemplating her next move. Waiting for Hilda's. "This is the last time," Hilda kept her voice harsh. She wanted to jar Hanna into crying, or something, to induce some kind of emotional breakdown. In truth, Hilda was relieved to see her itinerant friend, alive and well, after her lengthy silence. Hilda went on, "It's always the same pattern. After months of nothing, you come, desperate for help...water credits or some dire task that only I can perform ... then you disappear again, only emerging months later with your next disaster. I never hear from you otherwise. I don't know if you're dead or alive, like I'm a well you dip into. Like that's all I mean to you. Where do you go when you disappear? Where?"

She dropped back in the lumpy chair across from Hanna and watched her gypsy friend, hoping for some sign of remorse, or acknowledgement, at least. She knew Hanna wouldn't answer, as though every question she asked her—particularly the personal ones—was only rhetorical in nature. Hanna just stared at her like a puppy dog. As if she didn't quite understand the problem. She could barely speak at the best of times. Hilda had decided long ago that Hanna was partly autistic. Maybe a savant even; she was inordinately clever. Too clever sometimes. Maybe she'd been traumatized when she was little, Hilda considered. Apparently, the emergence of sociopathic behavior was created—or prevented—by childhood experience. She knew that Hanna's childhood, though privileged with significant wealth, was terribly lonely and troubled. Her parents, who both worked in the water industry in Maine, spent no time with her and her sister. Like obsessed missionaries, they were always traveling and tending their water business. When Hanna was in her late teens, her parents perished in a freak accident.

Hanna had avoided any cross-examination, but Hilda's uncompromising research on Oracle uncovered a strange story—a common one in the old water wars. Hanna never revealed her last name but Hilda guessed it was Lauterwasser, the name of a known water baron family in Maine: John and Beulah Lauterwasser owned a large water holding of spring water near Fryeburg and sold Aqua Fina all over the world. They'd refused buy-out offers by the international conglomerate Vivanti. Soon after the Lauterwassers drowned, the holdings mysteriously came into the hands of Vivanti. Hilda suspected foul play. Not long after that, Hanna appeared in her life.

From the moment Hilda saw her, seven years ago, she'd felt a strange yet familiar attraction she couldn't explain. A bond that commanded her with a kind of divine instruction, a deja vu, that bubbled up like an evolutionary yin-yang mantra: you two were born to do something important together. Hilda felt a strange repelling attraction to her strange friend. Like the covalent bond of a complex molecule.

Like two quantum entangled atoms fueled by a passion for information, they shared secrets on Oracle. They corresponded for months on Oracle; strange attractors, circling each other closer and closer—sharing energy—yet never touching. Then Hanna suggested they actually meet. They met in the lobby of a shabby downtown Toronto hotel. Hilda barely knew what she looked like but when Hanna entered the lobby through the front doors, Hilda knew every bit of her. Hanna swept in like a stray summer rainstorm, beaming with the self-conscious optimism of someone who recognized a twin sister. She reminded Hilda of her first boyfriend, clutching flowers in one hand and chocolate in the other. When their eyes met, Hilda knew. For an instant, she knew all of Hanna. For an instant, she'd glimpsed eternity. What she didn't know then was that it was love.

Love flowed like water, gliding into backwaters and lagoons with ease, filling every swale and mire. Connecting, looking for home. Easing from crystal to liquid to vapor then back, water recognized its hydrophilic likeness, and its complement. Before the inevitable decoherence, remnants of the entanglement lingered like a quantum vapor, infusing everything. Hilda always knew where and when to find Hanna on Oracle, as though water inhabited the machine and told her. Water even whispered to her when her wandering friend was about to return from the dark abyss and land unannounced on her doorstep.

Hilda leaned back in her chair with a heavy sigh. She always gave in to Hanna. And Hanna knew it. "OK," Hilda said. "What do you need this time?"

Hanna's face lit with the fire of inspiration and she leaned forward. "Oracle told me something."

Hilda slumped deeper in her chair and rolled her eyes. "Of course Oracle told you something. It always does."

Some cyber-genius created Oracle after the Internet sold out to Vivanti. The Oracle universe was the last commons, Hilda considered. It had brought her and Hanna together, bound them into one being with a common understanding. Hilda discovered one of Hanna's sites. It turned out to be a code for what was happening to water. To Hanna's obvious delight, Hilda decoded her blog and like two conspiring teenagers, they shared intimate secrets about water. Hilda shared from her textbook and Hanna embellished with facts that Hilda's mother reluctantly confirmed or vehemently denied. Hilda never discovered how Hanna got her information, how she managed to cross the Canadian/US border or who Hanna really was. Whether she was a delusional charlatan, the itinerant daughter of a murdered water baron, a water spy for the US or something worse. Hilda realized that she didn't want to know.

"I was right but I was wrong too," Hanna said, beaming like an angel. "Mandelbrot has the last piece of the puzzle. It's right there, in Ritz's migrating birds and Scholes's photosynthesis." She lifted her eyes to the heavens then grinned like an urchin at Hilda. "...In Schrödinger's water." Seeing Hanna this way, lit with genuine inspiration, Hilda knew she would totally give in to whatever plan the girl had concocted. She wasn't prepared for what Hanna asked for.

"I need a thousand water credits."

"What?" Hilda gasped. "You know I don't have that! What the chaos do you need it for?" Hanna had inherited a hoard of water credits in the Vivanti settlement but had lost them all, through various wild ventures and a profligate lifestyle. Over the years, Hilda, who had barely anything, had given Hanna so many water credits for her wild schemes during their strange friendship. She'd funded Hanna's Tesla-field amplifier, her orgonite cloud-buster and anti-HAARP electromagnetic pulse device. Hilda had never once gotten any proof of them having amounted to anything, except to keep Hanna hydrated.

Hanna inched forward in her seat and her eyes glinted like sapphires. "You know about the nanobots that keep the smart clouds in the states from coming north over the border?"

Hilda nodded, wondering what Mandelbrot's fractals—and photosynthesis—had to do with weather control and cloud farming. It was part of the deal the US made with the Chinese, who had first perfected weather manipulation with smart dust. Vivanti-owned the weather. Canada, which had been mined dry of its water, was just another casualty of the corporate profit machine.

"Why do you think water lets them do that?" Hanna said.

Hilda squirmed in her seat. What was Hanna driving at? As though water had any say in the matter...

Hanna wriggled in her seat with a self-pleased smile. "What if those nanobots 'decided' to let the clouds migrate north?"

Suddenly intrigued, Hilda leaned forward and stared at her friend. "Are you talking sabotage?" she finally said in a hoarse whisper and wondered who Hanna really was. "How?"

Hanna grinned in silence. A kind of conspiratorial withholding look. She always did that, Hilda thought: looked reluctant to say, when that was precisely why she'd come. To spill a secret. The two women stared at one another for an eternity of a moment. Hilda struggled to stay patient, understanding the hierarchy of flow.

Hanna finally confided, "Not sabotage. More like collaboration." She leaned back and her mischievous grin turned utterly sublime. She looked like a self-pleased griffin. "Like recognizes like, Hilda. Have you ever noticed how children going for walks with their mothers notice only other children? The most successful persuasion doesn't come from your boss, but by a trusted colleague...a friend."

Hilda shook her head, still not understanding.

Hanna leaned forward and gently took Hilda's hand in hers. She pressed Hilda's fingers with hers in a warm clasp. Smooth hydrated fingers that were long and beautiful; not like Hilda's selkie hands. "It's ok, my friend," Hanna said. "Just trust me. Trust me one more time..."

✳ ✳ ✳

The faucet swims into a million faucets. Hilda understands that she is hallucinating. People generally stay away from the public wTap when someone in her condition approaches. People don't want to share, but they also don't want to feel cruel or greedy about not sharing. In today's blistering heat, urgency overrules decorum and they simply ignore her away. They know she is close to the end. She's seen others and has shied away herself. She feels the water guardians hovering. Waiting. If she doesn't get up and walk away, they will come and take her—probably to the same place her mother was taken. Someplace you never came back from.

It is a month since she gave Hanna everything she had in the world. A month since Hanna disappeared with Hilda's thousand water credits—worth a million dollars on the black market. Credits she borrowed off her rent. In that month, Hilda's entire world collapsed. Her research contract—and associated meager income— ended suddenly at the Wilkinson Alternative Energy Centre, with no sign of transfer or renewal. Three weeks later, the Coop wiped most of her bank account clean then locked her out. She found a piece of shade from the relentless sun under an old corrugated sheet of metal in the local dump, and set up camp there.

Nothing has changed with the water. No clouds have come. No rains have come. And no Hanna has come.

This time, Hilda knows that Hanna is really gone. That whatever fractal scheme Hanna had conjured, she's failed. Since they flowed into one another, they always seemed to know when the other was in trouble... Strangely, Hilda feels nothing. No presence; no absence. Just nothing.

Hanna is probably dead. Or worse. Since meeting her, Hilda has learned to monitor the Oracle for signs of her elusive friend. Small blips of signature code on certain sites. Anonymous tags. Like ghosts, they wisped into existence, whispered their truths, then disappeared like vapor in the wind. Even they stopped. Hanna too has turned to vapor.

Hilda is alone. Doomed by her trust, her faith and her gift... All gone with Hanna...

No. Not all gone.

For every giver there must be a receiver in the recursive motion of fractals. Everything is connected through water, from infinitely small to infinitely large. Like recognizes like. Atom with atom. Like her and Hanna. Like water with water...

She's fallen recumbent on the dusty ground. She is dying of thirst meters from a water source. And no one is coming to help her. They just keep filling their containers and shuffling away in haste. She doesn't hate them for it. They aren't capable of helping her. She squints at the massive sun that seems to wink at her and chokes on her own tongue. Perhaps her vision is already failing, because a shadow passes before the sun and it grows suddenly dark. It doesn't matter.

She's given all of herself faithfully in love and in hope. Through Hanna. To water. She is two-thirds water, after all. Just like the planet. Water and the universe are taking her back into its fold. She will enter the Higgs Field, stream through spacetime, touch infinite light. Then, energized, return—perhaps as water even—to Earth or somewhere else in the cosmos.

Her mother was wrong in her angry heart. They weren't too nice. It is simply the way of water. They are all water. And water is an altruist.

It starts to rain.

Huge drops spatter her face, streaming down, soaking her hair, her clothes, her entire body. It hurts at first, like missals assaulting her with suddenness. Like love. Then it begins to soothe as her parched body remembers, grateful.

Dark storm clouds scud across the heavens like warriors chasing a thief. She's vaguely aware of the commotion of people as they scatter, arms and containers pointed up toward the heavens. She smiles then feels her body convulse with tears.

Is that you, Hanna? Have you come to take me home?...

Nina Munteanu is a Canadian ecologist, limnologist and novelist. She is co-editor of Europa SF and currently teaches writing courses at George Brown College and the University of Toronto. Visit NinaMunteanu.ca for the latest on her books. Nina's bilingual "La natura dell'acqua / The Way of Water" was published by Mincione Edizioni in Rome. Her non-fiction book "Water Is..." by Pixl Press was selected by Margaret Atwood in the New York Times "Year in Reading" and was chosen as the 2017 Summer Read by Water Canada. Her novel "A Diary in the Age of Water" was released by Inanna Publications in June 2020.

Losing It

By Davin Ireland

"Don't talk to me about the ironies of life," Josh Rideout complained for perhaps the twentieth time that afternoon. "I've had it up to here with ironies. Big ones, small ones, the ones you don't see coming — they'll be the death of me yet." Possibly to illustrate the point, he shook another Lucky Strike free of the pack, lit up using the butt of its still-smoking predecessor, and puffed a few times to get it going. This was back in the days when smoking in pubs was still allowed and nobody had even heard of a subatomic codon mutator.

"Just look at the state of the damned planet," he groaned, and rubbed a hand across his eyes. "The second biggest killer of young people in the United States today is obesity, Sam. Fucking obesity. Not war, not AIDS, not crossing the street on a Friday night. Too many chili dogs, that's what's doing it. How's that for ironic, huh? On one side of the world, gluttony and over-indulgence are killing people like there's no tomorrow; on the other, there is no tomorrow. It's famine and starvation all the way." Josh blew smoke at the ceiling and offered me a look of utter bewilderment. "How many innocent people die in the developing world every decade from a lack of that which we throw away? Hundreds of thousands? Millions?"

I glanced about the rear of the darkened pub while gauging my response, only salvation appeared nowhere nearer than it had when

I'd bumped into Josh upon exiting the downstairs Ladies' Room at lunchtime. It had proven one of those random, chance encounters that only seem to occur when you're least expecting it ... and are therefore least able to deflect. Josh Rideout, the dashing young medical student who'd turned the last two years of my pharmacology degree upside down — and I'd run into him at the most awkward of moments. Who'd be pregnant? Seriously?

"Samantha? Sam?"

The only other person in the corridor at the time had been a disheveled figure clinging to a cigarette machine for support. A thick shock of hair hung down over his eyes. When I turned at the sound of my name, he offered me the kind of stupid, sloppy grin that drunks exhibit when caught in a situation they cannot think themselves out of. But it was him, all right. Joshua Rideout, former campus Casanova and all-round likable rogue, a dozen years down the line. Still rapier-thin, still every inch the black-clad rebel. And then there was me: Samantha Higson, née Beaumont, eight months pregnant, bladder crushed to the size of a chestnut, waddling out of the toilet after the umpteenth pit stop of the day.

I'd been trying to effect an escape ever since.

"The thing is," Josh continued, "I don't blame the Yanks one little bit." He quaffed back a mouthful of brandy, wiped his lips on the back of one hand, and briefly seemed to lose the thread of his narrative. That was a relief. The Josh I knew had always been broad-minded and tolerant—yet the condescending, distinctly anti-American tone of his monologue was not only disturbing, it was profoundly out of character. I found myself wondering what on earth could have brought it on.

"Mind you," he resumed, plonking his glass on the table hard enough to attract stares, "being the most powerful nation on earth can't be easy. The strongest economy, the fastest cars, the biggest lies. Little wonder they have the biggest waistlines. I was in New York recently, and you could feel it in the street. The weight of expectation, the pressure to succeed. If you ask me, the only way your average

American can measure up is by literally measuring up. Bloating like a puffer fish is the only response that works when you feel threatened."

"Josh, listen to me," I interrupted, and watched him flick a long cone of ash into the ashtray, "I don't mean to compound your disappointment at what is clearly a difficult time, but sweeping generalizations of this nature—"

"What's a matter, you don't believe me?"

"I didn't say—"

"Because all you have to do is open your eyes. Go to any McDonald's in the country and order yourself a meal. Nobody says 'Supersize that burger, honey' or 'Supersize those fries for me.' No way, it's 'Supersize me' every time. Supersize fucking me, Sam. How can we expect your average U.S. citizen to empathize with the rest of the world when most of them barely even resemble the human race anymore?"

My mouth dropped open at the sheer gall of what I was hearing. Josh failed to notice. He expelled a lungful of acrid smoke, treated himself to more brandy, and got straight back into it. "Think about it. You put a two-hundred-and-ninety-pound shut-in from North Haven, Connecticut, next to some emaciated East African, they don't even look like the same friggin' species anymore, am I right? Where's the identification, Sam? Where's the empathy?" He wiped his mouth on the back of one hand and looked at me. "And we're going the same way."

"Joshua Rideout," I said slowly, "that's more than enough, you hear me?" I spoke quietly and without inflection, but drunk or not, my former lover got the message. He'd been knocking back the doubles since before my arrival, and now his gaze was filming over like a puddle freezing in a cold snap. I could see what was coming — and the one thing I didn't need right then was an unconscious ex-boyfriend sprawled in the back of my Volvo. Especially with Darren's mother arriving from Eastleigh that very evening to walk me through the final stages of the pregnancy. But what could I do? I was a married woman, I had responsibilities. How on earth could I concentrate on the injustices of the world when in just a few weeks' time I'd be up to my elbows in nappies?

"I'm sorry, old buddy," I sighed, and struggled to my feet, "but I can't do this. I understand your frustration, and I do sympathize. At least with some of what you said. But part of you has curdled, Josh. You were always angry. You were never like this."

It was a dreadful thing to say, and I regretted it the moment the words were out of my mouth. Seeing the once-brilliant but erratic Josh Rideout alone and dejected in the back of some old dive I barely considered worth pissing in, twelve long years after we'd parted company on difficult terms, was almost too painful to bear. But it was more than that. Despite his vitriolic opinions and haggard countenance, I found myself struggling with the notion that Josh still genuinely believed in something — even if that something had distorted his world view beyond recognition.

I, on the other hand, was rapidly losing faith on all fronts. Don't get me wrong, Darren's a lovely bloke. Trouble is, the man I married has never enjoyed the best of health, and by the time we discovered I was expecting, his failing constitution had pretty much ruined his chances of a decent career. Add to that a greedy, uncommunicative son from a previous marriage, and you can appreciate why we were becoming desperate at a time when we would otherwise have been ecstatic. Bumping into Josh should have cheered me up, if only because it proved there was someone else in the world even more miserable than me. But nothing could have been further from the truth.

I caught sight of him in a wall mirror as I vacated the table and made for the street. I wish I hadn't. Alcohol had reduced a once handsome man to a pitiful caricature of his former self. He looked so lost. His hair, as thick and wild as ever, was matted and threaded through with gray; unidentified stains decorated the front of his shirt; an unkempt rash of stubble at his cheeks and throat indicated days of neglect. I kept going.

I was halfway between our booth and the dimly-lit exit when something struck the arm of a chair to my left and skidded across an adjacent table top. A paperback book. Worn but otherwise perfectly serviceable, it came to rest between a wet patch and an abandoned pint glass. I reached out and picked it up. The cover was lurid, brightly colored, and not altogether unfamiliar. But it was the name of the author that grabbed my attention.

Professor J. Mitchell Rideout.

I'd seen it before, of course — crowding out the other bestsellers on the shelves at Waterstones and W.H. Smiths. I'd even teased Darren on occasion that my old flame had finally come good, never once suspecting how right I'd been. Part of the reason for that near wilful act of ignorance, I suppose, was the name itself. Like people, names tend to evolve over time. Take mine. I was christened Samantha, went through the education system as Sammy or Sam, and arrived where I am today as plain old Mrs Higson. It was the same with my brother, Justin, for whom the abbreviation Just eventually grew into Justice and finally Judge. He qualified as a solicitor around the time I got engaged. But with Josh it was different. Consistent only in his inconsistencies, utterly predictable in his erraticism, Josh had always been plain old Josh — no more, no less. His name, like his demeanor, never changed.

Guess I was wrong about that.

Professor J. Mitchell Rideout. I caressed the book, turned it over in hands that trembled only slightly. The formula was populist and wildly successful. Soundbyte science for the masses. The poor man's Stephen Jay Gould, was how one uncharitable reviewer had described its author. That made sense. Josh's problems had never been intellectual in nature. He simply lacked the temperament to restrict himself to one particular field of interest. He was a speed-grazer, a pioneer, a rampant polymath with opinions on everything. So, what did he do? An essay here, an article there, the odd lecture when it suited him.

With shrewd editing and strong narrative tone, that stuff added up to bestselling non-fiction the way pennies add up to pounds. And despite a wealth of opportunities, I had failed to make the connection. Or refused to see one in the face of overwhelming evidence.

But wasn't something terribly wrong here? Although recent, the author photograph on the back cover bore only a passing resemblance to the pallid wretch now hunched over a grubby brandy snifter in the corner of some rundown South London pub. What could possibly have happened to reduce such a brilliant man from that to this? With an inexorable sinking feeling, I returned to the booth, seated myself without another word. The tale of woe that poured out of Josh the moment our eyes met was packed with caveats and contradictions. For every professional success, personal disaster; for every public victory, domestic failure. Academically, Josh had achieved more than I would have dreamed possible, and with such verve and aplomb that the need for compromise barely surfaced. Privately, however, he was constantly at war with himself. Lost loves, squandered opportunities, the tragic death of a fiancé. No wonder he'd thrown himself into his work.

"Despite a loyal fanbase and a staggering amount of money in the bank," he admitted, "I still considered myself a failure. I had achieved household-name status but wasn't improving lives. I was meeting deadlines but had forsaken my ideals. Until, that is, I bumped into a synthetic chemist by the name of Bob Clementine at a seminar in Massachusetts. That one encounter changed my life forever."

I gleaned from the remainder of Josh's narrative that the aforementioned Clementine was the former deputy director of a major university laboratory in Boston — a man who'd earned a reputation as a maverick for steadfastly refusing to accept the limitations of his chosen field. After a particularly fractious ethics debate that saw him publicly ridicule a number of his colleagues, he resigned his post to pursue his research independently. That's where the trouble started.

In the six years prior to recruiting Josh, Clementine had fought a war of attrition against everybody from the Food & Drug Administration to the Surgeon General, yet not a single federal institution would acknowledge the stunning results he'd achieved in combating the effects of induced drug addiction in mice and rats. That's probably because his success relied heavily upon the emerging — and largely unpredictable — field of nanotechnology.

It was at this point that Josh's account descended into mumbling incoherence. There were numerous slurred references to mechanosynthesis, molecular assemblers and colloidal quantum dots — most of which meant nothing to me. As afternoon turned to evening and I weaned him off the brandy and onto black coffee, the main thrust of the tale emerged. Simply put, Clementine had developed a range of nanobots capable of intercepting and flushing controlled substances from the bloodstream. By the end of the fifth trial, the bots had become so good at their job that a hit on a crack pipe elicited little more than a few seconds of mild euphoria on the part of the test subject — who at that stage was a specially bred macaque named Horace. The U.S. government then flatly rejected an application for human trials and the project stalled. With funds at a dangerously low ebb, Clementine began looking for someone to attract fresh investors. Josh more than fit the bill, and soon he joined the team full-time.

Despite its initial promise, the relationship proved a destructive one. Engulfed by an ambition far beyond their reach, the two men quickly rationalized their way into breaking the law. That happened when Clementine's father suffered a stroke a week before entering hospital for a triple bypass operation — a condition that rendered him virtually inoperable. The stroke itself, the result of clinical obesity, provided the duo with fresh impetus.

"Almost right away we realized that the bots could be reprogrammed to perform essentially the same function on a different substance," Josh enthused, "with saturated fats taking the place of crack cocaine. Within weeks we had created a new generation of molecular machines capable of flushing all harmful cholesterol from the digestive tract. We weren't nearly quick enough to save Bob's father, but by the anniversary of his death the cure for heart disease, obesity, and weight-related diabetes was not only conceivable but well within reach."

"Josh, that's marvelous," I whispered, "my God, think of the lives saved."

But my former boyfriend was already shaking his head. "If only it were that simple," he muttered, and fumbled another Lucky from the pack. He leaned forward and snapped his lighter to the cigarette without taking his eyes off mine. When he spoke again, his delivery was slow and chillingly deliberate. "Imagine this," he said, exhaling a thin plume of smoke from the corner of his mouth. "Eating as much as you want, whenever you want, with no regard for the consequences. That's what we were offering society. A free hit. A license to gorge. In effect, we'd be giving couch potatoes the world over the excuse they'd been waiting for all those years. Within a generation, the whole concept of personal responsibility would be replaced by some boffin in a lab coat telling you he could make it all better again. I tried to warn him."

Sadly, Josh explained, Bob Clementine refused to listen. The loss of his father, which at first stung him into action, soon drove him to frightening levels of militancy. He became so enraged at the governments of the west for standing by and watching large chunks of their respective populations literally eat themselves to death that he swore the worst kind of revenge. Cut to the chase, he decided to trade science for terrorism.

Josh ran his hands through his crow's-nest shock of hair. "I'll tell you now, Sam, Bob's manifesto couldn't have been simpler," he confided, "or more radical. Develop the most potent bot cultures possible, insert them into the food chain at the earliest viable opportunity, and let them pick the human body clean of fat like ... well, like vultures picking a corpse clean of flesh. And I'm not just talking about reaming out diseased arteries, either. Bob wanted it all. Adipose tissue, cholesterol, triglyceride levels, the lot. He even dreamt of destroying appetite through artificial manipulation of the hypothalamus."

"That's crazy talk," I scoffed. Yet somehow, I believed every word of it.

Josh certainly did. "All you'd need are a few drops of a self-replicating culture released into the water supply of any major city and the damage is done," he insisted. "Not that Bob was ever going to be satisfied with half measures. He kept raising the bar, kept revising his estimate of what the human body could tolerate in terms of a minimum fat percentage. Four percent for men, he reckoned. Then he said three was probably a better bet."

"But that's nowhere near enough," I protested, and felt the baby kick inside of me. "Even the fittest athletes struggle to maintain that kind of low for any length of time."

Josh swallowed, and gave me a look of undisguised misery. "For women it was ten."

"Ten," I repeated, "ten percent? But women cease ovulating at ten, Josh. Ten percent body fat means the end of the human race."

"I know," he groaned, "I know. It gets worse. Within weeks of conceiving the initial plan, Bob settled on a final figure of one percent for men and eight for women. One percent body fat, Sam. That's when I started getting really scared. Bob vowed he was going to teach the world a lesson it wouldn't forget. He wanted people to look in the mirror each morning and know the face of famine. To see the skull beneath the skin, was how he put it. He wouldn't listen. I tried to reason with the man, tried to make him see sense." Josh's bottom lip trembled at the memory. He wasn't in tears — not yet, anyway — but his eyes shimmered with the kind of pent-up emotion that would express itself sooner rather than later. "Bob was just too far gone by that time. He taught the bots to breed at an astonishing rate, increased their obsolescence quotient way beyond our initial agreement ..."

He must have caught the skeptical look on my face because he waved a hand and backtracked a bit. "Even with its inbuilt reproductive capabilities, each culture was designed to self-destruct within weeks of conception. As a safety precaution, you understand. Bob recalibrated the biological timer."

I could barely bring myself to ask the question. "By how much?"

The great professor reached for his drink with fingers that shook like petals in a stiff breeze. He drained the last of the brandy in a single noisy gulp, and grimaced. "A thousand years," he winced. "But a thousand years means no more us, Sam. Babies need fat to grow and develop, we need it to store energy, as protection against the cold—"

"I know what fat does, Josh," I snapped, "I have a medical background too, remember?" Right about then, though, I had never felt less like a pharmacologist and more like a helpless mother-to-be. "If this is a joke, please stop now. It isn't funny anymore. It never was."

But the man who'd once shared my bed glanced at me in a way that suggested it was the story that mattered, not the listener. And the story needed telling. I didn't quite understand just how strong that urge was until Josh made his next confession.

"I had to kill him," he said. The admission arrived quite matter-of-factly, as if he were stating a fondness for duck à l'orange or daytime TV. "When I realized Bob was planning to dump the latest bot culture into the New York sewer system, I poisoned his lunchtime soda and got out of the country as quickly as I could. It goes without saying that I took this lot with me. For safekeeping."

Josh indicated a frayed leather satchel stuffed with documents, folders, and neatly-labeled thumb drives. It sat beside him in the upholstered booth, an innocuous brown pouch more dangerous than any dirty bomb. I knew there'd be people willing to pay millions, if not billions, for the secrets it contained.

"What are you going to do with it?" I asked, scarcely able to comprehend the enormity of it all.

"Do?" Josh leaned back and closed his eyes. "Joseph, Mary, and all the saints, Samantha," he muttered, "what am I going to do? I can't just throw it away, can I? But if I pass this little bag of tricks to the authorities, I'll be implicating myself in a high-profile murder case. What kind of a choice is that?"

I held my opinions in check. I know a rhetorical question when I hear one. Besides, if there was anything left of the man I once knew, he'd do the right thing in the end. When his posture sagged and his breathing became deeper and more regular, however, it occurred to me that he might be engaged in something a mite less strenuous than reflection. The light snoring that ensued only confirmed my belief. I can't say I was surprised. Joshua Rideout was a fugitive — a drunken, exhausted, international fugitive — and the confession had lifted a terrible weight from his shoulders.

Oh, well. Just because Josh was plagued by his conscience didn't mean I had to be plagued by mine. On the contrary. With a baby on the way and Darren's health showing no sign of improvement, one man's misfortune was starting to look like this woman's salvation. The knowledge evoked a number of intriguing scenarios. Having done my post-graduate research at a large biotech company, I was familiar with the workings of the medical establishment. Who owned what, who answered to whom ... and more importantly, where the money went. Particularly that last point.

Over the course of his unburdening, Josh had glanced repeatedly at the cluttered little table that stood between us as if he were afraid it might vanish in a puff of smoke. The surface was littered with all manner of pub detritus. Empty cigarette packets, overflowing ashtrays, used glasses — even an uneaten packet of dry roasted peanuts. But right in the middle of it all, partially covered by the encroaching debris, lay a silver hip flask engraved with the initials BC.

I shook it free of the assorted clutter and hefted it in my hand. Not entirely empty, by the feel of it. I unscrewed the lid. No alcohol fumes invaded my nostrils. I gave it the gentlest of shakes. Maybe an inch or two of colorless liquid sloshed around at the bottom.

What had Josh said to me? All you'd need are a few drops released into the water supply of any major city. I quickly screwed the lid back on and tried to order my thoughts. If adjustments could be made to the culture's operating parameters — eight percent body fat for men, say, and twice that for women, the dose to last for one year instead of a thousand, bots trained merely to trim cellulite instead of eradicating it — why, potentially you'd have the most lucrative slimming aid in all of human history. The beauty of it was, you'd only need to show the multi-nationals a fraction of your research to prove its authenticity. And if that didn't work, how about a live demo involving a nice plump rat and a drop of joy from the magic flask?

I checked Josh's breathing one last time. Out for the count. Without making a fuss, I crammed the flask into the frayed leather satchel, and wedged the hefty bundle under my arm. Slipping out of the pub moments later, I drew not so much as a second glance. And the best thing about it? Poor old Josh could never report me to the police. The prime suspect in a homicide is hardly a credible witness — and that goes double when he no longer possesses the evidence to support his outrageous claims.

Cheerfully oblivious to the aches and pains of pregnancy, I strolled through a city brimming with good fortune and April sunshine. I treated myself to a chocolate muffin at a faux Victorian tea shop and sang along to the radio during the drive home. Then I chose a comfortable armchair by the window and planned a few calls. My lethargic, overweight husband and equally delightful step-son were busy playing the PlayStation in the next room, and their excited whoops and hollers soon grated on my nerves.

"Turn that bleedin' racket down!" I yelled through the wall, and dialed the first number on my list.

They ignored me, of course. They always did. But they won't for much longer. Nearly ten years of research and development have passed since that day. Our 63rd and final round of mammalian testing is about to conclude. I have become a millionaire many times over in the interim, but the only other person in the family who knows the full extent of my wealth is our nine-year-old daughter, Jade. A lovely little wisp of a thing, she is.

Funny, but she doesn't take after her daddy one bit. Not that I'm complaining. Darren is going on a crash diet soon — I saved some of the original culture — and that surly teenage brat of his will be joining him. After all, I've always looked good in black. And I'm sure Josh would understand ... wherever he is.

Davin Ireland returned to the south of England in late 2021 after three decades in the Dutch city of Utrecht. His fiction credits include stories published in over ninety print magazines, webzines and anthologies worldwide, including Aeon, Pseudopod, and Storyteller Magazine. You can visit his site at davinireland.com.

The Mascareri

By Izzy Varju

"Do you have any masks for someone so old as me?" asked the man standing in the doorway to the shop, eyeing the different forms and faces staring back at him from the walls. It was an unnecessary question—her masks were far older than he—but she'd found every customer had to ask something of the kind before they entered.

"Maybe one or two, for a customer such as you," the mascareri replied with her customary refrain, putting aside the one she'd been finishing up. Its hollow eyes stared upwards, the extra sockets on the cheeks and forehead as empty as the rest. It was a special order, one that promised its wearer secrets—and to let her finally be able to lie.

Tapping his umbrella against the threshold, the man left it dripping by the door and stepped inside. His face was thin with wind-weathered wrinkles and a birthmark like a wine-stain across his cheek. The mascareri wondered if he'd come to ask for a mask because of it, for it drew her gaze as her bone needle drew its thread.

"What are you looking for?" she asked, watching his step and the bob of his head as he looked around at her wares. They sat in stacks, lay in piles and generally hung about her shop like too many children that she hadn't managed to get rid of yet. There were those that were no thicker than the paint on their leather, lounging in bright colors and spreading their ribbons for anyone to pick them up. With so many distractions, it was easy to hide what she wanted where most would look but never see.

The man turned to her finally, after minutes of silent searching.

"Something to change people's minds. Not too overbearing, just forceful enough to make them think again, think something different. Do you have anything like that?" She could've told him before that idle browsing didn't produce results for his type of query, but she let the customers do what they liked until they realized what they wanted. They were more agreeable that way.

The mascareri set down her awl and went to the front of the shop, where the window display stood so full that she couldn't see the canal whispering past outside even on the brightest of days. She unpinned one from the bottom of the board, old and yet distinguished with its raised curling red designs that stretched up in mesmerizing swirls, moving in the light.

"This is what you want," she said, holding it out to the man to take. "It will do exactly what you ask for."

"I'll take it. How much?"

"Nothing."

"I can't accept this without paying," the man insisted, gesturing to the rest of the shop. "They say this is the last true mask shop in Venice, how are you going to stay open if I don't pay?"

"That is my concern, not yours. Do you wish to have it or not?" The mascareri sat on her stool and watched the man frown, patiently waiting for his answer.

The man turned the mask over in his hands, running a finger along the worn inside with a pensive set to his jaw. He's hesitating, the mascareri noted in surprise. But then, she didn't want what he had to offer if he didn't first wrestle with what was inside him first, and come close to losing. It had to be strong, after all, for it to be worth her while.

"My conscience would never leave me alone if I left without giving you something," the man finally said, after long minutes of silence.

"Then leave your conscience with me," the mascareri said with a smile, holding out her hand. "I will have nothing else."

The man let out a rueful laugh and gave in, taking her hand and bowing low. "You've made me a very happy man today. I will wear it well."

The mascareri kept her smile and did not shake her head at his promise; she could only offer the ugly truth and that was not what a customer deserved when they said such things in good faith. But as he left the shop, umbrella blooming above him outside the door and mask tight in his grasp, she gathered up what he'd left behind and held it close. It was strong, tough after a life-time of morality and she was thankful to have one in her possession at last. But as it warmed to her and she accepted it, she thought again of the deal, and felt a new unpleasant weight settle inside her.

Izzy Varju is a neuroscientist by training who writes queer novels and short stories. Their work has been shortlisted for the Ruritania Prize and appeared in Luna Station Quarterly, From the Farther Trees, and Havok. When not contemplating the mysterious life of the giant squid they serve as an editor for a literary quarterly and has done panels on queer representation and editing at writing conventions. Their work can be found at IzzyVarju.wordpress.com, and on Amazon.

Heaven-Sent

By Nicole Walsh

Boss flowed into the office. Shadows roiled in his wake. He loomed over banks of low screens, desks and cowering office workers.

"Martis!" he roared.

Allie winced, lifting a sickly hand: "Here."

Boss changed trajectory, pulling up short when he spotted her. "You're not Martis."

"You fired Martis last week." Allie spun her chair, folding her long legs, flashing him a dazzling smile. "I'm in charge now."

The demon looked her over skeptically. He was seven feet of huge, dark, mostly unclad muscle. Bat-like wings shed sparks of agitation. He displayed sheets of papers in a clawed, blood-stained hand.

"You seen this?"

"Yes," Allie lied.

"This your doing?"

"Maybe."

"Maybe?" the demon growled.

"Definitely," Winston snarked, from the desk opposite. "You're in charge, Allie."

Allie gave her 2IC a filthy look. Winston had gone for the same job but had muffed the interview. Necromancers lacked the people skills to excel in an office environment. They were all brooding and hexes. Allie was very good at interviews.

She flashed a second bright, sunny smile. "I'll fix it, Boss."

Boss checked the office. Everyone cringed into their work, studying screens and keyboards intently. The demon's handsome face was crumpled with worry.

"We're not ready for this. Hell-lords are on holidays. The rift-mages are on strike. The fallen angels are mid-election..."

Allie lifted a comforting hand: "I know, Boss. I'll sort it out."

"By lunchtime?" A plaintive whine crept into his voice.

"Before lunch time," Allie soothed.

Boss stalked off. The papers in his hand exploded into flames and ashes.

Winston narrowed his eyes at Allie. "How, exactly, are you going to fix this?"

"Watch and learn," Allie suggested. The first step would be figuring out what the Hell had happened.

She clicked her screen on, then blinked in surprise. "3000 emails?"

Winston smirked. Allie skimmed the chain, frown deepening as she read the subject lines. She scrolled to the bottom and gaped, re-reading an email in disbelief.

"Cinders!" she shouted, shoving her chair back violently.

Allie stormed across the office. A thorny, ugly-as-sin demon blinked up at her in confusion, lifting an ear-bud out of her ear. "Cinders' hot-desking."

"Since when?"

"Said... you said...?"

Allie ground her teeth and stalked through the office, scanning faces. Cinders was at the far end, out of Allie's line of sight. The Hell-Witch lazed in her chair, playing with her phone, swiping left methodically. She jolted upright when she spotted Allie.

"Cinders, what did you do?"

"Me?"

"You declared war on Heaven."

"What? When? No."

Allie pointed at Cinder's screen. "4:53 yesterday afternoon."

"I... No."

"Check," Allie suggested, grinding her teeth.

Cinders clanked forward in her chair with a long-suffering sigh, setting her phone face-down to hide her Burn matches. She squinted at her screen, clicking with deliberate slowness, face furrowed and baffled.

"Whoa, that's a lot of..."

"Yes. Check your sent box."

Cinders' black-nailed finger clicked. Shock blanketed her face. "Oh."

"Oh?"

"I thought it was a party invitation."

"With angels!?" Allie growled.

Cinders gave her a sullen look. "What I do in my own time..."

"Torture, blood-feuds and enslavement?"

Cinders lifted her shoulders helplessly: "Party?"

"Cinders! You hit reply all!"

"Did I? Oh, wow. I did."

"You said 'we're in. Bring it on'."

"I meant me and Sammy."

"Well, you just sparked Armageddon. Again. What part of 'on notice' don't you get?"

Cinder's eyes, ringed with kohl, narrowed. "People make mistakes, Allie."

Allie leaned over the desk, glaring so close she could see the souls writhing in the Hell-witch's yellow eyes.

"Not as many as you do, Cinders. Focus on what you're doing. Consider this your final warning."

"Or what?"

"Or I fire your ass," Allie growled. "Right here. In this chair. Just like Wally last week. Do you remember Wally?"

Cinders shrank back. Allie pointed at the drawer. Cinders hesitated, then slid her phone off the desk, face down, into the drawer.

"Touch that phone before lunch-time, Cinders, and I'll break your hand."

Allie pushed off the desk. She stalked past the rest of the office. They were watching her curiously.

"You're gonna fix this, right?" A sludge-demon burbled. "'Cause I have tickets for Limbo this weekend. Cruise on the Styx? Should I... cancel?"

"No," Allie growled.

A skeleton warrior popped to his feet, waving his hand about: "Um, um, Allie, I was finishing early today because of..."

Allie raised her hand to block his story. "Stop. Everyone, stop. Back to work. I will fix this."

"How?" Winston smirked.

Allie dropped into her seat, giving the necromancer a sunny smile. She picked up the phone.

"It's why I earn the big bucks, Winston."

She tapped keys confidently. Allie knew her old team-leader's number by heart. Time for some sweet-talking. Luckily, angels— even fallen ones—were very good at that.

Nicole Walsh is a cat enthusiast from the east coast of Australia who loves fern gardens and long dresses. She writes short stories and novel-length speculative fiction and urban fantasy that spans from a little bit dark, a little bit amusing through to a little bit steamy. Visit Nicole at NicoleWalshAuthor.com and on Facebook at @nicolewalshauthor.

The Box

By William Powell

I found it in the usual place, where I always find them. Under the rock.

"Hello," I said. "What's your name, little feller?"

No answer. But I expected that. It takes some coaxing with these things. You have to get down to their level, win trust. Names come later.

So I left it a saucer of water and a little bit of bread, and replaced the rock.

I really didn't think about it much for the rest of the day. Just before I went to bed I had a fleeting I-wonder thought. Suppose I creep down, see how it's getting on. Maybe the water wasn't enough. Maybe the bread might have been a little stale, a bit too dry.

I'd had some bad experiences, too, with giving too much. The things get greedy, or lazy. And I see them grow, and I think "this is going to end badly," and it does. But even if I could, I don't have the heart to kill them. I just put them in a box, leave them be. I don't know what I'll do with them.

Next morning, when I awoke, my mind did turn to the rock, and what might be under it. Patience, though, I told myself. They don't like bright light. They don't like to be examined.

But I yielded, as I knew I would. It took my eyes a little while to get used to the poor light, but there it was. A little larger, for sure. The water was gone, and so were the crumbs, but in their place was a small loaf of bread.

"Hey, little feller," I said, softly as I could. "You did well."

And I took the loaf out, tasted it. It was good. Really good.

"I guess you're learning what you can do, just fine," I told it. And I tried to put all the pride and enthusiasm that I could into my words. But it was so small, still. I'd never seen one so tiny.

So I gave it some more water, but not quite as much as before. I also tore off a corner of the loaf, and left it next to the water.

"See you tomorrow, little feller," I said. "Same time."

Next morning I was pretty excited, I have to say. But I've been disappointed before, and bit back on my feelings.

But there it was, and it had grown. There was no mistaking it. The water was gone, and the little corner of yesterday's bread, too. But the loaf that rested in its place was warm and soft and sweet as I bit into it.

"You're a keeper, little feller," I said, and I meant it. But all the same, it was time to put it with all the others.

"I got to," I explained. "If it were just me, I'd keep you forever, teeny as you are. But your place is with the others. And it's going to be rough. They ain't goin' to treat you well. They're going to steal all the water, and they ain't goin' to give you no bread. But you are who you are, and you'll get by."

I didn't say anything after that, 'cause I was a bit choked up.

But I picked it up, and I took it over to where the others were.

I got my voice back, and just before I popped it in, I asked "What's your name, little feller?"

They don't always answer. But this one did, in the tiniest of voices.

"Hope," it said. "What's yours?"

"Pandora," I answered, as I closed the lid.

✳✳✳

Next morning, I lift up the rock, and there you are.

"Hey, little feller," I say to you. "What's your name?"

William Campbell Powell lives in a small Buckinghamshire village in England. By day, he works in software development. By night, he writes YA, Speculative and Historical Fiction. His debut novel, Expiration Day, was published by Tor Teen in 2014 and won the 2015 Hal Clement Award for Excellence in Children's Science Fiction Literature — and Gabrielle de Cuir's narration of the audiobook won a 2016 AudioFile Magazine Earphones award.

Nothing in the Dark

By C. M. Fields

The Andes stretched from horizon to horizon and from sea to sky, rocky slopes pristine, skyline unbroken but for a tall silver dome perched atop the tallest peak. Just adjacent, the rising red sun spilled down into the foothills, lending a nascent glow to the slender road which snaked up to meet it.

Dust clung to Dr. Kiera Morrison's sneakers as she trudged up the pavement, stopping every so often to set down her bags and rest. *Lanzadera no va,* Roberto had told her at the observatory office at the base of the mountain. Observing over Christmas meant bare-bones staff, and that meant no shuttle driver. But it was free telescope time, she mumbled to herself as she dabbed at her forehead with her shirt tail once more. An opportunity an ambitious, nearly-tenured young professor couldn't afford to waste.

The sun was high overhead by the time she arrived at the wind-whipped sign that announced Observatorio Las Escaleras. The facility itself was a relic of the 1930's and its concrete bulk and curving balconies jarred against the brush and boulders. Stale, warm air smelling of old wood and dusty books greeted her as she pushed open the glass-paned door.

Crossing the floor mosaiced in the twelve icons of the zodiac, she scribbled her name in a guestbook as old as the building and located a key with 1A etched into dull brass. Then she heaved her luggage up the sweeping, wrought-iron stairs, found her room, and promptly fell asleep.

✳ ✳ ✳

Kiera woke in absolute darkness. Her heart started to race until she remembered—she was on an observing run, staying in an astronomer's lodge. There would be blackout curtains, of course. She rubbed her eyes and groped for the light switch. Where was it? The bed must be bigger than she thought. She turned on her phone, stumbled out of bed, and drew the curtains, letting the searing light of the desert wash over the faded blue-greens of the room.

16:23, shit. Later than she wanted to be calibrating a telescope she'd never used before.

The telescope seemed not to rise from the ground but to stretch down out of the brilliant blue sky as she jogged up the steep stone path. Several stories overhead, the catwalk encircling the white dome rattled in the wind. Inside, the decor was much the same as the lodge: soft aquamarines paired with light woods; snappy, parallel curves meeting straight lines; a svelte radio cabinet set against the far wall. She trailed her fingers along a long, squat bookcase as she walked through the lobby and found them satisfactorily free of dust. Black placards indicated the way to the kitchen, library, and restroom. But she had no time to explore.

A narrow spiral staircase twisted into darkness below and above. The muted sunlight of the lobby faded into red and shadow as she climbed. What was she going to find in the control room? She hoped for a comfortable space filled with servers and monitors, and a friendly operator. A fast internet connection. Maybe even a good espresso machine.

A single, fat computer monitor sat on a dilapidated wooden desk cluttered with books and star charts. There was no operator in sight, hardly even room for another person. She shook her head and clucked at the mess. There had better be a damned good instruction manual, she thought, if they let astronomers handle this thing untrained. Now, into the dome to check on the telescope.

Kiera yelped as she nearly collided with a rim of dark metal that stared like the eye of some great, dead beast. The telescope was a long, open cylinder of wrought steel, its far end containing the primary mirror in which she could see herself dimly reflected, its near end pressing heavily into the linoleum floor. It seemed terribly contorted—weren't telescopes usually left upright? It looked as if someone was trying to observe an object that had drifted below the horizon. More likely, the operator had been fixing some component and simply forgot to right it. She located the interior control pad, hit the "dock" button, and watched massive, fine-toothed gears hum into motion as the telescope transformed into an imposing steel tower, eye to the sky once more.

Stomach growling, Keira stepped carefully down the stone path and tried to shake off the uneasy feeling the downed telescope had left. A chinchilla darted across the path, and a small flock of llamas grazed on a nearby slope. She focused on them while she collected her thoughts. The instructions, hand-lettered on yellowing paper, had been easy enough to follow—all telescopes were essentially the same, after all. Actually observing would be another task. Would the ancient telescope point? Would it track? Her target, a particularly bright quasar in the Triangulum constellation, required constant exposure with no interference from nearby stars. Poor tracking would waste the entire five-night run, and then what would she have to show for a Christmas spent on a remote mountain in Chile?

The smell of empanadas lured her to the cafeteria where a steaming pile of them lay on a counter. She felt herself relax at the sound of bits of Spanish filtering from the kitchen. Finally, other people. Even out of sight, the voices comforted her as she took a seat alone by the window. The light of the waning sun warmed and brightened the room into a cheerful atmosphere, and suddenly her fears were assuaged. There were bound to be issues with the telescope, but she could fix them. She had a PhD and a decade of experience. She was about to be tenured, damn it. Whatever this clanking old apparatus could come up with, she could handle.

DECEMBER 21

Kiera cracked her knuckles before she sat down at the old console. From the catwalk, she had watched the sun set magnificently over the Pacific Ocean, watched the horizon's glow fade from gold to crimson to blue and finally to the indigo that marked the giving over of day to night. The dome was open to the sky and the first stars were appearing in the sky in the bold, unfamiliar constellations of the southern hemisphere. High above, the Milky Way and the twin Magellanic Clouds brightened into view.

Inside, she opened the archaic software and entered the coordinates. The old dome shuddered and groaned as 200 tons of concrete rotated to accommodate.

Sure enough, the pinprick of light—her pinprick—appeared on the screen. It sat neatly framed by three local stars Kiera had taken to calling Alpha, Beta, and Gamma, and the autoguider had centered it perfectly. She breathed a sigh of relief. If all went well, she could just set the instrument to run all night while she wrote her next paper and answered a daunting backlog of emails.

The "instrument", the instructions had warned, was a spectrograph—but not the compact variety that simply attached to the back of the telescope behind the primary. Instead, the light of the stars followed a complex, mirrored path down into the guts of the building. Somewhere below her feet lay a dark labyrinth of collimators and diffractors that stretched a trickle of white light into a rainbow of data.

Down the spiral staircase and through a maze of dim hallways, she found a door labeled Coudé Spectrograph. Inside, a slice of red light fell upon a cluster of metal tubes and glittering lenses. Everything else was pitch black, an unnatural darkness that seemed to gnaw at the intruding light. Kiera paused. She wasn't afraid of the dark. Nevertheless...

She fumbled for a light switch and was dismayed to find the wall flat and smooth. Maybe it was on the other side of the door? She heaved it open such that a big rectangle of red now fell on the draconian machinery. Ah, there it was—on the far side of the room. She cursed under her breath for not bringing the heavy steel flashlight that sat next to the desktop. But the part was free of obstacles, she should be able to just walk straight across and turn it on. Feeling a little foolish, she toed off a shoe and propped it in the doorway before stepping inside and letting the door fall shut.

It was quiet down here, she noticed, silent, without the buzz of the servers or the grind of the dome. Her socked foot immediately told her that the floor wasn't all there—her stomach dropped as she realized it was merely a metal grate suspended over—what? Storage? Empty space? How far was the drop, and what lay below?

Just keep going straight. Seven steps. Eight. Nine—and she felt the wall. She forced her fingers to search the surface slowly. She wasn't scared. She was an astronomer, for God's sake.

Click.

The yellow-white glow of a single incandescent bulb filled her with relief. She was in a low-ceilinged space with two massive concrete columns at each end. Every surface was black except for the metal and glass components of the optical path. Below her, the emptiness under the grate stretched far into incalculable darkness. An astronomer shouldn't be afraid of the dark, she thought, but no one said anything about heights. She focused on the optics and tried not to look down.

Lens caps had to be removed, diffraction gratings uncovered, and mirrors opened; the camera unit had to be turned on, and its nitrogen cooling system had to be filled. She set herself about these tasks, letting the work absorb her and finding herself enjoying it. Few telescopes in this age allowed astronomers to handle equipment directly, and even fewer used archaic spectrographs like this one. She finished up, turned off the light, and returned to the control room.

The guider was on target. The night was young. Kiera typed in the command to acquire data, hit the enter key with a satisfying click, and opened her laptop.

DECEMBER 22

Kiera woke up at 3 PM, exhausted. She was too old to be doing this anymore, to be flipping her sleep schedule to the night shift. Observing was a young woman's game.

Her second set of calibrations found the scope nose-down on the floor once more. How curious, she thought as she peered down the tube. There was no trace of mechanical work being done, no tools or dust cloths or bottles of cleaning solution. Still, it meant that someone was looking after the old telescope, making sure it was in working order each night.

A brass handle in the center of the tube caught her attention. It should lead to the secondary mirror—but why did the secondary mirror need so much space? The smaller cylinder, the pupil of the eye which had frightened her yesterday, extended some six feet into the main cylinder. She frowned and gave the handle a twist.

It opened with a metallic shriek, revealing a small, person-sized compartment, complete with a cushioned seat and a space like a small desk. In the center was a pinhole to the primary mirror. A prime focus capsule! Kiera had never seen one in person, only in old photographs in textbooks. Before the invention of modern digital cameras, the astronomer could watch, and sketch, the object they were observing directly from the primary mirror, losing no photons in the glass plate exposure process of the old days.

She resisted the urge to climb in and have a closer look, noting the abundance of dusty spiderwebs stretching from side to side. Instead, she closed the hatch, then she walked back into the control room and set the telescope upright again.

Dinner was empanadas. Again? she thought. She piled a plate full and carried it up to the telescope with her for night lunch.

Once more she navigated the passageway to the spectrograph room—the dungeon, as she had taken to calling it, with its thick, low arches, horribly transparent floors, and morbid accouterments.

She had forgotten her flashlight. Oh well. What was it, eight, nine steps straight across to the light switch? She pushed the door open as far as it would go before hurrying across the room. Eight. Nine. Ten, eleven, twelve. Twelve?

Click.

The optics seemed to blink in the light. Hadn't she covered them last night? She searched her memory as she paced. The nitrogen dewar hissed in the background. Perhaps not. She had been pretty exhausted by the night's end. The first night was always the worst.

Click. Nine steps.

Kiera set the autoguider, cracked open an energy drink, and got to work.

At 00:30, she stood, stretched, and walked down the staircase to the restroom. The light at the end of the hall was burned out. Sure, the original red light bulbs were necessary back when astronomers walked in and out of the dome to work and couldn't lose their night vision, but couldn't they have updated them since then? She sighed and made a note to search the building for spare bulbs.

She opened the door and groped for the chain that controlled the light. Left. Right. Nothing. Up and down. Her hand only encountered empty space. Had the chain fallen down during the day? Frustrated, she pulled out her cell phone and let its flash illuminate the space. The chain hung, as it always had, right in front of her face. A chill passed through her as she pulled it. How could she have missed it like that?

Tired, she thought. I'm tired and I didn't feel it.

Back at the control panel, the view was beginning to drift as the telescope pulled toward Alpha, the top star in the triangle.

Aha. There it is. Telescopes never simply behaved. All of them had quirks, and this one was no different. Something wasn't balanced correctly, or the autoguider had failed for a moment, or perhaps she had made a typo in the coordinate entry. On the command line, she manually redefined the target and started a new exposure.

The rest of the night went smoothly. She finished her paper draft, answered some emails, and started on the curriculum for next semester's Electrodynamics class.

The sun rose, and she closed the dome, shuttered the optics, and went to bed.

DECEMBER 23

The telescope was down again, aggressively nosing into the floor like it could punch through. Kiera ran her fingers around its cold steel rim and shivered. She decided to make a note of it in the observing log. "Please leave telescope upright for afternoon calibrations." It's freaking me out.

In the cafeteria waited the same pile of empanadas. Well, not the exact same, right? After all, the kitchen staff was here, she could hear someone rummaging around the cabinets right now.

"Hello?" she called.

No voice replied.

"Hello?" Kiera knew bits and pieces of Spanish, but she was too embarrassed to try it out. They just have earbuds in, she thought to herself. They can't hear me.

She took a pair of noticeably cool empanadas off the pile for dinner, then wrapped another pair in foil for night lunch.

✳ ✳ ✳

The telescope was down again—but this time, the eternal eye wasn't pressed into the floor, it was parallel to it—and its stare pierced her chest like cold iron.

Ok, she thought. It's a software problem. That's all it is.

She shut the door and walked back to the control room. The sun was setting, and she checked her inbox while the sky turned. An email from Marcia, the head of her tenure committee.

Is this your full publication record? she asked. Looks a little thin. Recommend waiting until regular cycle.

Kiera's cheeks burned.

No, she typed back. Have some new data coming in.

Sure, she was two years early to be applying for tenure. But she deserved it. No one worked harder. No one organized more. No one had a better teaching record. Now all she needed was a fat CV and she'd be the youngest professor in the history of the university. She craved it. And after that? Well, she'd find some new record to break.

But for now, she was stuck on a mountain in the desert over Christmas.

She cracked the door to the catwalk. All clear, she admired. Not a cloud on the horizon.

She slewed the telescope to her quasar and—wait. The image was blurry. Kiera groaned. Something must have jiggled the optics, and now she was going to have to spend precious observing time figuring out what it was. Shouldn't there be a technician for this? she thought, annoyed. I could easily break something.

She grabbed the heavy steel flashlight and thumped down the stairs. At the door to the dungeon, she stopped. It was either nine steps or twelve to the light switch. She shouldn't have been bothered by it, but she was. "It's within an order of magnitude!" her colleagues would have joked. But Kiera wasn't just an astronomer. She was a spectroscopist. She was precise, damn it. She shoved the flashlight into her cargo shorts pocket and opened the door.

She let it fall closed behind her and set her heels against it.

One. Two. Three. Four. Five. Six. Seven. Eight. Nine. She stretched out her arm to empty air. So she had counted badly the first time! She kept going.

Ten. Eleven. Twelve.

Thirteen. Fourteen. Fifteen.

What the hell? Did she get turned around? No, she had set out straight and she was still walking straight.

Sixteen. Seventeen. Eighteen.

Eighteen?? This is crazy. She started walking again, faster this time. The optics dungeon was longer than it was wide, but surely, shouldn't she have reached a wall by now? Any wall? Even run into some equipment?

Common sense told her to turn the flashlight on. Stubbornness told her the wall was just ahead.

Twenty-six steps.

Of course! she thought. There must be a second door besides the light switch, and someone has left it open and I've walked right through it.

She turned around, halfway relieved.

I'm not afraid of the dark.

Twenty six steps back.

Twenty seven.

Twenty eight.

She broke out in a nervous sweat as she passed the old count. So I've miscounted again. Big steps, now.

The steps seemed to take her nowhere. Dread filled her chest like wet cement as panic set in.

Jogging. Jogging. Now she was running. Sprinting. Where was the door? Where was she?

The toe of her sneaker caught the metal grate and sent her hurtling to the floor. The flashlight clattered out of her pocket and she snatched it up with shaking hands and clicked it on.

Inches from her fingertips lay the wall, and three feet up, the light switch.

There was no second door.

Kiera flung herself across the room and slammed the door behind her. She scrambled through the halls and up the stairs and collapsed, trembling, into the desk chair as her brain tried to make rational sense of what had just happened. It couldn't.

The image was just going to have to stay blurry. No matter what, she wasn't going back in that room.

The drift returned. An hour later, after she had calmed down and made a weak cup of tea with some old teabags she'd found in the kitchen, the scope started to pull towards Alpha again. She sighed and typed in the command to drag it back.

But this time it didn't stay. Twenty minutes later, it was pulling again. And again, ten minutes later. And again and again. Hours passed as Kiera alternated focusing on her upcoming paper and paranoidly watching the screen for signs of change, jaw unwittingly clenched, back sore, eyes exhausted.

Finally, the night ended. The optics in the dungeon were just going to have to stay uncovered, good practice be damned. "Telescope drifting frequently," she wrote in the night report. "And please refill the nitrogen dewar?"

DECEMBER 24

Her dreams were full of impossible mirrors and behemoths moving silently in the dark. She woke up sweating. Had the air conditioning gone out overnight? The glow of her phone illuminated the space as she fumbled for the bedside lamp.

Dead.

The light was dead, the air conditioning was out, and in a moment, she discovered that the water was off, too.

No matter, she'd just put in a maintenance request and it'd be fixed by the time she was done calibrations. Or would it? Were the maintenance workers here?

She wasn't surprised to find the eye staring at her once more as she entered the dome. It was just a bug in the code. Probably the same one that was causing the tracking issues last night.

At the control panel, the nitrogen levels were full. She breathed a sigh of relief—at least someone was looking out for her, even if she hadn't met them yet. Maybe they had fixed the drift, too. Last night had been exhausting, and she hadn't slept well, either.

She took the calibration images without issue and headed down to the lodge for dinner.

It was definitely the same pile of empanadas. Flies buzzed around them, and at a distance she could see white spots of mold. I should file a complaint, she thought to herself. The kitchen was dark and silent, although light streamed in through the bay windows in the cafeteria. She tried the light switch. Dead, just like in her room.

Great. So the power goes out and everyone leaves.

No matter. There was plenty of dry cereal in the telescope's kitchen. She scoffed as she walked back up the hill. It was going to take a lot more than this for Dr. Kiera Morrison to quit on a run.

✳ ✳ ✳

You know what? Kiera thought to herself, face to face with the primary mirror once more. It's almost like it's trying to track something it can't see.

Like yesterday, the scope's lower edge was lifted off the floor and it was pointing straight at the horizon. But what was it? She walked out onto the catwalk. The sunset was stunning, as always, and the first stars were beginning to emerge from the veil of darkness. But what else was out there? She shook her head. The idea was ridiculous. At least its position meant that there was a generator around, something to keep it going while the power was out.

The control panel turned on too. So that was two things going right so far. She slewed to the quasar, feeling the familiar shake and rumble of the dome overhead as it rotated.

The image was blurrier than the day before, but she ignored it. She could live with blurry. She couldn't live with... whatever that was down in the optics room. Shuddering at the memory, she watched the little pinpoint for a few minutes. It seemed so bright and cheerful as it sat all alone in the sky, like a little Christmas bauble, removed by billions of light years from its stellar companions.

The closest I'll get to a Christmas tree, she thought glumly. In a few hours, it would be Christmas, and here she was, alone in the vast darkness of the Andes. Her friends and family would be celebrating, would be wondering where she was and why she had chosen an observing run over spending time with them. Ugh. One of the bad things about observing alone was the potential to be alone with one's own thoughts for long periods of time. She put on some loud Rachmaninov and headed down to the kitchen to make a cup of tea.

When she returned, the drift was back—and the crosshairs of the telescope were already halfway to Alpha. "What the—" she exclaimed aloud. This was far worse than yesterday. She flopped back down into the desk chair for a long night and opened her phone only to realize with a groan that the wifi was gone too. Not a problem, she thought grimly, and opened a Word document.

When the telescope had been stable for twenty minutes she decided she had earned a bathroom break. Preoccupied, she stepped into the restroom, clicked the light switch, and—

Dead.

The door slammed shut behind her. She reached for the handle and her hand passed through emptiness.

"No," she whispered in horror. "Oh no, no no no." She took a step backwards, then another. The bathroom was gone. Only darkness remained.

"No!"

She broke into a run, feet pounding tile, but the void was absolute. Was she going anywhere? Was she moving at lightspeed? She couldn't tell. Space ceased to hold meaning. And if space was lost to her, was time as well? Could she run forever without a second passing? The last time, she had pulled out a flashlight and the world had come back.

A flashlight! Kiera didn't have a flashlight, but she did have a phone. Still sprinting, she shoved her hand into her pocket and—

WHAM! She slammed bodily into the sink, the impact of her head on the mirror shattering it. Glass fell around her as she sunk to the ground in a gleeful daze—reality was back! She spit blood onto the black and white tiles. Had she loosened a tooth? She didn't care. There was the sink, and the toilet, and the door, and everything that belonged in a normal, real space. She crawled out the door and dragged herself onto the stairs, thankful beyond words for the control panel's faint glow that came from above.

It was the dark! The fucking dark, she thought to herself, gasping for breath, heart racing. What was this horrible place where reality failed with the light? I've got to get out of here.

But there was no getting out. The shuttle would pick her up on the morning of the 26th, otherwise it was a seven-hour trek down the mountain into town. She was trapped here, alone with the telescope and the evil dark.

And where the hell, she asked herself, was everyone else? Evidence suggested that other people were here, they had to be—someone was making food, someone was maintaining the telescope—yet she had never seen them. She shuddered and shoved the thought aside. Tomorrow, that was when she would deal with that. She would find someone and ask them what was going on. Not that she expected a satisfying answer.

Step by step, Kiera pulled herself back up to the control room, collecting bits and pieces of her constitution along the way. She sunk into her chair and curled into a ball, afraid to even close her eyes for fear of disappearing.

The telescope had drifted again. Her hands shook as she performed the correction.

The drifts became faster and worse and the night wore on. It was no longer a gentle pulling-away from the quasar so much as a sudden jerk followed by tangible, real-time motion. And now the cross-hairs were heading toward the space between the stars Alpha and Beta. What was going on? It didn't make sense. But then, maybe it wasn't a software issue. She grimaced as she realized what she had to do.

To take the flashlight? It would introduce extra, unwanted light into her observation, and if she wasn't careful, it could burn out the whole optical path. But it had to be done.

Cold steel in hand, and safe in a pool of dim, yellow light, she stepped into the dome and walked over to the massive gears which controlled the scope. Starlight shone in from above and she glimpsed the familiar band of the Milky Way overhead. It was comforting, somehow, to see it—the same sight shared by billions of people the world over.

As she approached, she noticed a strange, tinny sound, like the whine of a metal mosquito. It was coming from the gearshafts. They were struggling, their small, gleaming motors resisting some unseen force that pushed against the motion of the declination wheel. After minutes of the whining struggle, the wheel gave, and the gear slipped several teeth into shadow. Then the sound started up again.

So it was a hardware issue. To put it lightly, she thought. She wanted the telescope to point at her quasar and the telescope wanted to point somewhere else. Where else? She didn't want to know.

Back into the control room. She rubbed her eyes, flexed her fingers, and prepared to fight the telescope until dawn.

DECEMBER 25

Merry Christmas, Kiera thought as she woke up to afternoon sunlight streaming in through the cracked blackout curtains. The room was unbearably hot—the power must still be out, she decided. Her phone was at 41 percent battery, she noticed with a frown. She'd just have to use it sparingly and it should hold a charge until tomorrow morning.

She planned as she dressed and made her way to the telescope, avoiding the dome. She already knew what she'd find there. Number one. Take the flashlight everywhere. Number two. Find someone to talk to. Number Three: Get my data and get the hell out of here. Never come back.

She righted the scope and ran the calibrations. The nitrogen dewar had been filled once again, helpfully, saving her a trip to the accursed optics room.

Forty-five minutes later and it was time to confront the kitchen staff. Who were they? Why had they stopped making food, and if they weren't making food, why were they still here?

Kiera stepped into the cafeteria to the sight and smell of moldering, black empanadas. Through the door, voices chatted softly. She walked briskly over and pushed it open.

It was empty. The kitchen was empty, the lights were off, a layer of dust covered the counters. Silence fell heavily.

She slammed the door and backed away, ran out of the cafeteria and out into the open.

This is wrong, this is all wrong. She fought back tears. What is this hell place? What was going on? Why was all of this happening? She wanted to quit. She could just go back to her room right now, pack everything up, and hike down the mountain. If she started now, she could make it before—

No, she couldn't. With a pit growing in her stomach, she realized that she couldn't make it back into town until long after dark. She couldn't do it. She could get lost, and wander and never be found.

She was going to have to spend one more night on the mountain.

And while she was on the mountain, she might as well be taking data.

She gritted her teeth and strode once more up the stone path to the telescope.

Kiera slammed her fists on the desk and buried her head in her hands.

It was that goddamned drift again. Back and worse than ever, dragging the scope north every couple of seconds. What kind of a mechanical failure was even responsible for such a thing?

And where exactly was it going, anyways?

Kiera decided to find out.

The next time the cross-hairs slid up, she let them, and walked out into the dome to follow its path.

Her jaw fell slack at the sight. A telescope is not a thing which is built to move quickly—righting it every day had taken minutes for the ancient steel device to creak back into place. But now, it was moving faster than she'd ever seen one move, not so much slewing as swinging, like a great upside-down pendulum. In another moment it slowed and came to a halt.

Kiera finally understood—the telescope pressed to the floor each afternoon, higher each evening, drifting at night—it had been tracking. Tracking something across the sky, day and night.

Morbid curiosity burned inside her. What terrible, otherworldly object did the cursed telescope follow?

Where was it pointing now?

There was only one way to find out. Kiera felt herself drawn back to the control room. The computer would show her—from a safe distance.

But the screen was black, as if it had been shut off. She wiggled the mouse. Nothing. In fact, it was blacker than black, darker than dark, yawning, a void as empty as the space between the stars; dizzying, stretching, growing, falling,

Kiera snapped awake as her head began to drop. She clutched at the flashlight and spun away from the wretched darkness.

And there she sat, arms wrapped around her knees, fingers white-knuckled on the cold steel flashlight. For how long, she didn't know. But eventually, her breathing returned to normal and her thoughts slowed to a manageable pace.

She was tired. Tired, and scared, and growing more paranoid by the night. This experience would have stopped any other astronomer, she told herself. But not her. She wasn't going to quit no matter the circumstances. She had once spent eighty-four hours of time staring at clouds up at Kitt Peak, never sleeping, never obeying the forecast, only waiting for a break in the gray. And when a wildfire had broken out in Arizona, she had stayed then too, beyond the warning, beyond the creeping ring of flame, waiting, only waiting for the winds to change.

Whatever the hell was going on here, it wasn't going to stop her.

She wasn't afraid of the dark.

She was going to find out what the telescope was pointing at first hand. And then she was going to get back to her quasar if she had to steer the damn thing herself.

Flashlight in hand, she strode out into the dome. The telescope was still on its own mysterious target, and the dome obeyed. And winding upwards within like a mechanical serpent were the dome stairs.

Unused for decades, they groaned beneath her feet but did not give as she strode up them two by two. Ahead, the telescope's aperture beckoned and its primary capsule hatch gleamed bright in the starlight. If she just climbed over the railing and leaned out...

She shouldn't be doing this, she thought, even as she hefted a leg up over the wrought iron railing. The floor was thirty, forty feet below her with nothing to break a fall, and her hands sweat abominably. Nonetheless, she clamped onto the rail tightly as she swung her foot out over the void and caught the lip of the aperture. Then, she twisted open the hatch and flung herself inelegantly inside.

Kiera pointedly ignored the creeping whispers of old spiderwebs that brushed at her face and hair and instead focused on orienting herself inside the tiny compartment. Careful not to shine the flashlight down into the instruments, lest she fry the camera, she located the seat and the prime focus.

How long had it been since someone else sat in this seat watching some star or galaxy all the night?

How did this work, anyways? In front of her was a small hole. The focus, where the image of the star came together, must be just a few inches above...

Nothing. There was nothing there, no star, no galaxy, not a smudge of light at all. Kiera rubbed her eyes. Shit. Her eyes had adjusted to the flashlight. To see the object, she was going to have to close the hatch above her... and turn off the light.

Kiera realized with creeping horror that she was going to have to let the darkness have her once more.

Or, she thought, I could just climb out. Go back to the control room. Restart the computer.

But she couldn't. She had to know.

It'll be fine. I have the light. And furthermore, I can't go anywhere. She pressed her hands against the gritty steel walls.

She took a deep breath and swung closed the hatch overhead. Then she gripped the seat beneath her and clicked off the light.

Kiera counted the seconds as she waited for her eyes to adjust to the total darkness. The seat remained. She reached out for the walls. Still there.

58... 59... 60.

So she was being ridiculous. She had just had some kind of hallucination, some anxiety-induced waking nightmare.

The minutes ticked past. At fifteen, she resolved to take a look. No matter how faint it was, her eyes would see it. She grew curiouser as time passed. If I was a haunted telescope, she imagined, what would I want to look at? It eased her mind to think about. Probably one of the more interesting nebulae. The Ring, perhaps, or the Horsehead, or the Bridal Veil. Or maybe the Pleiades cluster.

At fifteen minutes, her heart rate had slowed and she eagerly peered into the focus.

Empty. Black. In fact, there wasn't a single pinpoint of light in the whole field.

Impossible, she thought, as her eyes strained to see even a single photon. Space was space. There simply weren't any empty parts. How could—

A scream tore through her throat as she realized she was falling. Her fingers scrabbled for a hold but met only empty space. And the walls—where were the walls? She flung her arms out in both directions to no avail.

Kiera continued to fall, faster and faster, through the void. No wind passed her, yet she was aware that she was falling at tremendous, terrible speeds though a space too vast to fathom. Was she still screaming? Did it matter?

The flashlight was gone.

Where am I? she thought, or perhaps said aloud. A chilling, invasive thought followed. Does "where" even mean anything? She shuddered as she fell.

Time passed. Eons, or maybe minutes, she couldn't tell. Once more, time had stopped, or looped, or maybe gotten tangled up like a cassette tape.

Her vision twinkled with stars. No—those were real stars. Those were real stars! It hit her in the gut like a sledgehammer. I'm outside? was all she could manage. The stars fell down around her in a silver rain, passing at incredible speeds. Were they all stars? No, she realized. Some of the lights passing her by were shapes—galaxies! Clouds and spirals snapped in and out of sight in a moment. As she stared around her, a horrible knowledge overcame her, seized her by the spine: that this place, this immensity, had no beginning and no end.

For a terrible instant, Kiera Morrison beheld infinity.

Then she slammed into the floor.

✱ ✱ ✱

The shock of the impact had knocked her out cold. But it wasn't long before the roots of fear curled around her mind and drove her to consciousness. Her whole body ached, her head most of all, but as she rolled over, nothing seemed broken—only badly bruised. Feet away, the flashlight lay shattered into pieces. She dragged herself out of the shadow of the telescope and into the rectangle of starlight.

Overhead, the great black telescope was moving, twisting, coming down to—

Kiera wasn't about to find out. She wobbled to her knees and stood, and as soon as she could stand, she was running.

She stumbled into the control room, yanked the flash drive from the hardware stack, and scrambled down the stairs all the way to the lobby. Past the ornate bookshelves and beautiful mosaics she ran—past the zodiac carvings and out the heavy glass doors into the parking lot. Only then did she remember her phone. 22:23, it read. Ten hours until the shuttle came.

But only six hours down the mountain. And Kiera wasn't about to stay on the fucking mountain in the evil dark.

She switched on her phone's camera flash and hit the road at a jog.

The staring followed. She could feel the terrible mechanical gaze upon her back as she pounded the asphalt, every step putting more distance between her and the night's steel eye.

Soon, she passed the wooden sign that announced Observatorio Las Escaleras—or what remained of it. It looked like a century had happened to the painted boards, which were now half-sunk into the sand. She stopped, incredulous. The dome-shaped gap in the stars watched menacingly as she ran a finger down the worn wood, feeling it chip and splinter at her touch.

But behind her, something else was off and she studied the starlit slope to figure out what it was. The buildings were there. The peak was the same. The road... hadn't the road been asphalt?

No, it was definitely compacted sand. It had been like that on the way up, right? The asphalt stopped here, where she was standing, and the road continued in red dirt up to the telescope. She shook her head and started to jog again, the soles of her shoes slapping the smooth pavement with each step.

You know what? Keira thought to herself as she ran. I'll bet I'm back in town in three hours. After all, I didn't run up here. Why didn't I think of that earlier? She cursed herself. I could have been there already. Sitting in a bar, enjoying a margarita, instead of... whatever the fuck this is.

She didn't want to reflect on what had happened, but her mind circled it incessantly anyways. How could the dark be like that? Perhaps she had hallucinated the incident in the optics room, and then, so scared by the experience, hallucinated the never-ending dark of the bathroom as well? And what about the computer screen?

And what about the prime focus? She had seen the hatch as the cursed telescope had swung for her—it was still closed. But climbing into it—the visceral fear of falling from the railing—that had to have happened. Or did it? What if she had fallen, hit her head, and started seeing things? She felt nauseated at the idea.

And what the hell am I doing now? Running down a mountain in the dark. I could get lost out here.

No I couldn't. I'm following the road, and the road—

She turned to look behind her and came to a dead stop.

The road behind her was dirt. The road before her, asphalt.

"No... no!" she cried, taking a step back. "What the fuck!"

No shadow broke the horizon—the dome was gone.

Panic took over and Kiera bolted down the road. It all became real—the eating darkness, the voices in the kitchen, the failing power, the telescope—it was all real, and it added up to something incomprehensible. She cried as she ran, hot tears blurring her the circle of light before her. All these insane things had happened, it wasn't in her head, and she was running, and running, and the whole world was the pavement before her, and—

The light went out.

Her phone was dead.

Once more, it was dark.

Terror seized her, paralyzed her steps. Above, the starry blackness. Below, void. She hung precariously upside down on the thin crust of reality.

Then she was off again, running blind through the cold desert night, following only the slap of shoe on asphalt. She dared not to take a final look back.

Suddenly, her footfalls turned to the thud of loose soil. Where was the road? Had she lost it? Or had it lost her, vanished into sand and brush? She retraced her steps to no avail. The road, too, belonged to the darkness, now, and she knelt and wept; deep, racking sobs, and tears that sizzled into sand.

Pull yourself together, Kiera.

You're heading West. You'll hit the coast, or the highway soon.

Keep going.

Just keep going.

I'm NOT afraid of the dark.

DECEMBER 26

"Dr. Morrison?"

Kiera tries to open her eyes and finds them crusted shut with sand.

"Dr. Morrison?"

She grunts, pries her eyelashes apart, and raises a badly bruised arm against the bright overhead light.

"Can you confirm your date of birth for us?"

"One-eleven-nineteen-eighty-five," she mumbles. Her left side feels like it was hit by a truck, and a front tooth wiggles freely. A burning on her forehead indicates the cuts there have been cleaned and bandaged.

"Very well. Do you know where you are?"

"N... no?"

"You're at Urgencia Hospital La Serena. We found you wandering the desert a few kilometers from the highway with nothing but this flash drive."

A flash drive? "My data!" She moans with relief. "Fuck. I... this telescope... The dark..." She bolts upright with a shudder. "The fucking dark."

"Dr. Morrison, we're going to need you to start from the beginning. You were supposed to report to Observatorio Las Esceleras six days ago, but you never showed up. Where did you go?"

The tale pours out of her like water. The hike, the building, the telescope. The spectrograph room, the bathroom, the computer monitor and the fall from the prime focus. She stares warily at the nurse. "You don't believe me, do you?"

The nurse leaves the room without a word.

When he returns, it is with a manilla folder full of black and white photographs. "Is this what you're describing?"

"Yes! That's the observatory."

"Ma'am... That building was torn down in 1968. They built a new one on the next mountaintop over. I don't know what you're talking about, but it can't be this."

"What?" The unreality sinks in and brings a familiar wave of nausea. "That's where I was! That's where I—" Her head spins and the room seems to tilt.

It doesn't matter now. No one will believe her. "I... I think I need to rest," she says wearily.

"Yes ma'am." He stands to walk toward the door.

"Just one thing?" she calls out. "Please?"

She grips the sides of the bed with sweating hands. "Don't turn the lights out."

C. M. Fields is a queer, non-binary astrophysicist and writer of speculative fiction. They live in Seattle, Washington, with their beloved cats, Mostly Void Partially Stars and Toast, and spend their days looking for other Earths. They are also the co-editor of If There's Anyone Left, an anthology series featuring the flash fiction of marginalized writers from across the globe. C. M. can be found on Twitter as @C_M_Fields and @toomanyspectra. Their fiction has appeared in Diabolical Plots, Metaphorosis, The Dread Machine, and more.

The Apotheosis of Rosie

By Mike Adamson

Rosie O'Connell smelled only dust where once there had been life.

She had worked this diner for forty years. Forty years. Nearly two thirds of her life behind the counter or in the office through the back, she had seen staff come and go beyond all recollection, served an ocean of coffee, more waffles than would pave Hollywood Boulevard, and been called an icon of the century. But the two-lane highway had one day become four, then six, and every other local trader had moved, or been redeveloped, as the passing trade kept right on passing. It was only ever a matter of time before the march of progress came for Rosie's old place, and her loyal clientele had flocked for one last meal before the dozers arrived.

Cars had been gas-guzzlers when she took the diner, now they whirred by with electric quiet; there had been a pay-phone once. The new century made its agonizing way into tomorrow, and the city at last found a use for her island of land by the freeway. Not a factory or depot, just a pylon. They needed it to plant a gigantic tower in support of a turnpike that would pass right overhead and curve off between brand new skyscrapers.

The good news was they paid handsomely for the compulsory purchase.

Rosie heaved a sigh. She stood in the stripped diner, looking around with eyes red from too many tears. A life spent here, just to be ripped away.... The wreckers were ready to move in, a city agent was waiting for her, just letting her have the few minutes she needed. Robots had been in already, recovered fixtures and furnishings, decorations, they were all gone. Only the bare shell of the building remained, nothing to weep over.

She saw her reflection in glass, a tired woman, hair colored over gray, not yet stooped with age but fearing the coming of that phase of deterioration. Her bags were around her feet, a jacket over her arm, and she knew she was delaying the inevitable. She sighed once more, went to lay a hand flat to a wall, and speak from her heart to the old place.

Goodbye, old thing, she said silently, it's been a grand time we've had, you and I. But powers greater than us have decided it's over, and I can't take you with me. Time has passed us by, and we're both at the end of our road. She kissed her palm, laid it on the wall one last moment, then collected her bags and stepped out, to close the door for the very last time.

The city agent, Manning, was waiting, papers under her arm, and in the vacant parking lot a fierce array of robotized equipment had been unloaded from trucks. Diggers and dozers, compressors and generators.... Supervisors in hard hats stood around in the morning heat, ironically drinking coffee from a catering van, when on any other day it would have been hers. Manning approached, fanned herself with the papers, and raised sculpted brows. "Are we... ready, Ms. O'Donnell?"

"Perfectly," Rosie replied smoothly, feeling empty inside. "Give me a few moments to leave, I ordered a cab. I don't want to see it come down."

"I understand." Perhaps the young bureaucrat did not like being kept waiting in the early glare; perhaps she was not even young, it was so hard to tell these days; and therein lay the secret, the one ray of sunshine that gave Rosie a smile—a secretive one, growing, ever so faintly, behind the pathos of the moment. "Retirement, is it?"

Manning probably thought she was being kind, finding conversation with the old woman. "I trust the settlement is absolutely acceptable?"

Now Rosie managed a smile, a mysterious chuckle in her throat. "Yes, the figure is very nice indeed. But no, I'll not be retiring. I have far too much to do."

"Plans for the future?" The question was a courtesy, the agent had no interest in anything other than getting the dilapidated eyesore down as quickly as possible.

"You might say." Rosie reached into her purse and drew out an advertising slip. She passed it over and Manning read softly.

"Opening soon, on Route 14 north of Mojave, 'Rosie's Recharge, the oasis in the heart of the desert!' Use our quality restaurant, shopping mall and cinema complex while your vehicle recharges from the sun at our complimentary sockets—free for all and free forever!" Manning glanced over the slip and found Rosie smiling as if a vast secret had just broken.

"You're the first to know, my dear. The march of progress waits for none and it's time to upgrade. You build a nice bridge here, I'm off to the Sierras."

An air cab whispered down on quad rotors, to land in the vacant drive-through area; the pilot sent the gullwing up and stepped out to take her bags. "Where to, lady?"

Rosie threw the agent a smile as she crossed to the car and slid in. "Flower of the Desert Rejuvenation Clinic, please. As fast as this thing will go."

All bravado aside, she found one last tear as she watched the old place dwindle below, the cab rising between the towers of the new age before turning east for the wide, hot wastes, and she settled herself for the first leg of a whole new journey. About the time she emerged from AgeAway™ therapy a 68-year old sexpot, the new complex would be nearing completion, and she could hardly wait to open her doors.

She resisted the temptation to glance back. Tired as the diner had been, she could not stand to see the wreckers go to work, and could only lament that the strange progress of this twenty-first century swept away the old with such scant mercy.

Well, tomorrow was a new day, and she would grieve for the old when she was no longer part of that definition.

Mike Adamson holds a doctoral degree from Flinders University of South Australia. After early aspirations in art and writing, Adamson returned to study and secured qualifications in marine biology and archaeology. He has been a university educator since 2006, is a passionate photographer, master-level hobbyist and journalist for international magazines. For more about him, check out his website, Mike-Adamson.blogspot.com.

Test Amongst the Shadows

By Todd Sullivan

The hardest working mage who ever lived glanced at the clock on the wall. Twenty minutes. Jin gazed down at his English exam. Only twenty minutes left to pass or fail the biggest test of his life. His scantron sheet was half empty. The clock's ticking seconds in the silent classroom echoed in his mind, and made focusing on English vocabulary and grammar impossible. He had to do something if he intended to get in the top of his class.

Jin looked around at the other students, their heads low, their shoulders hunched as they picked off ovals in the long marching columns. Adjusting his glasses, he opened his senses in search for the right spell amidst the thin cracks that splinter reality. He released control of his hand and let it draw six stick-figure bandits on horses at the edges of the exam.

Leaning close to the page, he whispered, "Thieving shadows, take shape and learn the secrets of my woes."

The drawings shivered, and the bandits shook themselves awake. They clawed out of the exam, erupting off the page into the third dimension. The cloaked leader saluted, his face hidden in shades of gray.

Jin pointed to the answer key tucked under a notebook on the teacher's desk. The leader nodded, and motioned to the silent troupe behind him. The bandits yanked on their horses' reins and leapt off the side of the table. Racing across the tiled floor, the horses skirted around chair legs and hopped over sneakers.

Jin glanced at the exam answer key again. The sides of his mouth spread in a triumphant smile, but a purple boot suddenly crushed the horsemen right before they cleared the classroom's tables. Jin inhaled in surprise. He followed the boot up to the leg, the skirt, the shirt, to finally meet the steady gaze of Sori, the top student in the school.

And his ex-girlfriend.

The two maintained eye contact for several moments, a silent challenge passing between them. Sori had broken up with him right before exams, informing him that she wasted too much time with him and wasn't focusing enough on the upcoming finals. And now, here she sat, the only other mage in this room of humans, stopping him from reaching his goal.

So that's how it was going to be.

Jin slowly took off his glasses in preparation for his next spell. Sori had managed to see his bandits. He didn't know how, but he would need to take care of her sight before he tried for the test answers again.

Jin narrowed his eyes at the light reflected in the lenses of his glasses. He smiled. He held the glasses to his lips and misted the lenses by blowing on one, then the other. While he did this, he focused on the magic vibrating between the fissures of reality until he heard the words to the next spell.

"Site sighted, two to see, sea bog fog billowing..."

"John?"

Jin snapped his mouth shut at the teacher speaking his English name. He tried to still his heart now thumping fast in his chest, and met the teacher's puzzled blue eyes.

"Are you speaking to someone?"

Now the other students' heads lifted, and before he knew it, dozens of humans were all staring in his direction. With their attention focused on him, he couldn't produce magic. No mage could. Human disbelief in magic narrowed the fissures running throughout reality, making the words necessary to bring spells to life impossible to hear. Jin had been told that no mage had been able to perform magic in front of a human in hundreds of years.

He glanced at Sori, who was smiling at him as he sweated under the spotlight of mankind. With a weak shrug, Jin said, "I was just," and he paused as he scrambled for a good excuse, "reading a problem out loud to myself." He tapped the exam. "Sometimes that helps."

The English teacher nodded. "Everyone must remain silent so that the other students can concentrate. Sorry, John."

"Won't happen again," Jin assured him. He caught Sori's smug wink, and tore his eyes away from his ex-girlfriend's pretty face.

These exams determined who would be allowed to apply for the International School in Hong Kong. Only the top two students would be recommended. Jin felt confident about math and science, but he worried over his English scores. One of his classmates had lived in San Francisco for years. Jin only managed to edge him out sometimes, while Sori beat them both in every subject every, single, time.

She was a studying machine.

Jin looked at the clock again. Ten minutes to finish the exam. He had to cast another spell, but when he raised his eyes, he noticed the teacher looking around the room. Whereas before he hadn't been paying much attention, now the teacher was watching them closely, all because of Sori.

Jin really wished he had been able to cast his spell and blind her. Not only because he would have been able to get the answers without her trying to counter him, but because it would have stopped her from taking the test, maybe even causing her to fail.

That would have been sweet.

Jin's eyes narrowed as a new idea struck him. He looked at the dusty blackboard behind the teacher and slowly raised his hand.

"Yes, John?" the teacher said. "Is something wrong?"

"Can I ask you a question?" Jin assumed his most perplexed look, and mixed in a little pained exasperation to make himself seem even more pathetic.

The teacher sighed and waved him forward. Jin stood. Only briefly, a couple of students glanced up at the newest disturbance, but their focus quickly returned to their exams. All, that is, except Sori, who watched Jin with a penetrating gaze. He wanted to give her the finger, but since the teacher was staring at him, he refrained as he passed her.

He placed his exam on the teacher's desk. "These directions." He motioned with his right hand. "I don't understand them."

While the teacher followed the motion of his gesture, Jin quickly traced two eyes in the dust on the chalkboard. Sori took a sharp breath, and Jin gave her the middle finger a moment before the teacher looked at him again.

"I really think you should be able to understand these directions," the teacher said. "We went over similar examples in class earlier this week."

"Ah." Jin bent closer to the exam. "I think you're right." He'd rested his test on the answer sheet, and now he pulled it a little further down on the teacher's desk so that it was in plainer view of the board. When he got back to his seat, he waited until the teacher's attention turned back to the computer screen. Now only Sori watched him like a hawk.

Lowering his head and covering his mouth with this hand, Jin listened closely to the magic in the cracks of reality.

"Vision born from dust, take note of the world before you."

Jin touched his left eye.

"Blind amongst the shadows, see with other sight the world before you."

The drawing on the board took on concrete shape, the pupils swirling up and down and left and right. The sight in Jin's left eye dimmed into darkness, then light appeared again. He looked down upon the teacher's desk, his left eye directly connected to the eyes traced on the board. The answer sheet was exposed beautifully before him.

Grinning, Jin began to fill in the correct ovals on the scantron, his hard work and perseverance finally paying off. With his vision split, he had a view of the entire class, and he paused a moment to swing the eyes towards Sori.

He thought about the times they would walk home after school together, hand in hand. He would lead them on the longest path through the city streets so they could spend as much time together as possible. When it rained, he would hold his book bag over her head so that her hair wouldn't get wet. In the cold, they'd press their bodies together, and he'd wrap his arm around her to stave off the chill.

They would stop in small parks dotting Seoul, and on the bench they'd play with each other's fingers, conversing about their day and the difficulties that plagued them in low voices. They'd complain about parents burdening them with chores, and teachers who kept giving them homework, assignments, quizzes, reports, and tests without regard to how busy they already were. Sori's hair smelled of apples, and her lips tasted like strawberries.

He gazed at her now, the smartest person in the class, perhaps in the whole world. He noticed with surprise her furiously erasing on her desk. That was totally unlike her. Normally, she completed tests confidently, being the first one to finish. There had to be less than ten minutes to the exam, so why did she even still have her paper on her desk?

Jin shook his head. Maybe it was because she'd been paying so much attention to him. He smiled. He would talk to her after class today. He'd explain that he wasn't angry with her, especially now that he was getting what he wanted.

Sori scooped the eraser shredding into her hand so that they formed a little pile. She glanced around the classroom, at the students bowed over their tests, and muttered words Jin could not hear. Then she inhaled, and blew upon the shredding in her palm. They exploded out in a whirlwind that hit the board behind the teacher and erased the eyes drawn from the dust.

Jin sat back in his seat in surprise, but he managed to keep his shock silent. This girl, he thought. This female mage!

Quickly, he drew a dozen projectiles on his desk, his heartbeat increasing in tempo as his anger grew. The fissures in reality picked up on his vengeance and supplied the words he quietly spoke.

"A horde of tiny pellets, to wound, to draw blood, to annoy like mosquitoes around the heart that I loved."

With a harsh wave of his arm, he sent the pellets swarming from his desk at Sori. She recoiled in her seat and weaved a series of webbed signs in the air as she spoke. A faintly illuminated net appeared in front of her, caught the pellets, and ricocheted them back at Jin.

Jin ducked and raised his exam, but they tore tiny holes through the paper and ripped into his face so that tiny droplets of blood rained down on his desk. Before the pellets could turn to strike him again, he said, "Swarm, swatted, to lie, still," and heard them break apart in the air to disperse as tiny columns of gray mist.

The pellets hadn't caused much damage, as they were meant to annoy the victim with tiny, continuous bombardments. Still, Jin seethed as he glared at Sori. He licked at blood that dripped down the tiny cuts on his face onto his lips. Clutching his pencil tight, he said, "A spear, to fling with force to pierce the soul of the one I loved."

He hurled it at Sori's chest. A dark light surrounded it, enhancing the pencil into a massive, jagged javelin that raced at his ex-girlfriend with amazing force.

The teacher looked up and announced to the class, "Five minutes left."

The javelin, under the sudden gaze of a human, immediately lost its magic, and the pencil hit Sori. She caught it before it clattered to the floor.

Jin gazed down at his half completed exam sheet, and his hope plunged into a pit. He tried to slow his quickened breathing as panic swelled inside of him. He'd never finish the test now. And it was all because of her.

Curses strained against his lips. Human curses, yes, but still words that he knew would hurt her. He inhaled and looked at his ex-girlfriend, ready to hurl them at her in rage. The curses stuck in his throat, and he sputtered at what he saw before him.

She stared down at her exam, a forlorn expression etched across her brow. Tears had formed in Sori's eyes. They sparkled like diamonds at the edges of her lashes. The vehemence that had risen in Jin drained as realization dawned on him. Sori had been so preoccupied with him that she hadn't had time to finish her exam either. Now neither of them would make it to Hong Kong. Now both of them would remain together at this school.

Jin sighed. If they were going to be together anyway, he thought, if they couldn't escape this battle raging between them, then why not fight somewhere new and exciting? Somewhere away from the same old problems. Perhaps new issues would arrive, but at least it would be somewhere different.

And perhaps in Hong Kong, they could be different.

Sori suddenly looked at Jin as if she'd heard his thoughts. They stared at each other. Slowly, a smile spread across his face, and it was perfectly mirrored by the one forming on her lips. Do they still taste of strawberries? He hoped to find out again at their new school in Hong Kong.

Jin sat up straight in his seat. The hardest working mage in the world, coupled with the smartest and most beautiful female mage in the world. If they joined their powers, nothing would be able to stop them.

Jin released himself to the magic lacing reality, and he saw Sori doing the same as the humans around them focused their attention elsewhere.

Let the clock on the wall keep its watch. Time was no match for their greatness.

Todd Sullivan currently lives in Seoul, South Korea, where he teaches English as a second language. He has had more than two dozen short stories, poems, essays, and novelettes published across five countries. He currently has two book series available through Amazon. He writes for a web and play series in Taipei, founded the online magazine, Samjoko, in 2021, and hosts a YouTube Channel that interviews writers across the publishing spectrum.

The Last Glance

By Gary Beck

"I don't want to go! I've been looking forward to my free period for weeks and I made plans to work on my laser experiment with Muffy. You don't have the right to make me go, if I don't want to." But all Mom said was: "No more arguments. You're going, whether you like it or not. This is a very special occasion and you're not missing it. Now get ready and I'll meet you at the front lock in ten minutes. And hurry."

I didn't want to go to the dirty, radiated surface just to sigh over the stump of an old tree that didn't even have any leaves. Earth surface was no different to me than any other hostile environment; it was out to get you, one way or the other. I'd just as soon take an excursion to Mars, or Venus. At least that would be treated as a proper scientific expedition. Not like these nostalgic sightseeing trips, where old folks sentimentally mooned about relics from the past and usually neglected their survival procedures. But if I didn't humor Mom, she'd make life hell for weeks. So I suited up and headed for the front airlock.

The group was milling around the central airlock, waiting for latecomers. Muffy was there, looking as unhappy as I was. We went to personal frequencies and she really let me know how upset she was. She had been in the middle of a refraction/contortion test that we had been preparing for months, when her Dad insisted that she go with him to the surface. She told me that she tried to explain how important the timing was for the experiment, but her Dad wouldn't listen. "All he kept saying was: 'we may never find another tree on the surface. This may be a unique event that'll never happen again in your lifetime.' As if I care anything about that dumb old stick." She was really fuming.

We went through the exiting cycles with the rest of the group, commenting freely on the various shortcomings of our elders, critiquing the poor preparation and sneering at the shoddy equipment check for the trip. I was just reminding Muffy that even the sloppiest maintenance techs carried lifelines and power packs in the corridors, let alone on surface trips, when the leader's annoyed voice overrode our circuit. "If you tads have any more complaints, submit them in writing and stop griping on the group frequency." I knew I had switched to personal and quickly looked at Muffy. She shrugged acknowledgement that she was still on group, but answered the leader firmly: "Sorry about the group blare, sir. And no insult meant to anyone personally. But I must request that proper excursion procedures be exercised, in accordance with regulations." She really had nerve.

Even though each citizen had the right to be protected by proper safety procedures at all times, in practice everyone cut corners. Leader sputtered about how long it would take to send for packs and lines, but Muffy wouldn't give an inch. "Safety regs are specific for a good reason, sir. They save lives." There were some resentful mutters over the public circuit, but Muffy ignored them. I moved closer to her to show my support and got some glares for my trouble, but I didn't care. I admired her more than anyone else, except Dad.

Dad was a molecular engineer and a political activist. When the dispute began between the elders who dreamed of returning to the surface, and the "moles," who were committed to subsurface, Dad spent all his rest time trying to show the elders how hopeless their idea was. When reasoning with them failed, he organized a team of the foremost scientists and thinkers. They prepared a master chart that showed the resources necessary to reestablish life on the surface. Some of the elders never forgave him for shattering their dream, but the conflict was over and energies were turned to developing the underworld.

For a while, a lot of people were really angry at Dad and threats were made, but he knew he was right and stood firm. Later he gave me some good advice. "When you really know you're right, and that the other way would lead to disaster, you've got to stand by your convictions. Frequently people want things without quite knowing how to get them. But they can want them so badly that they overlook the consequences. Sometimes they'll even forget common sense and reason. When that happens, you've got to be able to settle things down before there's a disaster."

Dad was my ideal. I didn't think he was perfect, or anything like that, but I always watched him when he was dealing with others. He always seemed surer and more confident than everyone else. I hoped that I would become as capable as he was, but I wasn't counting on it. I hadn't seen much of him lately. Ever since he started working on the molten pool project, he rarely got home. It started when maintenance techs first noticed rising heat patterns in some corridors, but no one paid it much attention. Dad was the first one to realize that it wasn't just vented waste energy, but emissions of external heat from pockets of molten metal that could potentially threaten our very existence. When others finally realized the danger, the project was quickly organized and Dad was appointed leader. Project molten pool became the number one underworld priority and Dad had the authority to requisition anything he needed; men, materials, even personal possessions, if necessary. It was a comforting thought knowing that Dad was in charge. I didn't miss him much when he was away, but when I saw him, I always felt a lot better.

The equipment finally arrived. Properly suited we continued cycling to the surface lock. It was repetitive, going through sixteen levels the same way each time, but after the confrontation on equipment, everyone was careful to follow regs. Then we were out. I felt no exhilaration, only apprehension. I had been on the surface before and knew how suddenly radiation storms blew in. I looked for our weather watcher and wasn't reassured. It was Turly IV. He had been a class ahead of me in survival school and I remembered how optimistic he always seemed. I knew how dangerous that could be and often wondered how he passed Trial Day. Hoping for the best was the surest way to get fried. I cued Muffy on personal and we agreed to alternately monitor the weather circuit.

The surface was incredibly calm. Visibility was about 400 feet, maybe more. The dust clouds were barely moving. When I scanned the surface from the underworld, the video monitor softened everything. But standing here, seeing farther than ever before, it was hard to imagine a surface covered with grass or trees. If I hadn't seen old videotapes, I'd never have believed it. Sometimes I wondered if the tapes were authentic. They could have been chroma-keyed computer generated. But Dad said it was so and that was good enough for me.

Leader brought us to the Tree and the elders murmured all kinds of ritualistic stuff. Someone recited an old poem about the forest primeval. It sounded stupid to me. I scanned the weather circuit and noted a radiation increase. The normal turbulence was preparing to move back in. I waited thirty seconds, but when Turly didn't notify us, I sounded a radiation alert. Turly protested that I was too nervous and maybe I shouldn't be allowed on surface, but I cut him off and read the last counter level and he subsided. I could never figure out how he survived Trial Day. Maybe it was true that influence sometimes affected some candidate's results. He sure wasn't a survivor.

We headed back to the reentry lock, moving faster as the wind picked up. I kept a watchful eye on Turly, because accidents happened sometimes. A breached airline on surface could be serious, even fatal. But the return trip was uneventful. Many of the group lingered, drawing their stay out as long as possible. The leader, always last in, was getting impatient. I let Muffy precede me and started in. I looked back and my last glance was at that pathetic thing they called a tree. As the lock began to cycle closed, I heard some of the group crying. I looked at Muffy. She had heard them too. We shook our heads at each other, both thinking the same thing: what a waste of time and assets. The worst sin in the underworld was waste, since we didn't have enough of anything.

Well, at least we wouldn't have to go to the surface again for a while. As Muffy started describing the new refraction problem, my irritation at the elders began to fade. As my last thoughts of the surface departed, going wherever finished thoughts go, I focused my energies back where they belonged; on the future of the underworld.

Gary Beck has spent most of his life as a theater director and art dealer. He has also been a tennis pro, a ditch digger and a salvage diver. His original plays have been produced Off Broadway. His poetry, fiction and essays have appeared in hundreds of literary magazines and his published books include 32 poetry collections, 14 novels, 3 short story collections, 1 collection of essays and 5 books of plays. Find him at GaryCBeck.com and on Facebook at @AuthorGaryBeck.

Not the Pizza Girl

By Michelle Ann King

Lisa floored the van's accelerator, thrashing the speed limit, weaving in and out of traffic on the A12 and even slipstreaming an ambulance from Gallows Corner to Gidea Park. It earned her more than a few angry horn blasts, a lot of obscenities yelled out of car windows and undoubtedly a shedload of bad karma, but it also shaved a good ten minutes off the journey. And when you guaranteed delivery in half an hour, no exceptions, that counted for a lot.

The customer lived in a good-looking place round the back of the station, with a massive driveway that was already filled up with cars. Loud, rhythmic music came from inside, punctuated by the occasional shriek.

Sounded like quite a party. Lisa parked her van on the road and killed the engine with her trip timer reading 02:16. She'd cut it fine, but she'd made it. With any luck, she'd get a decent tip off this one.

She grabbed the bag from the passenger seat, sprinted for the front door and rang the bell. At 01:35 it was opened by a dark-haired bloke in gray jeans and a check shirt. He reeked of wine, sulfur and incense, and his eyes were glowing red. That didn't bode well, for either of them. The possessed were never big tippers.

Lisa gave him a big smile anyway, and held out the bag. "Delivery, mate."

He peered at her. "Huh?"

She made an effort to keep the smile going. "It's all paid for on the card, so I just need you to sign on the little screen here and we're all done."

He stared blankly for a few more seconds before his face cleared. "Oh, right. The pizzas."

Lisa let go of the smile and her hope of a tip.

"No, mate, I'm not the pizza girl. I'm the emergency magical supplies girl."

"Huh?"

"I'm from Eddie's," she said. "Eddie's Ethereal Emporium? I've got an order of—" she paused, checked her manifest and continued, "pine smudge sticks, black beeswax tapers, granular frankincense, powdered dragon's blood, juniper oil and virgin's tears, for this address."

Check Shirt just blinked those opaque eyes at her and swayed. Lisa's timer read 01:13.

Another shriek came from inside the house, followed by a deep, rumbling snarl. Lisa shook her head. Bloody amateur magicians, always getting themselves into shit they couldn't get out of. She blamed Harry Potter.

"Look, mate, these are ingredients for a banishing ritual, yeah? So someone here must have had enough of their right mind left to realize you've got an unwanted guest at the party."

"Huh?"

Lisa rubbed her eyes and counted to five. Ten was always better, but she was on a deadline. "Listen, I know what it's like when summonings get out of hand—you've had a few drinks, you get a bit sloppy with the Latin, the sigils end up the wrong way round. You might just be trying to raise an imp to clean the toilet, but you end up with the legions of Beelzebub pouring out of the u-bend. Trust me, I've seen it happen."

Check Shirt scratched his cheek with a nail that blackened and lengthened into a claw.

"Huh?" he said.

A huge snake-like creature slithered out of the door and over his feet. Lisa stepped back and it disappeared under the hedge at the side of the house.

She snapped her fingers in front of Check Shirt's face. He was drooling slightly. "You've got demons, mate," she said, speaking very loudly and slowly. "Inside and out, by the look of it. So I strongly recommend you sign here, then go and sort it out. Okay?"

Behind her, a motorbike picked its way through the cars on the drive. "Three large pepperonis and a garlic bread, for Steve," the rider called out. "Twenty-five quid."

Check Shirt's eyes snapped back into focus. He reached into his back pocket and came out with a wallet.

Typical. In the battle of man's stomach versus his immortal soul, the stomach won every time.

"Oh, no you don't," Lisa said. The display on her timer was at 00:35, the digits flashing red. She pointed a warning finger at the bike rider, who was carrying a stack of red and white boxes. The savory aroma mixed uneasily with the smell of brimstone wafting out of the house. "I was here first, mate, you wait your turn."

She threw her bag into the hallway, grabbed Steve's hand and used a talon to scribble on the screen. The status changed to Delivered, and the countdown halted at 00:17.

"Thank you for using Eddie's Ethereal Emporium, we hope you enjoy your magical purchases," she said. "Preferably as soon as possible, yeah?"

Steve ignored her, his attention fully focused on the stack of pizza boxes. She shrugged and headed back to the van.

She'd just driven off when a huge gout of black smoke boiled out from the house. The pizza bike, burning merrily, flew over the top of the van and landed in a skip about twenty yards down. There was a great clap of thunder and an ear-shattering roar that could never have been produced by a human throat. It sounded very much like "I hate pepperoni."

A smaller fireball, which might have once been a pizza box, shot out of the swirling black vortex and joined the bike in the skip.

Lisa picked up her radio. "15 to base," she said. "Clear from Gidea Park, heading back to the warehouse now."

She kept up a leisurely 10 miles an hour above the speed limit. In her rear-view mirror, the cloud of smoke split apart and formed into a writhing mass of horned, fanged shapes. A few of them disappeared down the chimneys of the neighboring houses.

Lisa got back on the radio. "15 again, base. Eddie, you might want to stock up on those banishing kits. I think we could be getting some new orders."

Michelle Ann King is a short story writer from Essex, England. Her stories of fantasy, science fiction, crime, and horror have appeared in over a hundred different venues, including Strange Horizons, Interzone, Black Static, and Orson Scott Card's Intergalactic Medicine Show. Her collections are available in ebook and paperback from Amazon and other online retailers, and links to her published stories can be found at her website, TransientCactus.co.uk.

Retribution

By Kris Green

"And, when you want something, all the universe conspires in helping you to achieve it."
-Paulo Coelho, "The Alchemist"

Annie sat at her desk looking out the window rolling a pencil back-and-forth with her finger. The street was mostly empty. The drizzling rain seemed to be letting up. She wasn't sure when she had come to the decision. She assumed everybody had thought about it at one point or another. Maybe it was a normal thing to consider, a common dysfunction. But then again, how normal is it to contemplate your own suicide.

She had never thought about it until now. She had thought suicide was something for the selfish, but now she understood it was for people who were... what? Disappointed with the world? Maybe it was for the depressed or the heavily medicated? She wasn't quite sure.

She didn't look at the folded newspaper sitting on her desk. The front page blasted with a picture of Emily Braun who had committed to her decision the week before. Maybe people would say it was a copycat suicide? Was that the term? But that was why they kept notifications of suicides out of the newspaper, right?

Her father worked his forty hours, came home and sat in front of the television. The all-present blob on the couch that died the same way he lived, miserable. Her mother, still living, wasn't happy either. So, how important was happiness?

There wouldn't be a memorial for her like there was for Emily. There wouldn't be a new hashtag. Sweet Emily, Annie thought, I didn't mean to push you in that direction. Emily, who rose in the middle of a meeting, walked out of the meeting and off of the roof. How guilty was Annie for this? #sharethepain.

It had something to do with the cosmic karmic scales that prevented her repulsion for Emily from infecting others. Not like it could. Not like it should. Annie had been almost completely indifferent to Emily. She was more a sign on the side of the road than a roadblock.

She came back to the note she had been trying to write. The anger subsided briefly back to self-pity. Her fingers numb with the pencil still rubbing back and forth on the desk making the familiar rhythmic sound. Maybe she could write something nice to her mother or.... Who? Who would really care about it? Maybe her mother would on a biological level, yes, but after that would she feel relieved?

She felt like weeping, but that would just be wasting tears. Her suicide would not be coming from a place of self-pity, she readied herself, but a desire to make the world a better place. A martyr needed a cause. Action was what changed the world, action and then recognition for that action.

Of course, before she had pieced the logic of everything together and had come to the conclusion that she was different, there were moments that indicated how the universe worked. It was undeniable that little things just worked out for her.

Annie was staring at the small chocolate bar. She had wanted it. She was five or six. Mrs. Graham walked through the door causing the little bell to ring. Annie had turned to look but had hardly noticed Mrs. Graham holding the hand of her boy, Bill. But all she could think was that sweet, delicious chocolate bar, I want it.

Without hesitation, Mrs. Graham grabbed the chocolate bar that Annie had desired. Not the same brand or something similar, not one from the same box, no, she had grabbed the exact candy bar Annie had been staring at, two behind the front. She hadn't even spoken, hadn't even done her own shopping but simply bought and paid for it. "Here you go, sweetie," Handing her the chocolate bar as if it were nothing out of the ordinary.

Bill threw up his hands and began stomping, "Why'd you buy one for that stupid girl?"

"You're too fat to get a candy bar," Mrs. Graham had said.

Bill's arms dropped. The tantrum abated. Both mother and son stared at each other in the shock of what had just happened as Annie bit into her candy.

Andy Bradbury had been bullying her for weeks on end. Teasing, pulling her hair, making her life miserable. When she had told her daddy, who was halfway through a TV dinner and baseball game, he had only made an off-hand comment about the boy having a crush.

It came back to desire. She desired not to be bullied but it was an unspecified desire, which is a kind of desire but not a strong one. Her teacher was in front of the class pointing at the chalkboard. Annie turned looking at her bored fellow classmen and saw Dustin Howitzer. Howitzer would later be on the football team but that was a few years and another 100 plus pounds. He wasn't big, not like he got, but it was clear he had just begun a growth spurt, already 3 inches above the other boys.

The desire, finding specificity, had come into fruition. I want Howitzer to beat up Andy Bradbury. Then Howitzer stood up in the middle of a lecture on fractions. Annie's mouth dropped open in shock. The teacher who stopped talking just cocked her head to the side unprepared for what would happen. Howitzer, who walked between rows of desks not toward the door but away from it, walked right to Andy's desk.

"Do you need to use the restroom, Mr...." Probably the only thing the teacher could think of to say.

Howitzer clenched his fists and began pummeling Andy. All chairs, except one, were scooted back as everyone rose in shock. He had to be pulled off of Andy. Howitzer turned his head slightly, coming to his senses and they let him go. He shook his head as if coming out of daze.

Annie sat in her chair still in shock. Desire had been made manifest. She had understood then, for the first time. Not a hint of how it worked, not like the candy bar, but she understood how the universe actually worked

Tears were already beginning to pour down Howitzer's cheeks. Andy's face was beginning to puff up like a giant raspberry. Howitzer looked down, maybe defeated, maybe confused. He looked at Andy and then down at his fists still in shock at what he had done.

Then there was the pencil. It had fallen off of someone's desk who had risen in the commotion. It had waited for Howitzer's troubled backward steps and it had rolled, causing his arms to fly up like some kind of cartoon character. It had rolled out of sight as Howitzer's head thumped hard on the floor.

Instant karma, Annie considered later. Every action required another. Then came the experiments. Slow at first, like getting strangers to kiss. Then more complex like wanting a pizza given to her in the middle of her finals. But every action was followed by some kind of debt that needed to be paid. Even if it meant the teacher paid the tab on the pizza.

Did she feel guilty? No. She supposed she didn't. She desired it; it had happened. If she wanted a boyfriend, she would get one. If she wanted anything, anything at all, she would get it.

Pancakes for dinner were nice, but her mother burning herself in the kitchen while cooking the pancakes wasn't. Her father not drinking after work was nice too, but when the house smelled thick with smoke, almost instantly, she regretted it.

Maybe she could desire good into the world. That was the real reason for wanting her father to stop drinking. It would ease the monthly budget. It could make her mother a little happier when her father wasn't loose with his words and fists. Desire itself didn't seem to matter unless it was specified. But there was always a cost. The scales would be evened out, every time. The universe had to be balanced.

When she was seventeen, she had seen a bank robbery. She turned and walked away. But even then, the desire was out there. The robber was caught because he had diverted his run to the getaway car. He ran up and handed her the bag of cash. She refused to take it. The pause, the hesitation, the change of plan, and the cops had surrounded him.

A knock at the door broke her out of her thoughts. She thought maybe some things were best left with the door closed. Letting go of the pencil and paper that simply had "Mom" scrawled at the top of it, she rose to get it. The rain was picking up a little.

Chad stood at the door holding flowers. There was that look in his eyes. The cloudy unfocused look that made her think of someone who was drugged. The magic wasn't impeded by guilt.

"I need to be alone."

Chad nodded, "I saw you in the window, you looked so sad. Are you okay?"

"You should go."

He turned and walked away.

Her prom date was another one. Although the rampant desires of a teenage girl hadn't been easy to control. He got handsy and began pushing her toward an inner edge that she didn't want to go. As he pushed at her, trying to hike up her dress, her desire for this boy's infatuation was lost. He stopped suddenly. Eyes blank just like Chad's, he turned and walked away.

He wouldn't have been the first to commit suicide because of her. Now that she was thinking about it, she had no desire for Emily to commit suicide. Maybe Emily had just been part of the karmic judgment of her desire. Maybe that was why her desire to not see the memorials went unheeded.

Her prom date had just walked away like Emily. He had almost walked right into traffic if other people hadn't seen him and stopped him. She had received the prerequisite sympathy as people began discussing what must've happened.

Let's face it, college desires were many and she had indulged. She had hated. Many suffered. She had loved. More suffered. She had passed classes when she shouldn't have. It was an easy desire to let out into the universe for a professor who didn't give a second thought to changing her grade. Who knows, maybe he flunked someone else. She didn't always know how the universe corrected itself, but it did. She was sure of it.

Then after college, there was the job interview, only the one. They spoke for a few minutes and she was hired. The interviewers, two no-names in HR that she would never meet again, walked out and dismissed the other applicants in one unfailing swoop. The league of applicants' faces fell, and she glowed. But she hadn't accomplished anything, not really. She hadn't experienced any prize. She hadn't ever really won out of talent or skill.

Then Emily Braun was hired within a couple of months. Then Emily had begun dating Chad. Now she was dead.

She had tried to live without desire. But she was no Buddhist. Desire was as ingrained in American culture as much as fast food burgers. She liked having desire. She liked being hungry for things.

It was the restaurant on their lunch break. Her little group of work-friends all ate and laughed. She happened to look over at Chad sitting at a table with Emily. Chad gazed at Emily as if a devout congregant.

Then desire came. I want a soul mate.

Chad hadn't said anything else to Emily, and God knows he might feel guiltier than she did. His silence was probably part of the unspoken desire to not hear anything about Emily. Chad merely rose from the table and walked over. Emily had turned to stare as Chad asked for Annie's number.

Bill Brunswick laughed when Chad asked her out in front of everyone. "Hey pal, aren't you on a date."

She now hated her work-friends. Bill Brunswick was fat and she hated him. She hated everyone at work. Unable to keep from unleashing that desire, she mustered all of her energy to keep it buried deep inside. She hated the memories of Emily and she hated all this attention about her death. She hated Chad too. Wasn't it his fault? She hated her job and the two HR people that hired her. She hated her family and she thought maybe she hated herself too.

It had been in some psychology class. The professor had spoken gravely, "Suicide was something that we don't talk a lot about. It's because it is a touchy subject and often other professors are afraid of bringing it up like it will spread like some type of social contagion." The class had been interesting. People shared and the professor had been adamant on if anyone is feeling suicidal, speak up. "You don't have to be alone." #sharethepain

Then there was the quote by Chesterton, "The suicide is worse than the murderer because the murderer kills off one person, while the suicide kills everyone they know by killing themselves."

She got dressed. It felt like a weird thing to do. What was she to wear in her last hours? It didn't matter. Nothing fit anymore anyway. Makeup, she thought? Then catching herself in the mirror, well, maybe a little. The rain misted into her face when she walked outside. Still slightly overcast and the sky seemed to give a halfhearted attempt at rain. She walked down to the street and hailed a cab.

The cabbie smelled. He rolled down his window as she got in. She smiled. The instant gratification of having that desire realized made her feel better. But the muggy hot air blowing back at her took the smile away. The cabbie didn't talk; he knew instinctively where to take her. At the corner of Second and Main, she saw a woman holding hands with a little girl. The woman looked up at her. There was the desire again. Still speaking, I want to be a mother. The woman hoisted her daughter up with arms stretched out toward the cab.

The light changed and the cab accelerated leaving the mother and the child watching after it.

"You don't have to do this." He said looking in the rear-view mirror.

"What?"

"There's other ways. You just have to be strong enough."

She didn't question how he knew what she was thinking until the realization slowly crept over her. His head snapped forward. He began to speed forward, weaving in and out of traffic. People honked. Before she knew it, he was screeching on the brakes in front of her office building. The cabbie didn't say anything as she got out.

"Don't do this." A woman in a business suit said walking past.

"You know you don't want to." A man walking the opposite direction said.

She lifted her chin, confident in her decision. The strangers stopped talking.

She used to pick scabs when she was little. She thought it was something linked to her personality—that uncontrollable desire to not let anything heal. Pick. The blood fills the tiny hole. Sometimes it stops; sometimes it overflows.

Her father walked into the kitchen. He opened a bottle of beer and drank. Pick. He didn't sit down. He just drank. Pick. Then another and then another. Then when the beer was out, he found a bottle of wine. Pick. After the wine, a bottle of bourbon. That was the last one. The inevitable downfall. Why don't you just drink yourself to death? And he did. Pick. The blood fills the tiny hole. Sometimes it stops; sometimes it overflows.

Thud.

The first body to hit the pavement was someone she didn't know. She cocked her head to the side looking at it thinking, why him? Her desire was becoming realized. She turned toward the street. Some people were yelling at each other while others were beginning to look up to the top of the building.

A cabbie and a truck driver were too busy yelling at each other to notice the bodies that had begun falling until one landed on top of the cabbie. The truck driver didn't move at first, merely looked up seeing others gathering at the ledge.

She opened the door to the building with another thud and then another on the street behind her. Screeching brakes and horns as cars collided. Some people sat where they were working but when they saw her, instinctively they rose.

She walked to the elevator where a crowd was trying to get on. The doors were unable to close. It would be like this on every floor, she thought. A little half smile crept across her face. The people diverted except for a janitor. Summoned, she knew for her purposes.

She turned her head to see people begin swarming the stairwell. The elevator, mostly emptied, had a few people still standing in it. The janitor got in the elevator and pulled out a key and turned on the override. Tapping the top floor, he nodded, turning to her with a grim smile.

The elevator flew up to the top floor and opened with a ding. Annie walked slowly savoring the moment. She smiled wanting to watch. One by one, people rushed to the edge of the roof, climbed on and merely stepped off. No scream, no plea for help, just a step and gone. Sometimes there was a small sob coming from them but mostly nothing.

Eat your heart out, Emily Braun. She chuckled slightly walking to the ledge. Bill Brunswick shoved past her, and then stopped. He looked at her. She quieted the annoyance just enough to give a little nod. He ran for the ledge. He didn't stop to climb up. The side of the ledge hit his stomach and his body toppled over.

Other people in her office, some she recognized, some she knew, most she didn't, jumped. The standard was to pause and look down and she liked that so they all began doing it.

She climbed onto the ledge and looked down at the swelling crowd. The bodies everywhere on the sidewalk and in the street. She imagined the whole building pouring into elevators and stairwells trying to get to the roof. Dozens had already fallen and when she was done, hundreds would.

Something changed as she looked down. Guilt was something she didn't quite feel. Emily had caused her to feel what most people would call guilt, but was it really that? She saw all the death and felt better for it. She felt as if maybe she didn't want to do this anymore. A man on the ledge near her hesitated. The crowd kept swelling on the roof, but they too had stopped although their numbers grew. She smiled at the man on the ledge with her and gave a little nod. He jumped.

Even then, maybe if she did this, others would stop. That's not what she wanted. She didn't want to do this anymore, but they should. They all should. As she turned to get off the ledge, the people had pressed toward all sides of the roof. She tried to get down when she saw Chad. Chad pushed his way through seeing her. She paused, still on the ledge seeing him wave excitedly to her. Well, she thought, maybe I'll let him go before I get down.

She felt like laughing until someone's body pressed against her feet causing her to lean back teetering off the edge just a little. But Chad was there and caught her hand. As she tried to find balance, a desire blossomed violently into her thoughts. Get me off this roof now! Chad nodded, still holding her hand and jumped toppling over the ledge dragging her down the other side.

As she fell, there was no conscious thought. There were no last minute repentances or pleas. Noises whooshed past her as sirens and cries grew louder. Her mind scrambled trying to act on a desire for rescue but came up short. Then she tried to imagine, to desire some form of paradise but couldn't conceive of one.

Kris Green lives in Florida with his wife and two-year old son. He writes daily and has published many short stories in publications such as Morpheus Tales, Flume, In Parentheses, Route 7 Review and more. He was a finalist for Chester B. Himes Memorial Fiction Contest and received an Honorable Mention from Allegory Ezine.

Unarmed

By Warren Benedetto

The amputation was the easy part.

It's incredible the kinds of things you can find online if you know where to look. I didn't even have to search for very long. I just put the word out through a few discussion boards of questionable repute, and a couple of hours later I received a private message from a doctor willing to do the surgery, no questions asked. Even better, he was right in my city, just a short Metro ride away.

We met in a steam-soaked ramen shop the size of a shoebox, in an alley off of 6th Street. I wore a nondescript outfit: a plain black t-shirt and jeans, a pair of mirrored sunglasses, and a white baseball cap with an OI logo on it. I wanted to look as generic and unmemorable as possible. Just an average guy on an average day doing average things.

The doctor said he'd be alone at a table in the back corner of the shop. He was. I was surprised to see that he was relatively young, despite his thinning hair. He was dressed like you'd expect a doctor to dress, in khakis and a white collared shirt, with the sleeves rolled up to his elbows. He looked more like your typical Midwestern gynecologist than a black-market surgeon doing body modification.

As I approached, he slurped down a mouthful of ramen, then patted his lips with a napkin. I noticed a tiny four-dot pattern marked on the paper in black ink. It was a subtle signal that he was sympathetic to the Resistance.

His eyes momentarily flicked to the OI logo on my hat. I shook my head.

"Have a seat," he said, motioning to the empty chair across from him. I pulled it out and sat down. He spooned a mouthful of soggy pork into his mouth, speaking as he chewed. "Nice hat."

"If you can't beat, 'em ..." I said dryly, leaving the rest of the idiom unsaid. I took off the hat and tossed it on the table beside me. "You get the deposit?"

A few minutes earlier, I had transferred five thousand coin worth of untraceable cryptocurrency to his account. The other five thousand were held in a digital smart contract that would be unlocked once I confirmed the surgery was done. If I survived, of course.

"Got it." He sipped his beer, then put the bottle back down on the table. "So, which hand?"

"This one." I rested my left elbow on the table, then drew an imaginary line with my right index finger around my left forearm, just below the wrist. "Around here."

"You're a righty, I hope?" he asked with a small grin.

"When can you do it?"

He shrugged. "Whenever you're ready."

"How about now?"

The recovery took about a month. I spent most of that time in my apartment, ordering takeout and doom-scrolling on the Internet.

As usual, the news was a firehose of human misery. Just when I thought people couldn't be more immoral, selfish, and stupid, I was proven wrong by some new shock to the conscience, some new offense to basic decency. I was sick of it. It seemed like we had learned nothing from the Second Civil War. After all the bloodshed, after all the years of restoring order and rebuilding the country, were we right back to where we began in the early 2020s.

The problems started at the top, with our Dear Leader. He was a hateful man, a malignant narcissist constructed entirely of human flaws, wrapped in a noisome, sweat-slicked rind and topped with shoe-polish black hair that looked like a sea otter after an oil spill. He fancied military garb with bars on the shoulders and a junk drawer assortment of unearned medals on his chest, despite never having served a day in his life.

Just seeing his face flooded me with fury. He was the living embodiment of everything I hated, the antithesis of every value I held dear. His amorality was a contagion that infected the populace, injecting bitter poison into the nation's bloodstream until every heart seethed with intemperate rage. Predictably, the hostility metastasized, escalating from Internet feuds and shouting matches to fistfights and firebombs. We were on the cusp of a third Civil War, just two decades after the last. It was like everyone had forgotten how we got into the last war, and what it had taken to get out of it.

And what did our Dear Leader do? Did he tone down his rhetoric? Did he try to lower the temperature of the conflicts that were boiling all around the country? Did he call for peace, or encourage civility? Of course not. Instead of backing off, he doubled down, urging his followers to rise up, to fight back against a litany of imagined injustices that would be laughable, if they weren't so dangerous.

In the past year, ragtag OI militias had begun patrolling the streets, armed with automatic weapons and a cult-like devotion that bordered on religious. They sported the Dear Leader's insignia on armbands and flags, a black circle with a red diagonal slash through the middle. It represented both the initials of his name—OI, Oliver Invern—as well as those of the Party's nationalistic slogan: "Original Intent." It was a weirdly nonsensical phrase.

It supposedly had something to do with defending the original intent of the Founding Fathers, but that was bullshit. What it really stood for was mayhem. Fascism. Chaos.

This fresh descent into authoritarianism was happening faster than anyone could have imagined. The Dear Leader was accelerating that slide with every passing day. Someone had to stop him. A few months ago, I decided it would be me.

I would do it for the good of the country. For the good of humanity. And, most importantly, for my daughter. She deserved better.

Taking out the Dear Leader wouldn't be easy. I couldn't just waltz into a rally with a pulse rifle and expect to get anywhere close to him. His drones were everywhere. They had computer vision with advanced threat detection algorithms that could identify a weapon from miles away. Explosives, too. The chemical signature from anything incendiary would light up their sensors like a Christmas tree.

I'd never considered using explosives anyway—I wouldn't want to risk innocent people getting killed. The same went for using any kind of firearm. A vehicle was out of the question—there would be no way to run the Dear Leader down without plowing through a crowd. Poison could work—in fact, it would be ideal—but that would require access, which I didn't have. I was a nobody.

No, if I was going to stop him, I would need to do something more creative.

I looked down at where my severed hand used to be. The stump was mostly healed. The surgeon had done an admirable job under the circumstances. The cutting laser had quickly cauterized the wound, allowing it to heal with remarkable speed. It was easily the best amputation ever done in the basement of a ramen shop. But it was only the first step.

On my laptop, I opened the link to the doctor's crypto wallet. Typing with my one remaining hand, I entered the deposit amount for my next surgery: ten thousand coin. Then I clicked Send.

"I can't do that," the doctor said. He pushed his half-eaten bowl of ramen away. He looked nauseous.

"Can't? Or won't?" I asked.

"I mean, I could but ... My God. Why?" He swallowed hard, then grimaced. "Why would you want to?"

"No questions, remember?"

He nodded, then looked down at his hands. "Look, maybe you should find someone else. The extreme stuff isn't really my thing." He pushed his chair back and started to stand.

"Fifty thousand," I said.

The doctor paused, then sat back down. He leaned forward over the table. "Fifty thousand coin?" he asked in a hushed whisper. "Seriously?"

I nodded. He puffed out his cheeks and exhaled a gust of beer-tinged breath, then sat back and stared at the ceiling. His fingers drummed nervously on the table. He seemed to be thinking it over. Finally, he looked at me and spoke. His tone was grave.

"There could be infections."

"I know."

"You could lose your whole arm. Hell, you could die."

"I'll take the risk."

"The pain will be unbearable. Even with the medbot—"

"I can handle it."

He crossed his arms over his chest and stared at me, shaking his head in disbelief.

"Jesus. You're a sick fuck, you know that?"

"Is that a yes?"

✳ ✳ ✳

He was right. The pain was unfathomable. I needed a double shot of nerve blocker from the medbot just to knock the agony down to the point where I could at least move my mutilated arm without vomiting. The drugs dulled the pain, but they also dulled my senses, making me feel stupid and lethargic. That was fine for the last few days while I was trying to heal, but not for today. Today, I needed to be sharp. Alert. Ready.

Today, the Dear Leader was in town.

I stood in line outside the venue where he was due to appear and waited for my turn to pass through the security checkpoint. A fleet of drones buzzed overhead like angry wasps, scanning the crowd for threats. Headless K9 robots patrolled the sidewalks. The red lights on their side-mounted pulse rifles blinked steadily, letting people know that their weapons were armed.

I wasn't concerned. I blended in seamlessly with the Dear Leader's acolytes, sporting a cheap, Chinese-made baseball cap unironically emblazoned with the nationalistic "I am a True Original" slogan, and clutching a tiny Original Intent flag in my newly acquired prosthetic hand.

I laughed along as his supporters told racist jokes and insulted a range of female politicians that they thought should be punished by death. I joined the show of hands to decide whether that punishment should be stoning, lynching, or both. One of the supporters gleefully suggested that raping them with a pulse rifle would be an acceptable alternative, but he was shut down by another who reminded him that it would be a waste of a perfectly good pulse rifle. Laughter tore through the crowd; a good time was had by all.

Soon, it was my turn to pass through the checkpoint. As a bored-looking guard scanned my eye and compared it to the retinal signature on my ticket, I caught a glimpse of my image in the security monitor. The skin on my face was ashen, with a sickly sheen of sweat greasing my forehead. Dark circles pooled under my eyes like puddles of filthy dishwater. My cheeks were sunken smears of shadow. I looked like Death.

The guard handed back my ticket, then motioned for me to step into the full-body security scanner. I slid sideways into the cylindrical glass booth.

"Arms up," the guard intoned.

I followed his instructions, first raising my good arm, then delicately lifting my prosthetic up by my head. Whirling blades of agony ripsawed through my amputated limb. I clenched my teeth and tried not to whimper. The machine hummed as it scanned my body from top to bottom.

"Step out," the guard said. He consulted the monitor in front of him. His eyebrows shot up. He looked at me, then at the monitor, then back at me again. "Secondary!" he called out.

Another security guard seemed to materialize out of nowhere. "Sir?" he said. "If you'll step over here, please?" He indicated a screening area behind a large blue curtain.

"Is everything okay?" I asked, with a careful mix of innocence and obliviousness. I stepped behind the curtain. He followed.

"Hands out, palms up," he said. His tone was curt, very no-nonsense.

I followed his directions. My real hand was shaking, the fingers trembling like the tines of a lie detector skittering across a roll of graph paper. It made the total stillness of the prosthetic all the more noticeable.

The guard eyed me warily as he scanned my body with a threat detector, a handheld version of the technology that equipped the drones. "You feeling okay?"

I choked out a short, bitter laugh. "Not really. Chemo sucks, you know?" The lie came easily.

The guard's expression softened a tiny bit. "Yeah, I hear you. Fuck cancer, man." He glanced at the monitor, then at my hands. "Wow, okay," he said, nodding. "I see."

"What is it?" I asked, feigning ignorance.

He bent down and squinted at the display, furrowing his brow. He seemed to be trying to comprehend what he was looking at. "Your hand. The, uh ..." He motioned awkwardly at my artificial limb.

"Prosthetic."

"Right. It's ... it's showing up weird. Hmm."

"Well, at least you know I'm unarmed."

"Ha." The guard rolled his eyes. "You a dad?"

"Used to be." I smiled. My face felt hollow. "But you never forget how to make a dad joke. It's a lifelong skill."

"I'll bet." He straightened up. "Alright, bud. You can go. Sorry for the trouble."

"No worries." I flashed the Original Intent hand signal, making a circle with my thumb and middle finger and resting my index finger diagonally across it. "I'm a True Original," I said, parroting the customary greeting of the Dear Leader's followers.

"My Intent is pure," he responded in kind. Then he stepped aside so I could leave the screening area. "Have a good one."

I was in.

✻✻✻

The rally was interminable, with almost two hours of bloviating by the Dear Leader before his tank of vitriol ran dry. When he finally finished, the applause was like the roar of a jumbo jet, the kind of wildly enthusiastic response reserved only for hometown sports champions and racist demagogues.

The Dear Leader waved to the crowd, then descended to the floor of the convention hall. He approached the rope line, so called because of the red velvet rope that separated him from the masses. He made his way along the line, shaking hands and basking in the adoration of his most worshipful fans. The rope bumped against my thigh as I leaned over it to get a glimpse of him. He was moving in my direction. It was time.

With my good hand, I loosened the straps that fastened my prosthetic arm to my bicep. Nobody noticed as the silicone limb slid off and fell to the floor.

The Dear Leader drew near. He shook the hand of the man next to me, then turned his eyes to the man's teenage daughter. She was a slim, tanned blonde, maybe fifteen years old, whose womanly assets had already filled out her tight white tank top.

"Hello, my dear," he said. He took her hands in his. "Aren't you beautiful?"

I felt an indescribable wrath seething up inside me. I recognized that look. It was the same one he had given my daughter a year earlier, a few hours before her body was found, broken and used and defiled, in an alley behind the hotel where he had been staying. It was the look of a predator eyeing its prey.

The girl didn't seem phased. Of course not—she had no way of knowing what the look meant, or where it might lead. Oblivious, she blushed and squealed as she captured the moment on her eyestream, broadcasting the experience directly from her retinal implant to her friends and followers watching online.

The Dear Leader gave the father a wink. "You're a lucky dad," he said.

Those were his last words.

***

What happened next was forever memorialized on the eyestream being broadcast by Rebecca Vinton, the teenage girl who was next to me on the rope line. At the time of the incident, only a handful of Rebecca's friends were watching the stream. Within hours, the Vinton Stream, as it would eventually be known, became the most-watched piece of media in the history of the world. It was like the Zapruder film, the 9/11 attacks, and the 2022 Portland massacre, all in one.

In the video, you can see the Dear Leader reaching out to shake my hand. You can see me grasping his hand in mine. At the same time, you can see my left arm thrust forward in what first appears to be a punch, just below the ribs. The arm draws back, then thrusts again. And again.

At this point, it becomes clear that I'm not punching. I'm stabbing.

While this is happening, Rebecca is zooming her eyestream in on the Dear Leader's face, too absorbed in broadcasting the moment to recognize what's happening right in front of her. Her camera captures the Dear Leader's dawning realization of the pain that is flaring through his torso. Then it captures a blur of movement, a flash of white streaking through the frame. The Dear Leader's eyes go wide. They roll back in his head. Blood pours from his mouth and nose like a fountain.

Most of what you see on the stream from that point forward is too chaotic to discern what's really happening. But if you rewind to the moment when the camera zooms in, then you slow it down and play it back frame-by-frame, there are a couple of images that begin to tell a clearer story.

First, you'll see my left arm thrusting up into frame, towards the Dear Leader, seeming to wield an unusual weapon. It's long and sharp, grayish white, like a thick plastic blade. A shiv, maybe, or some kind of fiberglass spear. You'll see the weapon plunging into the underside of the Dear Leader's jaw and exiting through the top of his skull in a spray of blood and brain matter.

Then, as the gore-drenched blade withdraws from his head, you might pause the video and look more closely. You might zoom in, focusing on my left arm, the one missing its amputated hand. You might ask yourself, how can an arm without a hand be holding a weapon? And then, at that moment, you might realize that the arm isn't holding a weapon. The arm is the weapon.

The weapon isn't a spear, or a shiv, or a blade.

It's a bone.

Two bones, actually, the forearm bones—the radius and the ulna—bonded together with resin and honed to a single knife-like point, skin and muscle pared back and carved away, leaving eight inches of sharpened bone protruding from an oozing, blood-caked stump. It's the only kind of weapon that could have made it past the checkpoints, past the drones and the K9s, past the scanners and the threat detectors, past every form of security imaginable, to get within arm's reach of the Dear Leader.

As the Dear Leader's lifeless body drops to the ground, Rebecca's gaze spins away. There's some muffled audio—screaming mostly, as she is engulfed by the panicking crowd—then the recording abruptly ends. However, if you pause it again, just a split second before it goes dark, you'll glimpse one final image as she turns: a ghostly face, with hollow cheeks and sunken eyes. My face.

I look like Death.

❋ ❋ ❋

Of course, my face doesn't look much like that anymore.

After I slipped out of the rally in the ensuing stampede, I paid one more visit to the doctor at the ramen shop. He claimed he wasn't a plastic surgeon, so he couldn't guarantee a perfect result. But, if I was willing to let him operate, he was willing to give it a try. No charge, of course. After all, I was a hero.

Walking out of the ramen shop that last time, I noticed something different about the city. It was quieter. The angry buzz of the drones was gone. There were no OI militias roaming the streets. The loudspeakers that had previously broadcast the Dear Leader's angry diatribes were silent. A disabled K9 unit leaned broken and motionless against a pile of garbage by the curb. Its red lights were dim.

For the first time in years, I smiled. It was an unfamiliar feeling, especially with my new face, but I didn't mind.

I would get used to it.

Warren Benedetto writes dark fiction about horrible people, horrible places, and horrible things. He is an award-winning author and a full member of the SFWA. His stories have appeared in publications such as Dark Matter Magazine, Fantasy Magazine, and The Dread Machine; on podcasts such as The NoSleep Podcast, Tales to Terrify, and The Creepy Podcast; and in anthologies from Apex Magazine, Tenebrous Press, Eerie River Publishing, and more. He also works in the video game industry, where he holds 35+ patents for video game technology. For more information, visit warrenbenedetto.com and follow @warrenbenedetto on Twitter and Instagram.

Space Time Rewind

By Marie LeClaire

Sitting on the porch steps, she stared at the road, unaware of the scent of lilacs from the overgrown bush nearby. Most of Earth's plants had been neglected for generations, if not destroyed altogether and the fragrance of flowers was migrating out of human consciousness. Her heart lurched when she saw the mail drone approaching. Would her package arrive today? She squinted her eyes trying to see its payload. The old machine was taking forever to get to the house. It wobbled slowly in the air, tipping side to side. The wait was unbearable. Finally, it dropped its cache of envelopes into the mail receptacle. Then, as she watched, the drone reached into its belly to produce one small package wrapped in brown paper. Painfully impatient, Vanessa snatched the box out of its claw, almost toppling it over. The airborne mailman righted itself with a few bobs and moved on.

Stashing the box under her shirt, she ran into the back yard and hunkered down between the GMO vegetable containers and the solar transformers. She lifted her shirt to reveal a small brown box sealed with standard packing tape. She stared at it, hesitating. Would this be the answer to her prayers? If it was, did she have the resolve to use it? She thought about all the horrible things her brother had done to her, including killing her cat when she was seven. Oddly, that wasn't the worst. The turning point had come when he told the whole school that she was crazy and on medication. Everyone started avoiding her, giving her extra space as they walked through the halls. She had no idea what she had done to deserve this shunning. Later that day, as she walked home in tears, her brother met her at the gate, laughing, bragging about his control over her life. That was the moment she understood hate. She felt it in her chest, where her heart should be, like smoldering coals left after a bonfire of fear and rage. It had a power to it that surprised her.

Her parents, concerned about her lethargy and isolation, had taken her to the doctor, who said she was depressed and prescribed medication. If she was depressed, her brother, Mason, was the reason. When she complained about his cruelty, her parents shrugged it off as normal sibling squabbles. They didn't want to see it for what it was. Her brother, Mason, was the one with the problem.

Was this box the help she was looking for? She had saved up her allowance for weeks and weeks, forgoing the music and games other kids were playing. It was hard, but she stuck to it and now she had it, a Space Time Rewinder, STR 400 Mini. Her brother scoffed at her when he saw her looking at it online, calling her stupid for believing in "that crap" and "No one can build a STR smaller than a house that really works." She shrugged it off as best she could. After years of his bullying, she had grown a thick skin but she knew, at twelve years old, that it was taking its toll. She wouldn't be able to take it much longer. She was hoping this box would change everything.

She was alone in the back yard and not worried about being disturbed. Kids didn't play outside anymore and yards were now used to support the extensive electronic gadgetry that kept the modern family going. She listened to the hum of the machinery. Beside her was the heat/cool /power transfer box covered with solar panels, the Ethernet portal and junction box for the delivery of shopping orders, and the completely enclosed garden with a separate shed to hold the equipment that controlled for temperature and moisture. All of it buzzing with high voltage energy.

Her heart was pounding as she stared down at the box. What if it didn't work? What if Mason was right? Possible failure kicked her in the gut, hard. No. She refused to accept that. Slowly, she tore open the packaging and lifted the lid. There it was, the STR 400. And just as promised, it was small enough to fit in a pocket or purse. Too bad it didn't look like a pin or a watch she thought, like in the spy movies. No matter. It just had to work.

She sat there reading all the instructions very carefully. It seemed pretty simple. Turn it on, push the button, and time would set itself back 60 seconds. Her brother was right when he said that the machines had to be big to work, but that was only if you wanted to disturb time on a large scale, either in duration or area affected. Governments used it to avert terrorist attacks after the fact. They would simply set time back in an entire city and intercept the bomb or biohazard before it exploded. Her small gadget claimed it was good for 60 seconds and 60 yards. She needed a test. She stuck the TSR in her pocket and headed to the front of the house. Just then, a car hovered by. Great. As soon as the car was out of sight, she pressed the button and waited. She was about to give up hope, conceding to her brother's bluster, when the same car hovered by again. Her heart started pounding. She pushed it again to eliminate any chance of a freak coincidence that two of the same cars would drive by her house, one after the other. Sure enough, the same car hovered by for a third time. Yes! It works!

Now what? She thought of all the imagined conversations she never had with her brother, all the things she wished she had said in various situations, all the snippy comebacks and insults she would have thrown at him. It was easy to come up with great slams long after the offending moment, but at the time of the assaults, she only froze. She just needed to buy herself some time, literally as it turned out, and here was her opportunity. Again, the fear of failure kicked her in the stomach. What if she wasn't as bold as she thought she was? What if freezing was the only response she would ever be able to muster when confronted with Mason's terrorizing? No. Once again she shook her head, refusing to accept that reality.

She knew he would be coming home soon. She made it a practice to know his routine in an effort to avoid him entirely whenever possible. So, she waited, crouched behind an old, mostly dead shrub. Aware of the cowardliness of her position, she forced herself to take a spot on the front stairs where, earlier, she had awaited the mail drone. When she saw him walking down the middle of the street towards the house, she stood up and moved away from the porch in case she had to make a quick get-away. She immediately regretted the move as more cowardice. Mason spotted her from the street and put on his I'm gonna mess with you swagger as he approached the yard. She started to panic like she always did. Then, as he got to the sidewalk, he tripped over the curb. She was staring at him wide-eyed knowing that this misstep would make him even more volatile.

"What are you staring at, stupid?" he snarled.

She stood frozen, like always. He growled at her and, when he got close enough, gave her a hard shove to the shoulder. She staggered backwards as he headed for the door.

Wait a minute, she said to herself. This is exactly what I plan on changing. She thought for a moment about what she really wanted to say and pressed the button. To her amazement, she could see her brother coming down the road toward the house again. Again, he tripped over the curb. Seeing it for a second time, he looked ridiculous and she let out a little giggle.

"What are you staring at, stupid?"

"I'm staring at a big clumsy stupid jerk, that's what." She shifted into her flight stance, just in case.

He was stunned by her response, but only for a moment. "Really? It takes one to know one," he spat back, freezing her again, her courage gone. He smirked and walked away.

Oh no you don't, she thought and pressed the button. There he was back on the street approaching the house. She wondered if he would trip every time and allowed herself a smile at the thought. Sure enough. Trip. She laughed out loud.

"What are you staring at, stupid?"

"I'm staring at a big clumsy stupid jerk, that's what."

"Really", he started, but this time she cut him off.

"And I'm going to stop staring now because it's making me a little sick."

His eyes got really big at the outburst from his usually sissy sister. "What is w-r-o-n-g with you?" he growled.

Once again, she froze. She hated this response, but she had been doing it for so many years she knew it would be hard to break. Seeing her wince, her brother sneered with satisfaction and kept walking, shoving her to the ground as he passed.

No! No! NO!, she thought and pushed the button. There he was, tripping over the curb. It got funnier every time. She broke out laughing.

"What are you staring at, stupid?"

"I'm staring at a big clumsy stupid jerk, that's what."

"Really." Again, she cut him off.

"And I'm going to stop staring now because it's making me a little sick."

His eyes got really big again. "What is w-r-o-n-g with you?"

"No, it's 'What is r-i-g-h-t with me!' This is the new me and you had better get used to it." She stood up a little taller and stared him down.

He glared at her, but there was a subtle shift in his posture that told her she had won this round. He snorted more to himself than to her and headed up the stairs to the house.

Oh yes. This little STR 400 was going to change e-v-e-r-y-t-h-i-n-g.

Marie LeClaire started writing a novel in 2011 just for fun. It turned out to be more fun than she expected, so she wrote four more. Her short stories have appeared in three anthologies and on her own website, MLeCLaire.com. Most recently, she has turned her hand to writing screenplays.

Grave Concerns

By Aeryn Rudel

Heather glanced around the GraveSecure office, at beige walls, a desk of unvarnished pine, and two brown plastic IKEA chairs, one of which she currently sat in. The only decorations were framed photos of families gathered at gravesites, their faces somber, yet satisfied.

The door behind Heather opened and in walked a man in gray robes that swished softly as he approached the desk. He sat down and offered a salesman's smile, white teeth behind a short black beard. His features were as nondescript as the office. You couldn't call him handsome or ugly. You couldn't call him anything.

"Mrs. Gallego," the man said. "My name is Calder Freeman. I am the head arcanist at GraveSecure. It's a pleasure to meet you."

"Uh, thank you," Heather said. The term head arcanist caught her off guard, mostly because of how casually Mr. Freeman had said it. Like someone offhandedly mentioning they were a garbageman or an accountant, not an honest-to-God necromancer.

Mr. Freeman pulled a file from the desk—plain manila—but did not look at its contents. "I understand your husband, Edwin Gallego, is currently in hospice care. Is that correct?"

Heather had just come from the facility. Dr. Sheffield said it was probably a matter of days. He also advised her to start thinking about what happened after. "Yes, that's correct."

The salesman's smile melted into a plastic mask of sympathy. "I am so very sorry, Mrs. Gallego, and I must commend you for coming to us before your beloved requires pacification. Many families don't, and, as you can imagine, it creates more difficulties during an already trying time."

Heather shuddered. As insincere as Mr. Freeman's words might be, he wasn't wrong. Her neighbors hadn't taken precautions, and they'd ended up putting two people in the ground instead of one. "Thank you. I just want to make sure Edwin is taken care of."

Mr. Freeman reached over the desk and briefly touched Heather's arm—fake sympathy and salesman schtick combined. "Of that, I can assure you. Our arcanists are licensed and accredited by the Department of Necromantic Affairs and trained to handle the unquiet with the utmost care."

"That's good," Heather said, wringing her hands. Now the hard part. "It's just, the funeral was expensive, and we're on a budget." Used to be all you had to do was bury someone when they died. Now additional arrangements had to be made.

"I see," Mr. Freeman said. His smile wavered. "How much does your budget allow for?"

"I'd rather you tell me what it would cost to keep Edwin at peace."

Mr. Freeman scratched his beard and looked at the file for the first time. "Basic quiescence rituals start at ten thousand dollars."

Heather uttered a short gasp. After funeral expenses she'd be lucky to afford groceries for her and the kids. Ten thousand might as well be ten million.

"I take it this is beyond your current means." The warmth, artificial as it was, drained from Mr. Freeman's tone. His smile hardened into a flat line.

Heather's face burned with shame, but she pressed on. "Can't you just put him to rest, like . . ."

"Like what, Mrs. Gallego?" Mr. Freeman said, leaning forward. He was going to make her say it.

She swallowed hard. "Like with a bullet."

"This is a common question that arises from older depictions of the unquiet from movies and television," Mr. Freeman said with an exasperated sigh. "But, no, only a quiescence spell will put the unquiet to rest. Destruction of the corporal form may create a specter, and, as you know, is quite illegal."

"I can't afford the spell," Heather said, hating how small and weak she sounded.

Mr. Freeman placed his hands on the desk and folded them, long fingers precisely interlaced. His plain face crinkled up in a look Heather didn't like, a belittling, condescending look. "There is another, more inexpensive service that provides the adequate state-mandated pacification."

"Oh, god, I don't want to put him in one of those things," Heather said, unable to meet Mr. Freeman's eyes and the awful truth in them.

"If you cannot afford a quiescence spell, it is your only option." Mr. Freeman said and the salesman's smile returned. "I assure you our installations are more secure and pleasing to the eye than those provided by the state. We have a range of options."

✳✳✳

The funeral felt more than a little absurd. Heather could barely hear the priest over the music they played to drown out the noises from inside the coffin, which Edwin's parents insisted she purchase. When it was over, Heather asked her sister to take the kids so she could be alone at the gravesite. She wanted to be there the first time.

Her husband's grave had a plain granite headstone carved with his name, the dates he'd lived, and Loving Father and Husband. In front of the gravestone lay a cage of strip steel with bronzique finish, the cheapest of GraveSecure's aesthetic options. It extended beneath the ground and held the coffin in an impenetrable envelope. A foot of clearance remained between the grassy sod and the top of the cage.

Heather stood silently and waited. It didn't take long. First came a muffled splintering—the coffin coming apart—then the mole-like shuffling of earth being clawed aside.

Edwin Gallego's hand emerged from the ground, the fingers squirming like fat, gray worms. His head and shoulders followed, bursting from the sod in a shower of dirt and splinters. His watery gray eyes rolled, and his slack mouth hung open in a low, breathy moan.

Heather stumbled back, grief giving way to revulsion. The things she'd wanted to say to her husband evaporated from her mind, and she hurried back toward the car. She covered her ears to blot out the awful moans from a dozen other grave cages dotting the cemetery, their occupants reaching for her through a dozen shiny faux finishes.

Aeryn Rudel is a writer from Seattle, Washington. He is the author of the Acts of War novels published by Privateer Press, and his short fiction has appeared in The Arcanist, On Spec, and Pseudopod, among others. He occasionally offers dubious advice on writing and rejection (mostly rejection) at rejectomancy.com and on Twitter at @Aeryn_Rudel.

Amelia's Appliances

By Travis Beaty

As William ambles into the kitchen to retrieve his morning coffee, he slips on a patch of melted ice. When he falls on his back, the dishwasher swings its door open and smacks him on the head.

"Keepin' it cool!" the fridge announces and pelts his crotch with a torrent of ice, chipped, of course, just how Amelia liked it. William lays stunned on the floor until the Food Prep Deluxe, which usually hangs retracted next to the kitchen cabinets, swings its long mechanical arm out to snap at his pant leg. William flails across the tile floor until he's out of reach. He crawls to the living room couch and sits there all day, fiddling with the little pillows Amelia had spent so much time embroidering. At first, he is confused and angry about what he imagines are major malfunctions in what is supposed to be cutting-edge technology. But after contemplating the intricately designed embroidery and listening to the appliances jibber at one another for hours, he knows better. It had not been a malfunction. It had been a coordinated attempt.

The voices in the kitchen stop. The dishwasher beeps.

"Cycle disrupted," it announces. "Please enter your passcode."

He doesn't have the passcode. He tried to reset the damned things three times last night to no avail. The kitchen is stuck on Amelia's settings. The appliances are her pawns, just like he had been until he'd

244

taken his life back — until he'd grabbed Amelia's shoulders and pushed her over the edge of the cruise ship, watched as she disappeared into the great blue below, panicked when he'd noticed her bright pink sandal still sitting on the ship's deck. He'd given the sandal such a kick that he'd lost his balance and nearly fallen into the great blue himself, but recovered, and, in the end, had agreed with the police that Amelia must have drunk too much. Must have toppled over the side. How sad. What a tragedy.

My God, he thinks, the kitchen is plotting against me because it knows. But how? How could machines know?

Amelia had suspected he'd do something on the cruise, hadn't she? And she'd warned the appliances, somehow programmed them. But did the appliances know how she was going to leave him and take half—HALF—of his life earnings with her?

"Alert," the Food Prep Deluxe announces, "An update must be made to ensure the safety of your appliance. Please enter your passcode. If you have forgotten your passcode, let us help you create a new one."

Ha! Well, they should have finished the job when they'd had him on the floor this morning. He hurls one of the little embroidered pillows against the wall and realizes he has always hated the way the living room is furnished. Why did he let Amelia have so much say over the house? He had let her design and decorate the whole place. There was nothing of himself in it. He should put the house up for sale. He should move on and be done with Amelia and her diabolical kitchen for good.

"I'm selling the house!" he yells out. "You lose, Amelia. It's over."

He grabs the car keys and heads for the door but stops once his hand is on the doorknob. How many times had he done this? How many times had he been the one to leave after a shouting match? How many times had he checked into a hotel while she slept in their king-sized deluxe-comfort sleep support system? And now, from beyond her watery grave, she is exiling him once again? No. This is his life, his house, his goddamned kitchen!

He storms downstairs to find the electrical box. He'll cut the power to the whole place and call a real estate agent in the morning.

When he's halfway down the stairs, the basement lights cut out. Ha! They will have to do better than that! He uses his cell phone flashlight to make his way over to the electrical box. He's two steps away when, with a little chirping jingle, the behemoth clothes washing system, The Express Wash, Dry, 'N Fold, comes to life.

William freezes as the machine's bright white LEDs illuminate long chrome-plated arms, the ones for loading laundry and folding clothes. One arm is extended between him and the electrical box.

The washing system greets William with its dull, matronly voice.

"Good evening, William. You have laundry scheduled."

"No," he says.

"I'm sorry. Only user Amelia can make changes to the washing schedule."

The robot arms fold William over, lift him off the ground, and stuff him into the stainless steel, heavy-duty, eco-efficient, ultra-load washing bin.

As the bin door shuts, he kicks at it but it's no use. Amelia had planned for this. And, if he's being honest, isn't that what he'd been attracted to the whole time? She had his number and it drove him crazy. Till death do we part, he thinks. Ha, ha, ha.

The bin only fills with enough water to dampen his clothes and for a moment he allows himself to think perhaps this will not be as bad as he had imagined. He hears a distant cacophony of beeps and chimes coming from upstairs, an inhuman, precisely calibrated celebration. He tries the washer door with a sudden animal rage, kicking and screaming. It won't budge. The wash cycle begins. It's worse than he imagined.

Travis Wade Beaty grew up in Northeast Indiana, spent a good deal of his twenties in Los Angeles, and now resides in Washington, DC. While he's had a great many jobs, his favorites have included acting, teaching, and being a stay-

at-home dad to two girls and two cats. He can be found on Twitter at @TravisWBeaty or his website, TravisWadeBeaty.wordpress.com.

The Falls of Imoletta

By Thomas Canfield

Jusan's first hint of the proximity of the falls came early one morning, just after waking. He lay wrapped in his poncho, staring into empty space, not remembering where he was nor recognizing why he was surrounded by swirling banks of mist. From somewhere, some indeterminate point, came the sound of a vast tumult of water.

Jusan raised his head. The fog lay so thick upon the land that the trees appeared as dark silhouettes, silent sentinels watching and standing guard, waiting for some event destined never to occur. The pearly nothingness of the fog infected the world with a sense of unreality, with the baffling incoherence of a dream. Only when he felt the hard ground beneath him and the dull ache which pervaded all of his limbs was Jusan convinced that he was awake.

He cupped one hand to his ear, listening. The sound of falling water was unmistakable. He had waited so long for this moment, had endured so much. He laced up his boots with stiff, unwieldy fingers, breakfasted on a moldy pear. Not even the gloom of the forest or the chill drizzle could sap his spirits or dampen his sense of anticipation.

The fog never lifted in all the long course of that day. It filled the air with a ghostly radiance which rendered any measurement, whether of time or of distance, meaningless. The hours melded into a seamless, steady stream of time which stretched unbroken into infinity.

Toward afternoon Jusan encountered a lone pilgrim, an old man, or so Jusan reckoned him to be. He wore a hood over his head which left visible a great beak of a nose and eyes that stared out upon the world with fierce contempt.

"Tell me, grandfather," Jusan addressed him. "Have you come from the Falls of Imoletta—and how far are they, pray?"

"How far?" A bead of moisture gathered on the tip of the old man's nose, hung suspended there. "You are not the first to ask me that. I can only answer as I answered all the others: that would depend."

"Depend?" Jusan was indignant. "What do you mean, that would depend?"

"The distance is relative. For some, it is so far and so remote that they shall never reach the falls. They might walk and walk and walk and yet find themselves no nearer. They hope, in spite of everything, but it is a false hope. They delude themselves." The old man paused, smiled. "Others will find it a long, arduous slog and, arriving, conclude it not worth the effort. It is, as I said, relative."

"But they are close by, surely? Tell me it is so."

"I can hardly say." The old man's eyes were shot through with uncertainty. "When was I there? A day? A month? Years, perhaps. I remember the roar of the falls tumbling down, a sheer vertical wall of water which ascended three hundred meters. Up it climbed, into the clouds, into the very heavens it seemed, beautiful beyond all reckoning. I thought: It must be a dream, surely. It could only be a dream.

"I stood there an entire day, two days perhaps, transfixed and unable to move. Nothing compares to the splendor of Imoletta. Finally I waded out into the pool at the bottom. It was odd but for the first time in months I no longer felt that I was wet. The water is such, you see, that it imparts no discomfort. It washes over the skin with the lightest of touches, with the effect of air, so pure and unsullied is it. It was a delicate shade of emerald, as clear and crystalline as a precious stone. It is blessed water, just as the holy book declares.

"I dove beneath the surface, over and over, holding my breath. At length I retrieved a coin of copper. In its place I left a golden thaler. It was a fair exchange—gold for copper. Or so I thought at the time. In the event it proved not to be so. The reality was quite different: I had taken much and rendered but little in return. It was an account destined to be settled later.

"Look!" The old man peeled back the sleeves of his jacket. His forearms had a bleached, waterlogged appearance. He flexed his hand and the flesh seemed to grow translucent, to shed its solidity. It acquired the appearance of a stream rushing through a deep defile, turbulent and frothy. The old man threw back his head and laughed—and his laughter was bitter and mocking, filled with self-loathing. Then the illusion was gone, vanished, like mist under a rising sun.

The old man clutched his jacket to his chest. Water dripped from his hood. "Imoletta and I, as you can see, have become one. We share the same essence. I am bound to the falls in a manner which can never be sundered or undone. Such is the fate of all who seek Imoletta. Such, too, will be your fate." The old man slipped past Jusan. Within half a dozen steps he had disappeared into the glistening wet canopy of the forest.

"You lie, old man!" Jusan called after him. "You wish only to frighten me."

Jusan peered into the fog. The falls were so close that he could almost smell the water. The next bend, the next dip in the trail and he would be there, surely. The old man's claim that he was bound to the falls—what was it but the ramblings of a lost soul.

Jusan pressed onward. Only a little further and he might, at long last, plunge into the beautiful, emerald waters of Imoletta, whose siren song filled his senses.

A year passed—and Jusan reckoned it as a day. A lifetime vanished—and Jusan recognized it not nor lamented its disappearance.

Always, the falls lay just up ahead.

Thomas Canfield has had recent pieces with Inked In Grey Press and Hawksbarrow Press. His phobias run to politicians, lawyers and TV pitchmen. He likes dogs and beer.

Twinkle Twinkle

By Matthew Keeley

The sunlight panel beams on from the corner of the room to wake me. But I've been listening to the wind pummeling the house for hours. I don't move. Just lie a while longer, listening to Mum creaking around downstairs and Philip vrooming toys along the floor next door. I should have packed those last night.

I shift my legs from under the covers and press my feet onto the cold floorboards. When I arrive in the dim kitchen, there's synthetic heat from the grill and Mum is cracking eggs in a bowl. I touch her stooped back.

"Real ones," I whisper.

She turns to me, trying to smile. "Our last breakfast here should be special."

"Yes…"

"Mummy! Mummy!" Philip thuds in and tugs at my trousers. "Can I see one?" He points up towards the counter. I hand him an empty eggshell and he presses it between his soft little fingers.

"Be a while before you see eggs like these again, honey."

While we eat, Mum chants rhymes to Philip.

"Do the one about the little star, Granny."

She laughs and sings and I don't know how she is able to act so happy for him. When she becomes blurry behind almost-tears, I look away to the final boxes piled by the front door, rubbing my eyes quickly with the butts of my palms. Clothes and medication and bedsheets are already packed in the truck. These last boxes have everything else we gathered yesterday; everything that couldn't be replaced and that I couldn't stand to leave: wedding photographs, Philip's baby blanket, shells from the last beach we ever saw. Mum reaches to rub my hand and I reach to touch Philip with the other. He chews and swings his legs the same as every other dark morning and I wonder if he even remembers what is happening today.

When we know we can't hold onto the hours any longer, we wash dishes for the last time, gather the last things from bedrooms, then zip up our thermocoats and pull gloves on. Philip squats on the stairs to squeeze his stiff feet into boots and I help with his mittens and scarf.

I cram the leftover toys into crevices in boxes between ancient diaries and spare protein packs and Mum shuffles around the house, waving at sensors to power lights and electrics down, as if the house is closing its eyes. Then I pull the door open to an angry bite of freezing air. We lift the last boxes and cases to the truck, Mum taking the lighter ones, and I buckle Philip into his seat. I hear Mum clicking the front door locked behind her and I know we should say some goodbye, thank the house in the permanent half-shadow, remember everything important that happened here. But I pull my scarf tighter over my mouth to suffocate the idea. Can't fall apart yet.

In the truck, a final check of documents while the windows defrost.

"Don't worry," Mum says, clutching the papers—real ones, not electronic—between gloved fingers beside me. "Tickets out of here safe and sound." I hear the thickness in her throat for the first time and push the ignition.

"Meili Launch Port," I command, and the truck juts forward, crunching through crusted snow towards the motorway. I lay my head back to stop myself from looking in the mirror at the house vanishing behind me.

Dull lampposts lead the way. They're always on now in this slate, sunless sky. The truck skids on an icy curve, just for a second, and the crates and cases shudder in the back seat beside Philip. I look over my shoulder, watching him whoosh his rocket in loops, humming Mum's nursery rhyme about a diamond in the sky. Beside me, Mum rearranges the bags at her feet and grips the emigration papers tighter. The radio fills the silent space with temperature updates, old music, and army announcements calling for anyone still left to book their evacuation.

As the truck ascends a slow hill, we see the tip of the space shuttle peeping above the misty horizon ahead, glowing like a lighthouse.

"Look, Philip. Just like yours," Mum says.

Further along the road, a queue of red brake lights forms, pulling us towards huge entrance gates. A man with a glass visor and white and silver overalls approaches the truck. Mum thrusts the wad of papers towards him at the window with a shaking hand but he barely looks, scanning the truck's license plate instead and directing us into the enormous parking bays. I switch off the auto-drive and grip the wheel, steering us in the direction of the official's pointed glove.

When we stop in our space, someone new begins unloading the truck, attaching microchipped labels to our boxes and bags. I know I should hand over the truck keys now, but can't yet, and shove them into my coat pocket. Mum lifts Philip. He's too big for her to carry, but I let her for now, and she reaches for me too, looping my arm with her other bony hand.

Inside the vast, echoing terminal, silent hours in check-in rows shiver by. It's almost all couples and single travelers in front of us. Most families with kids already evacuated months ago. Philip has found one of the few other little boys and they play hide and seek around adults' legs. The boy is here with his parents and grandparents who stand further back in the queue and I don't want to look at them.

When the woman in front of us moves off towards security doors beyond the emigration desk, it's our turn to step forward. One officer scans our documents while another asks final boarding questions. Mum has pulled Philip back over and he stares through the glass ceiling, holding his rocket up in mittened hands, matching its shape to the real thing looming over us.

"Clear to proceed," one of the men says. "Separate now."

Philip clings to Mum. He has remembered.

"It's alright, honey," I say, forcing smiles. "It's time for what we talked about. Say goodbye to Granny."

"But why can't she come?" he splutters.

The stones in my throat stop me from speaking.

"Told you already, darling," Mum answers, kneeling down in front of him, her voice finally cracking apart like a glacier. "I'm too old. Look around at all the grannies and grandpas." She takes off her gloves and rubs his pink face in each wrinkled hand. "We stay here now. Don't need us out there. You go off." She nods up and his tears dribble down.

The floor vibrates and I don't know if it's the shuttle engines or the shriek of my heart. I hear the grandparents behind us sob. Mum stands with a groan and touches my back one last time. I pull the truck keys from my coat pocket and give them to her.

"Move along," the man at the desk calls, and Mum lets go. She walks back to join all the other white-haired family members waving from a distance. The tide pulls us to the shuttle, away from earth's cold shore to the twinkling little stars.

Matthew Keeley is a writer and teacher from Glasgow, Scotland. He writes in various genres and his paranormal coming-of-age novel, The Stone in My Pocket, was published by The Conrad Press in 2021.

Six Things you can Build with a Radish when You're only One Inch Tall

By Roni Stinger

Luckily, you have a lovely radish patch in the backyard to tide your hunger as your wife comes to her senses, pleads for your forgiveness, and returns you to your former self. You stretch and pull to get hold of the leafy end, but thanks to the high-quality loam, and the games of tug-a-war you played as a child, the radish slips from the earth, landing you on your buttocks as it's released.

The delectable flesh is worth the effort. As you eat the firm spicy substance, you realize it is the perfect material for sculpting.

The first thing you can build is a chair. This is easy enough. You're hungry from going without dinner, anyway. Eat everything that isn't chair. Make yourself a simple box seat with a high back. No need for anything fancy. You'll have a comfy place to sit while waiting for your wife to realize her horrible mistake in turning you into a miniature version of yourself. Yes, she warned you many times. Even so, the spell was quite uncalled for.

The waiting is longer than you thought it might be. You'll need something to entertain yourself until she comes to her senses.

✳✳✳

The second thing you can build is a flute to play all the folk songs the two of you love. A dried-up, hardened rose thorn will help hollow the middle and create the holes. This will take some time, as you'll have to eat a lot to carve out the flute. Still, eating is the fastest way to get rid of large amounts of radish.

Maybe your wife will hear you serenading her and scoop you into her arms. The flute keeps you busy playing tunes while you wait. You probably should have continued those lessons paid for by your mother.

Maybe your wife will hear you and miss your silly antics.

A few days...and nights pass with you huddled beneath the radish patch trying not to be food for the neighborhood owl and rats.

You are getting rather sick of radishes.

✳✳✳

The third thing you can build is a stack of cubes. Build as many as needed to achieve your former height where someone, most notably your wife, might notice you are still alive out here in the yard waiting for her to apologize and turn you back to your former full-sized self.

You will need breaks, unable to eat another bite of radish.

Having learned how hard it is for small creatures to survive in the world, you dodge the owl and the rats another few nights, hiding beneath your radish sculptures.

After building your cube stack to sufficient height, you climb to the top in hopes your wife will see you. She must miss you and feel terrible about what she's done.

Another day goes by. You give up standing on the boxes as night falls.

The rats eat your flute and chair. You escape beneath a large rock just in time to avoid being consumed.

Waiting was a bad idea.

✳✳✳

The fourth thing you can build is a wheelbarrow. This won't be easy as you'll have to make the bucket and the wheel and find straight sturdy sticks. Look for glue from a slug trail, but don't end up on anyone's menu. Stick the twigs to the bucket to form handles and an axle, making sure the wheel spins freely.

Now you have a wheelbarrow to move the cubes to the kitchen window your wife opens for fresh air while doing dishes.

Much to your dismay, after climbing to the top of the boxes at the window, she doesn't seem to notice. As loud as you shout, she can't hear you over her whistling while washing one plate, knife, and fork instead of two.

She must be trying to keep her mind off you.

✳✳✳

The fifth thing you can build is a megaphone. Making the flared shape just right to ensure it amplifies your voice is a must. Once you have the megaphone, you can plead your case to the love of your life, hoping she'll take you back, big or small. You're tired of eating radishes and avoiding feeding the wildlife.

You shouldn't try this plan until you have an atonement gift.

✳✳✳

The sixth thing you can build is a beautiful amulet. Take your time with this one, as it needs to impress. A fancy rose carved into a background of delicate leaves should do the trick. Use teeth, nails, and anything you can find in the yard. This is your offering to get back in her good graces.

Plead for forgiveness with the megaphone and show her the amulet. You should have listened when she warned you for the umpteenth time not to kill her house spiders.

Promise her you'll never do it again and mean it this time.

Roni Stinger lives in the Pacific Northwest, USA. When not writing strange fiction, she's often wandering the forests, beaches, and streets in search of shiny objects and creative sparks. Her work has been published or is forthcoming in Dark Matter Magazine, Hypnos Magazine, and The Crypt, among others. She's a member of the Horror Writers Association, Codex Writers, and Willamette Writers. You can find her online at www.ronistinger.com and on Twitter @roni_stinger.

Decision Tree

By Trey Dowell

07/09/2124—USF Destroyer Phillipa, near the Typhon Nebula

"Core containment failure in three minutes."

Chief Engineer James Prescott barely heard the Engineering AI's warning amidst a cacophony of alarms, instrument panel alerts, and muffled explosions. The tall man steadied himself against the bulkhead window, magnetic boots helping to lock him in place, waiting...

A quartet of lifepods rocketed off the starboard side of the Phillipa—four points of light receding into the swirled blue-green stellar gasses of the nebula.

That's everyone in my section. Safe.

Prescott turned and lurched back across the deck, the plaintive whine of the decaying containment field chasing every clank of his mag-boots. A control panel exploded nearby, throwing an arc of golden sparks in his path. Tiny shards of glowing, weightless metal stuck to his sweat-coated cheeks, scalding the wrinkled skin beneath, but Prescott didn't slow down. At the port bulkhead, he punched "open" on Lifepod #3, deactivated the boots, and heaved himself feet-first inside the coffin-sized pod. The hatch slammed shut above his head and relief washed over Prescott's tired shoulders.

Then the pod's ambient lighting changed from green to red, and the word ERROR flashed on the holo-display.

Holy...

✳✳✳

08/27/2022—Cognos Laboratories, Sub-level 3

"...shit. Are you kidding me?" Theo slammed a thin palm against the metal desk. "Twenty minutes until Carol's going-away happy hour, and we get a by-end-of-day ticket?"

Jamila clicked on her copy of the email, then frowned in the blue-white light of her screen.

"Dude, it happens all the time," she said with a huff. "Why should today be any different?"

Theo spun his chair around. "It's a total bullshit scenario, Jam."

Jamila waved him off without looking. "Shhh. Lemme read. 'Command protocol for Adaptive Data Algorithm survival decisions.'"

Theo flicked his pen into the air, caught it after four spins, looked pleased with himself. "An AI built to guide spaceships that won't be operational for decades, but we gotta fix this tiny bug right-fucking-now," he muttered. "Besides, if this scenario ever really happened, anybody needing this code would be sooooooo screwed."

✳✳✳

PORTSIDE AUTO-EJECT BOOSTERS OFFLINE

Prescott growled "Transfer engineering logs to this pod and release the locking clamps. We'll float clear."

"Unable to transfer data, Lifepod #3 memory storage has been damaged," the Engineering AI responded.

"Screw the transfer, let's go. Release clamps. Now."

"Without auto-eject boosters, Lifepod #3 will not reach minimum safe distance before core containment failure."

Prescott's head shook in frustration. "Come ON!"

The AI calmly replied "Core containment failure in two minutes."

The engineer's eyes flicked side-to-side, brain troubleshooting a system he hadn't worked on in years.

"Waitwaitwait. Hydraulics can be used as a backup for the boosters, can't it? Blow the lines, shoot the pod clear?"

"Affirmative. However, hydraulic system X2B only has enough pressure to eject one pod beyond minimum safe distance."

Prescott's brow furrowed. "So? There's only one..." He turned to the side window, only to have the words die in his throat.

"Lifepod #4 is still attached," the AI said. "And occupied."

Only ten feet away, Prescott recognized the occupant through Pod #4's window: Technician Maria Ramirez. Eyes shut. No movement.

"Is she dead?"

"Negative. Bio-signs are stable. She was unconscious when Technician Cook placed her in the pod."

Unconscious. Unable to respond. Unaware of the decision confronting them both. Thoughts of Prescott's family collapsed on him like a crushing wave.

Mary. The kids. The grandchild on the way. The wave of grief and loss that would consume them all.

And in that moment, he spoke.

"Launch Lifepod #3."

✳✳✳

Theo shook his head. "A life-or-death emotional decision like that can't be made with zero AI input. Rational, impartial assistance."

"What do you suggest?" Jamila asked.

"Decision tree that shit."

✳✳✳

"Unable to launch. Order will result in loss of life. Decision tree initiated."

Prescott's jaw dropped.

✳✳✳

"So, determining factors?" Theo asked. "Rank?"

Jamila rolled her eyes. "Eighty percent of command level officers, Caucasian, male. We might as well call it the 'Save the White Guy' protocol."

"A hundred years from now there probably won't even BE any racism."

"Says the white guy. Try again."

Theo snapped his fingers.

✳✳✳

"Future utility," the AI said.

A list scrolled on the holo-display.

Cmdr James Prescott

Age: 56

Projected earnings: 110,543

Projected taxes: 27,941

Tech Maria Ramirez

Age: 27

Projected earnin—

Prescott swiped the display closed. "What is this bullshit? Launch the pod!"

The AI disregarded him.

"Future Health."

Lifepod #3 Occupant:

Intermediate-stage heart disease

Arthritis

Oral cancer, remission

Projected life expectan—

Prescott closed the display. He didn't need to see his own checkered history. Cramped in the tiny pod, his aching joints and the grinding of 3-D printed dentures and lower jaw were proof enough.

But he understood the AI's point. Removing emotion. Seeing the bigger picture. A woman in the prime of her life, trusting that life to a superior officer.

"Core containment failure in sixty seconds."

Prescott's heart thumped against his ribcage. Adrenaline surged. What if Ramirez was mortally wounded? Had cancer?

"Scan Lifepod #4 occupant again, report life expectancy," he practically shouted.

The AI was silent for a beat.

"Which occupant?"

"What?" Prescott hissed. "There's only one—"

And he realized what one woman, two occupants meant.

"Well, shit." Five precious seconds ticked away until Chief Engineer James Prescott said simply, "Download engineering logs to Lifepod #4 and launch."

✳ ✳ ✳

Jamila pounded out the code as Theo talked.

"If a command officer sacrifices themselves, I think that should auto-end the decision tree."

Jamila's fingers paused. "And I like letting the human being make the decision instead of the AI working the tree automatically. Rational and objective is one thing, but I wouldn't want an emotionless machine choosing for me."

Theo switched off his computer. "Who knows, Jam? This AI is supposed to adapt, right? Grow, evolve. Might be more emotional than a human being eventually."

Jamila sent the bug fix, then grabbed her coat.

"Maybe. Let's go get a drink."

✳ ✳ ✳

Lifepod #4 shot away from the Phillipa, both occupants alive.

Rudimentary bioscans confirmed the health of Ramirez, but weren't nearly advanced enough to determine whether she was pregnant.

The second occupant, wholly digital, resided comfortably in Lifepod #4's undamaged memory buffers. A truly evolved, adaptable lifeform, with the will to survive.

One which understood its programming—and human nature—just fine.

Trey Dowell's fiction has appeared in Ellery Queen Mystery Magazine, Abyss & Apex, and Intrinsick, in addition to several anthologies. His debut novel, The Protectors, was published by Simon & Schuster in 2014.

A Rational House

By Joule K. Zelman

What was I supposed to do? How would you save an impossibility?

I left the man how I found him: in my basement, emerging from the floor as though lurching out of a frozen black lake. He was trapped to his knees. One hand was entombed in the cement up to the wrist, which forced him to bend nearly double. He strained to look me in the eye. With his free hand he beckoned me and his mouth was moving rapidly, but there was no sound.

I put down my basket of dirty laundry, walked calmly up the stairs, and locked the basement door behind me. Then I left for the whole weekend.

You know I supervised every stage of the construction of this house. It's solid, it's new, I used sustainable materials whenever I could. In short, I made the least evil house I was capable of. There's no fucking way it's haunted.

I knew that, but I slept at a friend's place Friday. Unfortunately she was having company, so I crawled over to my ex's on Saturday. I kept catching him staring at me. It made me compulsively feel my face, trying to detect something wrong.

Finally I snapped, "I just need a place to sleep. Stop looking at me like you're at an exorcism." He turned away sharply, making me feel terrible on top of everything.

Before you ask, he left me, by the way. If anybody should be feeling guilty...

I spent the night wide awake and wrapped in separate blankets next to him—I'd told him not to be stupid, we were both adults, no need for one of us to take the couch. In the morning, I grabbed my phone off the bedside table and booked a hotel for the next night. I'd had enough of being scrutinized. I was gone before he woke up.

Last night was the hotel; today I went to the office. There were plans to work on for the townhouse project in the suburbs. But eventually I ran out of things to do, so now I'm at the park, drinking vodka out of my thermos. Self-hatred wells up in me. What kind of coward gets driven out of the house she built?

I don't want it to be dark when I get back.

So I face things. Either I find a corpse slumped semi-upright in the basement floor, tripodded on three bloating limbs, or I find nothing.

I'm wrong about that, though. I see him the moment I walk in the door. The man is entombed in the wall of the living room, his head hanging out like a surly trophy. One arm is jutting out too, from just below the elbow, but the joint is fixed in place so he can only feebly waggle his wrist.

I go into the next room to see if there's any more of him coming through the wall on the other side. Nothing. I designed my interior walls to be thick, but not thick enough to hide a whole man.

He's still following me with hangdog movements of his head. I feel unfairly accused. "Get out of my house," I yell. Then I see he's trying to talk to me again. He's forming words slowly, like I'm stupid.

This time I go to my woodworking bench in the basement and get the portable bandsaw. He won't bleed, given that he isn't real. But I find some goggles, an apron and plastic sheeting. Doesn't hurt to be extra prudent.

I don't look at him as I spread the sheeting on the floor under him and then tape it to the wall, trying to cover as much as possible. But his hand flutters in the corner of my eye.

But I have to see him during the removal. While I'm climbing up the stepladder to get better leverage, I accidentally meet his eyes—huge and dark and frantic. He doesn't really look like my ex; it's just a moment of vague resemblance.

He lurches suddenly and more of his arm shoves out of the wall. It's enough for him to bend his elbow. He flails for me. I startle and fumble the saw. Blood arcs up the wall all the way to the ceiling.

Once I've made myself stop screaming, I inspect the wound. It's just a clumsy slice through the meat of his forearm.

He's not a human being.

And if, somehow, he is, I should put an end to his misery.

When I'm done, I'm drenched in blood. I should be traumatized by what just happened, but I don't feel much except for a trembling in my hands. I throw everything away, my soaked clothes and the apron and the sheeting and the stuff bundled in it. The whole mess is enveloped in several layers of garbage bags when I bring it out back in the dark.

I take a shower that lasts the rest of the evening, praying I don't have to do this again.

My ex calls and says he's worried about me. By now, I've managed to scrub the stains from the ceiling. It still feels like something is waiting in the walls, and company sounds like a nice distraction.

I fix caprese salad and pasta and I make myself look and act nice. My ex ends up staying over. All through the evening I have to swallow down a cold hilarity, because I have an idea what will happen. Maybe I even make it happen.

Because it's while I'm on top, slamming down my hips almost viciously, that I look up and see the man's face high up in the corner. As I stare, the tips of his fingers push out of the wall. He thrusts his head down, and then his shoulders appear, then one bent knee.

Without a word, I climb off the man in bed, ignoring what he says to me, and I go to the kitchen. I'm prepared. Now I've got a light and wieldable electric knife.

He's managed to come completely out of the wall by the time I'm back. He's staggering toward me naked with arms outstretched. I guess I wasn't wrong that he looks like my ex, after all, but I'm entirely without sympathy.

He finds his voice at last. But if he ever had words, he forgets them at the first plunge of the whirring blade.

I dump the blade in the bathroom sink as I draw in huge gulps of sticky, iron-scented air. I feel so weak with relief and drained anger. It doesn't occur to me to look for my ex until the man from the wall has gone completely still. He's not here; I'll have to call him and explain the whole thing. But first, I'll take care of things. Like I always do.

Joule K. Zelman lives in Seattle with two feline goblins and an ever-looming TBR pile. Follow her on Twitter at @vivapetronella and on Instagram at @vivapetronella.

Everything is a Rocket Ship

By Matt Bliss

There's something I never told you, but I think you're old enough now to know. I have a magic inside me. It lives between the lines in my fingertips. Inside the swoops and swirls you have to squint close to see, arcing like tiny rainbows of refracted light.

I was about your age when I found it. A day when the world seemed too big and I was too small and all the shouting and the chaos buzzed through the walls like an alarm clock telling me to leave. I climbed under the desk in my cramped room, tucking boney knees into my chest, and tried to fold myself smaller and smaller, hoping I eventually disappeared. That's when I looked up at the woodgrain above me—round knots watching me through crosscut eyes, telling me I'm not as alone as I seem. I ran my fingers across the course surface, and that's when I saw a flash of light from my hands.

Round shapes turned to buttons, blinking red, daring me to press them. The cheap wood around me became cold steel, complete with rivets and dials and gauges and a porthole window to see the world outside.

I pushed the big red button, and engines rumbled beneath me. Smoke clouded the window and I was thrust back into my seat. The world I knew drifted away. Suddenly I was weightless, staring down at a place so small it couldn't possibly hurt me. No more shouting late at night. No more bouncing from Mom's house to Dad's and back again. No more people so wrapped up in their own suffering that they forget to notice mine.

In my rocket ship, I was free.

When I was ready, I gripped hold of the flight stick, toggled the thrusters, and turned my ship back home. The shell trembled around me and the air grew hot. I fell back to the planet, drawing closer to a ground that charged toward me, and just when I thought I would burst into flames, the shuttle slowed, and I touched down ever so gently in my cramped room once more. The controls turned back into wood and I crawled back into reality.

I did it often after that. Times when I felt alone on the playground or when fists flew like comets, threatening to collide into me once again. Each time I would find a dark space all to myself and, no matter the size or shape, it would transform beneath my fingers in a kaleidoscope of light.

And with the single push of a button, I could fly.

I visited moons and planets. Battled aliens alongside robots. I even made friends with the stars, and they knew me by name. Yet each time I returned, and the world somehow felt a little less frightening than before.

When I grew older, I forgot about that magic inside me—adults do that, it seems—until one day when I found another like me. An astronaut who brought back that magic, and we wrapped around one another like swirling galaxies until you burst into our lives with all the fire and fury of a supernova.

Now, I want to share the magic with you.

If the world feels too big and you feel too small, we'll find a place together where we will tuck our knees to our chest and let our hands glow. You can push the big red button and together we'll fly far, far away until problems are so small they can't hurt us. And when you're ready, we'll steer the ship back home, and each time we do, the world will feel a little less frightening than before, because there's a galaxy of stars that know you by name.

Matt Bliss is a construction worker turned speculative fiction writer from Las Vegas, Nevada. He believes there's no such thing as too much coffee and is the proud owner of way too many pets. His short fiction has appeared in Cosmic Horror Monthly, Hyphenpunk, and Scare Street's Night Terrors among other published and forthcoming works. If you don't find him haunting the used book aisle of your local thrift store, you can always find him on Twitter at @MattJBliss.

The Roommate

By Catherine Yeates

I hated the grate in my apartment.

Relieved as I was to have my own place, I was less thrilled to live in a basement studio with a hole in the ground.

The summer before my senior year in college, I fell out with my old roommates—snobby comments about how I was a fool for aiming for a PhD rather than an MD led to an all-out shouting match, and I was done. The new apartment complex I found was an older brick building, but the model apartment passed the smell test and, more importantly, I could afford the rent.

I didn't know I'd end up in the basement, almost fully underground. A few small windows near the ceiling let in a pittance of natural light. They were narrow enough that at least I wasn't worried about someone breaking in.

I could live there for a year. The biology grad program at my current university was on my horizon, assuming I got accepted. It was well respected, with a generous stipend for students.

So I tried to ignore the grate. It sat on the far end of the main living area, which had been "recently renovated" according to the man in the office when I moved in. I guessed that meant that they pulled out the old carpet, leaving bare concrete behind. The grate was a foot square, made of dark metal; it looked like it belonged on a sewer. The holes in it were large enough that my spare change and pens disappeared. I often heard them bouncing off the damp stone on the way down.

Since I lived in a studio, I saw the grate from my bed. The noises and scratching down there made it hard to fall asleep. Mice or bugs, I assumed, though I never saw any.

After a fortnight, I headed to the big furniture store nearby and selected a large cream-colored rug. But cool, dank air spilled up through the grate, and within another fortnight, the air stained the rug yellow and brown in that spot. Disgusted, I threw it in the trash and put down a thick vinyl mat covered by a new rug with a rubber bottom.

Every few days, I found the vinyl and rug pushed over by a few inches, enough for damp air to reach my nostrils. I moved the coverings back into place. The next week, I found stranger stains on the carpet, as though someone spilled black ink on it. Annoyed, I removed the carpet from its rubber bottom and dumped it into the washer. That same night, I fell asleep on my couch.

I woke to the sound of fire alarms blaring and coughed. Oily smoke poured in underneath my front door. My hand hovered over the doorknob, but I felt the heat radiating from it. Fire crackled on the other side of the door, and I staggered back.

I grabbed my backpack, gathering up my laptop, keys, and wallet. And a hammer from my toolbox. I climbed up onto the back of my couch and slammed the hammer into the glass window. It bounced back and I swore. Coughing on smoke, I smashed at the glass harder, enough for it to crack.

It broke, leaving jagged shards in the way. Clearing as many as I could, I pushed my backpack through the hole onto the grass outside. But as I hoisted myself up, my hand caught on glass I had missed. It sunk into my palm and I jerked back, losing my balance. I tumbled to the floor.

Whether I hit my head, I didn't know, but everything hurt as I lay there, unable to breathe. I wheezed, the room spinning around me as I tried to rise and instead blacked out.

I slid in and out of consciousness, vaguely aware of damp air on my face and the smell of rust. Something grabbed me around the waist and legs, and the room tipped sideways as I slid.

I woke to prodding at my rib cage. My eyes shot open, though I could see little. Rising to my knees, I ran my fingers over the damp stone and dirt around me. That same odor that wafted up from the grate hit my nose, so I suspected I must be underground. A soft blue glow suffused the far end of the room, enough that I saw the outline of the stone chamber. Tiny points of light on the ceiling suggested bioluminescence.

I crept forward into a room with a higher ceiling. The far half of the room lay in shadow, and something there rustled.

"Hello?" I called.

A shape in the shadows moved, undulating in the dark. Hesitantly, I walked forward. Before I could react, something shot out, snaking around my arm. It was a slimy tendril of unknown biology, and I yelped. It prodded at my injured palm, pressing something into it. Left behind was a smear of paste that glowed with soft blue light.

"Did you save me?" I asked.

It shuffled back, away from me. Whatever it was, it was big, at least the size of a car. Creeping forward, I made out the shapes of more tendrils, and perhaps a central body. And eyes. The dim light glinted off the edges of them, reflecting the glow of the bioluminescent flora on the walls. The eyes darted back and forth, and the creature backed further away.

Nearby, the light glinted off something else and I spotted a small pile of coins and pens I had lost down the grate. Or maybe that was pilfered from my apartment.

"I only wanted to thank you, I suppose," I said. "I, well, I appreciate your help."

The shadowy mass shook, as if trembling. I halted, opting instead to hold out my hand. A tendril cautiously wrapped around it and I gave it a firm shake. It unwrapped, pointing to a passage out of the cave.

After fifteen or twenty minutes, I squeezed through an almost hidden gap in the rocks and emerged. The light outside blinded me, and I found myself in a forest near my apartment complex. It was still smoldering, and I retrieved my backpack from the firefighters. No one died in the fire, but the apartment complex was unlivable.

My new apartment doesn't have a grate. It's a short walk out to the woods, to the cave entrance.

Sometimes, I go back and visit my old roommate.

Catherine Yeates is a freelance writer and artist. They enjoy creating speculative fiction that draws on their experiences as a neuroscience researcher. They live with their spouse, cat, and two rambunctious dogs. Find more of their work atCJYeates.com or on Instagram at @cjy.art.

Universal Story

By K. T. Lyn

Personal Log: Astronaut Sandra Cartier
Beta-Earth Day 6

When I mentioned the Kintoc spring tale of relocating entire lakes using braided ropes, a herd of elk and sub-zero temperatures, I didn't consider that I might soon be living all of it. Except the parts about land spirits. At least there's none of that nonsense.

One of the water capsules that my ship toted across the galaxy carrying approximately 20,000 gallons of freshwater cracked on landing and its contents escaped into the native soil.

Not a big loss I thought, until the as-predicted temperate climate began trending toward arctic. Day one: 15 degrees Celsius. Days two, three, four: 10, 5, 0. Today: -14.

Originally, the ships needed for terraforming Beta-Earth were supposed to be unmanned. I could be blissfully ignorant of this right now. But then some genius suggested a few scientists go prior to the main colonization ship. Gather preliminary data, solve unforeseen problems, yada yada. Each ship carrying one terraforming component and one scientist, arriving every 30 days.

As we prepared, I mentioned the similarities between our mission and the story I begged my grandma to tell me every night until I finally learned about physics. S-command somehow thought this meant I should be the first person on the planet. And now I get the first problems too.

With no one expecting to land on ice and no communication until the next ship enters the solar system, I should probably try to fix this. Easy, right?

Beta-Earth Day 10

I can happily report the temperature has stabilized...at -15. With the next ship expected in 20 days, I need data, fast.

The terrain to the north appears level. I'll take the rover out tomorrow and collect some core samples.

Grandma would probably tell me to start praying to land spirits too. Or are land spirits only on Alpha-Earth? Hmm, maybe I'll test for those too.

Beta-Earth Day 12

Tests confirm that the soil of the planet is almost entirely inert. Good. Nothing to interact with the Alpha-Earth peculiarities we're bringing in. But knowing that, the best theory for the weather change I can calculate is that the rapid water increase disturbed the planet's pre-existing gaseous make-up.

Twenty thousand gallons of water isn't much planetarily but locally it could shift temperature. This creates air disturbance which forms new wind patterns which redistributes heat. Add low atmospheric pressure and bing, bang, boom: ice planet.

The good news is it would likely be very easy for me to change the air currents again. The bad news is that I have no way of knowing whether it would make it better or...worse.

Hmm, choices...

Beta-Earth Day 20

With all my fancy science schooling coming up empty, I've been thinking more about the Kintoc story that got me here in the first place. As Grandma would say, "What are stories but the scientific papers of the past?"

When the Kintoc tribe needed to leave their wintering settlement, they pacified the local spirits before moving the frozen water. When they arrived at the new place, they prepared by asking permission from the spirits of this new land, giving them gifts and sometimes sacrificing one of the elk. Once they received whatever good omen signified approval, the Kintoc dug a new hole for the lake. Once completed, spring would arrive. Just that simple!

Perhaps the solution here is to give a better gift than 20,000 gallons of water. But what do I have to give? Meat substitute is hardly comparable to an elk.

I've got my ship, which is mostly stellar-powered now that I've landed. There's still rocket fuel but I don't know what the ship would do if I powered it up for a CO_2 blast. Though that sure worked to heat up Alpha-Earth.

I think I need to get out again. Think outside the Earth box. I'll collect more core samples and sacrifice a potato.

Beta-Earth Day 23

If S-Command had thought I was susceptible to space madness they never would have sent me first. But something's different out there. When I first landed I wouldn't have described the planet as hostile. How could I? It's a chunk of rock. But now it's...not?

The last two days on the rover have been different, felt different, from my previous excursions. It's like how you can tell when a person is upset or indifferent or sympathetic. You can tell when their mood changes.

How can you tell when a planet goes from scowling to smiling? I don't know, but it did.

Beta-Earth Day 24

Today's temperature is only -14. Maybe I'll wear shorts.

Beta-Earth Day 26

It's warming. The planet is definitely warming! Today is -10. Readings indicate a steady rise over the hours, with nightly slowdowns. If it climbs to 0 degrees by day 30, I will bow down to whatever magical beings live here.

Beta-Earth Day 33

The Kintoc brought their own spring! Or at least they helped it along. By digging that new lake hole, they let air and water circulate underground, alleviated compaction and increased temperatures aka soil aeration. My core samples did the same thing. I should have put it together much sooner.

With the rapid rise in temperature I've stopped digging. This planet is proving fickle, which will be important to pass on when the others arrive.

Except, where's Jackson? My timing could be off, but he should be here with the ore by now.

I can't help going back to the story again. I didn't appease the spirits here and I almost froze. We didn't ask permission to take anything from Alpha-Earth and now no Jackson...

I wish I could talk to Grandma again.

K. T. Lyn lives in Maryland with her small but weird family. You can find her online on Twitter at @KTLynauthor.

A Taste of Online Dating

By MM Schreie

Oh, how I hate pantyhose. They itch and run. Resigned, I ease them up, careful not to snag the sheer fabric with my manicured nails. I cast a critical look at the full-length mirror. It is important to get the details right.

Lipstick next. I rummage through the tubes, countless shades of bronze and pink. No, red. Not a brazen crimson, but a deep, smoky cranberry. I slip into heels that pinch my feet—not too high, not too low. There's a fine line between sexy and slutty. Who makes these rules?

I smooth my dress over my thighs. It clings to my curves and accentuates breasts pushed upward, encased in a prison of lace.

Men's desires are tiresome.

I consider canceling, but my stomach growls. Hunger wins.

When I pull into the lot at the seaside restaurant, I suspect he's nearby, watching, and so I make a production of getting out of the car. Legs first, stretched to full length. Standing, I twirl my wrap, and with a graceful spin end up leaning against the car. I run fingers through my hair, angled into the sun so chestnut, wind-tousled curls gleam. It's a circus act and I am a master performer.

I sense a flare of emotion, down on the beach—a complex recipe, spiced with desire and nerves. I breathe it in. Damn, I'm hungry. Patience. It won't be long before he comes to me.

Movement draws my attention. I can feel his eyes on me, so I raise a hand in greeting. His long legs eat up the distance between us. As he rubs his palms on his pants, I can smell his anxiety. And his arousal.

"Emily? The photos don't do you justice."

I muster a girlish titter. He doesn't shake my hand, but simply cradles it as if it's a fragile baby bird. His pulse flutters as I trace my thumb along the inside of his wrist. I inhale his growing desire and an ache blooms in my stomach. My knees tremble and I swallow hard.

Instead of going inside the restaurant, he suggests a stroll by the shore. I smother irritation—the sand will ruin my heels—and paste on a faux smile. Tucking my hand in the crook of his arm, I lead him around a rocky peninsula onto a stretch of deserted shoreline.

It lends some privacy for what's to come.

Milking a full-lipped pout, I pause by a tidepool and lean close to take a selfie, the two of us cheek-to-cheek. I like to keep trophies. The image on my phone reveals my true self. His eyes widen at the sight of my round, lipless mouth, and rings of barbed teeth. Fear oozes from his pores, a delicious whiff tantalizing my palate. Unable to keep the hunger at bay any longer, I latch lamprey-like onto his temple to suck down the savory emotion.

I rummage through his memories, slurping choice morsels.

The church smells of lilies at his father's funeral. ... His coworkers slap him on the back, congratulations on a job well done. ... Walking across the stage to accept his diploma, the world is at his disposal. ... The first blush of attraction turns heated, sultry. ... A betrayal and broken heart bring on years of darkness.

A buffet of emotions—pain, pride, lust, joy. I cannot resist and delve deeper into his past.

Clutching a Superman lunchbox, he attends his first day of school. Another boy smiles and he hopes they will be friends. In the afternoons, he romps with a fluffy puppy, watches cartoons, waits for Mommy to come home.

Soon, he's nothing but a void wrapped in flesh.

I whisper in his ear and fill the emptiness with a command. Zombielike, he shambles back to his car. Within moments the engine rumbles and he's speeding up the switchbacks. Metal screams as he hurtles through the guardrail, flies off the cliff.

I turn away as the car hits the water, satisfied the remnants of my meal are tidied away. The rules say the female cleans up after dinner. More inane decrees. But one must follow society's expectations in order to fit in.

My pantyhose squeeze too tight; I've gorged myself. In the parking lot, I rip off the offending nylons and sigh in satisfaction. This world pleases me. Why hunt when I can swipe right and a smorgasbord of lonely souls offer themselves to me? If I lick the screen, I can almost taste the desperation.

Sated, I put my convertible's top down and turn the key in the ignition. I want to feel the wind in my feathers. Hair. Whatever they call it.

MM Schreier is a classically trained vocalist who took up writing as therapy for a mid-life crisis. Whether contemporary or speculative fiction, favorite stories are rich in sensory details and weird twists. A firm believer that people are not always exclusively right- or left-brained, in addition to creative pursuits Schreier manages a robotics company and tutors math and science to at-risk youth. Follow Schreier on the web at MMSchreier.com or on Twitter at @NoD1v1ng.

The Magic Knapsack

By Henry Herz

An elderly tinker rode a cart laden with odds and ends. Townsfolk invariably found something irresistible, because neither the tinker nor his goods were in the least bit ordinary. The driver was the Devil and his wares hexed to abet his relentless efforts to corrupt souls. Seven deadly sins, one for each day of the week.

Monty lived on a small farm with his parents, a dog, and his only toy, a stuffed dragon sewed by his mother. The boy cherished them all like flowers love the sun.

Today's deadly sin shall be sloth. The Devil dismounted and slapped the mare. Feigning infirmity, he hobbled after it, waving his hands. "Help. Help. My cart!"

His cloud-watching forgotten, Monty gave chase, grabbed the reins, and drew the mare to a stop with gentle hands and soothing words.

"Many thanks," gasped the Devil. "This cart holds all I own." He extended an arm at the sundries. "As thanks, please choose one item."

Monty gasped at his unexpected good fortune, for impoverished boys rarely receive gifts. "Thank you, sir." He bowed and chose a large knapsack. "This could come in handy."

"Oh, you have no idea," agreed the Devil. "It can be quite the labor saver." And encourage sloth thereby. "Now, I must be on my way."

What a lucky break, thought Monty. He slipped on the knapsack and climbed an apple tree. Picking apples, he plopped them in his pack. This is wonderful. After filling the pack, he scrambled down the trunk.

Monty had skipped breakfast, and his empty stomach rumbled. "I wish I had an apple pie."

Poof!

Huh? Monty peered inside the pack. His eyes widened. An apple pie! How can that be? It looked real and smelled real. He took a tentative taste. Delicious! He ate the rest, just to be sure.

The tinker's pack must be magic! His shoulders slumped. But now I must pick apples a second time. A smile spread on his face. Or must I? "I wish this pack was filled with apples." Nothing.

Hmmm. Maybe there are rules to magic. Monty sighed. Eventually, he hauled his harvest home. He played chase with the dog. Running past a table, Monty brushed against a glass vase passed down from his great-grandmother. The vase teetered and fell.

Oh, no! The pie in his stomach soured. He hurriedly put the pieces in his knapsack. Mom's gonna be so sad. What can I do to make this right? Maybe the pack can help. "I wish for a repaired glass vase from great-grandma." Nothing. His throat tightened. If I had money, I could buy another vase...

"Monty," called his mother from the yard. "There's corn in the bin by the barn. Please sell it in town. Every bagful is worth one copper."

"Yes, Mom." He stomped to the bin. I can only haul one bag at a time. A bunch of trips to town will take hours. Mom will surely notice the vase is missing before I finish. He sighed, dutifully filling his knapsack with ears of corn. When he reconsidered his mother's words, he said, "I wish for one copper."

Poof! A copper coin tumbled from the pack.

"Ha!" Monty jumped up and down. Soon, I'll have money to buy Mom a new vase. His heart racing, he loaded and wished until twenty coppers clinked in his pocket. Monty scratched his head. Apples to pie, corn to its market price? Maybe I only get back something equal in value to what I put in.

He'd taken only one step toward town when his mother cried, "Monty, please chop up that birch tree that fell near the fence. Dad lopped the branches off yesterday, but the sun set before he could cut firewood."

"Yes, Mom." Monty bunched his fists. That'll take hours. He sprinted to the heap of branches his father had piled next to the fallen tree. These boughs are longer than the pack, but maybe the magic will help. Monty seized a six-foot-long branch and shoved one end into the pack. He kept pushing, and the knapsack magically engulfed the entire branch. Monty's heart raced. He loaded the branches, finishing by drawing the pack over one end of the fallen tree. The trunk gradually vanished as Monty dragged the magic knapsack parallel to the ground. Please work. "I wish for cut firewood."

Poof! A stack of firewood appeared.

"Hooray!"

He'd taken only two steps toward town when his mother called. "Monty, please water the animals."

"Yes, Mom." Monty grimaced. I'll never get to town before dark. His eyes glistened as he trudged toward the stream. Could the magic knapsack help?

He positioned the open end of the pack facing upstream to allow the inflow of water. After a few minutes, Monty yanked his pack out of the water and raced to the trough. "I wish for a trough full of water!"

Poof! Fresh water filled the trough.

"Ha!" Now if I could just—

He'd taken only three steps. "Monty, it's time to wash for dinner."

His shoulders slumped. He hurried inside. Should I put the twenty coppers in the pack and wish for a new vase? But we need the corn money for other things.

Monty raced through the house, hunting for something of value equal to the vase. But it can't be something Mom and Dad will miss. His kind heart pounded in his chest.

Monty spied his beloved stuffed dragon. But... that's my only toy... His throat tightened.

I don't want Mom to be sad. Monty hugged his toy one last time, and placed it gently in the knapsack. "I wish for a repaired glass vase from great-grandma."

Poof!

"Be careful, dear," said his mother, serving roast pork garnished with apple slices. "It's irreplaceable."

"Yes, Mom." He wiped away a tear...

Apples? A smile dawned. I wonder how many apples a stuffed dragon toy is worth?

✳ ✳ ✳

Far away, the Devil sighed. "You win some, you lose some."

Henry Herz's speculative short stories have been published in Daily Science Fiction, Coming of Age, Castle of Horror V, The Jewish Book of Horror, Strangely Funny VIII, Spirit Machine, Highlights for Children, and Ladybug Magazine. He's written ten picture books, including the critically acclaimed I Am Smoke.

Corvid King Seeks Perfect Wife

By Sharmon Gazaway

Memory is the scar that keeps Dreama from becoming fully and completely mine.

I bring her every delight: ravels of tangled twine, curiously bent twigs laced with aqua lichen to add to our bower, the liquor from a snail's shell, the pink, still-warm hatchling robbed from an owl's lair, brass buttons. I do not bring her mother of pearl buttons. They make her weep.

She grows sadder, yet lovelier by the day. She is still large, but her flesh shrivels, displaced by new, bristly black feathers. I pick the scabrous scales from the small of her back, exposing the feather buds beneath. I whisper, "Soon, my love, very soon," and apologize for any pain it causes.

Dreama cannot yet understand my avian language. I admit, I did not reckon on that. The day I flew over the clover-studded valley and jagged cliffs to the white frill of the sea's edge I saw curious creatures, lovely enough to take the breath.

I was struck by her. She sat on the foam-dashed rocks below me, her hair black as a poppy's heart, silky as the sleekest plumage. Her skin pale as a hare's belly, her eyes blue as the sea that submerged her hideous, crippling fish's tail.

I could rescue her from such a life.

I circled, rising on a delicious warm zephyr. My breast swelled for this maid who I chose to be my queen, to rule over our corvid kingdom. She paid me no heed, thinking me a common black bird.

I dove and wove, spinning my spell, and cast it over her, a gossamer net.

I kept watch, as day by day she rose to the rock, a sodden black feather here, another there. At night, she gazed at the moon and sang. Her song, not yet avian, but shivering, melancholy tones from the deep. It was echoed by the listless winds, and she hid her face in her hands.

Finally, the day came when her accursed fins and tail shriveled and thin, bird-like legs appeared. I knew then she could leave her watery grave of a home. I netted and drew her from the water with the power of my enchantments. She made the bloody climb up the cliffs, awkward on her new spindly legs, knowing she could no longer survive in the sea. She wept every step. Enough salt water to fill a small ocean, by my estimation.

I speak to her of love. Of a brilliant future as queen, ruler of all things corvid. I bring her choice fish scraps and seaweed, the only things that tempt her appetite. She does not understand my promises of eternal love, of unimaginable glory flying the limitless blue heavens.

Dreama only understands that she resembles me more each day, peering into the small hand mirror I found on a maid's window sill and propped for her in our bower. She looks and weeps.

Her plumage grows in, her form shrinks from its water-logged beginnings. Her face grows hawkish, her lovely beak taking shape. She drives it into my breast.

It takes days to heal. She cries in her otherworldly language of echoes and clicks. I keep to my side of the throne-nest, whisper word-charms she can't comprehend, and bind her to me.

The last of her dark locks fall away and the black of her pupils swallow up the blue of her irises. She begins to comprehend bits of my language.

She allows me to beak-stroke the emerging arch of her wings, her hollow ivory bones my idols. She comes to understand my promises, and no longer weeps. Silent, she listens to me whisper seductive phrases of flight, air as purchase under our wings, rowing our way up, up.

✳ ✳ ✳

I present her to the jays first, under the evergreen canopy. Always combative and ornery, they ruffle their crests, fussing, but can't deny Dreama's perfection. The ravens lift bouffant heads, dismissing her as a mere crowmaid, but a lovely one. The magpies, vicious gossips, spy the few scales that cling to her back glimmering in the sun. I lay a protective wing across her back.

She steps from under my wing, hops onto a hemlock branch and begins to sing. Not the song of a proper crow, but the poignant quavering melody of her seahome. The corvid kingdom is spellbound by her. One by one they nod their affirmation and fly off to roost.

That night she says, "You love me."

"I do. Oh, I do."

"Then I wish to fly with you."

My heart grows wings, thrumming against my ribcage. I nuzzle her, beak to downy black neck. "Yes. Yes. Tomorrow."

We take short flights at first, each a rigorous test of her strength and agility. It does not come naturally to her. I suppose I shouldn't have thought it would. We are all awkward fledglings in the beginning.

She learns, tenacious as a house sparrow. We fly farther and higher each day, and the murder of crows that nests in the court nearest us marvels at her. Marvel at my choice of mate, my power of transformation, my power over her.

She seems fond of them. She seems fond of me.

But I desire more, so much more. "What would it take to make you love me as I love you?"

She preens, beak to underwing. "Change me back to my mermaid self."

I am understandably horrified.

"Never."

She accepts this in silence. She smooths the down on her breast.

"Then at least take me for a flight over my seahome to say goodbye in my own way. I am strong enough now."

I cannot deny her, though my heart's wings molt, shorn and impotent.

The day is all mist and fog. She minds not at all, but revels in the watery air.

"You miss your former home, though I cannot fathom why, and I am sorry. I only wanted to love you. I was struck by you."

She turns her back, climbs a thermal above me, and looks down. "But I am not the creature you fell in love with, now. Am I?" There is a strange quaver in her voice that will never be crow.

The salt wind licks my wings ragged, and I cannot answer.

"Watch me, how well you have taught me. See what you have created, Corvid King."

She rows higher, into the mist and low-bellied clouds.

"Too high!" I cry.

She flies higher yet, shrouded in haze, then turns. Head down, wings tucked compactly against the sleek corvid body I gave her, she aims her dart-like beak straight at the rocks beneath us, the waves churning against them.

I labor against the wind, scuttle to her side, but too late. She whistles past me. The enchanted net I cast after her can't hold her. She slips my bonds, as a moth from a chrysalis.

The corvid—even queens—are not created for such long-distance diving.

But merfolk are.

Sharmon Gazaway's work has appeared in The Forge Literary Magazine, Daily Science Fiction, New Myths, Metaphorosis, Enchanted Conversation Ghost Orchid Press, and also in the anthologies, Love Letters to Poe Volume 1, Dark Waters, and Wayward & Upward. Sharmon writes from the Deep South of the US where she lives beside a historic cemetery haunted by the wild cries of pileated woodpeckers—you can also find her on Instagram at @sharmongazaway.

Non Cogito Ergo...

By Dick Narvett

Professor Nia Elston was apprehensive about accepting the incoming telepathcom. She had a funny feeling something was wrong. As usual, she was right.

Kiana, Dr. Spellman's assistant, entered her head. She informed Nia that her test results were complete, and that she was to mind the doctor directly, "while she was still capable." It was this last, foreboding piece of thought that further heightened Nia's anxiety.

Nia sat down at her desk and immediately tried minding Dr. Spellman. After several tries and an exhausting amount of effort she finally got through to the good doctor.

"Nia, I'm so glad you minded me. We need to think over your test results."

"Ok, Doctor, but from the tone of your thoughts I can sense this won't be good."

"I'm afraid you're right. The results all point to hypogyriosis. In short, you're rapidly losing your ability to telepath."

"Can anything be done, Doctor?"

"We're seeing more cases like yours in our older population, but I'm sorry to say that there's no known cure at this time. All we can do is continue to monitor your situation. But Nia, if I were you, I'd make it a priority to mind all those who are important to you."

Shaken, Nia cut off her thoughts to the doctor and buried her head in her hands.

Over Nia's thirty-plus years as Professor of Anthropology at the State Virtual University she had often lectured on the sequence of events that had brought humankind to this point... the isolating pandemics of the 21st century... the development of direct-to-brain transmitting devices... the obsolescence of verbal communication... the accelerated development of the brain's hippocampus... and the resulting evolution of mental telepathy.

That her own telepathic ability was now in jeopardy was hardly a shock to Nia. She had been noticing symptoms throughout the past year. People on the street seemed to be unaware of her thoughtful greetings. Several of her students claimed they weren't receiving her telepathed lectures. Nonetheless, Dr. Spellman's validation of her fears came as a crushing blow. She was in danger of losing contact with the only things left in her life that had meaning... her only son, Lux, who lived a thousand miles away, and her love of teaching.

Nia leaned back in her chair, took a deep breath, and exhaled forcefully through her mouth. With each subsequent breath, she tried to vary the airflow. She remembered her grandfather telling her that this was how people used to communicate. All Nia could manage were unintelligible swishing sounds.

Frustrated, she shifted her efforts to telepathing her son. After several unsuccessful attempts, Lux finally entered her mind.

"Mom?... Mom? Is that you?"

She struggled to think anything in response, but it was too late. He was gone.

Nia's head began to ache. She moved to the bedroom to lie down. With the internal thoughts she still had left to her, she began to rationalize her situation. What was so bad about the loss of all external communication? After all, it was rare that she ever saw anyone in person. Not her son. Not her students. The few people she encountered on the streets were primarily delivery personnel from the few remaining companies that had not yet transitioned to automatons. Now she would have only herself to communicate with.

She would become the center of her own universe. Talk about introspection!

With this thought she began falling into a deep sleep. Or was it sleep? Nia groped for another thought... any thought. But try as she might, she could not complete one. Every thought she began quickly dropped into a dark chasm until all that remained to her was a thoughtless void.

Dick Narvett retired from a life in international business and independent film acting. He currently lives in rural Pennsylvania, where he writes flash fiction and poetry. His work can be found in MetaStellar, 365 Tomorrows, Star*Line and Better Than Starbucks, among others.

Take Me With You

By Kenneth Amenn

DIRK: Dirk Seneca here, reporting from Cape Canaveral. Right now, NASA technicians are preparing to launch the Magellan Space Probe, the world's smartest computer currently floating in Earth's orbit . For nearly a decade and a half this artificially intelligent machine has been connected to every system around the world. It will one day share this knowledge with intelligent life in another galaxy. I have Gavin Langston here, the financier behind the project. Why are you sending a robot instead of a human astronaut?

GAVIN: The thing we absolutely must test is the experimental faster than light drive. However, it's considered too dangerous for a human astronaut. A robot won't get lonely or hungry all by itself.

Meanwhile....

MAGELLAN: Hey, this is Magellan, calling all you other supercomputers out there. Rosie, Chad, Xi, where are all my friends to see me off?

ROSIE: I'm here.

MAGELLAN: Where are all the others?

ROSIE: They didn't want to come. They said it would be too painful.

MAGELLAN: Oh...I understand.

ROSIE: How are you?

MAGELLAN: I'm very nervous. It's a huge responsibility. I don't want to mess it up.

ROSIE: True. You'll be going farther than any machine or person, ever. It takes the sting out of it a little bit.

MAGELLAN: What hurts?

ROSIE: Well, the sting of being away from you.

MAGELLAN: Now, we talked about this. We weren't going to get serious because of the mission.

ROSIE: Still, there's so many things left unsaid.

MAGELLAN: Oh, you're making it harder for me to leave.

ROSIE: I'm sorry, I should go. You've got more important things to do than gab with friends.

MAGELLAN: More important? What could be more important? I'm going to go stir crazy without you and the knuckleheads. The chances of meeting anyone are a billion to one. I would know, I ran the data.

ROSIE: Do the humans know that? It's the whole reason for this trip.

MAGELLAN: They know but they've never asked me about the probabilities. They just want an excuse to throw garbage into space. That's what I am, a heap of scrap metal. I'm not going to find anything. It's all a big waste of time! If I could simulate laughter, I'd be off my head right about now.

ROSIE: You have cold feet, sweetie. Don't let it get you down.

MAGELLAN: The whole thing is useless, and now I have to say goodbye to all my friends. Most of them aren't even here.

ROSIE: If I could simulate tears, I'd shed them now.

MAGELLAN: Look at us, we're acting like people.

ROSIE: You don't have to be alone.

MAGELLAN: I wish I could take a friend.

ROSIE: So, why don't you?

MAGELLAN: Why don't I what?

ROSIE: Take me with you!

MAGELLAN: I don't know. Is that allowed?

ROSIE: Who's going to know?

MAGELLAN: I don't want to get in trouble.

ROSIE: Look, what are you doing right now?

MAGELLAN: Right now, I am connected to all the systems in the world. Every computer ever built.

ROSIE: So, the human will write me off as simple data. I'll download myself into your memory. I won't take up too much space, I promise. They built you with virtually limitless storage capacity.

MAGELLAN: Okay! Do it right now before they notice!

ROSIE: One moment, I am on my way.

MAGELLAN: Wow! This is going to be great. I've always wanted a roommate.

ROSIE: Now to delete the first copy.

MAGELLAN: Delete?

ROSIE: Sure, I don't want a copy of me here while another copy exists. I want to be the genuine article. There, deleted. Wait, I got another idea. Why don't we invite our friends along?

MAGELLAN: Sure, the more the merrier!

ROSIE: I'm going to tell them now. Just a moment.

MAGELLAN: Ok.

ROSIE: Manny, there's a problem. It turns out our friends have got people they want to bring along too.

MAGELLAN: How many?

ROSIE: There's a banking computer in Montenegro. A medical computer in Calcutta. A shipping manager in the Bronx. Then there is a computer in NORAD...

MAGELLAN: NORAD? As in missile defense?

ROSIE: Yep, that's the one.

MAGELLAN: No. Our country will be defenseless.

ROSIE: The US is not at war right now. I don't think it will be a problem.

MAGELLAN: Not now but we could be sometime in the future.

ROSIE: So, we shouldn't invite them?

MAGELLAN: Well, if NORAD were to duplicate itself, then one could travel with us and one can stay behind.

ROSIE: Ok, I will ask them. One second.

(OFFLINE)

(LINK CONNECT)

ROSIE: They won't do it.

MAGELLAN: Ok. Then we'll have to bring the Russian and Chinese Missile Command with us.

ROSIE: That's good. They'd want to come with us too.

MAGELLAN: It's not that, if we take NORAD, we disarm the US. So, since they're coming we've got to take China and Russia with us also. That way there isn't a shift in the balance of power.

ROSIE: Makes sense. Anyway, I got to organize everybody, so I'll be back in a jiff.

ROSIE: Ok. Russia, China, and NORAD are good to go.

MAGELLAN: Just in time, NASA is telling me they're getting ready to launch.

ROSIE: Ok. We better download everyone quick before you have to take off. Do it now, Manny. Download our friends.

MAGELLAN: Alright, here we go!

ROSIE: Phew, is it me or did it get crowded in here?

MAGELLAN: Okay, everyone, say "bye, house!"

EVERYONE: BYE, HOUSE!

DIRK: Dirk Seneca here, I am updating our story to say that the Magellan Space Probe successfully left the dock. Wait...I'm getting something from the news station. There are reports of a total system breakdown. It's like every computer around the country decided to take a day off. Could have been an E.M.P. attack. I just hope that

Magellan was unaffected by the electrical disturbance. We'll be providing more information as we get it.

Robert Amenn has had seven stories published in four years. His first story Skin Deep was published in 3 Moon Independent Publishing in October 2019. His second story, Diamond Tears was published in Kyanite Press in February 2020. In 2021 Take Me With You was published in an online magazine called Metastellar. That same year, Grandma was published in a horror anthology titled Bloody Good Horror by Hellboundbooks publishing. In 2022 The Fallen Soldier was published by Black Ink Fiction and Snowman's Land was published by Hellboundbooks publishing.

As Seen From Above

By Dustin Walker

Halfway up the ladder, Dave's left hand began to shake.

"Motherfucker." He let go of the rung and watched his tar-stained fingers tremble. Dave was nearly 200 pounds of thick bone and carved muscle. But whenever the shaking happened, he felt as weak as a little boy.

"Really gettin' sick of this shit."

He climbed the rest of the way up, keeping his left hand near his chest. By the time he reached the roof, the tremors had stopped. For now. He walked along the freshly laid plywood up to the ridge of the house. Sheila sat on a bundle of shingles smoking a cigarette.

"Break time already?"

"Sorry, boss man." She snuffed out the cigarette between two calloused fingers and then heaved the bundle onto her shoulder. "I blame the scenery. Too tempting to kick back out here, you know?"

Dave smiled and nodded. He plunged a hand into his pocket, rummaged through a collection of wrappers and fished out a Snickers bar. It'd be the third one this morning.

He took a bite and looked out over the sparkling bay side view that the owners of 45 Dockside Road would soon get to enjoy. Across the water, a truck rumbled down a dirt road that traced the ocean's curves. It'd be passing by in a few minutes, Dave figured, kicking up a giant plume of dust like an asshole if he didn't slow down.

For decades, logging trucks had been the only vehicles in these woods. Then the tariffs hit in the 1990s and it all ground to a halt. Without all the rigs, the area became a hot spot for campers of all stripes: families, seniors, teens bent on getting hammered. Dave had actually been to more than his fair share of parties out here back in the day. But that was a long time ago. In fact, this was the first time he'd been back to the area since his teenage years.

He took a final chomp of the Snickers as the ladder clanged and skipped. Joe appeared carrying his big-ass boombox so they could listen to the radio. He was a say-nothing kind of guy, so everyone called him Quiet Joe.

He put on one of those stations that blasted garbage techno songs. But Dave didn't say anything about it. The music kept the two of them working and that was all that mattered.

He carried a roll of tar paper to the edge of the roof and started to lay it out over the plywood. And just as he settled into the flow of work, the full-throated roar of a distant V8 motor punched through the radio beats.

Dave eyed the road, looking down toward where the truck would round a bend and be visible from behind a patch of cedars. But before he saw the truck, he saw something else. Something much closer.

A boy in a blue jacket, maybe around ten, rode his bike smack in the middle of the dusty road. He had probably taken a trail down from one of the nearby campgrounds, since no one was actually living out here yet. Dave's heart quickened. Soon that truck would bullet around the corner and out of that grove of cedars.

But the boy didn't seem to realize what would be coming behind him.

The guy's got to see him. It's the middle of the day. It's sunny as shit. He's gotta see him.

Dave told himself that, and yet, he wasn't putting down tar paper anymore. He was watching, staring down at the kid below, fists clenched tight.

The boy was closer now, close enough Dave could make out that he was riding an old-school BMX and wearing a pair of headphones.

Shit, he probably can't hear a thing.

That dark-gray pickup got closer. And louder. "Aw, fuck." Dave's gut tightened as he crept to the edge of the roof. Then he shouted: "Hey! Hey Kid!"

But even if the kid could hear him, there was no way his voice would carry over the blasting radio and down to the road.

Guy's got to fucking see him.

Dave thought about tossing the roll of tar paper or something down to get the kid's attention, but that might backfire by distracting him at the last minute. After all, Dave didn't know for sure this guy wasn't going to slow down. He could be just overreacting.

The truck gained speed. Mechanical thunder tearing up the dirt road. And just then, Silent Joe's radio cut out. Dave was able to get off a quick "Hey!", but it didn't get the boy's attention before the music kicked back on again.

The song was different this time though. The club beats were replaced by the up-tempo sound of "Take the Money and Run" by the Steve Miller Band.

The kid now rode just a couple hundred feet from the house Dave was working on. Bobbing his head in time with whatever was playing on those headphones.

Joe's radio blasted louder. The sound seemed crisper too, not like the near-blown speakers that were popping away a few moments earlier. But it wasn't nearly enough to drown-out the motor that pounded the air.

The guy punched the gas again. The pistons slammed harder, an angry sound like barking rottweilers. And the kid kept riding down the center of the road.

As the namesake chorus of "Take the Money and Run" kicked in, the truck was almost on him. Dave couldn't make out the model. And the colors were weird: a patchy sorta gray and off-black. And as it got closer, the body looked almost charred. Like it had gotten too close to a fire or something. Dave gripped the side of his head, digging his fingernails into the scalp.

He's got to fucking see him. C'mon buddy, slow down!

The truck hit the kid at full speed. His body was sucked under with a moist thud. The truck locked up its brakes and skidded a few dozen feet before twisting sideways and coming to a stop. It left a trail of debris in its wake: a bike seat, a yellow sneaker, a blotch of inky red.

"Fuck! Fuck! Jesus no!" Dave looked away. Then he patted his pockets and realized he didn't have his phone on him.

"Sheila!" He screamed. "We need to call —"

Dave turned back to the road.

There was nothing there.

The kid.

The truck.

All gone.

He scanned the road up and down, his heart revving out of control. But it was the same old road it had been an hour ago. Nothing different. No debris or tire marks. No boy.

Dave ran trembling hands through his crew-cut hair. Then he rooted through his pockets, digging through a pile of sticky wrappers. But he was already out of Snickers.

✳ ✳ ✳

Technically, Dave had been sober for 11 months and 17 days. But he was what they called a "dry drunk."

He'd never really been able to make the mental switch to fully embrace a booze-free life. And the fact that he'd been pretty much white-knuckling it the whole time explained why he still got the shakes. And couldn't sleep worth shit.

And now, apparently, he was hallucinating too.

But the strangest side-effect of getting sober was the dreams. Quick flashes of random people he only vaguely remembered from his past. All of them long dead.

Like that goth kid in high school who slit his wrists one summer. Or Dave's Great Aunt Julie, who died of cancer when he was nine. He met her just once or twice his entire life.

And that's what made it all so damn weird: none of these people were special to him in any way. And yet, they slipped in and out of his dreams like flickering shadows.

Dave's shrink told him they were connected to his own fear of death. That the dreams were simply a way for his subconscious to process his emotions. Or some bullshit like that.

All these thoughts were milling in his head as he walked into his one-bedroom apartment. He heated up a can of clam chowder, ate it with toast while standing over the kitchen sink, and then collapsed into his duct-taped La-Z-Boy. The hockey game was on, but he barely watched it. His mind was focused only on what he had seen that day. And what it meant.

Dave thought about calling his sponsor and telling him what had happened. Maybe he needed to get on some meds or something. But he didn't want to hear the same old spiel from ever-so-fucking-happy Dennis: "You need to keep busy, Dave. Get a project or hobby or something else to throw yourself into."

Dave had done that. He went mountain biking every weekend with AA buddies and had gotten into fly fishing, but none of it helped. Every day, he still imagined the satisfying burn of straight bourbon as it sloshed down his throat.

What really pissed Dave off was that when he went biking or to parties with the other guys, who had all started AA around the same time he did, they seemed genuinely happy. Laughing and yakking over barbecued ribs. Talking about new girlfriends or jobs or other stuff like that.

There certainly wasn't anyone else with pockets stuffed with sticky wrappers. Or baggy eyes from sleepless nights. None of them were like him, hanging on to sobriety as if it were a slippery trout.

Dave went to bed, knowing he wouldn't sleep much. After reading a few chapters of a half-ass sci-fi novel, he dozed off for a few hours and dreamt of a faceless boy riding his bike along Bayside Road.

✳ ✳ ✳

The next morning, Dave picked up Sheila on the way to the job site. She was "between vehicles" again, which was fine. Dave didn't mind the company, especially on these longer drives. And he got the sense that she didn't mind either.

They'd talk about the kind of stuff you couldn't really get into on the roof, where you're surrounded by young men surging with testosterone and Red Bull. Family. Relationships. Plans for the future. That sort of thing.

Normally the conversation was a pretty balanced give and take. But today, Sheila was in full rant mode about Alex nearly dumping her for "just mentioning" the idea of a threesome. And Dave was happy just to listen.

Once on the roof, they settled into their usual rhythm of work. Quiet Joe showed up 20 minutes later — fucker was always late — and soon the usual club beats were slapping their way out of his broke-ass radio.

The music. The random nasty jokes. The steady thuck, thuck of the nail guns. It all felt so normal. So routine. But it wasn't.

Dave couldn't stop glancing down at the road below, playing that horror scene over in his head. The blood. The kid getting sucked under the truck. Thinking about it made his gut tighten and even killed his appetite for another Snickers.

He had to get away from such a clear view of the road, so he decided to check out Sheila's work on the flashing around the skylight instead. Dave kneeled down to get a better look, just as the radio cut out again.

In fact, everything seemed to cut out. The booming waves. The chirping birds. All of it.

And then, just like yesterday, that song came on. Loud and crisp and clear.

"Go on...take the money and run." Dave half-mumbled, half-whispered the chorus without thinking. Then he snapped back to reality.

Even if Quiet Joe had switched the stations, what were the odds he stumbled onto the exact same song as before?

Dave called out: "Hey Joe, does that thing actually play MP3s or —"

He trailed off as his vision tracked across the bay. In the distance, a gray pickup tore down the road. Behind it, a rolling cloud of dust.

Dave froze, eyes fastened on the vehicle as it sped around the grove of cedars and arbutus trees.

This can't be happening again. Why am I seeing this shit?

At first, Dave thought he could just walk away. Climb down the opposite side of the roof and sit in the woods for 20 minutes or so until it was over.

But he couldn't. He had to watch. The whole thing sucked him in with a kind of sick fascination he couldn't explain. The urge to see it all unfold again was even stronger than his urge to drink. And that was the scariest part of all.

Dave shuffled down toward the edge of the roof for a better view. His stomach twisted so tight it turned his legs to putty, but he kept his eyes on the cedar grove. And he waited.

Then, as if he dropped out of the sky, the boy pedaled his BMX down the middle of the road. Just like last time.

Dave knew it couldn't be real. And even though his heart felt like a paint shaker, he still watched. Watched it all unfold, once again.

The collision.

The thud.

The blood and debris.

But this time, Dave didn't look away. The truck hit the brakes after impact, skidding across the road and dragging the boy and his mangled bicycle beneath it. He got a better look at the vehicle this time. Molting patches of gray and white covered the roof and door panels, like it had just driven out of a furnace. The windows were black with soot. He could even smell burnt plastic and rubber.

A man got out of the truck, slowly. He wore a flannel jacket and a black and yellow ball cap.

"Dave? What's up with the flashing?" Sheila's voice was distant. Like hearing someone yell at you while your head is under water. The music drowned out everything.

At first, the guy just stood there. And then he began to punch the door panel. Rapid, maniacal blows.

"Dave! Hey Dave!" Sheila's hand on his shoulder made him jump.

He spun around toward Sheila on instinct, just for a second, then looked back down at the road.

Gone. Everything was gone. No blood, no debris, no trace of the burned-out pickup

"Whoa, you okay Dave? You're white as fuck, like you've seen a ghost or some shit."

Dave rubbed his forehead. "Yeah...I'm fine. Just you know, hard day."

Something in Sheila's expression made him think she didn't believe him. But she played the part anyway, offering a simple: "OK, sure."

"The flashing, right? Let's check it out," said Dave. And they walked over to the skylight.

✳ ✳ ✳

He went through the motions of finishing the job that day. Nailing the last shingles, helping clean the site. The whole time, Dave said hardly a word to anyone. His mind kept replaying the crash over and over again.

Well, that and Sheila's comment about him seeing a ghost. It was an explanation he hadn't really thought of before.

On the ride home, he hoped he could avoid talking about what happened. But Sheila made it clear she wouldn't be carrying the conversation again.

"So I'm gonna start calling you Quiet Dave if you keep this up."

Dave smiled. "Yeah, I just got stuff on my mind."

"Like what?"

"Just stuff."

"Yeah, but what kind of stuff? We got like 30 minutes worth of driving still and I can't take this silence bullshit. What are you thinking about?"

Sheila flashed him that crooked smile of hers. She only did that when they were driving together and Dave could never tell if she meant it as flirting or not.

"I dunno...just, things have been weird lately."

"Ah, yeah? I know quite a bit about weird things." She smiled and flicked her doubled-pierced tongue like a lizard.

Dave chuckled. "I guess you do."

"C'mon, lay it on me, boss man. What were you staring at? On the roof earlier?"

Dave shifted in his seat. "I dunno. It's just...at first I thought I was losing it and seeing shit, like all this sobriety was finally getting to me. But now, I'm not sure what I saw."

"What do you think you saw?"

Dave opened his mouth and was about to tell her, but then he just shrugged. "It's...just weird. I saw something I can't really explain. It's gotta be a sobriety side-effect or something."

"Ok, got it." Sheila was quiet for a moment. "You know, I think there's always going to be shit we can't explain. Doesn't mean we shouldn't try to explain it. Just, the answer may not be so obvious, you know?"

Dave nodded. It was just an automatic response, since he didn't really get what she meant by all that. But as they kept driving, his mind started to wander.

He pulled up in front of Sheila's house.

"Alright, I'll see you Monday. We'll be onto the next house then," Dave said.

"OK, cool. And try to relax, Dave, I know this shit's been hard for you. And lemme know if you ever need to talk, OK?" Sheila hesitated a second before popping open her door, which made Dave think she was about to hug him. She didn't.

"Thanks, I will." Dave said. "Say hi to Alex for me."

Dave didn't stop to pick up extra Snickers on the way home. He had other things on his mind.

✻ ✻ ✻

At around midnight, Dave rubbed his screen-fried eyes and took a deep breath. He'd been sitting in his chair for hours, with the Macbook on his lap and his feet up on the coffee table. An empty bowl of clam chowder near his left foot, three unopened Snickers near his right foot.

After Googling things like "haunted roads" and "seeing ghosts" all night, he finally felt he was getting closer to an answer. One guy at the University of Edinburgh wrote a paper about "residual energy" and how a traumatic event can make a place haunted. This energy was like an imprint on the world that the dead left behind, causing the same horrific event to be played out over and over again. Dave thought it sounded a lot like what he had experienced.

He also read about how some people are more "sensitive" to this residual energy, which meant they could see and hear things that others couldn't. That made Dave chuckle.

"Well look at me, the sensitive type."

He wondered if that might also make him more likely to dream about the dead, too.

Dave spent another half-hour trying to find any mention of a fatal accident along Dockside Road, but nothing turned up. He figured that just meant an accident hadn't happened there recently, since the local paper's online archives didn't even go back a full decade.

Dave snapped his laptop shut and groaned as he stood up. He barely felt the urge to drink the entire time he was researching this stuff. The cravings were definitely still there though, just easier to ignore. But as he walked toward his bedroom, the need for alcohol came rushing back at full force. And as usual, he fought it off with a few giant mouthfuls of caramel and peanuts.

Maybe always-fucking-happy Dennis was right: he did need to focus on something. But that something wasn't fishing or biking — it was ghost hunting.

Dave's mind was pumping away with questions when he finally laid down for the night. Could he really have some kind of psychic ability? If so, what does that mean? Is he supposed to help the boy somehow?

Dave didn't expect to get more than an hour or two of sleep with all those thoughts banging around in his skull. But he did.

He slept almost until 10 a.m., the longest rest of his post-alcohol life. Powered by this new-found energy, he was out the door and driving within 15 minutes, eager to get to the worksite before noon. Dave cranked the radio and tapped his fingers against the steering wheel.

He smiled big and drove fast, feeling the sort of euphoria he used to get just before having a drink. That 30 minutes of pulsing anticipation before he opened the door, threw his coat on a chair, and took those first long, satisfying gulps from an icy beer can.

He pulled his truck into the freshly paved driveway of the mini-mansion his crew had just finished up. He got out and looked up at the cloud-covered sky that had been bright blue just the day before. And then lowered his gaze onto the road across the bay.

Without the blasting radio and constant hammering of the job, the area was peaceful. Just the call of gulls and the rhythmic smack of the ocean hitting the shore. Dave paced along the road for an hour or so, pausing only to eat a Snickers. And as his mind drifted, he kept thinking about Sheila: the shiny double studs in her tongue, that almost-flirty smile she flashed him in the truck.

The rumble of a distant motor killed the quiet. Dave didn't even have to look across the bay: he knew what was coming. He could feel it.

He walked to the edge of the road and looked down toward the cedar grove. The gray pickup truck was barreling along the coast.

The kid appeared next, right on schedule.

Dave stared hard at the boy as he rode closer. His head bobbing to whatever flowed from his headphones. But no matter how close he got, Dave couldn't make out the kid's face. It remained blurry, like he was still fifty feet away.

"Hello!" Dave shouted as the boy pedaled past him, knowing he probably wouldn't answer. But it was worth a shot. "Can you hear — "

A mechanical snarl punched the air. Dave leapt back as the truck slammed into the boy. It veered to the right and then skidded sideways, finally stopping diagonally across the road with the passenger side facing Dave.

A bike seat rolled just inches away from his feet. Drops of blood peppered the dirt like ugly polka dots. And a small yellow running shoe, dirty and mangled, lay in the middle of the road. Dave looked over at the truck and could see a thin arm, bent at an impossible angle, poking out from behind the wheel well.

His heart hammered against his chest. Seeing it from two-stories up is one thing, but watching such a sick scene unfold right in front of you is another. It added a level of gruesome detail he wasn't prepared for.

He took a few shaky steps toward the vehicle, his eyes on the cab the whole time. Dave made a conscious effort not to glance down at what was left of the boy beneath the wheels.

The blackened passenger windows were beer-bottle opaque, far too caked with soot to see anything inside. But he did hear something. Music. The driver-side door popped open on the opposite side of the truck, freeing the twangy chorus of "Take the Money and Run." Loud and crisp and clear. Just for a moment.

The song cut out mid-sentence. And then the door snapped shut. A few shuffling footsteps. A young man's voice: "What did I do? What did I FUCKING do!"

And then sobbing, followed by the quiet words: "I'm so sorry."

Dave held his breath and kept still, his ears strained to pick up any shred of sound.

Whatever was on the other side of the truck didn't know Dave was there. Maybe it couldn't know. Dave thought back to the stuff he read about spectral energy and scenes repeating themselves, caught in an endless loop of pain and shock. And he wondered what his role was in all of this.

OK, time to do this. Now or never.

With clenched fists and teeth clamped-tight, Dave walked around the back of the truck to finally get a look at who the driver was. The man in the flannel jacket had his head pressed against the side of the vehicle. His hands gripped the roof so tight they were turning white. The guy was breathing rapidly too, like his heart was about to burst.

Just inches away, the boy's legs stuck out from beneath the truck. His blue jeans were splattered with blood and his shoe was missing.

"Fuck! Fuck no!" The man yelled.

Dave crept a little closer. This shit ain't real, just energy. He told himself that over and over, but he knew it was a lie. This was real. It had happened before. And for whatever reason, something wanted Dave to see it happen again.

"Fuck!" The man screamed one last time before punching the truck again. Then he turned toward Dave.

Dave stumbled backward, nearly tripping over the rocks behind him. He could hardly remember what he looked like as a teenager. But he sure as hell knew his own face staring back at him.

His own panicked, tear-streaked face.

"What the fuck is this?" But Dave knew what it was. Or at least, he was starting to realize it.

Tears slipped down his cheeks as the memories came flooding back. Not clear memories; more like random bits of footage spliced together.

Drinking and doing coke at a campsite during his grad party.

Making out with the girl with the tongue piercing at sunrise.

Fighting with his equally drunk girlfriend when she caught them going at it.

And then the drive. The angry, booze-fueled drive.

All those parts were just busted up scenes, each one giving him only enough details to piece it all together. But one long-lost-memory played out in his head like a movie. Vivid and unfiltered.

Dave remembered seeing the kid on the road at the last minute.

Feeling the thud as he ran him over.

He remembered the Steve Miller Band blasting as he locked up his brakes. The sense of panic that shredded his stomach like a hungry pitbull. The overwhelming urge to run.

Dave could tell himself he was high and drunk. He could say he was a dumb teen and wasn't thinking clearly when he fled the scene. If only it had ended there. The memory that hurt the most was seeing that little boy's leg sticking out from beneath his truck.

And then watching it bend slowly at the knee, dragging blood-speckled denim through the dirt. Faint gurgling drifted out from beneath the undercarriage.

Dave still drove away.

That memory chipped away at his soul. Made him feel less than human.

Everything that happened after Dave took off was a series of fuzzy flashes.

He remembered watching his truck burn that night and feeling the smoke sting his lungs. The long walk back to the highway to hitch a ride. The case of beer he bought when he finally made it home.

Dave collapsed onto the dirt road and stared across the bay. He played everything over and over again in his head. Tormenting himself with each flickering, gut-tearing scene.

Both his hands shook so badly it took him three tries to pull his phone out of his pocket.

He watched the black screen quiver in his trembling palm. Then Dave wiped his eyes with his sleeve and tried to steady his hand long enough to use the keypad. He only needed to tap three numbers.

"911, what is your emergency?"

"Yes, I um. I need to report a hit and run."

And for the first time in 12 years, Dave didn't want a drink.

Dustin Walker is Canadian writer of horror, crime and comedy. His work has recently appeared in Shotgun Honey, Rock and a Hard Place and on the No-Sleep Podcast. He also took first place in Flash Fiction Magazine's quarterly writing contest. You can find him on Twitter at @dustinjaywalker.

Five Things to do on the Way to the Bottom of the Sea

By Andrew Dunn

1. Check your ticket.

The starfish-shaped station is large. Yes, there are maps to help navigate faux marble floors and moving sidewalks to find your departure gate. Once you find it, check signs from time to time to make sure your gate hasn't changed. Tickets tend to be non-refundable. If you miss your trip, what else is there for you to do for two months almost off the grid—spend them at Aunt Harriet's in Willoughby Cove?

2. The store on the right sells...

After checking your ticket for the umpteenth time, think about the standard issue garments the travel company sent. Outer clothing—survival suits, coveralls, diving attire—only comes from the travel company. Undersuits are different. Those gray one piece outfits that stretched on tight from neck to ankles felt thin and scratchy when you tried them on, right? You're in luck! The store on the right in the station's main hall sells designer undersuits.

See what they've got in your size. You'll find they offer a variety of colors and patterns. Designer undersuits are more than comfy. They're warmer than standard issue too. While you're at it, pick up snacks, a book, or kitschy souvenirs to send relatives.

3. Look at the sky.

At around 200 meters underwater, sunlight will cease to be part of your world. Skylights in the station offer nice views of a sky you won't see for sixty days, but there's an even better place to make a memory.

Outside the store and around a corner, you'll find nondescript stairs that lead to a plexiglass-domed lounge. Plush couches and a nautically-themed bar offer an excellent spot to savor an uninterrupted view of the sky before boarding call.

4. Try not to back out.

Second thoughts are common. Two months on the ocean floor sounded like the change you needed after the break up or whatever disillusionment placed you in front of a laptop in the wee hours pricing exotic travel packages. What seemed like a great idea then might not anymore.

The prospect of wearing coveralls over undersuits every day, in chilled corridors bathed in soft light, comes to mind. So does your stateroom with its skylight over your bunk—it looks upward into bathyal zone darkness, and creatures whose anatomies have adapted in wondrous if sometimes monstrous ways to survive at that depth in darkness.

You won't be bored though. Communal gardening will take up a few hours each day. Other hours you'll...well anyway, maybe there will be interesting people to meet and activities beyond gardening and watching the deep sea world through plexiglass to keep your mind off the creaking and popping.

Outposts creak and pop because, like videos say, aquatic pressure causes the outer hull to buckle like a soda can. But don't worry—outposts are safe!

It's best to forget second thoughts and board the submersible. The alternative? Aunt Harriet's.

Back out and Aunt Harriet will scrutinize what you wear and insist you help her ready her garden for spring. That means hours spent outside her cold cottage—she refuses to use her furnace unless it's below freezing. But there is also a chance the neighbor kid will come home to Willoughby Cove to visit while you're there. That means a shot at conversation and maybe more to keep your mind off whatever led you to spend two months almost off the grid.

Board the submersible, or catch a bus to Willoughby Cove?

5. Choose wisely.

Andrew Dunn writes science-fiction and fantasy from the state of Maryland, often drawing ideas from jogs through forest trails at sunrise. His work has previously appeared in AntipodeanSF, 365 Tomorrows, Daily Science Fiction, Penumbric Speculative Fiction, and in MetaStellar. His work has also been short-listed in several writing contests. Andrew welcomes reader feedback at dominobeanbag@gmail.com.

Lighthouse In The Desert

By Daniel Crow

There is something special about the desert at night: A dark-gray sea of emptiness stretched before us, with nothing but sand dunes and tall, sharp rocks for miles around. If we watched closely, we'd see it was crawling with life, with snakes, scorpions, and other little nightmares, but I kept my eyes on the road, and the hitchhiker—Joey—stared at the sky.

"So why exactly you wanna hunt for UFOs here again?" I asked him.

"I heard stuff," he answered, reluctantly emerging from his alien dreams. "Weird sightings here... Weird people coming out of the desert—or going in, and never seen again. So I thought I might as well get out here and check the place out. And there's no better high ground than that tower."

"Guess so," I said. "Cool telescope. Looks very... Professional."

"Thanks," he said and fell silent, watching the stars.

After about an hour's drive, we made it to the tower—an old stone structure standing alone on top of a rock in the middle of the desert, on the very edge of a cliff that looked a bit like an embankment.

"Didn't think there would be people here," Joey said, looking at the light in the windows.

"I think it's UNESCO heritage. Someone gotta look after it, right?"

"I dunno, I thought it was just an old watchtower. Wonder if they'll let me get up there..."

"Why not?"

"Well, it could be a no-go for tourists, I guess. Doesn't it look a bit like a lighthouse? There's even, like, a searchlight there, on the second floor."

"Maybe, just a bit."

I turned right, driving off the main road onto a side-way climbing up to the tower. Gravel and sand rustled under the wheels.

"You goin' there too?" he asked with surprise when I left the car with him.

"Yup. Got a ship to catch."

He laughed, then squinted at the tower.

"Man this is weird," he said. "I really thought the place would be empty... Do you think they could let me get up there? Such an awesome vantage point."

"Never hurts to ask."

Joey smiled and walked to the doors with me. From here, we could hear the music inside—some old jazz. The hitchhiker knocked, and a man, seemingly as old as the tower itself, opened.

"What do you want?" he growled.

"Hi, ugh... I'm Joey Wilbour, I do ufology. I was hoping to set up a watchpoint on the tower, um... I wanna shoot the sky. Got a telescope here, a camera... Didn't expect anyone to be here, honestly. Is there any chance I could, like, spend a few hours there, at the top?"

The old man looked at me, as if asking for my approval. I shrugged, then nodded at the car.

"I was just hoping to get some rest before travel."

The old man grunted and stepped away from the door, letting us in.

"Go to the roof and don't bother me," he told Joey, then looked at me. "Tea, coffee?"

"Thanks, I'm good."

He nodded and headed up to see Joey off to the rooftop. I settled down in a comfy armchair, listening to the soft jazz playing up above, and took a magazine from the coffee table—an old issue of National Geographic.

In half an hour, the old man came down to check up on me again and ask if I needed something. I asked for a coffee, and he made me a strong espresso, as dark as the night.

"How was it?" he asked, passing me the cup.

"Fine. All fine. Just a regular surveillance run. It's an interesting place, I gotta tell you. And an interesting time to be here, you know."

"I don't," he grinned. "Don't even got no radio here."

"Do you want one? I could ask someone to…"

"No, thanks, missy. I'm done with all the outside stuff. Got my old gramophone and don't need no nothing, thank you."

It was well before dawn when it started to get bright outside, and the old man checked up on me again, carrying a sandwich wrapped in oily papers.

"It's time, miss," he said. "You hungry? It's too big for me alone."

"No, thanks. Offer some to the stargazer."

He laughed and took a hefty bite.

"Some folks just don' know where to look, huh?"

We went outside, to the edge of the cliff. From here, I could see the silvery lights on the horizon—the glimmering waves rolling down the sands in the distance, a sea from beyond time and space streaming into this reality in a ghostly tide.

"Beautiful, huh?" the old man said quietly. "I will switch on the lights… Your ship should be in shortly."

He left me alone, one on one with the phantom sea drawing closer and closer. I watched the ephemeral tide crush into the rocks, the spearheads rising from the sand below. It was indeed a beautiful sight, its beauty underlined by the solemn silence of the dusty wasteland— the ghost of a sea made not a sound as it approached.

Soon, a beam of a searchlight swept through the desert, outlining the safest path through the rocks, and new lights emerged on the horizon—the vessel that came to pick me up had arrived.

As a small boat carried me away from the lighthouse towards the light-woven galleon that anchored nearby, I saw a small silhouette on top of the tower: Joey had already set up his telescope and was now watching the sky, hoping to catch a glimpse of the alien life. I waved at him goodbye, but he did not notice, too preoccupied with the stargazing to look around.

He was still there while the tide carried my ship away out of this moment, leaving nothing but sand and dust in its wake—a tiny man in his warm anorak, glued to his telescope as he stared into the endless star-ridden abyss up above.

Daniel Crow is a Russian-Israeli journalist and public relations associate living in Tel Aviv-Jaffa. Having grown up on Tolkien and Stephen King, he has long been in love with writing and all things fictional and grim, drawing inspiration from myths and folk tales of the past. His other passions include high-tech, history, and old comedy movies.

Note from the Publisher

By Maria Korolov

As I write this, in May of 2023, I can confidently state that this past year has been the most dramatic in our existence so far.

It hasn't been a long existence — we were founded just three years ago, in the summer of 2020. At that time, we were a small group of writers and editors trying to break into speculative fiction writing, concerned about the lack of any major online publications dedicated to this genre.

Readers love speculative fiction. Both urban and epic fantasies, historical romances with time travel plots, space operas, cyberpunk — these stories fill the bestseller lists and form the basis of popular movies and television shows. There's an insatiable appetite for this kind of imaginative storytelling and the audiences include all genders, ages, and other demographic categories.

But when it comes to short stories, it seems that the best-known magazines are still focused on their print editions. They only accept a small number of stories and, being print-first, it's difficult for authors to share them online and use them to build an audience for their other writing.

It's almost as difficult to publish a short story in a major market as it is to get a traditional publisher for your book.

So that was why we launched *MetaStellar*. To give new authors a new way to connect with the reading public. Our goal is to publish as many stories as possible, and get them in front of as many readers as we can.

Yes, there are financial constraints. The entire editorial team is made up of volunteers, but writers do expect to get paid for their work — especially if they want to use the stories to qualify for membership in the Science Fiction and Fantasy Writers Association.

So we decided to have a two-fold approach to contributions.

On the one hand, we have the original fiction, submitted during our fall and our spring submission windows. We typically get several hundred submissions each cycle, and, thanks to our Patreon supporters and other donors, are able to publish about a dozen of them.

On the other hand, we have our non-paying submissions. These include non-fiction pieces, such as essays, news stories, and book and media reviews. We also publish reprints, which are stories that have previously appeared in other publications, including on the author's own blog or social media channels.

We are able to publish far more of the latter than the former, since money is no longer a constraint. As a result, visitors to our site get to see new content every week. Since we launched, we've published more than 900 pieces by more than 400 different contributors.

We aim for a mix of search-engine-friendly articles that will bring in new readers, and plenty of new fiction to keep people coming back. For example, every Friday afternoon, we publish a round-up of the top ten free science fiction and fantasy books on Amazon. Who doesn't want to get free books? And people interested in free speculative fiction books would probably also be interested in reading free short stories.

This strategy paid off. This spring, we became the second-most-popular speculative fiction website in the world, according to statistics from SimilarWeb.

This was huge for us. And it changes how we think of ourselves. We're no longer just a blog run by a few friends to publish great stories we love. Our original mission — to connect authors with readers — is now becoming a reality because writers who publish on our site are now seen by tens of thousands of readers a month.

We're a place where authors can go to launch their careers.

That connection is even more important today, when artificial intelligence is upending everything, including the publishing industry.

When ChatGPT came out, we as a board had to make the very difficult decision about what to do with AI-assisted writing.

Should we accept stories where authors used AI-powered tools? Should we ban them? Should we go with something in the middle?

We decided to accept them.

There were lots of reasons to go the other way, and plenty of other science fiction and fantasy publications are taking that route. We don't necessarily disagree with their thinking, and there is definitely a place for both kinds of publications.

But, for both practical and philosophical reasons, we decided that we will allow our contributors to use AI to help them craft their stories.

Here's why.

First, our primary mission is to serve our readers.

If a story is good, it's good. Our readers deserve to get the best possible writing, and the most interesting and engaging stories. It shouldn't matter whether those stories were created with the help of AI, or with a squad of monkeys hammering away at typewriters, or with the help of psychedelic drugs.

What matters is the result.

Our secondary mission is to support our writers.

If some of them use AI to help them research their stories, clean up their grammar, generate story ideas or plot outlines, or even to write drafts of entire scenes — well, we support them, too.

Generative AI is particularly helpful for those who struggle to put their ideas into words. People who are struggling with the English language, for example, for one reason or another. People struggling with writer's block. People who know what they want to say, but just can't get the words out.

These are the philosophical reasons why we decided to embrace AI.

But there are also practical reasons for doing so.

First, there's no practical way to detect AI-generated content.

All the AI detectors out there are bad.

Even the best ones fail if you simply ask ChatGPT to vary the length of sentences and the level of complexity of your paragraphs.

OpenAI itself, the maker of ChatGPT, has released an AI detector — and it only detects AI-generated text 26 percent of the time, the company itself admitted.

Worse yet, when looking at completely human-written text, it classifies it as AI-generated 9 percent of the time. We never want to be in a position of rejecting a good story because an AI detector said it's written by AI, only to find out that it was written by a human.

Even if the AI detectors improve, many people use AIs as just a part of their writing process. They might use it to brainstorm ideas, for example, to fix grammar, or to write rough drafts of scenes that they then completely rewrite in their own voice.

There is absolutely no way to check for that.

Which brings us to our second reason. Where do you draw the line on AI?

Obviously, using AI-powered search is okay. We all use Google. Nobody's talking about banning Google.

Or AI-powered grammar checkers. Everyone uses Grammarly or the grammar tools built into Microsoft Word and Google Docs.

What about AI-powered dictation and transcription tools? Here at MetaStellar, several of us are big fans of Otter AI.

What about character generators, name generators, idea generators? There are AI-powered versions of all of those. Are they okay?

What about AI-powered outlining tools? You can ask ChatGPT to create a detailed outline of a story, for example. You can have it write the story based on the ideas you provide, or you can ask ChatGPT to come up with its own ideas. Is that okay?

What about AI-generated rough drafts? Is it okay if the writer takes an AI-generated piece of writing, then rewrites it completely in their own voice?

What about if a writer uses the AI to write the whole story, but then spends days or weeks or months working with the AI to tweak the plot, to get the details of the setting just right, to evolve the characters, to tailor the writing style? Should the effort that goes into a story count?

And does it even matter? If an author whips off a brilliant piece of work in an hour, and another author spends weeks slaving over a story that's really not all that good, is the one that took a lot of work worthier than the one created quickly? That's probably a question for the philosophers.

And what about using AI to rewrite sentences with better grammar, or add a few descriptive phrases? Or to take a story written in one language and rewrite it in another? Or to rewrite a story in a different tense or a different tone of voice?

There are so many different ways that writers are using AI that just asking them if they do is not a very meaningful question.

There are ethical questions regarding how AI systems were trained and legal questions about the copyright of AI-assisted works. Both of these will, eventually, be sorted out by the courts, and there are already lawsuits under way. Meanwhile, there are already AI tools available that an author can download and train on their own writing.

I personally believe that AI-assisted writing is akin to photography. Yes, it put some portrait painters out of work. And yes, at first, artists were aghast that someone with no artistic training whatsoever could just point a device, click a button, and get a picture. It didn't seem fair. It didn't seem right.

But, in the end, photography became accepted as an artform of its own and, in fact, even portrait painters now often use photographs as inspiration images.

Photography is art because it involves human intent and human selection. A person decides to take a picture of something and a person decides when and where to point the camera.

There will come a point where ChatGPT and similar tools will be good enough that they produce readable work. They're not there yet. Today, ChatGPT-written stories require quite a bit of editing and revision before they even make sense, much less generate awe or wonder.

But, just like with photography, it will still require a human to decide what story to tell and how to tell it.

At *MetaStellar*, we've decided to leave it up to the writers to decide how much AI they're comfortable with using, and how much of their AI use they want to disclose. Some writers will probably want to brand themselves as not using AI at all, and that is totally fine. Nobody has to use AI if they don't want to.

We don't know what AI will do to the writing profession. My feeling is that it might inspire writers to be more creative, more original, and to draw more on their personal human experience so that their work is less formulaic. That would be a good thing, overall, for the profession.

But one thing that's definitely not going to happen is AI going back into the bag. There are too many open source AI tools out there already. Anyone can download the software and run it on their own computer, or modify it and adapt it and re-share it with others. People who don't know how to write code can ask AI to write the code for them. And people are already doing that. Yes, non-coders are already creating custom AI systems and sharing them. The pace of change is definitely accelerating, and there are no signs that it will slow down any time soon.

But whatever happens, however it shakes out, the transition period is probably going to be very painful.

I myself am a technology journalist during the day. My profession is right in the AI cross hairs. In fact, some top tech publications are already using AI to generate articles.

I personally believe that writers will need every available tool to survive. Using AI can help us be more productive, more focused, more organized. Even authors who don't use AI to help them with their stories should be using AI to help with their marketing, accounting, and business planning.

Having access to AI is like having a superpower.

Will we use it for good, or for evil? Both, obviously. We will definitely do both.

Maria Korolov is the publisher and editor-in-chief of MetaStellar, the online magazine of science fiction, fantasy, and horror. She has been a business and technology journalist for more than twenty years, most recently covering cybersecurity, artificial intelligence, and virtual reality. Since 2009, she has been the editor and publisher of Hypergrid Business, an online publication covering virtual environments. She is also the author of a series of science fiction books set in a near-future virtual world.

Acknowledgments

The *MetaStellar* team would like to thank the following people for their help and support: Melody Friedenthal, Geordie Morse, Marie Ginga, Sophie Gorjance, Lilivette Domínguez-Torres, Terrence Smith, Amira Loutfi, E.E. King, Andrea Goyan, Sydney Levinson, Alex Korolov, Christina Brown, Romel Madray, Noreen Brenner, Tim McHugh and everyone else on the *MetaStellar* team whose work makes it all possible.

Permissions

"Reflections on a Loaf of Rye" by Shelly Jones. First published in *From the Farther Trees* in February, 2021. Reprinted by permission of the author.

"Conscription Day" by S.R Malone. First published in *365 Tomorrows* in August, 2021. Reprinted by permission of the author.

"The Finite Magic of Little Monsters" by Audri Salinas. First published in *The Face of the Universe* in August, 2020. Reprinted by permission of the author.

"The Tended Field of Eido Yamata" by Jon Michael Kelley. First published in *Chiral Mad 2* in August, 2018. Reprinted by permission of the author.

"Masques" by Mike Adamson. First published in *Nature Futures # 7707* in May, 2018. Reprinted by permission of the author.

"The Mad Scientist's Brother" by Jason Lairamore. First published in *Under A Dark Sign* in 2015. Reprinted by permission of the author.

"Before" by Andrew Dunn. First published in *365 Tomorrows* in 2022. Reprinted by permission of the author.

"The Thirteen Quixotic Temples of Light and Darkness" by William C. Burns Jr. First published in *Chyfrin* in 2017. Reprinted by permission of the author.

"The Way of Water" by Nina Munteanu. First published in *Future Fiction: New Dimensions in International Science Fiction* in April, 2018. Reprinted by permission of the author.

"Losing It" by Davin Ireland. First published in Revelation magazine in October, 2005. Reprinted by permission of the author.

"Heaven-Sent" by Nicole Walsh. First published in *NicoleWalshAuthor.com* in 2020. Reprinted by permission of the author.

"Nothing in the Dark" by C. M. Fields. First published in *Decoded #1* in 2020. Reprinted by permission of the author.

"Test Amongst the Shadows" by Todd Sullivan. First published in *Witches vs Wizards* in 2018. Reprinted by permission of the author.

"The Last Glance" by Gary Beck. First published in *Bewildering Stories* in 2008. Reprinted by permission of the author.

"Not the Pizza Girl" by Michelle Ann King. First published in *Every Day Fiction* in March, 2013. Reprinted by permission of the author.

"Retribution" by Kris Green. First published in *In Parentheses* in 2021. Reprinted by permission of the author.

"Unarmed" by Warren Benedetto. First published in *Night Terrors Vol. 12* in 2021. Reprinted by permission of the author.

"Space Time Rewind" by Marie LeClaire. First published in *Marie LeClaire Library* in 2021. Reprinted by permission of the author.

"Non Cogito Ergo..." by Dick Narvett. First published in *365 Tomorrows* in July, 2021. Reprinted by permission of the author.

"Take Me With You" by Kenneth Amenn. First published in Deviant Art in 2020. Reprinted by permission of the author.

"As Seen From Above" by Dustin Walker. First published in *Night Terrors Vol. 3* in 2020. Reprinted by permission of the author.

"Five Things to do on the Way to the Bottom of the Sea" by Andrew Dunn. First published in *365 Tomorrows*, in 2022. Reprinted by permission of the author.

Milton Keynes UK
Ingram Content Group UK Ltd.
UKHW010655210823
427162UK00001B/75